Cinder-Nanny

PRAISE FOR SARIAH WILSON

The Seat Filler

"Wilson (*Roommaid*) balances the quirky with the heartfelt in this adorable rom-com."

—*Publishers Weekly*

The Friend Zone

"Wilson scores a touchdown with this engaging contemporary romance that delivers plenty of electric sexual chemistry and zingy banter while still being romantically sweet at its core."

—*Booklist*

"Snappy banter, palpable sexual tension, and a lively sense of fun combine with deeply felt emotional issues in a sweet, upbeat romance that will appeal to both the YA and new adult markets."

—*Library Journal*

The #Lovestruck Novels

"Wilson has mastered the art of creating a romance that manages to be both sexy and sweet, and her novel's skillfully drawn characters, deliciously snarky sense of humor, and vividly evoked music-business settings add up to a supremely satisfying love story that will be music to romance readers' ears."

—*Booklist* (starred review), *#Moonstruck*

"Making excellent use of sassy banter, hilarious texts, and a breezy style, Wilson's energetic story brims with sexual tension and takes readers on a musical road trip that will leave them smiling. Perfect as well for YA and new adult collections."

—*Library Journal, #Moonstruck*

"*#Starstruck* is oh so funny! Sariah Wilson created an entertaining story with great banter that I didn't want to put down. Ms. Wilson provided a diverse cast of characters in their friends and family. Fans of *Sweet Cheeks* by K. Bromberg and Ruthie Knox will enjoy *#Starstruck*."

—*Harlequin Junkie* (4.5 stars), *#Starstruck*

Cinder-Nanny

a Novel

SARIAH
WILSON

Text copyright © 2022 by Sariah Wilson
All rights reserved.

Published by Montlake, Seattle

www.apub.com

Amazon, the Amazon logo, and Montlake are trademarks of Amazon.com, Inc., or its affiliates.

ISBN-13: 9781542030588
ISBN-10: 1542030587

Cover design by Philip Pascuzzo

Printed in the United States of America

For Alison Dasho:
thank you, thank you, thank you for everything

CHAPTER ONE

"Alice? Hi! It's me. I got it. I got the job!" I couldn't help but squeal the last word. I was still in shock that this had all happened. I'd done it. The so-amazing-it-felt-like-I-had-dreamed-it-up job was mine.

"Diana?" my sister asked, sounding a little groggy. Sometimes that happened after dialysis, depending on how fast they'd had to cycle her blood. Or maybe she'd been taking a well-deserved nap. I thought I'd waited long enough after her session to call her to share this incredible news, but maybe not. "What job?" she asked, sounding slightly more alert. "The one at Carl's Crab Shack?"

"No." That had been my original plan, to take on a third job waitressing on weekends at a nearby tourist restaurant. But instead I was going to be a nanny, across the country in Aspen, Colorado. For three months, and I was going to be paid forty thousand dollars.

Forty thousand dollars that we desperately needed.

"I got that nanny job," I said.

"The one that you're completely unqualified for?"

"Hey!" That she was correct was beside the point. "I'm qualified enough. I've done a ton of babysitting. Not to mention that I've looked after Jenna and Jasper thousands of times." Babysitting Alice's seven-year-old twins had been like watching twenty kids at once.

"When they said 'professional experience,' they meant as a nanny. And if I'm remembering right, which I admit is hit-or-miss these days," she said, "you also needed to be fluent in French, have a master's degree in childhood development, and be an Olympic-level skier."

"Zero out of three ain't bad," I joked, but she didn't laugh. "Oh, come on. Your twins have given me all the child expertise that I need. And I can probably get some French CDs from the library to listen to. Plus, how hard can skiing actually be? You're just strapping yourself to some long boards and coasting gently downhill."

Even though she didn't respond, I could feel her disapproval here in Maine all the way from Florida.

I knew what Alice wanted to say but wouldn't. Ever since she'd taken me in at the age of sixteen, we'd made each other a promise: That we would never be like our mother. That we would always be honest. When a coworker of mine had sent me the job listing for the nanny position in Aspen via email, she had meant it in a "can you believe this is real?" sort of way, but I'd applied once I'd seen the salary.

The Crawfords had ridiculously high expectations for a short-term nanny for their five-year-old son, Milo, and I had lied and said that I met each and every one of them. Mrs. Crawford seemed very pleased about this; I suspected that was because it was two days before they were set to arrive in Aspen, and obviously, no other person on the planet actually had the qualifications they wanted. (I was also supposed to be a math whiz, certified in teaching small children, and an etiquette expert. Ha.) This was also why they were paying so much money. I had to imagine that they'd kept increasing the offer until they'd found someone.

It had taken very little effort to create an online presence with social media that backed up my tall tales / lies, and my two roommates had served as my "references." It was a good thing Mrs. Crawford hadn't done a background check, because everything would have unraveled fairly quickly. Fortunately for me, she had bought it all hook, line, and sinker.

At least my con-artist mother had been good for something.

Alice sighed her disapproval but still stayed quiet. Which was good, because I would have been very honest with her in that moment if she'd made me explain myself.

My sister was in renal failure. Her kidneys had stopped functioning entirely, and she now had to go to dialysis three times a week, four hours at a time. I was a match and could be her donor, but her soon-to-be-ex-husband, Chad, was messing everything up. She was fighting him in court for alimony and child support, and in retaliation, he'd removed her and the kids from his health insurance. The court had ordered that she and the children be added on again, but now Chad was fighting that ruling. The legal system moved slowly. Too slowly.

Which meant that she didn't qualify for health care assistance because legally, technically, she was supposed to already have private insurance.

It was maddening.

I didn't know how much time she had, and I wasn't willing to wait.

We'd been able to work out a deal with the hospital (with some grants from local charities), and it was going to cost $37,632.13 to get the operation performed. This gig was an answer to my prayers. There was no way, even working three jobs, that I would have ever come up with that kind of money. I was already sending Alice all the extra cash I had so that she could buy groceries.

And in my defense, I'd managed to keep the pact she and I had made for the last seven years. I had always been honest. Sometimes painfully so, avoiding even the white lies that seemed so small and simple and harmless but could easily lead into bigger and bigger lies.

But to save Alice, I would have lied to and/or made a bargain with the devil himself. I would have happily committed any number of felonies to make sure she got the operation. I didn't feel any guilt over what I'd done with this job, because it was going to keep my sister alive. I was going to give her the entire amount. I was probably supposed to pay taxes on the money from the Crawfords so that I wouldn't be jailed for tax evasion, but I was going to deal with one possible felony at a time.

"So you're really going to do this?" she asked.

"Yes."

She must have heard the conviction in my voice, that there was no way for her to talk me out of it, because she didn't press me any further. Instead she asked, "When do you leave?"

"Tomorrow," I said.

"Tomorrow. You're going to Aspen tomorrow. I can't believe that. You staying in some high-end resort in . . . oh wait! Do you know who's supposedly in Aspen right now?" she asked, and I couldn't help but nod in satisfaction. I'd won this round, and she wasn't going to give me a hard time about it.

I leaned against the sofa. "Chase Covington?"

"No." She brushed aside my answer with a sound of disgust. "Griffin Windsor."

"Who?"

"He's a British lord."

"Does that mean he's a count? 'One, two, three British lords, ah, ah, ah,'" I said in a bad Transylvanian accent. When Alice didn't respond, I helpfully added on, "The Count? Like that purple Muppet on *Sesame Street*?"

I could practically hear her rolling her eyes through the phone. "He's not a count. He's the Earl of Strathorne."

"I still don't know why I should care."

"He's part of the royal family."

Oh, now I was getting why she was bringing up his title. One of her dialysis buddies was a woman who practically worshipped the British royal family and all of its many branches and had somehow managed to suck my sister into her obsession.

"And?" I asked, wondering why she was telling me. I'd made it pretty clear on previous occasions that I didn't care about British royalty.

I'd told her once that we'd fought the Revolution so that none of us had to care, but that hadn't gone over too well.

"It's not confirmed that he'll be in Aspen, but a couple of high-profile magazines are reporting that they're almost certain, thanks to an unnamed source, that he was headed to the US for a ski vacation."

These magazines sounded a hundred percent legit and like their highest concern was verifying actual facts, but I let my internal snark slide. "Do you know how many ski resorts there are in the whole country? Let alone Aspen? I could play the Powerball and have better odds of winning than meeting him."

"Is that device you claim is a laptop nearby?"

It was on the wooden boxes that my roommates and I used as a coffee table (and our dining table). My laptop was nearly as old as I was, but it still sent and received emails, and I had no other options. "Right here."

"I sent you a picture of him already. Check it out."

It took a ridiculously long time to download the photo (with the Wi-Fi we borrowed from a neighbor), but it finally finished. Sandy-blond hair, light eyes (green or blue? I couldn't tell), dimpled smile. This Griffin Windsor was cute.

Okay, he was ovary-exploding hot, but my sister did not need the encouragement. "Why are you sending me pictures of this Englishman?"

"In case you run into him. He's England's most eligible bachelor at the moment, and there is a long line of women trying to snag him."

I didn't doubt it. "So I'm supposed to succeed where so many of my British sisters have failed?"

"Duh, it's not the same thing. You're down to earth, and if you would ever watch an actual rom-com, rich guys love that kind of thing. He'll fall for you and whisk you off to his castle."

Her logic did not seem sound, but I wasn't going to argue with her. "What if he doesn't have a castle?" I teased.

"It doesn't matter. You'd be happy if he owned a studio apartment."

Alice wasn't wrong. Living somewhere without a roommate or a landlord was the dream. That, and having my own art show for my paintings in some world-renowned gallery.

Sometimes I dreamed very small, and other times I dreamed ridiculously big.

A trait my sister seemed to share with me, so I indulged her. "Okay. If I meet this Griffin guy, I'll do my best to make him fall in love with me so that we can live in his castle."

"That's all I'm asking," she said, as if I were being the unreasonable one here. "And if he's not there, maybe look around for a good guy. One who won't clean out your bank account and steal your cat and then ghost you."

I had no intention of looking for any kind of relationship whatsoever. I was going to fake my way through this job and that was that. Fortunately, my roommate Tammy came into the room and waved her hand, pointing at the phone. "Alice? Tammy needs to use the phone. I'll call you later. Kiss Jenna and Jasper for me!"

Alice said goodbye, and I handed the phone to Tammy. She thanked me, and sat down on the sofa in the spot I'd just vacated. My roommates—Tammy and Evelyn—and I shared a landline that was included as part of our rent. All three of us were desperately poor, as evidenced by our sharing a loft space over a garage that seemed to be infested with both raccoons and cockroaches. I'd spent many a night wondering why the raccoons didn't eat the cockroaches. Weren't they omnivores? If those little masked bandits would just do their part, our infestation issues would be solved. The cockroaches would be gone, and the raccoons would be too stuffed to move and wouldn't steal our food.

Anyway, shared miserable circumstances were why Tammy, Evelyn, and I did our best to help each other out whenever we could, like when they had pretended to be my references for Mrs. Crawford. We were friendly and kind to one another, but our schedules hadn't really allowed us to get close. I'd felt bad about leaving them with such short notice, but Evelyn had a friend who had already started storing her things in our tiny space in anticipation of moving in as soon as I was officially gone.

Part of me wished that I had gotten to know these girls better, but there just wasn't time. I felt bad that I wasn't really going to miss them and they weren't going to miss me.

Then again, maybe that made things a bit easier.

I grabbed my laptop, walked across the room to where my mattress rested on the floor. I packed the laptop and its charger and then lay down. I'd already thrown everything else I owned into the tattered duffel bag that had been a gift from Mick, the boyfriend I'd followed to Maine. He was another in a long line of men I'd dated for too long in some kind of perverse desire to see just how red he could make his flags before I bailed.

I hated that I'd left Alice and the kids, but to be fair, everything had been fine when I'd headed up north. She was healthy and Chad was still pretending to be a good husband and father. I couldn't have predicted any of this.

Or that I'd be unable to earn enough to go back to Florida, given how expensive the cost of living was in this part of the state.

That was all about to change. I was going to make enough money to fix Alice and to get back home. Everything was going to work out, no matter what I had to do.

I thought briefly of the picture of that Griffin guy. If my mother had given me one good thing, besides Alice, it was the ability to dream and wish for things that couldn't ever possibly come true. I gave myself a moment to entertain the idea of candlelit dinners and sleigh rides in the snow and tiaras, unicorns, and castles before I made myself come back down to reality.

There was no way that this Griffin was going to be part of my world. There was only one boy that I had to worry about, and that was five-year-old Milo Crawford. I'd never met a kid who I hadn't been able to eventually win over. Mrs. Crawford hadn't told me much about him other than the typical mom stuff, that he was bright and sweet and funny, and I wondered what kind of situation I'd be walking into. The money might have been because the Crawfords couldn't find the perfect person, but maybe it was because this Milo kid was a terror and they were willing to pay for someone to handle him. Which was fine with me. There wasn't anything this kid could throw at me that I wouldn't put up with.

I was very happy to be trading the gray, slushy streets and vermin of my current life for the powder snow and luxury suites I'd have starting tomorrow.

I couldn't wait.

CHAPTER TWO

I flew into Denver, and from there took a smaller plane to the Aspen/ Pitkin County Airport. Flying in the snow was not my favorite thing, and I white knuckled the last leg of my trip, letting out a sigh of relief when we didn't skid all over the runway.

Mrs. Crawford had told me a driver would be waiting for me, and I found him holding up a sign that said DIANA PARKER. I said hello and told him that I was Diana. Although he didn't immediately say anything, he did give me and my tattered duffel bag the once-over. Which made sense—he probably didn't pick up people like me every day.

"The hotel is about three miles away," he said. "I should have you there in no time."

I thanked him as I climbed into the back of the luxurious SUV. I made sure to put my seat belt on, because it had started snowing in heavy flurries shaped like giant globs of cotton candy.

As he eased out onto the road, I wondered if I should have done more to prepare for what was about to happen. Any intense drilling by Mrs. Crawford, and I'd be toast. Like, what if she was already fluent in French? What if they spoke it at home? It wouldn't take much for her to figure out that the only French I knew was a dirty lyric from a famous song and the words used by Miss Piggy.

My mom's voice echoed inside my head: *Always do your homework.* She hadn't meant real homework, the kind schools assigned you. She meant learning everything I could about a potential mark so that they'd be easier to exploit.

My mom, a notorious con artist, had been caught the day before my seventeenth birthday. She had been arrested, tried for her many crimes, and incarcerated with a twenty-year sentence. She had raised me and Alice as her partners in crime, teaching me how to manipulate people to get what I wanted before I could tie my own shoes.

I hadn't known that what we did was wrong. Obviously, there had been no kind of morality in my life other than "take what you can get and don't get caught." I assumed that everybody around me lived a life like mine. That other parents were just like my mom. I hadn't really had many friends growing up because she kept me out of school as much as she possibly could, telling the district that she was homeschooling me. That was a lie—she needed my schedule to be open so that I could be available to help with her schemes.

I'd never graduated from high school. Which in turn made college an impossibility. I wasn't dumb, and I had always spent all of my free time reading, but I lacked mastery over a lot of the basics. My mother had always hated that I read, which made sense, given that it opened my eyes to an existence beyond my own. That everything in my life was completely messed up and totally abnormal.

Alice got away first, and when she was married and settled, she came for me. She rescued me, and I would always, always owe her for that.

I'd promised Alice nothing but honesty and here I was, about to spend the next few months lying my face off. I knew how disappointed she was, even if she stayed quiet about it.

That slightly guilty feeling returned, since I was ashamed that I'd broken my promise to her. Not to mention the one I'd made to myself—that I would never, ever be like my mom. No matter what. I wiped that regret away quickly by reminding myself that nothing mattered more than Alice getting better.

I wasn't like my mother. This was different.

Despite wanting to keep the memory of my mom and her instructions at bay, I had actually done some homework. John Crawford was an executive for a huge conglomerate with offices all over the world. He seemed to travel frequently. Sheila Crawford had started up an organic / health food home-delivery service that had exploded in popularity.

Their pictures surprised me, though. My now former roommate Tammy had done nannying for a few years. She had warned me that the kids were almost never the problem; the parents were the people I'd have to watch out for. She'd shared horror stories about inappropriate husbands, demanding and entitled moms, being forced to do jobs she wasn't being paid for, how she had to fill in for the parents' neglect. So I was expecting the Crawfords to be horrible. To hate each other.

But in all their photos, they looked genuinely happy together. It was a trick I'd learned early on—to tell the difference between people who tried to appear happy and those who actually were. (Unhappy people were easier to manipulate.) I could tell that the Crawfords weren't faking it.

And in all their photos with Milo I saw the same thing—parents who adored their child and were loved in return. Tammy's words hung in my head, though, and I wasn't sure what to expect.

There was such a thing as being overprepared. I had to believe in myself and my skills, and everything else would hopefully fall into place. Milo and the Crawfords would be won over and they'd be sad when I left in three months.

That was the thing about how I'd grown up—I was this confusing mix of insecurity and distrust, balanced out by flexibility in new situations and a confidence in my abilities that I probably didn't deserve.

The driver pulled up to the largest hotel I'd ever seen in real life. He opened my car door and I was hit with a blast of frigid air. He ran to the back to get my bag while I got out of the SUV. I pulled my threadbare jean jacket around my torso, wishing that I'd had the funds to buy a real coat before I arrived. I thanked the driver and wondered if I had a dollar in one of my pockets that I could tip him with.

He seemed to know what I was doing and offered me a bright smile. "Don't worry about it. The Crawfords took care of everything."

We said goodbye and the SUV drove off. I stood in the snow for a moment longer, steeling myself against what I was about to do. Resolved, I walked in through the massive sliding glass doors. The lobby was all marble and shining chandeliers and had a kind of elegance that my mom had always pretended to possess but had never actually achieved.

I felt completely out of my element.

The man behind the registration counter seemed to agree with me. "Is there something I can help you with?" His tone was dismissive.

"I'm here to work for the Crawfords." I shivered, and I didn't know if it was because of how cold my skin still felt or if the full weight of what I was doing had finally settled onto my chest.

"You're Diana Parker?" he asked, one eyebrow perfectly arched.

"That's me."

He frowned, as if not certain whether to believe me. I got it. I didn't look like I belonged, and I had learned at an early age to view everyone around me with suspicion.

I couldn't get offended when somebody else saw me the same way. In large part because, in the past, they would have been right.

The snooty man typed some things into his computer and then slid a keycard through a device before handing it over to me. "The Crawfords are staying in the Presidential Suite on the thirtieth floor. Your keycard will give you access to that level. I will call and let them know that you're on the way up."

I gave him a brilliant smile and said, "Thanks so much." Just because he was being rude and dismissive didn't mean that I had to play his game.

When I got into the elevator, it took me a second to figure out that I had to insert the card first and then push the button marked "30." I kept up my internal mantra that everything was going to be fine. It was all going to work out. Nothing bad was going to happen.

The elevator opened and I walked down the short hallway and stood in front of the door. I took a deep breath before I knocked.

Sheila Crawford opened the door a moment later. She looked just like her photos but was much taller than I'd thought. As tall as me, and I was pretty tall at 5'10". Other than that we didn't look much alike—she had short blonde hair, pretty blue eyes, and tan skin. I was pale with dark brown hair and dark brown eyes. She was Cinderella to my Snow White.

"Diana! I'm so glad you made it. Come in!"

The penthouse suite had the same level of luxury and elegance I'd seen in the lobby. Expensive flooring, a granite fireplace, twenty-foot ceilings. A view of the nearby mountains that was breathtaking. This was no regular hotel room—it was like a massive apartment with rooms far beyond what I could see from this front living room.

Against my will, I found myself mentally calculating the price of the art around us—the Chagall lithograph on the wall, the Lalique crystal vase sitting on a side table, the Piaget clock on the mantel. I wondered if the items I saw belonged to the hotel, or if the Crawfords had brought them.

It doesn't matter how much anything is worth, I hissed at my mercenary brain.

"Wow, this is some place!" I told her, doing my best to shut down my worst impulses.

"I know, it's a little over the top," she agreed. "My husband grew up with the best of everything. So sometimes we spend more than we should."

"Like paying nannies' salaries," I said teasingly.

She laughed. "I knew I was going to really like you. Come in and meet Milo."

I could almost hear my mother, like she was in the room with me. *Good. Get her laughing. Listen. Don't interrupt. Put her at ease. Find out everything you can. Make her trust you.*

"Stop it," I muttered as I followed Mrs. Crawford.

She turned her head. "Did you say something?"

"No," I responded, trying to smile. I worried that everything my mother had taught me had been so ingrained that I couldn't help but take advantage of other people. I suppose in this case I sort of was, but not for a selfish reason. It was for Alice. Okay, maybe that was selfish because I needed her alive. There was no one in the world I loved more than my sister.

But I wasn't ripping them off. They were paying for a service that I was going to render. Just maybe not in the exact way that they had hoped for.

I was going to have to watch my thoughts, what I said. Telling these lies to get this job had been too easy. It was like having a coat that was too small, too constricting, and shoving it to the back of your closet, then pulling it out years later and finding that it was comfortable and fit perfectly.

It was a slippery slope and I was going to have to be careful.

I'd had all these questions about Milo, wondering what kind of kid he would be. If he'd be easy to get along with, or if he was the type who hated his nannies and would try to get me fired. Considering his mother's unrealistic expectations for this job, I had to imagine that she had the same sort of expectations for her only child. There were probably all sorts of things he was forbidden from doing. Like eating sugar or watching TV or playing video games. All things I could use in my battle to win the boy over.

Milo was lying on a couch, playing with an iPad. He had light brown hair, wore black-rimmed glasses, and had a very serious expression.

"We don't spend a lot of time on devices, but today Milo earned some extra screen time, didn't you, sweetheart?" Sheila's voice was warm and tender as she spoke both to and about her son. "Milo, I need you to put it down for a second and meet Diana. Do you remember when we talked about her? She's going to be with us for a little bit and will watch you while Daddy and I work."

I mentally cataloged the fact that Milo liked screen time. Definitely something I could use in the future. Determined to make this kid like me, I crouched down so that we were more eye level. "Hi, Milo! Nice to meet you."

His expression stayed somber. "It's nice to meet you, too. I have rickets. That means my bones are soft." He made a show of attempting to raise his arm, and it seemed to take a good deal of effort.

I looked up at his mother, alarmed. She hadn't mentioned that he had soft bones. That seemed like important information to have.

"No, he doesn't have rickets. What he has is an overactive imagination. Which I'm sure you'll be able to handle with your early childhood development degree."

Yes, I knew just how to cure a child who pretended he was wasting away from a disease I'd never heard of.

"I also have consumption," Milo told me, as if his mother hadn't spoken.

"Milo, you don't have tuberculosis or any other Victorian-era diseases," his mother said, her voice a bit more stern this time. "Ten more minutes and then it will be bath time."

"Did you want me to do that?" I offered, ready to hit the ground running.

"No, but could you come into the kitchen with me for a few minutes?"

"Sure." I stood up and put my bag strap back over my shoulder. "I'll see you later, Milo."

He nodded sadly. "Yes, you will, if my brain hasn't been destroyed by mad cow disease."

Okay. I nodded, not sure if I should respond. I followed Mrs. Crawford into the kitchen, which was enormous. Shiny chrome appliances, sparkling stone countertops. I sat at an island that could have seated thirty people. She pushed a tiny pile of electronics and a black binder toward me.

"What's this?" I asked.

"The binder has Milo's schedule, his current curriculum, and all the notes I think you might need to know about him."

I picked up the binder and it was ridiculously heavy. I didn't know what to say.

"The most important thing you need to know is that when John and I are here, our workday stops between six o'clock and eight o'clock. That's our family time, and it's sacred. We eat dinner, spend time together, give Milo his bath, and get him into bed. Which means your workday is done at six if one of us is home. Obviously if we're gone, we'll need you to stay and be with Milo. Or if John and I go out on a date after Milo's in bed. But we'll always clear it with you first to make sure you're available."

I was always going to be available. I'd do whatever they wanted. Including washing those massive windows in their family room. "Of course." I nodded. This was far more generous than I had expected.

"Like tomorrow night. There's a charity dinner I have to attend. Would you be okay staying here with Milo?"

"Of course!"

She nodded. "Thanks. Usually we always try to eat here at home when we can, and you're welcome to join us for dinner whenever you wish."

During the time she'd just called sacred? I was pretty sure I'd just grab something out of that massive fridge or walk-in pantry and call it good. "Thanks."

"And this is a laptop and a cell phone for you to use. Everything's all set up and ready to go."

I'd lied to her when she'd asked about me having a phone. When she'd offered to chat with me via text, I'd told her some kind of nonsense about wanting to live off the grid and not being tied to a device in order to explain why we had to arrange our phone interview from my landline. Now she was giving me a phone?

This was too much. "Oh, no, Mrs. Crawford, I couldn't possibly—"

She held up one hand and I stopped speaking. "First, I'd love for you to call me Sheila. And second, when you told me that you didn't have a smartphone or a computer with a fast CPU, we got these. It's important for us to be able to contact you whenever we need to. I already put my and John's numbers in there. I also want you to have your own computer to download lesson plans, find art projects, or just print out whatever you need. We've done the same thing for our other nannies."

Still not quite able to process what was happening, I seized on the least important part of the sentence. "What happened to your previous nanny?"

"Gail? She was amazing, but she wanted to stay in California."

"That must have been hard to let go of someone with so much experience." Sheila looked a little confused. "Someone who . . . has the same set of skills as me?"

"Oh, no. Gail didn't have any of that. She just played with and watched over Milo."

Wait. Why was it so important that I meet some laundry list of impossible qualifications then? At my quizzical expression, she continued, "John was offered a promotion and a transfer to his company's office in France, and it will mean such great things for our family. His travel will go down from twenty-one days a month to just seven days. And I can do my work from anywhere in the world—I just need a good Wi-Fi connection. We've already got a French nanny all lined up once we arrive, and we need you to help Milo prepare for his life in France. Our home in California sold really quickly. Faster than we expected. And we're waiting for the lease of the current tenants in our new French home to finish up, so we're spending the next few months here. On vacation."

This was kind of like a stopgap, then. "A vacation where you still have to work."

Sheila smiled at that. "Yes. I prefer to go to the business center during the day because if I'm home, I just want to spend all my time with Milo. And while we're standing here in the kitchen, please know that you can help yourself to anything and everything. We keep it pretty well stocked. Our home is going to be your home, and I want you to treat it that way."

I nodded, still feeling like I was in an actual dream. And not sure that I could ever feel at home here.

"Okay," she continued. "Grab your stuff and I'll show you to your room."

There was another hallway and Sheila opened the door farthest from the kitchen. We walked into a cavernous room, just as lush and gorgeous as everything else I'd seen. There was a massive dark wood dresser, a matching entertainment center with a seventy-inch big-screen TV, a comfy-looking sofa, and several wingback chairs. But I saw only one bed. "Am I sharing this with Milo?"

Now it was Sheila's turn to look confused. "No, Milo has his own room. This is just for your private use. You have your own bathroom, as well, just through that door. No one will come in here except the cleaning staff. So if you're running low on supplies, just leave them a note and they'll make sure to restock."

Tammy had warned me that at her last nannying job, she'd had to sleep in the closet of the little girl she was caring for, and I'd actually expected something similar. What I hadn't expected was a room bigger than my sister's entire home. That feeling of "too much" came rushing back, but I was just going to accept it and go on. "Thank you. This is amazing. I can't believe all of this is for me. I've never lived like this before."

"You'll be surprised at how quickly you get used to it," Sheila said with a wink.

She wasn't wrong. I already didn't know how I was supposed to go back to cockroach/raccoon living ever again.

"So I'm going to get back to Milo, and you're free to settle in or go out and explore the city. Maybe do some shopping?"

I definitely needed some better outdoor clothing. "Shopping sounds fun, but I . . ." I hadn't told her that I was completely broke. I wasn't sure how to explain that without her asking more questions, but somehow she seemed to understand.

"I've already transferred half of the money to your bank account. Like we agreed on."

We'd agreed on that? Yay, past me! I didn't even remember that part of the conversation, probably because I'd been so excited that a literal answer to all my prayers was happening.

Although I should have just said thanks, instead I blurted out, "That's so much money. I can't believe you're paying this much." Like I'd half expected to be human trafficked or locked up in somebody's basement when I got here.

"We paid our last nanny a hundred and sixty thousand dollars a year, which works out to forty thousand for three months. We're happy to pay a lot to have the best."

"And you really couldn't find anyone else?"

"We wanted the perfect person. And you made us wait until it was almost too late, didn't you?"

At that I cringed. I was so not the best or the perfect person. Ugh. I felt terrible. I did finally manage a weak "Thanks."

"You'll need to get up with Milo at seven. And anything you need to know should be in the binder, but text or call if you need anything else, okay?"

I nodded.

"We're all so glad that you're here." Then she left me alone and I put my bag, new phone, and laptop on the bed. Despite the size of the room, it felt a bit like the walls were closing in on me. So much for my conscience being totally clear.

I'd thought the Crawfords would be the worst and had rationalized my actions with that belief in mind. Now that I could see it was untrue?

I had to go somewhere that was not here.

I grabbed my wallet and the new phone and headed toward the front door. Sheila and Milo were sitting in the family room, reading a book together. When I came into the room I said, "I am going to go out. And buy some things."

"Is that what you're wearing? You should take one of my coats." Sheila got up and headed to a closet in the hallway, taking out a coat and handing it to me. "Try it on."

Part of me wanted to protest again, but she was right. It was too cold outside to be wandering around in my jacket. Her coat fit perfectly, like it had been made for me.

"I would guess we wear the same size," Sheila said, smiling. "Have fun!"

"I will. Thanks for letting me borrow your coat!"

She waved her hand like it was nothing and went back to join Milo on the couch. I wondered whether I should say something more, but instead I left and headed down to the lobby. An employee, not the snooty guy from earlier, asked if they could help me. I told them I wanted to go shopping and they pointed to a large white van out front, saying it was a shuttle and that I could call them when I was finished and they'd come pick me up.

It took only a few minutes to get to the "historic downtown" area, and the driver told me there was a pedestrian mall. He let me out on a busy corner, and I found myself facing three different skiing-supply stores. Which made me think of how Sheila believed I could teach Milo to ski.

Oh man, what had I done? My heart felt unsteady, like it might stop beating altogether.

Taking a deep breath, I tried to calm myself. Maybe things weren't the way I had anticipated, when I'd imagined myself as some kind of modern-day Robin Hood, taking from the terrible, selfish, spoiled rich people and giving it to my deserving and very poor sister.

The only way to get through this would be to do the best possible job I could and hope they never, ever found out the truth about me. I would work really hard and do whatever they asked me. If they needed to yell at me and give me extra chores, I was ready. Whatever it took.

I would be as honest with them as I could within certain parameters. I couldn't tell them about not having actual experience or that the only French I knew was fries and kiss, but I would be as authentic with them as I possibly could be, and would have to hope it was enough.

For the Crawfords, and for my own peace of mind.

Right then a man smacked against my shoulder, making me drop my new cell phone. Of course. This was karmic retribution for what I'd done. Get a new phone, the universe breaks it into tiny pieces all over the sidewalk.

Before I could lean down to pick it up, the man who'd hit me grabbed it first and handed it to me. Something about him made my heart beat hard in my chest.

A jolt of electricity hit me when he spoke. "So sorry. No damage done, though. Here you go."

I focused on the unbelievably still intact phone so that I didn't stare at him. My gaze darted around so that I saw only small bits of him—a blinding smile, stubbled jawline, light hair, that foreign accent, and the expensive and yummy cologne he wore.

Before I could respond, he was already walking away. Tall, broad shoulders. I felt a strange twinge in my stomach, and I was struck with an overwhelming desire to run after him to find out his name. If I'd tried to explain this moment to my sister, she probably would have made fun of me. Crushing on some stranger who obviously wasn't the least bit interested in me.

So instead of following my completely inappropriate urges, I turned my attention back to my phone. The handsome, polite man and my unbroken device felt like some kind of cosmic reassurance that things were going to be okay.

It was all going to work out.

CHAPTER THREE

I woke up early the next morning and got ready quickly. I heard Milo singing a song and washing his hands in the bathroom. I wondered if I was supposed to go in and wake him up at a specific time or just generally try to be awake at the same time he was.

He came out of the bathroom and looked up at me, his enormous glasses hanging slightly crooked on his face, and muttered, "Breakfast."

"Sure thing. What do you normally eat?"

"Cookies." He said this so hopefully I almost didn't have it in me to disappoint him. I filed away the fact that cookies were motivating for him.

"Sorry, buddy, I don't think your mom will be okay with that."

"She wants me to have oatmeal with banana slices and Greek yogurt," he said with a sigh and climbed up onto one of the stools next to the island.

I went into their pantry, and it was literally like walking into a grocery store. Another bad assumption on my part—I thought for sure that Sheila would have her house stocked with only the most organic and freshest of ingredients. Like the kind where I'd find small woodland creatures making themselves at home on the shelves. Instead, there was a little bit of everything, including sugary and processed foods. It took me a couple of minutes to locate the oatmeal with Milo shouting unhelpful directions at me from the island.

The fridge was also stuffed to the gills, and the Greek yogurt was eluding me. Milo finally got off the stool and got the yogurt himself. He got a spoon and I made a mental note of where the silverware drawer was. He climbed back onto his stool while I took the lid off his yogurt and grabbed the oatmeal.

"You have a tag," Milo said, pointing his spoon in my direction. "Is that a new shirt?"

Huh. He was more observant than I would have thought. There was a tag sticking out from my armpit. "Yes. I did some shopping last night. I didn't have warm enough clothes for the mountains."

I'd been very careful with my spending. I needed almost all of my earnings for Alice and enough to fly back to Florida, and everything here was so expensive. I did get a coat, gloves, a hat. A few shirts and a new pair of jeans, along with a pair of boots. I hoped it would be enough.

I was reading the directions on the back of the oatmeal container when Sheila came in the room.

She didn't look very well. She coughed, and it definitely sounded phlegmy.

"Good morning," she said, sneezing as soon as she finished speaking.

"Are you okay?" I asked.

She waved her hand. "Just feeling a little under the weather."

Milo bore his signature solemn expression when he offered, "Maybe you have consumption, Mom."

"I don't have consumption and neither do you, Milo." She went over to the coffee maker and pushed a button.

"Can I get something for you?" I offered.

"No, I'll be fine. I'll just take a couple of DayQuil. I have a lot to do today."

I reached for the binder and patted the top. "So do we!"

She smiled, then left the kitchen, presumably to find that cold medicine she'd mentioned.

I opened a few cabinets until I found a bowl, and then I filled it up with water and stuck it in the microwave. It took me only three tries to figure out how to use it.

While I waited for the water to heat up, I opened the binder and began reading Milo's schedule.

7:00 a.m. Wake up; bathroom

7:10 a.m. Breakfast

I felt a tiny bit of pride that we'd already managed to do the first two things on his schedule. Check and check.

7:25 a.m. Change clothes; brush teeth

7:30 a.m. French—vocabulary

8:00 a.m. Masters of the Renaissance—sixteenth century

9:00 a.m. Calculus—fractals and patterns

10:00 a.m. French—present-tense conjugation

It continued in that vein—there were breaks for lunch and snacks, one for playtime, one for screen time ("if Milo behaves"), one for skiing practice, and then it was a list of topics and assignments that would have made a graduate student cry. I didn't understand most of the words, and it seemed they were all written in English.

My experience with other small kids said they preferred Play-Doh and snowflakes made out of Popsicle sticks over Renaissance masters and fractals.

Maybe this was just Mondays. I flipped through the binder and every day was just as full and busy as the one before it.

Wow.

"This is some schedule, Milo."

He nodded mournfully. "I know."

"Your parents know you're five, right?"

"I keep telling them that." He shrugged. "And it's very hard for someone with the plague to do it all."

25

"Let me see your fingers."

Slightly confused, Milo held up both of his hands.

"Just like I suspected. If you had the bubonic plague, your fingers would turn black."

"Really?" He sounded very interested in this revelation.

"You don't have the plague."

"Smallpox?" he tried.

"Not smallpox, either. Not even chicken pox."

Sheila reentered the kitchen and pulled a coffee mug from the shelf. "What were your plans today?" she asked.

I gestured toward the binder, not sure what I should say. Teaching young Milo how to take over the world?

"Our current lesson plans are in there, but you should feel free to adjust those however you wish."

"Okay." I should have gone through the binder the previous night when I got back from shopping so that I could have been better prepared.

"If you want, you could delay today's work until after lunch and spend the morning exploring the hotel with Milo. There's a lot of amenities."

Exploring sounded much more up my alley. "That would be fun. What do you think, Milo?"

He grinned and shrieked/said, "I'll get dressed!"

Sheila smiled as he ran through the kitchen, but slumped against the counter once he'd left.

"Seriously," I said. "What can I do? You seem really sick."

"Nothing. I'll be fine. I just need rest and fluids. We try not to talk too much about sickness around here," she said and I nodded. That seemed smart. If someone in the Crawford household got the flu, Milo would probably proclaim that he was dying from Ebola.

Her suggestion that we go out suddenly made more sense. She probably wanted a chance to be sick in private without Milo seeing it.

"There's a card for your expenses." She reached over to flip to the back of the binder and pulled out an envelope, handing it to me.

A black American Express card slid into my hand.

My mother would have been drooling.

As it was, I might have salivated just a teensy bit. The words *no limit* repeated on a loop in my mind. "Expenses?" I repeated.

"For buying food or snacks or whatever activities the two of you might want to do," Sheila said.

Receipts. I was going to get a receipt every single time I used this card and stick it into this envelope. For the Crawfords' benefit as well as my own. I'd make myself accountable.

Milo came back into the kitchen wearing cowboy boots, shorts, goggles, a scarf, and no shirt. "I'm ready!"

"Maybe we should go pick out some clothes that would be better for the weather," I said, slipping the AmEx card into my back pocket. I'd never understood the expression "burning a hole in my pocket" before, but I totally got it now.

"And after you get changed maybe you could show Diana where the slopes are, so that the two of you can try it out later." Sheila sounded hesitant, which surprised me. Until now she'd seemed so confident about everything.

"No skiing!" Milo's expression was hard to make out with his goggles covering half of his face, but he sounded very unhappy.

"It's John's favorite thing in the whole world, but Milo is afraid of it," she said to me in a low voice and then loudly added on, "even though we will be really careful and safe and take it slow!"

"No skiing," he repeated.

Part of me was relieved, thinking that my lack of skiing ability was not going to be revealed, but this was what they'd hired me for. Using my supposed psychology skills and knowledge of how child brains worked to convince their son to learn how to ski. This made it all worse. How was I going to get him to do it?

"Why don't you show me your room and we'll find something to change into?" I asked Milo, now wanting this conversation with his mother to be over.

He grumbled, but Milo led me to his bedroom and I found a pair of sweatpants and a long-sleeve shirt for him to put on. I left him to change and went into my room to brush my teeth and put my hair up in a ponytail.

Milo met me in the hallway, but he didn't seem happy about his required wardrobe change.

Oh well. There were worse things in life. He needed to be in warm clothes because I was not going to have him get sick for real. I couldn't imagine he was a very good patient, what with the thinking he always had some kind of deadly illness.

I tried to get him thinking about other things as we went down to the lobby. "Is there any place special you'd like to show me?"

"There's some cool stuff, I guess. Like the pool and the waterslides."

"Which way is that?"

Milo pointed to the left and I followed the signs to the indoor water park. And no joke, there was a lazy river, an Olympic-size pool, a hot tub, and a variety of waterslides. It smelled of chlorine and the room echoed with the shrieks of small children. "Why do they have all this?" I asked. "Don't most people come to Aspen just to ski?"

I realized my mistake just a moment too late, and Milo's face fell again. Maybe it would help to talk about it.

"Why don't you like skiing?"

"I don't know. I just don't like it. It's scary. Do you want to see the playground?" This perked him up a little and I followed him until we came to a large play area with swings and slides and equipment to climb on. It was pretty empty.

"There's not many kids here," I commented.

"It gets busier when school is out." Milo wandered over to a bench and I sat down next to him. He watched the other kids playing with a wistful expression.

"Why aren't you in school?" I asked him. I couldn't remember Sheila mentioning her reason for keeping him out of kindergarten.

"My mom worries. She likes me being at home and having nannies and tutors."

"Why?"

He shrugged one shoulder. "I was sick. I had cancer."

"Was this the kind of cancer you got from the plague?"

"You can't get cancer from the plague," he scoffed, as if I were the one who made up medical conditions. My smile faded as I realized that he was being serious. "When I was little I had Hodgkin's lymphoma. I was in the hospital for a long time."

I did not know what to say to that. I settled on "I'm sorry."

"I'm fine now. And Mom says that when we move to France, maybe I can enroll in school there. Do you know what the best part of that will be?"

Getting away from his mother's insane and totally unrealistic schedule? "What?"

"I think when I go to school that I'll finally have a friend."

That made my heart plummet down into my stomach. "What do you mean? You've never had a friend?"

"I don't know how to make friends. I was in the hospital for a long time. I didn't get to play with other kids." He looked so lost and forlorn that I was ready to take on the world for him. How could he not have friends? I'd known him for less than twenty-four hours but I was already prepared to stab somebody to protect him.

"It's actually pretty easy at your age to make friends. You just find someone you like the look of and ask them if they want to be your friend."

Milo didn't respond, and wore an expression that said he didn't believe me.

"Tell you what," I said. "We'll come back here tomorrow, later in the afternoon, and I will help you make a friend." I held out my hand. "Deal?"

He perked up, excited by my offer, and shook my fingers enthusiastically. "Deal!"

Now I had to hope that the kids here would be nice and not terrible snobs who might reject Milo. Children were usually easy to read. It shouldn't be too hard to find a kind one.

He jumped off the bench. "Let me show you all the restaurants!"

"Sure," I agreed and stood up. I turned to go but felt a burning sensation at the base of my neck, almost like I was being watched. Not in a creepy way, but there was this feeling of . . . anticipation. Or recognition. As if there were someone I needed to find. It was so strange and I scanned the area, back and forth, and noticed a little girl about Milo's age on the jungle gym smiling at me. I waved to her, and she waved back.

But she wasn't the one who had been looking at me.

So odd.

Milo tugged at my hand and I followed him toward the restaurants. I thought of the little girl and hoped that she'd be at the playground tomorrow so that I could help her and Milo become friends.

That was at least one thing I could do for him. Other than keeping him alive and all his limbs intact.

I imagined sharing this story with Alice, and knew she'd be rooting for that little girl to have a cute single dad so that I could make a new friend, too.

That wasn't what I was here for, though. I was going to focus completely on Milo and the Crawfords. There just wasn't room for anything else.

CHAPTER FOUR

The hotel was basically like its own city. In addition to several restaurants, it also had multiple stores to shop in. I could have spent the whole day exploring everything. I also attempted to get Milo to just walk out on the slopes, but he refused.

We spent the rest of the afternoon trying to do his schoolwork as best we could. I was going to have to do some serious research tonight. I'd be learning this material alongside him. He wasn't very enthusiastic about the stuff we had to do, and I went to YouTube more than once to look up how to properly pronounce French words. Milo seemed to prefer my mispronunciations and kept using those instead of the right words.

At five o'clock, as I was supposed to be drilling Max on some verbs, Sheila came into the kitchen.

"Mommy!" he said, and ran over to her. He threw his arms around her waist and almost knocked her over. She actually looked worse than when we'd left that morning.

"Milo! Why don't you go run and get your iPad?" she said, sounding congested.

Needing no further encouragement, he shot out of the kitchen.

"You look and sound sick," I told her.

"I am. I think it's just a bug, but there's this fancy charity thing I'm supposed to go to tonight." She sneezed and pulled a tissue out of her robe pocket.

Yeah, she'd mentioned that to me yesterday. "Well, you're definitely missing that."

"I can't. Bonnie Southworth runs this event every year, and if somebody's not in our seats, she'll block us from coming in the future. She takes empty seats personally."

"Aren't you supposed to be on vacation?" I asked her.

"There's vacation, and then there's vacation the way we have to do it. Still working. And since we're out here every January for the skiing, the dinner is such a great networking event for both John and me. He was actually supposed to be here tonight but they were having some kind of emergency out in Palo Alto and he had to go take care of it."

I was about to offer to make her some tea or chicken noodle soup when her eyes lit up.

"You can go!"

"To Palo Alto?" I asked, confused.

"No, to the dinner!"

Maybe her cold was making her delirious. "You want me to go to a formal charity party? I have nothing to wear." I was worn out after today, still had a full night of studying in front of me—the last thing I wanted to do was go to some boring charity thing.

"But I have a million dresses you could borrow! Come with me!"

Before I could protest that I knew nothing about this kind of stuff, she was pulling me into her bedroom and then a walk-in closet that was bigger than my apartment.

"Which designer do you prefer? Or color?"

"I . . ." I was distracted by everything around me. There were too many hues and fabrics and I wanted to spin in a circle to take it all in slowly.

"I've got it. The Dior." She grabbed a dark red dress that went all the way to the floor. It was so silky looking that I was afraid to touch it when she held it out to me, so I took it by the hanger.

"I couldn't possibly—"

But Sheila cut me off. "I've always wished for a daughter that I could share my clothes with. It took us so long to get pregnant with Milo and we had to have so many interventions . . . but I do hope it'll happen again. Maybe someday soon, once our lives settle down. But for now, what size shoe do you wear?" she asked.

"Ten."

She looked discouraged for a second. "I wear an eleven. But you can just stuff some tissue into the end or something." She grabbed a pair of black high heel Louboutins that Alice might have sold her twins for.

Sheila handed me the dress and the shoes and all I wanted to do was protest. This had to be outside the scope of my job, but how could I say no? It was obviously important to her and I reminded myself that I'd do anything the Crawfords asked me to do in order to assuage my guilty conscience.

Walking over to an ornate makeup table, she picked up an envelope. "Here's the invitation. The address is on there. You can tell them our name at the door. There will be dinner and then dancing. It should be fun."

I glanced down at the dress and shoes. Even in her weakened state, my sister would literally kill me if I missed out on a chance to go to a fancy party in an expensive dress. "I'll go get changed," I said, mind made up. Sheila nodded, obviously delighted, before she started a long coughing jag.

"And I'll go back to bed," she said. "I think I just need a good night's sleep."

"Do you want me to go put Milo into bed first?" I asked. It was something I could easily take off her plate.

"No, you can get ready. It's starting soon and Bonnie doesn't like people to be late, either."

Great. One more rich lady I had to keep happy tonight. I plastered a smile on my face, not very enthusiastic about this event. I headed back to my room. I didn't have much makeup with me, but I was good at making do with very little. Besides, with this gorgeous dress on, no one was going to notice my face. I undressed; carefully put on the dress, which did fit me (I'd been secretly hoping it wouldn't so that I would have an excuse to stay home); and did my hair into a messy bun. I probably should have tried for something more elegant, but I was running out of time.

The shoes were too big, and I did stuff some tissue into the toes. All that did was make me more uncomfortable, and they were only kind of staying on. My heels kept sliding out, so I located a couple of Band-Aids to help create a barrier that would keep the shoes in place.

I gave myself a once-over in the mirror and headed out toward the front door. Milo and his mom were watching a show in the family room and I stepped inside to say good night. So that she could see I was doing what she'd asked.

"Wow! Diana looks like a princess!" Milo declared, and I will admit, it did make me feel pretty.

"She sure does!" Sheila agreed, and then blew her nose. She gave me a watery smile, and I could see that this was making her happy.

"Thanks, guys! I'll see you in the morning!" I waved and grabbed my coat from the front hallway. I didn't actually plan on staying out that late—just long enough that this Bonnie person would see me sitting in the Crawfords' seats during dinner, and then I'd make my getaway when the dancing started. Despite Sheila's hope that I might have fun, I had to imagine that most of the people there would be either way too old or, if they were age appropriate, probably not dysfunctional enough to be attractive to me.

I wished that were something you could just decide. That you would like only nice, sweet men from now on, instead of the kind who made you question all of humanity.

When I got to the lobby I discovered that Sheila had hired a driver for me, and the driver gave me a card with his number so that I could call when I was ready to leave. Her thoughtfulness, even while sick, was a bit overwhelming.

It made me feel like a truly terrible person all over again. I pulled out my new phone and looked at the photo that Alice had recently sent me, a selfie with her kids. This was why I was doing this.

It took only a couple of minutes to reach the party, and the outside was kind of . . . dull. I didn't know exactly what I had imagined when Sheila had mentioned the event—maybe people taking photos or a red carpet. Instead there was just a bored-looking man in a suit with a headset asking for my name. I told him Crawford and he didn't even ask me for an ID. It was actually a bit of a disappointment, not only in that I had wished this whole thing might be more glamorous but also because there had been the slight hope that he might tell me I couldn't come in.

Instead he waved me inside and I checked my coat in the lobby. I passed through a couple of smaller rooms before reaching the main ballroom, and there were people standing around talking and I felt very . . . conspicuous. In the past I'd stood out only when I'd chosen to, and this was making me uncomfortable. It felt like everyone was staring at me.

When my mom was convicted, the media had posted family pictures that had both me and Alice in them. Honestly, I was always a bit worried that somebody obsessed with her story or doing a podcast about her crimes would identify me.

People were standing around talking while waiters circulated with trays of champagne and hors d'oeuvres. I passed on both, wanting to stay alert enough to study when I got home and to have enough of an appetite that I could eat dinner quickly and then leave.

This segment of the evening was probably part of that whole networking thing Sheila had mentioned, but I did not need new friends. Instead I walked around each table, looking for the Crawfords' names. It took me a bit to find them, at one of the center tables not far away from the stage where the DJ was playing classical music. I sat down just as the DJ announced that dinner was about to begin.

That I was now even closer to making my escape pleased me. An elderly woman sat down on my right and said, "You don't look like a John."

"No," I said with a small smile. "I'm filling in for the Crawfords tonight."

"What a coincidence! I'm filling in for my daughter."

"Oh, that's nice."

Now, this was where the conversation probably should have ended. She was sitting with a man who was presumably her husband, so she had someone else to talk to, and I wasn't really encouraging her.

She leaned over and said, "My name is Margery Brown. This is my husband, Sal."

"I'm Diana. Nice to meet you both." Her husband didn't look up from his phone.

That was my first clue that things were about to take a turn for the annoying. I quickly studied Margery's face, the intent in her eyes. In my previous line of "work," it had been easy to read cues from people, to see who they were and what they wanted. I realized that this woman was the talkative type and I was going to be trapped by her monologue for the next forty-five minutes.

I hated it when I was right.

Dinner was some kind of chicken dish, and I could barely even taste it. Margery went on and on about traveling out to see her daughter and grandchildren and how that son-in-law of hers was no good. At one point I saw her husband secretly smile, and I assumed it was because I was the one dealing with this conversation instead of him.

I nodded, made appropriate sounds, and tried to eat quickly. But Margery was the type who seemed to talk without taking a single breath, so there was no chance to excuse myself. Not only that, but she was somehow managing to eat, too. That took real skill. I would have admired her if I hadn't been so out of my mind with boredom.

"You should meet my youngest son. He's . . . How old are you?" Margery asked.

What? She wanted to know something about me? "Twenty-three."

"Oh." Her face fell and she said, "My son is only twenty and at Brown. Where did you go to college?"

For one whole second I entertained myself with the thought of being totally truthful with her about my life story. But then I reminded myself that I didn't know what kind of connection she might have to the Crawfords and I couldn't indulge my sometimes self-destructive nature.

Wait, she was filling in for her daughter. There probably wasn't any connection.

Okay, maybe I could indulge it a tiny bit. "I didn't go to school."

"Your poor parents must have been so disappointed."

I couldn't help myself. "Not really."

Margery made a sputtering noise at this, but we were, thankfully, interrupted.

"May I have your attention, please?" A woman at the microphone who looked very much like a Bonnie began to speak and thank their donors and sponsors and everyone attending this evening. I'd never, in my entire life, been so grateful for the mind-numbing speeches portion of the evening. At least here I could let my mind wander, think about what I was going to do with Milo's lessons. I didn't come up with any good solutions other than to google everything, but this was more entertaining than anything I'd gone through so far that evening.

The DJ started up some soft rock and I could finally, FINALLY, leave. I said goodbye to Margery and a clearly disappointed Sal, and headed for what I assumed was the exit. There were multiple sets of

Sariah Wilson

doors throughout the room and I picked the wrong ones. Instead of going out the way I'd come in, I had gone into some kind of enclosed terrace. There were several sofas and tables, a fire burned in the fireplace against one wall, and the snow fell silently just beyond the large windows.

I walked closer to the windows to see if I could make out any of the view, and that's when I tripped and fell, flying out of my right shoe. I hit the ground so hard it was like my soul temporarily left my body.

"That looked like it hurt. Are you all right?" The voice was very masculine, very British. Posh sounding.

Up to that point, the only thing I'd had going for me was that no one here had seen me humiliate myself. Of course that couldn't be the case.

I turned to see a ridiculously handsome twentysomething man staring down at me with concern. Like the kind where he was so good-looking that he didn't seem real. My eyes were drooling. Or maybe crying over his hotness.

If this was Margery's son I was going to punch somebody.

Although it might be worth having her as a mother-in-law if I got this guy as my husband.

I found myself staring at him, taking in his smile, his strong jawline, tousled brownish-blondish hair, his light eyes. I loved the way the light caressed the planes of his face, the curve of his mouth. I wanted to paint him. Everything was so working for me. Realizing that I hadn't replied I said, "It wasn't great. But I'm okay."

"Here." He reached out his hand. "Let me help you up."

I felt this tingling awareness, like this was some fated meeting. That everything in my life had been leading to this moment. Which was so stupid, but it was like he'd walked out of my dreams and into my ballroom.

"Thanks." I put my hand in his and the electric feeling of his hand wrapped around me made my knees go weak. It was a good thing I was

38

still sitting on the floor. He pulled gently but firmly and it took a second for me to make my legs work. I did get up, though, and my whole body swayed toward him. He put his hands on my shoulders, as if to steady me, but that seriously only made things worse. Heat burst under his touch and made me shivery everywhere.

He was tall! So tall. Taller than me. And he was wearing an expensive Tom Ford suit that fit him very, very well. Wow. So attractive.

I stepped back slightly on my bare foot, feeling a little like a cartoon pirate with a too-short peg leg, given that I had one shoe off and the other still on. He released his hands and I felt a chill pass through me. My stomach felt hollowed out, and I didn't know if that was caused by him or the fall.

"I'm good," I said. Whether that was for his benefit or for mine, I wasn't sure. I went to get my other shoe, but he got it first and picked it up.

Something about him crouching down felt very familiar. Like it had happened before. I saw realization dawn in his eyes at the same time.

"You're the man from the pedestrian mall."

"And you're the woman who dropped her mobile." He said it in a teasing voice, like I was some perpetually clumsy person he had to continually rescue.

That this had been true so far was beside the point. "After you slammed into me."

"Slammed into you?" he repeated, now sounding slightly offended. "I barely grazed you."

Enjoying his mock outrage I said, "Oh, really? It was like a move from the WWE."

"The what?"

"Professional wrestling."

"Which is fake, correct?" Now he was triumphant, as if he'd caught me.

"So? You still hit my shoulder."

He bowed gracefully at the waist, as if I were the princess Milo had proclaimed me to be. "My deepest and sincerest apologies, my lady, for any injury, fake or otherwise, that I might have caused you." He straightened up, his smile full of a mischief I was finding a bit irresistible. "It seems you're quite desperate for my attention. You don't have to leave your things on the ground hoping I'll speak to you."

"I'm not doing that."

"No?" His eyes were teasing. "Because all evidence points to the contrary. Although, now that I have your shoe, according to fairy-tale law, I get to keep you."

That made my heart beat faster, in a good way. "What?"

"Cinderella? My grandmother read it to me as a warning for the kind of woman I should avoid."

"Women who think they can talk to animals and have ball gowns conjured out of thin air?"

That made him laugh, and I felt my insides warming from the rich sound. "Not quite. My granny saw her as the ultimate gold digger."

His words triggered something in my brain. Not just because I once had been that kind of gold digger, at my mom's insistence and direction, but the accent, the fairy-tale thing, the familiarity of his face. It wasn't just because of the phone-dropping incident.

I knew exactly who he was.

"You're Griffin Windsor."

CHAPTER FIVE

His smile flickered, fading off his face. My revelation seemed to displease him, but it was like I couldn't shut up.

"You're that prince or duke or whatever."

"Not a prince. Or a duke. Just an earl." That teasing lilt in his voice was gone, but I couldn't focus on that. All I could think about was that this entire situation was completely impossible. How had I ended up at a party, one that I wasn't even supposed to be at, with the very man Alice had hoped would be here? It was like she was reaching out with her puppet master hands, tugging at my strings, willing this entire encounter into being.

For a second I wondered whether I was having some kind of guilt delusion, a wonderful fantasy that I'd conjured up to share with my sister, but it was very real.

And he was looking at me like I was a ditzy airhead.

Which might have been warranted, considering how I was gawking at him with my mouth hanging open. I snapped it shut.

"My sister's obsessed with you." The words were out before I could snatch them back.

"With me, specifically?" He edged back slightly, as if afraid I might rush him.

"No, your whole family. She . . ." There was no way to tell him about my conversation with Alice and her sending his photo to me without us sounding like weirdos. "She's just a fan."

He squared his shoulders. "Could I ask a rather large favor? Would you mind not mentioning to her that I'm here? I don't want anyone to know."

"I . . . She won't tell anyone." I could have lied to him—easily and in a very professional way—but I found that I didn't want to. "She's really sick and this will bring her so much joy. To know that we met. She's not on social media or anything. I'll swear her to secrecy and she won't tell a soul. I promise."

Griffin hesitated, as if unsure how he wanted to respond. That charming smile of his popped back onto his face. "So long as I have your word, I suppose it's fine, then."

I let out a breath I hadn't realized I'd been holding. "Thank you. That'll mean a lot to her."

"I'd rather hoped no one would recognize me."

Walking around with that face? Not likely. "How did you think that was possible? I have it on very good authority that you're England's most eligible bachelor."

He ducked his head, as if embarrassed. "No one here knows who I am. I can usually stay fairly anonymous in the States."

"Until me."

"I've actually never been recognized outside the UK. Although I suppose that if I wanted to be truly incognito, I should have worn a mask to this event."

"I'm sure that wouldn't have drawn any kind of unwanted attention to you at all." He smiled at my slightly sarcastic jab, and it was then that I realized that he still hadn't given me my shoe back. "So, were you planning on keeping my shoe or were you going to return it to me at some point?"

That mischievous glint was back and I was realizing that I had no power to resist it. If he'd been wearing this expression when he asked me to keep things about him from Alice, I might have done it.

"If I'm remembering the stories correctly, one can only return a shoe with a marriage proposal."

I knew he was joking, completely joking, but I swear I had a moment where I imagined myself in a white dress walking down an aisle toward him.

Which freaked me out. I had to take a deep breath before I said, "I'm sorry, but that only applies if you're a prince."

"Just a lowly earl, I'm afraid."

I still didn't get how this whole nobility thing worked. "I don't even know what that means."

He nodded seriously. "No one really does, but they all pretend as if they do."

"Is saving damsels in distress part of your earl thing?"

"Yes, but only if they're in mild distress. Dropping a mobile, losing a shoe. There's a special license required to slay a dragon."

I couldn't help myself. He made me laugh. He grinned at me in response and it was doing funny things to my insides. I pressed a hand against my stomach, trying to calm down. I couldn't remember ever being this attracted to someone who wasn't also sporting a neck tattoo.

Maybe I was growing as a person.

He was undeniably attractive, though. The way the light hit the golden strands of his hair, and how I would have to get much closer to be able to figure out the actual color of his eyes . . . Again my fingers itched for a canvas and a brush. Then my stupid mouth, the one Alice had tried to teach to be only honest, decided to let him know what I was thinking. "You're a lot prettier than I thought you would be."

I wanted to die. I wanted a giant hole to open up underneath me and suck me down into oblivion. What was wrong with me?

Not to mention that *pretty* was wholly inadequate for how he looked. *Gorgeous. Handsome. Perfect. The kind of face that would make a nun forsake her vows.*

He apparently found it funny. "Just what I've always longed to hear. How pretty I am."

I could feel my face flush, and I didn't know how to respond. I was currently afraid that if I tried to speak I might say something else ridiculous.

"I'm afraid you have me at a disadvantage," Griffin said, changing the subject for me.

I'd like to have you at a disadvantage, I thought and then immediately hushed myself. "How so?"

"You know my name but I don't know yours."

Name. I had a name, right? What was it again? It took me a second before I finally blurted out, "Diana Parker." I felt actual relief that I had remembered it.

"Pleased to meet you, Diana Parker. You have a lovely name."

"Thanks. I got it for my birthday."

He chuckled and then asked, "Were you named for the Roman goddess of the hunt?"

Hardly. My mom had chosen it because she thought it sounded regal, and that it would make people trust me more if she named me after a famous and beloved figure. "My mother loved Princess Diana."

"She was a distant relation via marriage. Did you know that?"

"No. But everything I do know about your extended family I know against my will." He smiled again, and before I got suckered into the beauty of his face I asked, "Can I have my shoe back?"

Because at some moment he was going to notice my toes and I was going to be humiliated. All the women he dated probably had perfect pedicures, and I had cracked toenails—plus my left pinkie nail had fallen off after I'd stubbed it hard against a chair.

Not to mention I could feel that the Band-Aid I'd put on the back of my heel was only partially hanging on.

"Yes, I've been holding on to this for a long time, haven't I? I hope you don't think I have some sort of foot fetish."

"I didn't before, but now you're kind of making me question. I also need it back to keep my foot warm. That way when I stick it in my mouth it won't be cold."

"What if I think it's cute when you stick your foot in your mouth?" When I didn't answer because his flirtatious tone was short-circuiting my brain, he held the shoe out. "Here. A lovely shoe for a lovely woman. And I am not interested in drinking champagne from it or whatever it is that people do."

He handed it to me while I tried very hard not to fixate on the fact that he'd just called me lovely. Maybe it was just some British thing and he thought everything was lovely. The slushy, blackened snow surrounding the parking lot. Lovely. My missing toenail. Lovely. Margery Brown's conversational skills. Lovely.

Griffin started to kneel down, like he was going to help me put my shoe back on me. I did not want him that close to my feet. "It's okay. I've got it."

He straightened up, looking a little confused, but when I bent at the side to slide the shoe onto my foot, he offered me his forearm to hang on to. It was an impressive and gentlemanly move, but it also made me think about the fact that it meant he had a lot of experience helping women get their shoes back on.

Why would England's most eligible bachelor be interested in someone like me? I wriggled my foot into place and let go of his nicely formed forearm. With the return of both heels, I was nearly as tall as he was. And by straightening back up, I had somehow moved closer to him. Which was inappropriate and I was invading his personal space like I was the Roman Empire, but in my defense, he smelled really, really good.

Griffin cleared his throat. "Your shoes. That's my grandmother's favorite brand." It was interesting, this statement from him sounded a little off. Like he was trying to distract himself or couldn't think of something else to say, so he'd settled on that. I got the impulse, but why would he feel the need to do that? He struck me as the sort of man who always knew the right thing to say.

Stepping back and then teasing him was obviously my only recourse. I used his own words. "Just what I've always longed to hear. That I remind you of your grandmother. Is that the same one who read you Cinderella as a warning?"

He nodded.

"Who uses a fairy tale as a dating guide?" I asked.

"Controlling people," he responded grimly.

Well, I definitely wanted to know more about that, but from the way his eyes shuttered, I saw that he wouldn't be very amenable to further questions.

Not that he gave me a chance to ask. "What made you run from the ballroom like you'd just committed a bank heist?"

"Do most robbers you know wear an evening gown to commit crimes?"

There was no mistaking the interest in his eyes as he studied my dress. "I don't know any criminals."

That made one of us.

"Why did you follow me?" I asked, realizing that if he'd seen me fleeing, he had obviously been watching me.

Griffin put his hands in his pockets and shrugged slightly. Like he knew exactly how charming that particular gesture would be. "Perhaps I was hoping to ask you for a dance."

"What?" My stomach fluttered. It was like my brain was not understanding his words. Because despite some flashes of possible attraction, men like Griffin did not like women like me. "Why?"

"Why does any man ask a woman to dance?" His voice seemed to have dropped an octave and the deliciousness of it was making me feel weak.

I couldn't be taken in by this act. It had to be an act, right? Nothing else really made sense. "Usually because he wants something."

"Yes. The pleasure of your company."

"My company is pretty bad, actually."

"Shouldn't I be the one to judge that?"

"Or you could just take my word for it," I said.

"I prefer to discover things for myself."

I crossed my arms, ignoring the little tingles racing through me at his declaration. I was not going to be taken in, no matter what his game was. Because everyone had a con, didn't they? Some sort of scheme in every interaction? Something they wanted? I walked over to an armchair and sat down. "I would have said no. I don't like to dance."

He followed me, undid the button of his suit coat, and sat on a sofa right next to the chair, so close that our knees were almost touching. The phantom warmth floating against my kneecaps was making me feel a teensy bit woozy.

"If you don't like dancing, what do you do for fun?"

"Eat."

He laughed, but I was dead serious. Eating on the regular in the hotel had so far been the best part of my experience with the Crawfords. I realized he might have been figuring out just how serious I'd been in my reply when his laughter trailed off and he studied my face, intently.

"What about you?" I asked brightly, hoping to distract him. "What kind of stuff do you do for fun? Doesn't it involve crumpets and . . . what's it called? The sport you have that's like baseball, only stupider?"

"Cricket?"

"That's the one!"

Griffin leaned forward and I had to back up so that our faces wouldn't be close together. "Cricket is excellent and crumpets are delicious. But I thought we'd already established that in my free time, I enjoy rescuing damsels. And if you'd let me ask you to dance, I would have rescued you."

"From what?"

"That terrible Margery Brown woman. She cornered me before the dinner and wanted me to spirit her daughter away from her son-in-law. I saw you seated next to her and you've had my sympathy all evening."

"You should have joined us."

"Perhaps if I were a braver man."

"Or a masochistic one."

"That too." He grinned. "She spent a long time telling me how much she loved visiting London although it was clear she's never actually been. I told her I hadn't been there, either, but she didn't believe me. She's one of those people who assumes everyone with a British accent has been to London."

I didn't tell him that I thought he lived in a castle there. "You haven't?"

"Oh no, I grew up there, I just very much wanted the conversation to end."

I smiled. "I completely understand."

"I also happen to be a very poor liar, as it turns out."

Again, that made one of us. But he did not need to know that. "While she was busy trying to convince you to woo her daughter, she was trying to off-load her youngest son on me. Although I think she rescinded the offer when she found out I hadn't gone to college."

"Really?" His eyebrows lifted slightly, reminding me that I probably shouldn't have shared personal information, but what was the harm? It wasn't like I was ever going to see him again. He asked, "You didn't go to university?"

Right. He assumed I was like him. Which wasn't a big jump, given the clothes I had on and the fact that I was here. "No. Did you?"

"Oxford."

"Of course." I should have known. Honestly, it was a bit surprising he hadn't already brought it up, as people who'd gone to prestigious schools usually did. "Do your business cards have 'Oxford alum' on them?"

"No, they say 'Earl of Strathorne.'"

Right. He didn't need to boast about anything. His entire life was one big brag.

There was more than one new thing happening in this conversation. The first was that I'd never had this experience before, this rush of getting to know someone for no other reason than I was just honestly curious about him. There was nothing I was trying to take from him, no information I wanted to extract to use against him later, no manipulating him to get what I wanted. Every relationship I'd ever had contained some element of manipulation on my part—it had been an incredibly hard habit to shake. I'd worked to overcome it, justifying it at the time by telling myself that the type of men I dated needed to be handled.

But there was nothing I wanted from Griffin. He seemed like a decent person. It was just this organic encounter, and while on one hand it was wonderful, it was kind of scary on the other.

My mom had raised me to fake confidence in any situation I stepped into. Because confidence, real or otherwise, would carry you through just about anything. But I was sitting here realizing just how out of my depth I was with the Earl of . . . whatever, that place he'd just said. That was my second realization—he lived a completely different life than mine.

I didn't know what I was supposed to do about it. Just leave?

If I did that, I didn't think Alice would ever forgive me.

But if I stayed . . . I hadn't ever met a man quite so charming and all around yummy in every way imaginable.

It might be dangerous if I stayed.

"Is there somewhere you have to be?" Griffin asked.

I knew what I should do. What the smart thing would be.

No one had ever accused me of being smart, though.

CHAPTER SIX

"No. There's nowhere else I have to be. Tomorrow I've got to spend time with a five-year-old, but tonight I'm free."

My eyes widened in shock at my own stupidity. Again, it was like he'd hit me with some kind of truth serum and I was confessing things I'd planned to keep quiet about. Because I liked that—thanks to my couture dress and designer shoes—he thought I was like him. Moved in the same circles. How could he not come to the wrong conclusion? It would be kind of hard to keep up the illusion if he knew I was a nanny.

Although maybe that would be the right move. He would quickly excuse himself and I could sneak past Margery Brown and go back to the hotel and focus all of my energy on the Crawfords.

Why didn't I want that to happen? Why did I want to stay in this romantic room with the snow falling outside and the roaring fire next to us and this impossibly sexy man sitting near me?

Huh. I think I just answered my own question.

"Five-year-old?" he repeated. "Wait, were you at the playground at the Royal Paramount yesterday?"

"Um, yes?" How did he know that?

"Is that a question or an answer?"

"An answer."

He grinned, and it was utterly disarming. "I saw you there. That's three times in two days we've been in the same place at the same time. I think we were fated to meet, Miss Diana Parker."

I had been feeling the exact same way for the last couple of days—but it was entirely different hearing him say what I'd been thinking.

"That or you're moonlighting from earl-ing as a stalker," I told him.

"No. Definitely fate."

"I don't believe in fate." Karma, yes. But fate? Fate was a fickle wench who had no place in my life.

"One doesn't have to believe in something for it to be true." His entire body shifted toward me and for one panicked second I thought he was going to kiss me. For reasons I couldn't have explained, I could not go there with him. I didn't think I'd ever recover.

Where was the tough girl? The one my mother had so carefully cultivated? Who could hurt people without thinking twice? The one with no heart to hurt? Something about this man made me feel all exposed and vulnerable. As if the act of accepting this job and coming out to Colorado had made me leave all of my old armor out on the battlefield so that this entire exchange was starting to make me feel a little shaky.

Griffin seemed to pick up on this as he leaned the opposite direction, against the back of the couch. Making a lot of space. Which was both a relief and a disappointment. "Does that mean you're staying at the Royal Paramount?"

"Yes. In the Presidential Suite." I didn't know why I'd added that last bit on.

Okay, in the spirit of radical honesty (at least when it came to admitting things to myself), yes, I did know why: I was trying to impress him.

And from the raise of his eyebrows, it seemed to have worked.

I assured myself that I wasn't technically lying about anything. Whatever conclusion he jumped to was out of my control, right?

Yeah, I wasn't buying it, either.

"We tried to get that particular suite, but it was already taken."

"That's not surprising. Apparently the Crawfords reserved it well in advance." I sucked in a big breath. So much for not tipping my hand.

"Who are the Crawfords?"

My employers. "The people I'm staying with."

"Friends."

In a manner of speaking . . . "Yes."

"Ah. Is that where the five-year-old comes in?"

I seized on that explanation. "Yes. Milo. He's a great kid. A total hypochondriac, but fun."

"I may understand that better than you think." I waited for him to explain. Was he a hypochondriac? Knew someone else who was? But instead he asked, "Is this your first time in Aspen?"

"Yes!" It was kind of a relief to have something that felt so nonconfrontational and possibly not threatening to my secret identity.

"It's the first time for me, too. Perhaps we could help each other explore."

That put all kinds of inappropriate images in my head as I imagined exploring him. I cleared my throat. I couldn't commit to spending any kind of time with him when I was here for a job. I pulled out one of my tried-and-true maneuvers and focused the conversation back on him so that he'd forget all about me. "Are you staying at the Royal Paramount as well?"

His expression let me know that he recognized my subject change, but thankfully he let it slide. A part of me was impressed that he seemed to pick up so easily on what I was doing. "Yes. I needed a place to hide, and an old chum of mine from *Oxford*"—he put a big emphasis on the word, apparently to mess with me—"recommended we join him here."

"Hiding? From what?" Or who?

"The paparazzi. This and that." He waved his hand as if it were unimportant, but there was so much he wasn't saying.

I both did and didn't want to know what it was. "I guess we all have secrets." Some worse than others.

"Indeed?" he asked.

"And how's that hiding thing working out for you?"

"Until today? Very well."

"I won't tell anyone."

"I know." He held my gaze for a moment and I saw something there I didn't recognize. I didn't like that he wasn't easy for me to read. "My mate from *Oxford* is why I'm here tonight. His wife's involved with this charity and they asked me to come. I had been really regretting it until I met you."

My breath caught and this time there was no mistaking his implication. The way he caressed the last few words he said had me totally enthralled, wondering what he would say next.

Definitely dangerous. Alice or no Alice, this night needed to come to an end. I wasn't strong enough to resist this guy forever and I had a very serious commitment over the next few months and would not have the time to be hanging out with a bored earl.

Because after my most recent "relationship," I had promised myself that going forward I was only going to date guys where there could be something more. Someone I could have an actual future with. And since that wasn't the case here, it seemed pointless.

Not to mention that much like the real Cinderella, this prince had no idea I was basically a servant, and this would all go away the second he found out. I was already hard-core crushing on this guy—I didn't need to add painful emotions when he inevitably left. I had to be responsible and mature. "Your friends are probably wondering where you are. You should get back to them. I'll just call my driver and have him meet me out front. It was really nice to meet you."

I stood up and he shot out of his seat so quickly we almost slammed into each other. There was this moment that hung heavy between us, where his breath was mine and I was so aware of every inch of him that

I couldn't process anything beyond his nearness. My limbs felt thick and heavy and my stomach tightened in anticipation. My mouth tingled with want.

I stepped around the coffee table to put an object between us because of how tempted I was to fuse my lips against his.

If I'd doubted whether I could be honestly attracted to a nice guy before, well, that matter had been thoroughly settled. I felt like I couldn't catch my breath.

"What about a drink? With me?" he asked, and there was a tinge of desperation in his voice that I related to all too well.

"I don't think that's a good idea," I told him. I got out my phone and the driver's card and sent a text. He responded immediately, saying he'd be here in ten minutes. "My driver's on his way. So, good night then."

"Wait, that's it?"

"Why do you sound so surprised?" Surely he'd been turned down at some point in his life. And I hadn't been flirting, right? Definitely bantering, but that was just the polite thing to do. I wasn't putting out any "ask me on a date" vibes, was I? Although . . . I had felt conflicted and confused by his prettiness and he might have picked up on it, but I was shutting things down now. Nothing good could come from this. We had our fun, and now it was time to go our separate ways. "I don't think tonight went the way you thought it did."

Griffin looked thoroughly dumbfounded. "You're saying I didn't win you over with my wit and dashing good looks?"

Completely, but this wasn't what I was in Aspen for. "Sorry." Lie, huge lie, but it felt necessary. Because it wouldn't take much from him to get me to change my mind.

"And you know who I am? Vulgar as it is to mention, I do have money. An appalling amount."

He really was pulling out all the stops here, and there was too much of my mom in me not to be curious about his financial background, whether or not I wanted to be. I shook my head hard, willing myself to stop going down that road.

"It's not about that."

"So the title doesn't sway you." Again, he acted like this was a completely new experience for him. "I realize I'm reacting badly here. But this has never happened to me before."

I kind of wanted to hug him. But you know, only from a human viewpoint of wanting to be compassionate to another human being. Not because I wanted to feel all those strong muscles of his pressed against me and . . .

Clearing my throat I said, "There's a first time for everything."

But apparently accepting defeat gracefully wasn't Griffin's strong point. "And I wasn't charming? Prince-level charming?" He kept going, like there was one right thing he could say that would change everything.

"I thought you weren't a prince."

"No, but I was raised with them. Also, I have been, as you Americans say, giving you my A game."

"Yes, I noticed, and it's been quite the struggle to keep my clothes on." I'd discovered that there was a good way of being honest without other people realizing it. Like now, where I said what I was actually feeling but did it in a sarcastic tone so as to throw them off the scent. "Look, Griffin, I know people say this all the time and don't mean it, but this time it really is me and my current situation. There's nothing wrong with you. Unfortunately, there isn't anything you can say to change things. You won't be able to talk your way out of it."

"To be fair, I have talked my way out of many a situation."

I completely believed him, considering how much I wanted to agree to go out with him.

"But," he continued, "if that is how you feel, then I understand." He paused for a beat and then said, "So you're saying that in some alternate dimension you might have fallen for me?"

Uh, like a piano falling on a cartoon character's head. "There's a distinct possibility."

He grinned at me. "I hope alternate-reality me understands what a lucky sod he is."

"I'm sure alternate-reality me is making sure of it."

Griffin glanced down at my mouth and it was making my insides shivery. Then he said in that low, lyrical voice of his, "I don't doubt that," and shivering turned to full-on trembling. He cleared his throat, like he was remembering himself. "I do apologize for any unwanted attention. I thought you were enjoying spending time with me."

"It's not that. I did enjoy it." More than I should have.

"Logic would dictate that if we like spending time together now, we might like spending more time together later. Like over dinner."

That conjured up an image of us at an intimate candlelight setting, leaning in close, forgetting that there was food because he was far more delicious and . . . I sucked in a deep breath. "You would think, but I've got a lot going on in my life. I'm not really in a date-y kind of place. But thank you."

What? I could feel my face flush. Everything I'd just said felt so inadequate and . . . stupid. Date-y? Thanking him? I was like some middle-school girl with her first crush.

"Friends, then?" he offered.

I had no plans to see this man ever again. "Sure. Friends. I really should get going, though." My resistance had become paper thin and I was ready to tell him to forget about the friends thing and just make out with his face.

"Then as your friend, may I walk you out?"

Again, I should have said no, but how was I supposed to turn that down? "Okay."

"I suppose this means you passed the gold-digger test," he said as we went toward the exit. I noted that he opened the door for me and let me pass through first.

"Why do you think I'm a gold digger?" We headed into the ballroom and located the correct set of doors for leaving the building. We walked over to the coat check.

"I personally don't, but I will say that according to the ancient texts and my granny, gold diggers are notorious for leaving behind a single shoe as a devious trap for poor unsuspecting noblemen."

"Oh, so we're calling fairy tales 'the ancient texts' now?" I asked as I handed my ticket to the attendant so that he could grab my coat.

"Well—" he said, but he was interrupted by the attendant returning with my coat. I thanked the man and to my surprise, Griffin reached for the coat first.

"This is your coat?" he asked with a bit of surprise and it took me a second to register that he probably expected me to have something designer or made of mink. The coat was good quality, but definitely not something the other women here would be caught dead in.

"I don't hurt small, furry animals. Like fairy-tale princesses, I have even let them live with me." Let him think I was some eccentric heiress who had an army of ferrets roaming in my mansion instead of a starving artist who couldn't get the raccoons to go away.

But my declaration didn't seem to faze him. "May I?" he asked, holding my coat aloft.

It took me a second to realize that he was offering to help me put my coat on. Which was weird. Why would he do that? No one had ever done that for me before. I was fully capable of putting on my own outerwear.

Instead of arguing with him about it, I decided to just accept his kind gesture. "Sure."

I turned around and quickly realized the genius of his plan. As I slid my arms into place, he had to stand close behind me and my back was enveloped by his warmth, his nearness. His breath was on the back of my neck and I briefly considered stepping back so that we would touch.

Instead I walked forward and managed a breathy "Thanks. I'm just going to go . . ." I pointed toward the doors. "Outside." It was cold out there, but it was better than being stuck in this little room with him with the attendant hanging on our every word.

"I'll grab my coat and join you," Griffin said.

I nodded and pushed hard against the door, letting out a giant breath when I got to the sidewalk. My driver hadn't arrived yet, which meant more standing and talking to Griffin. Somehow the temperature had managed to drop yet again, and I shivered.

"Here."

I hadn't even heard him come outside and suddenly he was standing in front of me, taking a cashmere scarf from around his neck and wrapping it around mine. It smelled just like him and I had to resist taking in a big whiff.

"Thank you."

"My pleasure."

He moved to stand next to me and I felt guilty. Here he was being chivalrous and nice and I'd turned him down flat. Which was obviously my right, but it wasn't like he had just misread the situation. I had definitely been putting out a vibe. I was probably still doing it.

I wanted to reassure him. "Hey, so, tonight was fun. And you shouldn't doubt your prince-like qualities. This whole night had a very Cinderella feel to it."

"You know, in that tale, despite my grandmother's disapproval, the couple do end up together."

"Right. But that's in the fairy tale." This was very real life, where beloved sisters needed new kidneys.

"You can say that now, but if a pumpkin carriage arrives to take you home, then you'll have to concede that I was right about us being fated to meet."

Was it strange that I was disappointed because I knew that wasn't going to happen?

As if on cue, my driver arrived, but parked about fifteen feet away. "See?" I said. "No pumpkins. Just a black sedan."

"Perhaps it's an overly ripened pumpkin that has turned black. Did you consider that?"

He was such an optimist, seeing the world through a lens I couldn't comprehend. I was always so wary of humanity and rarely disappointed in my pessimism. I could see the appeal of getting to see life the way he did. I wondered what it would be like to date someone like him.

Too bad I was never going to find out.

"Good night, Griffin."

"Diana . . ." He reached for my elbow and I stopped, wishing I could feel the touch of his hand against the skin of my arm. "May I call on you?"

I didn't even know what that meant but I shrugged and said, "Sure." I figured that meant he wanted to call me and would ask for my phone number, but he didn't.

Instead there was another moment, another heavy, staring-into-each-other's-eyes moment, our breaths misty in the cold air as they intermingled, and I was basically running on willpower fumes at this point.

Gulping, I said, "Okay. I'm going to go." I didn't know why I kept feeling compelled to announce all of my movements, but I did. He released me and I stepped into the parking lot. The parking lot full of slush and snowdrifts. I tried to step over them, but I could feel my shoes coming loose. I couldn't risk walking out of one again. He would take it as some sort of sign and say something darling and romantic about it and I would throw all of my newly found scruples out the window and let him have his way with me. I suppressed a groan as I thought about how good he probably was at that.

Without looking at him, I slipped my shoes off and darted across the parking lot. Why couldn't the car have parked closer? The driver was waiting for me with the back door open and I jumped inside. He shut it behind me and I let out a deep breath, not wanting to think about how stupid I must have looked.

There was a knock at the window.

Griffin.

Of course. Could I not have one moment to lick my wounded pride tonight?

I rolled the window down.

"I may be a visitor to your country," he said, "but isn't it usually customary to keep your shoes on when traversing an icy parking lot?"

"They're slippery," I said. "I might have fallen."

"Then I would have caught you."

I knew it! Darling and romantic! Gah!

My heart started to flutter helplessly in my chest and I was literally seconds away from asking him to get in the car with me.

"Good night, Miss Diana Parker."

He pounded on the top of the car, and the driver pulled forward. I rolled the window up and then collapsed against the back seat, letting out a massive sigh.

"You should have kissed him," the driver said, and I couldn't help but agree with him. It did seem like a wasted chance—the perfect way to cap off this never-to-be-repeated event.

I tried telling myself that I needed to think of it more as dodging a bullet instead of a missed opportunity. I should just enjoy what I'd had. Because what I'd had? Wow.

And I couldn't wait to tell Alice all about it.

CHAPTER SEVEN

When I got back to the hotel, I sneaked in quietly, making sure to hang up my dress when I got to my room so that it wouldn't get wrinkled. I threw my coat on the floor but the Burberry scarf I unwound carefully, folding it up and placing it on my nightstand. I didn't know how I was supposed to return it to him.

It would be my one souvenir from what had been a magical evening. I again thought of my driver's words. Maybe I should have kissed Griffin. To have something I could tell my grandchildren about someday.

I wanted to call Alice, but she was two hours ahead of me and while I assumed she would be happy for me to wake her up with this story, she needed her sleep. It could wait.

I washed my face, brushed my teeth, but I was way too wired to sleep. I got out my new laptop and started researching ways to teach Milo and what he should actually be learning. It seemed off to me that a kindergartner was supposed to be learning calculus.

According to the experts on the internet, I should be focusing on age-appropriate stuff, teaching him critical-thinking skills and things like looking for patterns. To use play and fun to teach him concepts.

I read and read, trying to absorb everything into my brain instead of thinking about Griffin. Not that I was perfect at it. I did look up British titles at one point and might have read a few British tabloid–website articles about him and he really did get around. He was constantly photographed with some beautiful woman on his arm. I wondered if he was settling for me because there were no supermodels or actresses or heiresses here in Aspen, which was very disappointing the more I thought about it. I decided to stop looking. Because the more attention I gave Griffin, the more I would want to know.

I resolved to focus on stuff for Milo, and fortunately, the longer the night went on, the easier it got to concentrate on what I was supposed to be doing instead of on Griffin.

At some point I must have nodded off, because I awoke with a jolt when my alarm went off. I should have been exhausted—I'd had only about two hours of sleep—but I was strangely energized.

I climbed out of bed, got ready, and found Milo in the kitchen. He sat at the island in his pajamas, looking extremely depressed.

"Hey, Milo. What's up?" I went over to the fridge to grab his yogurt.

"Is my mom going to the hospital?"

I turned to look at him, not sure I'd heard him right, and saw from his face that I had. "Of course not! Why would you think that?"

"Because she was sick."

"Oh, Milo, no. She just caught a bug. She's going to be fine."

As if to prove my point, Sheila came into the room looking about a thousand times better. "Good morning!" As if she knew what we'd been talking about, she turned directly toward Milo. "I'm feeling better today."

"That's good, Mom, because I have psoriasis."

"No, you don't."

He pulled up his sleeve. "Look! I have a rash."

Cinder-Nanny

"You colored your skin with a red marker," she pointed out. "I've got to go to California today to take care of some issues, and so I wanted to take you out to breakfast this morning. Go get dressed!"

Milo whooped and ran out of the room and Sheila said to me, "I should be back tomorrow evening, if that's okay."

She did not need to run any of her plans by me. "Of course! Anything I can do to help. Milo and I will have fun."

"I know my little boy is in good hands," she said with a smile. "And that you have all of his educational needs well in hand."

Untrue. Even if I was trying my best to make it truer.

"About that," I said, leaning against the counter. "I noticed yesterday that Milo was struggling with his lessons. He had a hard time sitting still and paying attention. Some kids learn better from doing instead of just listening. Maybe he's more of a tactile learner?" It was a term I'd picked up last night during my research and it seemed to impress Sheila.

"You think so?"

If she was impressed by that, she should hang on to her hat because I was about to hit her with . . . "Maybe. It would probably be good for him to go to a kids' museum, where he can be hands-on. Or a painting or pottery class. I've read that art can help with math. It teaches critical-thinking skills, how to visualize problems, pattern recognition, that sort of thing."

Heck, at this point I was impressing myself. Behold the powers of memorization and the learned ability to make it sound like I actually knew what I was talking about.

"That sounds good. We had a professor friend of John's arrange his current curriculum. We're hoping to enroll Milo in school when we move to France, and we don't want him to be behind."

Behind the other kindergartners? I could teach the kid to trace his hand on a piece of paper and eat paste. Kindergartners were not learning about the Renaissance. "I get that. But he's not going to be able to learn French in three months."

63

"I know. I just want him to start to have some familiarity with the language."

That was a relief. We could just find some French animated shows and watch those. My obsession with K-dramas had definitely taught me a tiny bit of Korean. Like saranghae and gajima—*I love you* and *don't go*. Two romantic phrases I'd never had need of in my regular life. But if I ever went to Korea and a hot guy there said them to me, I would be ready to go.

Sheila continued, "It sounds like you've got a great plan in place."

Guilt. "I also want to make sure Milo's got plenty of time to move around. More than he has on his schedule now." I hadn't been with him long, but yesterday he had been moving the entire time he was supposed to be learning. I figured that meant he one, was bored and two, had excess energy he needed to burn off.

"You're the expert. Whatever you think is best!"

That pang of guilt pierced me again, but I just nodded. Sheila left the room, calling for Milo to hurry up. I reminded myself that the Crawfords had spent a long time trying to hire someone to take care of Milo. What were the odds that if I quit in a moment of conscience they would quickly find a replacement? They needed me and I needed them.

This was a symbiotic relationship. Even if only half of the pairing was aware of it.

When I heard the front door close behind them, I went to my bedroom and shut my door. I checked the time and figured out that Alice would be in dialysis. Which meant I was going to have a completely captive audience.

She answered the phone. "Is this my younger sister on her pilfered phone?"

"It wasn't stolen, they gave it to me," I said defensively.

"Under false pretenses."

"To make it so you don't have to sit in that uncomfortable armchair three days a week attached to a machine."

There was a pause. "Touché. Although I still think we could just figure something else out."

"I'm not here to climb on board the good SS *Guilt Trip* with you." I was doing more than enough of that on my own. "I have news. News that is going to make you freak the freak out."

Now it was my turn to pause. I continued, "That pause was for dramatic effect. Because when I tell you what I have to tell you . . . whew. You're going to lose it."

"Does any of this involve me wiring bail money to you? Because I'm not sure I can afford it."

"No. But when I tell you, you need to hold the phone away from your face because I don't want to lose my hearing."

"Diana!" she protested with a laugh. "What is it?"

"Last night . . . at a party . . . I met . . . Griffin Windsor."

There was no shrieking, no invoking the names of any deity, just silence. Completely dead silence. I checked my phone to make sure the call was still connected.

"Alice? Are you there?"

"I'm here."

But that was it. Nothing more. No questions. "He also kind of asked me out, but I told him I had other things to worry about." I'd worried that part might upset her, that I hadn't gone out on a date with him, but figured it was best to share it now if she was going to be acting weird.

Her voice was so quiet that it was a strain to hear her. "Are you screwing with me? I am deathly ill, in case you forgot."

"I know that! I'd never lie to you about this. Never. I really met him and spent most of the evening talking to him and he was charming and adorable and you would really like him. Also, this entire thing feels like some kind of cosmic joke that you personally orchestrated."

Another long pause. "I want proof of life."

"Alice, seriously, I'm not lying!"

"Given our shared background, are you surprised that I would question it?"

Me taking this job had made her suspicious that I might go back to my old ways, which meant her caution was warranted but still felt unfair. I grabbed his scarf and took a photo of the label and texted it to her.

"This is his scarf. Burberry. It's cashmere and expensive. He put it around my neck last night because he thought I was cold, which lets you see how sweet he is. And a gentleman. Which I've never experienced in real life."

Then I finally got the reaction I'd been anticipating. She shrieked so hard and so loud I was pretty sure she'd broken the sound barrier. I held my phone at arm's length and waited for her to calm down.

Which didn't happen. The screaming did, probably due to the other dialysis patients and medical professionals in the room with her, but then the questions started.

"Are you serious? You met him? He's so gorgeous. And he asked you out? Why didn't you go? What's wrong with you? I knew it. I just knew it when I read that article. You made fun of me but I told you I was a little bit psychic. I knew you guys were going to meet and hit it off. I knew it. Also, I am so, so jealous of you right now."

"Jealous? Why?"

"I can't believe this has happened. I feel like my heart is going to give out. They're going to have to schedule me for a heart transplant, too, because I am *dying*. I mean in an excited way, and not the usual way. Okay, tell me everything. And don't leave out a single detail. I want all of them."

Obviously, I couldn't give her every detail. Like the ones where I had considered kissing him more than once. I needed her to see this as a fun little escapade, never to be repeated. Just something to take her mind off her problems.

Alice laughed and asked question after question about everything, probably to make sure that I didn't leave anything out.

She sighed when I finished my story after I rolled the window back up. "This is everything I ever wanted. Amazing. Like a movie."

"You're not kidding. He's like some old-fashioned character from a historical novel or something. He's so . . . proper."

"That's the best kind."

"What do you mean?" I asked.

"Those buttoned-up types are the ones who are all wild underneath. Primal."

"That . . ." I could feel my temperature rising as I pictured what she was describing. "I don't think that's true." A more accurate statement would be that I personally couldn't have handled it if it were true. "He's kind of goofy."

"Goofy hot."

"That's not a thing."

"It is now! Griffin Windsor, Earl of Strathorne, is goofy hot." Alice let out a loud gasp. "Just think. If you married him, you'd be Lady Diana."

"I'm not marrying him, we're just friends, and that's not how British titles work. I looked it up."

"Who cares how British titles work?"

"I'm pretty sure British people do." I realized that I was probably tipping my hand, that I was more invested than I'd let on, but I did want to know more about him and his world. I would have been Lady Strathorne, not Lady Diana. Not that I thought it would ever happen, but it was fun to get carried away for a little bit.

Which was why I understood Alice's compulsion to do the same.

"Oh, just let me have this, Lady Diana. It gives me something else to think about."

When she thought about her illness and what the outcome of it might be, I knew her main concern was her twins and what would happen if she passed away. I told her I'd look after Jenna and Jasper, but we both knew there wouldn't be any way for me to get custody. Chad wasn't abusive or anything, just a deadbeat.

But I couldn't worry about the future. Right now my main concern was getting money to my sister. Once I'd figured out how much I needed to buy an airplane ticket to Florida, I'd transferred all the extra to Alice. Her retirement fund was almost completely emptied out and pretty soon there wouldn't be anything left. They needed all the help they could get and I needed a judge to force Chad to pay what he owed.

"Have you heard anything about the continuance?" I asked.

"Because he has a new lawyer, it will probably be granted." Chad kept switching lawyers and asking for continuances in order to delay everything. It was maddening. "You know how it is. It's like one step forward and then two steps back and then your husband runs off with all your money and both your kidneys stop working."

"I would happily give you an alibi for any day that Chad has a horrific accident."

"Diana!" Alice never liked it when I joked about things like that.

"Fine. Sorry. But I do wish I could do more," I told her.

"You're already doing too much," she said.

There was a lump in my throat at her words. There was no way I could ever do too much. She'd saved my life. The very least I could do was return the favor. I changed the subject, talking to her about Milo. Alice had actually been a schoolteacher before she got sick, but at a junior high. She shared some of the stuff that she'd learned while she was still in college about younger children, suggesting activities Milo might like.

Talking about him was not the distraction I'd hoped it might be. Alice said, "The Crawfords are going to figure this out. That you're not who they think you are."

"If that happens . . . then I'll deal with it then." There was no need to borrow trouble.

"That sounds a lot like something Mom would say."

My stomach dropped to the floor. It was literally like Alice had reached through her phone and slapped me. There was nothing she could have said to me that would have been meaner, which she seemed to realize.

"Diana, I'm so sorry. I didn't mean—"

"It's okay. Don't worry about it."

She paused and then said, "Tell me something else about Griffin. Something I don't know."

I took the olive branch she offered. What else could I tell her that we hadn't already discussed? I quickly ran through the whole evening in my mind. There wasn't anything I hadn't already shared. Other than my personal feelings about him. Or how I kind of wanted to live in a perfume commercial with him. I thought of the first time I'd seen him, how he'd looked in that soft light. "Um, he's much better looking in person."

"Listen to you. I can hear you smiling over the phone. You like him!"

I made my face go lax as I realized I had been smiling. "I do not."

"Yes, you do! And now you need to prove that your statement about his appearance is true. Get me a picture the next time you see him."

"There's not going to be a next time."

She let out a short *ha* and then followed it up with, "It doesn't sound that way to me."

"Then get your hearing checked the next time you're at the doctor." Alice ignored me. "I want daily reports."

"There aren't going to be daily reports. I'm not seeing him again."

"You're staying in the same hotel."

"This place is massive. It's not like I'm going to accidentally run into him."

I heard another voice—someone was speaking to my sister. Alice asked me to hang on for a second, but then I remembered her dialysis buddy who loved the royal family. When Alice got back on the phone, I said, "Hey, Griffin said I could tell you he was here as long as you didn't tell anyone else. So I need you to keep it secret."

"Why?"

Good question. It was something I'd also wondered. "I don't know. But he doesn't want anybody to find out he's in Aspen."

"Okay. Send me a picture and I will."

"Fine. If I see him again, I will get you a picture." There. That wasn't going to happen, so I wouldn't have to hold up my end of the bargain.

"Also, when you see him again, be nice. Don't let your issues get in the way."

"I don't have issues," I immediately retorted, and then even I had to acknowledge how stupid that was. "Maybe I have issues."

"Diana, I love you, but it's not 'maybe.' It's 'how many.'"

I laughed, which had been her intent. We talked a bit about the twins and then I heard Milo and Sheila returning from their breakfast. "I have to go."

"Okay, and just know that the next time I call it will be from the edge of my seat. Where I will be dutifully perched until the next installment."

I laughed again, told her I loved her, and we hung up. As I went to greet the returning Crawfords, I thought about my older sister's interfering ways. This thing with Griffin wasn't new. She'd been trying to set me up with one nice guy or another for the last year or so. I worried that her pushing me was due to the fact that she'd considered the possibility that she might not live and wanted me to have someone.

Alice dying was a thought I refused to entertain.

But for the other part? Having a good guy? This was the first time I could see myself with the sweet man she was rooting for. Not that it mattered. It couldn't happen.

I did let myself secretly admit that if things were different, I wouldn't have minded having someone like him in my life.

CHAPTER EIGHT

Sheila rolled her suitcase into the living room and explained that, with getting the California house packed up and trying to adjust to telecommuting for her business from France, this would be just one of the many trips she'd have to take. I told her not to worry, that we had things in hand. She kissed Milo goodbye, told me to call her if I needed anything, and then she was gone.

Once Milo and I were alone together, I worried that he might cry about missing his parents. "It must be tough to have both of your parents gone."

He seemed to take it all in stride, though. "They always come back," he told me.

I couldn't decide if he was really well adjusted or screwed up.

"We have to do our work," I told him and he groaned and collapsed against the couch.

"It's not that bad," I told him. "Maybe we should talk about stuff you'd like to learn."

"Not math. Or writing. Or skiing," he said.

"Okay." He really was dead set against skiing, and I still didn't have any good ideas on how to entice him into trying it. "You still haven't told me what you do want to learn." I'd hoped finding things he was interested in would make his class time go more smoothly.

"I don't know." He shrugged. "Dogs?"

"Dogs are good. What else?"

"Diseases?"

That didn't seem like a great idea. This kid did not need more ammunition.

"Legos?" he added on when I didn't respond.

"We can definitely play together. And we're going to work on that making-friends thing."

"Not today. I'm not feeling like being a friend today," he said. I figured that meant he was sadder than he was letting on and probably needed some time to miss his mom and dad.

"Maybe we should take things easy. How about we go downstairs and buy some art stuff? I love to paint and we can make some cool things together. We can also watch some of your favorite TV shows while we work. How does that sound?"

Of course he agreed, and it didn't matter what show he picked because I'd recently discovered that I could select French as the language and the whole thing would be dubbed. If he protested I'd tell him it was a game to see if we could understand what they were saying.

We went shopping and picked up a bunch of supplies, and I bought him some things that I thought a five-year-old kid should have, like Play-Doh. We could work on making shapes out of it. The day actually passed by quickly and we colored together while watching a couple of French-dubbed episodes of *Phineas and Ferb*. Later we ate dinner in one of the hotel's restaurants, because Milo really seemed to love eating out. Much as I would never have admitted this to my sister, I found myself keeping one eye out for Griffin.

But as I'd predicted, we didn't see him.

I did make sure to put all the receipts back into the binder. That was where I found Sheila's detailed walk-through for Milo's bedtime, and going through each of the steps seemed to soothe him. He was asleep before I'd read the first page of the book he'd picked out. I waited a minute or two more and then sneaked out of his room.

I had decided to grab myself a snack and head back to my room to do more studying when I heard a knock at the door.

At first I wasn't sure what to do. This wasn't my home. Should I be answering the door? It could have been one of the Crawfords, if they'd lost their key or something, but wouldn't they have called first? Or gone to the front desk to get another card? Maybe it was a member of the hotel staff.

The only way I was going to find out was to answer it. I grabbed one of the knives from the butcher block, just in case. The Crawfords were rich. What if someone had come to steal Milo? It was my job to protect him and I was ready to do that.

When I got to the front hallway I looked out the peephole. I saw a shoulder. Definitely a man. Who was standing off to the side. Why? So as not to be seen? Now I was officially freaking out.

I opened the door, keeping the knife at my side.

It was Griffin.

I felt relief that there was no kidnapper, but now I was freaked out that he was standing there. "What are you doing?"

"Knocking on the door," he said with his beautiful smile. "Isn't that why you opened it? Because you heard me knocking?"

He was messing with me via his excess of charm, but I was so confused by seeing him here that I didn't know what to do.

"You didn't stand in front of the peephole," I said in an accusing tone.

He shrugged, and I understood that to mean that he'd done it deliberately. Did he think I wouldn't open the door if I knew it was him? That little bit of insecurity on his part was endearing.

It was then that he saw the knife I held. "I know I didn't call first, but I don't think that my breach of etiquette merits a stabbing."

Griffin stepped closer to me, which surprised me, and while he was busy giving off all that masculine-scented warmth, my hand went lax. Fortunately, he noticed. He grabbed my wrist and the shock of his skin on mine, his strong fingers wrapped around my arm, caused my own fingers to tighten so that I gripped the handle tightly.

"Careful. That was pointed at my feet," he said. "It would have been bad if you'd taken off one of my toes. I'm rather attached to them."

"I know you assume that's clever and funny, but you do know it's just a camouflaged dad joke, right?" I tugged my wrist free and then set the knife down on a side table. I wondered what the penalty was for dismembering the toe of a relative of the queen of England and what our extradition situation was with that country. My heart, furiously pumping away first from fear and then from something else, finally started to calm down and I felt like I could breathe again.

"I already knew you were dangerous, I just didn't realize it was also in a physical sense," he said.

Dangerous? Me? He was the one who was dangerous. Standing there in clothes he probably thought were casual—Gucci jeans and a merino-wool, dark green sweater, his hair slightly tousled, looking way too handsome to be real, teasing me. And even his dumb dad joke was funny.

Heaven help me.

"How did you know where I live?" I asked, still not able to believe that he'd just shown up. Like I'd conjured him or something.

"I realize my showing up here isn't helping my earlier assertion that I am not, in fact, a stalker, but you told me you were staying in this suite."

Oh. Right. I was the one who had been passing out information on my whereabouts like it was candy and I was Willy Wonka.

He added, "I had my secretary double-check, just to be sure."

"Secretary?" I said, picturing a buxom blonde sporting 1950s horn-rimmed glasses. I irrationally already hated her.

Griffin smirked, as if he could read my thoughts. "Yes, secretary. A fifty-three-year-old man named Louis who is more of a snob than my grandmother."

"Oh." I did feel better and told myself that my reaction was way over the top—I had no rights to this man, despite the fact that I wanted to climb him like a mountain and plant my flag on the top of his head in order to stake my claim. "So you're stalking me by proxy."

"Not quite." He grinned. "Just attempting to uncover some useful intel."

Panic rushed through me. "What kind of intel?"

"If you'd invite me in I could explain."

Did he know? Was he about to confront me? He probably had access to really good private investigators. It wouldn't take much for him to unravel my entire life and tell the Crawfords everything. Had he come here to expose me?

I took a deep breath. I was being irrational. He wouldn't be grinning at me like that if he was about to blow up my whole life. I was letting my paranoia get the best of me. Plus, hadn't I promised Alice a picture?

He was still standing in the hallway and I wondered whether anybody was listening in on our conversation. It would be better to have him come inside. Right?

Then again, I didn't know what the rules were. The Crawfords had never said I couldn't invite someone over. But that could have just been an oversight; it probably hadn't occurred to them that I might.

I glanced toward the kitchen. Knowing Sheila, the answer to my question was in that binder. But that would take some explaining that I didn't currently want to do.

"Are you arguing with the angel and devil on your shoulders?" he asked.

Constantly, ever since I'd met him. I decided to let him in, but to make him stay in the front entryway. Where we would stand with several feet of distance between us. Remaining vertical so that I wouldn't be tempted to go horizontal. "Come in."

I backed up and he put his hand on the door, letting himself in, then allowed the door to shut quietly behind him.

"We need to keep our voices down," I told him. "I'm babysitting and Milo's asleep."

"Understood."

Crossing my arms, I asked, "Why didn't you call or text?"

"I don't have your number," he said triumphantly.

"You know which room I'm in. You could have called the front desk and asked them to connect you."

The look on his face let me know that he'd considered and then rejected this idea. "You've caught me. I should have rung you, but I wanted to see you in person. You did say I could come by."

"I did? When?"

"When I asked if I could call on you."

"That's what that means?" I asked. I'd had no idea.

"Do you often agree to things you don't understand?"

More often than I was about to admit. "Sometimes. But the things I agree to don't usually involve people doing their best *Mission: Impossible* impression."

He looked sheepish at my words, and we both stood there, as if unsure what to say next. It became awkward and strange and I didn't know what to do.

Then Griffin broke the tension by speaking. "Now I understand why that prince held on to Cinderella's shoe."

His statement was so far out of left field all I could say was, "What?"

"He had the perfect excuse to see her again. It would be all right and proper if I was returning your shoe."

"It would be weird," I told him, taking in what he'd just said and then focusing on the important part. "You wanted to see me again?"

"Of course. Why wouldn't I?"

Because I'd already rejected him? Was he a glutton for punishment? "If it would help you out I could get you one of my shoes."

"No need," he said, mirroring my stance, crossing his arms as well. "I've already been caught out not having a plan. I was hoping I'd see your lovely face and something would come to me."

I ignored the way my stomach quivered over his use of the word *lovely*. "Has it?"

"No. I've never been good at reacting quickly to situations where I have to make a snap decision, so it shouldn't surprise me that this would all blow up and you'd think me strange."

I tried to hide my smile. "I don't think you're strange."

"You don't?" he asked, as if it were the most important thing in the world that I think well of him. The expression in his eyes was so endearing, so adorable.

He was not charming. I was not charmed by him. Not.

"You'd think someone with a degree from Oxford could have come up with a good excuse," I said.

Shrugging his shoulders playfully he said, "Yes, I've shamed the hallowed halls of that institution. But is it my fault that you render me incapable of coming up with a decent lie?"

His words made me want things that couldn't be.

"Can you stop doing that?" I asked him.

"Stop doing what?" He seemed genuinely confused. As if he wasn't aware of what he was doing.

I waved my hand. "This. This whole charm offensive you're trying to launch."

"I can turn the charm down, but I don't believe I can turn it off completely," he said with a disarming grin that proved his point.

Fine. I could deal with a charmed-down man. Just barely, but it was possible.

What I couldn't do, however, was control my mouth. "What's wrong with you?"

"A great deal, I'm sure. What specifically were you curious about?"

"Most men that I'm a . . ." I'd almost said *attracted to*. Out loud. With my whole face. Wow. I really was losing it. "Most men that I meet are usually messed up in some major way. They tend not to treat women very well."

"Whyever not? I find women to be incredible creatures."

"Creatures?" I repeated with a note of disgust.

"It's a term of endearment."

"For a bunny. Not for a woman."

He took a step closer to me, and my heartbeat kicked up its pace. "You wouldn't like it if I called you Bunny?"

Uh, I would like that very much, please and thank you.

I got a mental image of him murmuring *Bunny* against my throat and I nearly spontaneously combusted. "No," I said, clearing my throat. "No, I would not like that and there would probably be a blunt object accompanying my outrage."

"Duly noted," he said with a laugh. "Perhaps that's what's wrong with me."

I had to shake my head to stop those mental images from proceeding. "Are you a cheater?"

"At cards?"

"No, with women."

"I never have, no."

Why did I find that so hard to believe? "You've never cheated on anybody?"

"Do most of the men you've met do that?"

"Yes. Every single one that I've ever met."

Griffin studied me for a second, like I was a puzzle he was trying to figure out but he couldn't find the corner pieces he needed to get started. "I have an aunt that I adore and her husband has cheated on her their entire marriage—going on thirty years now. I've seen the pain it's caused her and how it's broken her spirit. I could never do that to someone I care about."

"Why doesn't she divorce him?"

"Because she would stop being a marchioness."

"So?" That literally made no sense to me.

"To some people that's everything."

In what world? "Well, it doesn't mean anything to me."

He grinned. "That's why I like you."

I wanted his words to mean something. To not be some charming, flirtatious response that he had probably doled out to dozens of girls before me. "You only like me because you can't have me."

He raised both eyebrows and shrugged one shoulder in a way that very much said *not yet*.

Now I was annoyed. "Do you think that's going to change?"

"Life is about change."

Despite his assertion, nothing was going to change here. Not the way he wanted it to, anyway. Time to talk about something else. I recalled what he'd said when he first arrived. "Earlier, you said something about gathering intel?"

"Yes, well, we left things a little muddled last night, didn't we? With how we ended things. Or didn't."

"What are you referring to specifically?" Because I felt like I'd been pretty clear. Well, clear-ish.

"You said we could be friends. Does that mean we can hang out? Spend time together?"

I was far too excited at this prospect. Which should have been a flashing neon sign to tell him no, he'd misunderstood, shake his hand, and send him on his way. Especially with all his "life is about change" nonsense. "Technically, yes. I suppose."

"Brilliant. Why don't you give me your number so that I can ring you properly next time?"

The digits of my phone number—which I hoped were right, considering I hadn't had the number for very long—just fell out of my mouth, and he put the number into his cell. Some part of me kept repeating that this was a bad idea, but I had already agreed to a friendship. It just seemed rude to say no to that now, particularly given that I'd just told him (again) that we wouldn't be dating. It wasn't Griffin's fault that my ovaries wanted to throw a parade every time I saw him. I could control myself.

I could. And I would.

My phone buzzed and I glanced down to see a hi text from him. That reminded me of what I'd promised Alice.

"Can I ask for a weird favor?"

"Anything," he said in a way that made my stomach all twisty with anticipation.

"Can I get a photo of you?"

"Of us together?" he asked.

"No, just you."

"Why?" His tone was suspicious and I realized that he was probably worried that I might try to sell it to a tabloid or something.

"Do you remember my sister? The one who's a fan?"

"Ah yes. The sister with excellent taste."

"She asked me to send her a photo of you. To prove that I wasn't making this up." It might do me good to have a picture of him, too. Because sometimes I wondered if this was some kind of fever dream that I'd accidentally walked into and I was going to wake back up in my old apartment surrounded by vermin.

"Anything for your sister."

"Thanks."

I held up my phone and he angled his body toward me. "How's this? Debonair enough?"

Instead of just smiling and maybe waving like a regular person would have done, Griffin was . . . posing. His face—he was *smoldering* at my phone. Seriously. I thought it was going to melt in my hand. Like this was a professional photo shoot for some designer brand and he had modeling experience. Which, for all I knew, he might have. His expression was so sexy it took me a full four seconds before I finally remembered to click the button to take the picture.

"There we go!" My voice was weird and high pitched. "Alice will love this." Saying that reminded me of the photo I'd sent her earlier. "By the way, I still have your scarf."

While he probably didn't understand my subject leap, he didn't question it. "I wish I'd realized that earlier. I would have saved myself quite a bit of dignity if I'd remembered. It would have been a convenient excuse."

If my Burberry scarf had been borrowed, I would have not forgotten it and not rested until it was returned to me. It amazed me that anybody could own so much stuff that they didn't know when something was missing.

"It would have been much better than just tracking me down." I said it lightly because honestly? I was nothing but flattered. "It's in my room. I'll go grab it."

Most of the men I'd ever dated would have taken my words as an invitation and followed me into my bedroom. But not Griffin. He stayed put and I realized that my Things Men Should Do bar was so low that I was impressed by this small gesture.

I reminded myself of all the reasons that getting involved with him was a bad idea. That there were layers of variables that currently existed in my life, all of them lying on top of one another and tainted with the scary risk of the Crawfords discovering my true identity. Dating Griffin would just end up being a ticking-time-bomb relationship lasagna. Possibly tasty but, as he had said himself, dangerous.

But when I came back into the hallway, it was like I forgot all of my good intentions because somehow I kept forgetting just how attractive he was. He didn't say anything, but I saw the way his eyes lit up when he saw me, the smile that hovered on his lips, and I swallowed. Hard.

The man had needed to come over to clarify my meaning about "friends" because I had been sending out all kinds of mixed signals and here I was, doing it again. I should have handed him the scarf, thanked him for coming by, and sent him on his way.

Only I didn't do that.

Instead I held the scarf out to him and he grabbed the end closest to him. The rational thing would have been to let go.

But nobody had ever accused me of being rational.

CHAPTER NINE

Instead of asking what was wrong with me, Griffin's eyes darkened and he tugged on the scarf, first with one hand and then the other, pulling me closer and closer to him, so close that I was practically on top of him. I didn't resist. I couldn't have even if I wanted to. The space between us was arcing with electricity, heating me up and making me shiver all at the same time.

I thought about trying to move away, but I didn't. I was frozen in this spot, holding my breath. His gaze flickered from my eyes down to my mouth and my heart came to a complete halt under my rib cage.

Kiss me. Kiss me. Kiss me. The words thundered in my head, but he didn't seem to hear them. My body leaned toward his, like he was still pulling me to him, even though my feet weren't moving.

I heard the husky intake of his breath when I canted toward him again, making our chests lightly graze one another. My head felt light, my stomach doing somersaults. It reminded me of when I was a kid playing on the playground merry-go-round and had been knocked loose, landing with a thud, not able to catch my breath but still feeling like I was twirling.

He released a breath against my cheek and my skin literally ached in response, needing his touch more than anything in the world. Wanting beat hard through my veins.

This had to stop. I had to be the one to stop it.

"Thanks for lending it to me," I said in a soft voice. I wondered if he could hear what I was actually trying to say.

"Thanks for returning it." His voice was low, and also full of unspoken want.

Of things that had to remain unsaid.

It felt as if his nose grazed mine, but the sensation was so fleeting that I couldn't be sure. "Just friends, huh?" he asked.

"Just friends," I whispered. It probably would have been a lot more convincing if I could have said it in my normal voice.

Another ten seconds of this and I was going to kiss him. Which, for reasons I couldn't currently recall, wasn't allowed. I tried to summon up a mental image of my sister to give me strength, but all I could think about was his shoulders and how strong and broad they were. What it would feel like to run my lips across the stubble on his jawline. Whether or not his hair was soft.

No! I couldn't afford the distraction. Not even one this cute. Somehow I got my feet to move and then I was opening the door. "Thanks for coming by."

I felt his hesitation, his confusion, as he stood next to me, but I didn't make eye contact. I couldn't.

"I'll text you. Good night, Bunny."

That nickname sent a spear of heat through me, but I somehow managed to stay upright.

He went through the door and not only did I manage to close it, but I locked it as well. I leaned against it and then finally gave in to my urge to slide into a pile on the floor.

I'd told my sister I wouldn't accidentally run into him, but I had not counted on him doing it deliberately. Or him saying that he wanted us to hang out.

What did I do now?

~

While I did manage to do more work on Milo's lesson plans, I spent many hours that night thinking about Griffin and what to do about the situation I found myself in. He intrigued me. I wanted to get to know him better and I wanted to spend time with him. I could acknowledge that to myself, at least. I was very physically attracted to him. Very. It was nice to discover that I could be interested in a man who didn't seem determined to ruin my life.

I probably should have tried to go to bed, but with my brain buzzing like this, there was no way I would have slept. I'd been dealing with bouts of insomnia on and off my whole life. The one time Alice had convinced me to go to a shrink, he'd suggested that it might be related to guilt I was feeling over things I had done. It might have been true and so it would make sense that I'd be unable to sleep now. I felt a lot of guilt, even if I tried to suppress it most of the time.

That was the problem with spending time with Griffin. It would be like tugging a loose thread on a cheap sweater. It would be okay in the beginning, just one or two missing patches, but eventually everything would unravel around me. He would figure it all out, and there was no way to predict the fallout. But I'd seen enough schemes go bad to know that it would start with the relationship falling apart and then move on to destroying what I had with the Crawfords.

I was walking a tightrope here and I had to be careful. I had done my best to stay calm around them because if I was constantly stressing about my fears that Sheila would find out the truth, she would sense that something was off. I had to believe the lie to convince everyone else around me. I hated doing this because I liked the Crawfords so much, but what else could I do? It wasn't like I could raise money by selling my kidney or something. I needed to give it to Alice.

Not wanting to think about it anymore, I gave in to my desire to know more about Griffin Windsor and grabbed my laptop, opening a web browser. It didn't take long to discover that he was twenty-seven and a Gemini. I don't know why I bothered looking that last part up; it wasn't as if knowing his astrological sign would tell me anything about him. He'd gone to some fancy school and then Oxford and apparently had never had a relationship that had lasted longer than a week.

Since I liked only dysfunctional men, that had to be his thing. That he couldn't commit.

Which I shouldn't have cared about. I currently couldn't commit to anything, either. As I'd already decided, there couldn't be a relationship here.

Nobody is saying you have to date him. Just have some fun, a voice inside my head whispered to me. Maybe it was that proverbial devil on my shoulder that Griffin had asked about.

A short fling certainly had its merits. Who would be better at it than Griffin?

But I discovered that I didn't like the idea of him being a womanizer. I preferred for him to be the kind of guy who wanted to adopt a golden retriever and then live happily ever after with me in his castle with a white picket fence.

Not that any of this actually mattered, because despite the temptation, I absolutely could not get involved with this man. I convinced myself that learning more about him was actually a good thing. Had to do my homework so that I knew what I was dealing with.

As I continued on my search, a link showed up that had his name and the word *tragedy* in the title. I read it and found out that Griffin's parents had died in a car accident when he was just seven years old. It was so, so sad.

At that, I closed my laptop. I didn't want to see any more. Picturing Griffin as a lonely little seven-year-old absolutely broke my heart.

I grabbed my phone, going to the gallery to look at the picture I'd taken of him. Yep, still scorching hot. I forwarded the picture to

Alice. She really was going to need that heart transplant after she saw this.

At least one of us could be deliriously happy.

~

I woke up the next morning to a text block from Alice that was just a line of EEEEEEEEEEEEEEEEEs and a bunch of emojis that I didn't want to try to interpret because I got the general gist. Then she'd told me to call her ASAP to discuss everything.

Yawning, I texted back that I had to get up and work and would call when I got the chance. Some part of me thought it served her right to have to wait, what with her willing this whole situation into being and making the universe send him to me.

Then I felt bad about being petty when my sister deserved all the happiness in the world.

She quickly responded, asking, Up all night again?

I've had eight hours of sleep. It's just taken me the last four days to do it.

I half expected her to write me back and tell me that my insomnia was the price of lying, but she just told me to have a good day and sent me a heart emoji. I texted the same one back to her and got up to start my day with Milo.

On my way to Milo's room my phone buzzed. I was about to tell Alice I was serious about the whole I'd-talk-to-her-later thing, but it was a text from Sheila. She said that she was planning on being home that evening. So Milo and I spent the day learning about things he wanted to learn about, playing games, and it felt like he was more engaged in the stuff I was trying to teach him. I still felt completely unqualified to be doing any of this, but I kept trying my best.

After lunch we spent a lot of time talking about what it meant to be a friend, and how you should treat people with kindness and respect, and he soaked it all in like a tiny little sponge. We role-played and practiced having conversations with other kids and it was so cute how seriously he was taking it.

During all of this I couldn't help myself—I kept checking my phone to see if Griffin had texted me. Not that I would have responded, because I was busy, but shouldn't he have done what he said he was going to do? I was seriously miffed.

Milo and I decided to go down to the playground at about three o'clock to try out the friend thing. He put on a play hard hat and an orange vest over his shirt and sweats, and I couldn't help but take note of the subtext of how he was trying to protect himself. I grabbed a couple of juice boxes and emptied the snack bin into a large tote bag. I didn't know how much of an appetite Milo might work up and decided it was better to be safe than sorry.

He didn't say much on the elevator ride down and when we arrived at the playground, Milo was nervous and hung back. Unfortunately, I couldn't do everything for him.

"Go out there and see if there's a kid you'd like to meet. Then just do what we practiced. I know you can do this. I believe in you! I'll be waiting right here for you." I sat down on an empty bench that faced the playground. There were a lot of kids running around and screaming and Milo headed into their midst. I couldn't believe how anxious I was for him. I made a wish that things would work out and I waited. If he was having a hard time, we'd talk about what went wrong and how we could try again tomorrow. He looked so small and lost on the playground that I nearly rushed out there to tell him it was okay, he didn't have to do this.

"Diana?"

I turned to my right and saw Griffin. With a little blonde girl hanging on to his right leg. My heart did a happy jig at the sight of him.

My first thought was that he was even prettier in full sunlight than he had been in dim-room lighting.

My second was that he had a child and was obviously married and now I knew why I was attracted to him. He was a Cheating McCheater who also lied. Of course I liked him.

Karma was seriously going to smite me for flirting with (and lusting after) a married man.

I sat there for a moment, unable to process what I was seeing. "Griffin! You . . . have a daughter." This changed everything I thought I knew about him. Married and a father. How could he not have even mentioned it to me?

"Not quite. This is Sophie, my niece. Sophie, say hello to Diana."

My chest caved in with relief. "You're not married?"

If he thought my question was strange, he didn't show it. "Of course not." His phone rang and he looked at the screen. "Pardon me for a moment."

Sophie untangled herself from her uncle's leg and ran over to me. She was wearing a pink sequined shirt with an orange tutu over purple tights. She should definitely be friends with Milo.

She cinched that belief for me when she held up her hand with all her fingers outstretched, her bubbly grin reminding me so much of Griffin. "My name is Sophie and I'm five years old."

"Hello, Sophie, nice to meet you."

"You're Diana?" Her accent was part British, part something else that I couldn't identify. "Uncle Griffin talked about you last night on our Zoom call with Papa. Papa laughed and said you weren't a bird Uncle Griffin could easily pull and he understood the appeal because that's how I happened. I don't know what that meant."

I figured *bird* must be like the American *chick* for a woman, and *pull?* Did her dad mean that Griffin couldn't get me? That had to be the definition because even if Sophie didn't understand the adult conversation, it was making sense to me. Apparently Sophie's mom hadn't given in to her dad's charms until she did and then Sophie was born.

Which was not going to happen here.

Instead of explaining I said, "I have someone I'd like you to meet. Milo!" I called his name and waved him over. He was still wearing that dejected expression and I pointed to Sophie. "This is Sophie. She's your age. Sophie, this is my friend Milo."

Sophie jumped up and down slightly, clearly excited. "Hullo, Milo! Did you know that in four billion years the surface of the planet will heat up and kill all life on the surface?"

"I think I have Lyme disease," Milo responded.

Ah, the beginning of a beautiful friendship.

"Brilliant! Let's be friends!" she said, grabbing him by the hand and pulling him along with her to the playground. Milo shot a glance at me over his shoulder, and I could see that he was smiling. I put my hand over my chest. How did I already care so much about this kid and his happiness?

Speaking of people I cared too much about after knowing them for only a few days, Griffin sat down next to me. His profile was strong and attractive, but even from this angle I could see that his expression was troubled. To my surprise, he didn't say anything.

I closed my eyes, taking in his warmth and that delicious clean smell of his. It was kind of weird how into his scent I was, but the last guy I'd dated thought his natural deodorant actually worked, so a hygienic man was a literal breath of fresh air.

When I opened my eyes again, it was then that I noticed those small details that other people probably missed. The way his shoulders hunched forward, how his hair looked a little crazier than normal, his clothes a bit wrinkled.

"You look disheveled," I said to him.

He turned his face toward me, giving me a wry expression. "That's not very gallant of you."

"I've been trying out radical honesty for the last few years." I mean, there'd been some huge but necessary deviations from that recently, but for the most part I did really try to always tell the truth. Even if it was painful.

"Radical honesty?" he repeated. "Is that where you get to just insult people and not worry about the consequences?"

Now I was certain something was up. "You sound grumpy. Do you want a snack?" I picked up the tote bag, showing him the inside.

He smiled at my attempt to distract him, feeling more like the regular Griffin to me. "Do you have any raisins?"

"I don't know." I started pawing through the bag. Sheila was really into healthy and organic snacks. It took me a few seconds, but I emerged triumphant, holding up a small red box. I handed it to him. "There you go."

Griffin looked down at the box. "Right. You were supposed to say no, and then I would have said, 'That's okay, do you have any dates?'"

"I see what you were going for there."

He nodded. "I would hope so, because it wouldn't have been very subtle."

"Foiled by your own cheesy pickup line."

"Tragic day indeed for us Oxford graduates."

"Indeed," I agreed, and he grinned.

"I do want to point out, though, that the line worked."

What? "It did not."

He relaxed back against the bench and put one of his arms behind me. Not touching me, but I was keenly aware of it being there. "The point of those lines is to initiate a conversation by making someone laugh. And hopefully have them agree to go on a date."

"Neither one of those things happened."

"The conversation did. You're talking to me right now. That par-ticular line has a one hundred percent success rate."

I did not want to think about his past and him talking to other women. At all. "You already know me, so it doesn't count." I didn't mention that the success of that line was most likely due to the person saying it. Griffin Windsor was a hard man to say no to. "Plus, you're not supposed to ask me out on dates because of the friend thing we've clearly established."

That was a lie, because nothing was clear where he was concerned.

"Friends can ask each other out on dates, can't they? You never clarified that they couldn't."

"It's universally understood," I said, mildly frustrated. That was the entire point of being "just friends."

"Not by me." He leaned in slightly toward me. "But if you want me to stop asking, to stop flirting with you, tell me and I will. I can take a no."

Here was my chance. To tell him exactly that. That nothing could or would happen between us and he should not ask me on a date.

All I had to do was say the actual words.

CHAPTER TEN

The words rattled around in my head: *Stop. Don't ask me out. We're only friends.* Around and around they swirled and it was like my mouth couldn't grab hold of any of them and actually speak the words.

"You're not saying anything," Griffin pointed out helpfully, but even him annoying me wasn't enough to get the words out. "You didn't say no."

"I didn't say yes, either."

He nonchalantly shrugged one shoulder, as if to say he disagreed with my assessment but wasn't going to say so. Instead he said, "You were worried that I was married."

That teasing lilt was back in his voice. I'd probably given him false hope that I would eventually say yes, which I shouldn't have done. I should take it back.

I didn't, though. "It was a reasonable conclusion to draw."

"Not really. I don't wear a ring and I wouldn't be asking you for dates if I were."

Which was why it had shocked me so much to see him with Sophie. He didn't seem like the kind of man who would be cheating on a wife. Especially after that story he'd shared with me about his aunt.

But I could give as good as I got. "So maybe you aren't married, but if we had to go to trial to determine whether or not you were a stalker, I'm pretty sure today would be enough to convict you."

I should have known he'd be ready with a retort. "I'm not stalking you, this is a coincidence, and are you carrying any knives that I should know about?"

"This is what happens when you don't really know someone. I might always keep knives on me. I could be a hired mercenary or an assassin."

"Yes, the kind who can't keep her shoes on."

He was laughing at his own joke, and I nudged his arm. Things felt casual and easy, and I was glad we were back to that.

Then he turned to look at me and wrecked that whole feeling.

"Green," I whispered. His eyes were definitely green, not blue. In this light I could finally see what color they were. Viridian green. It made me want to run to the local craft store and get a tube of that exact color and cover an entire canvas with it. "I wondered about that."

For some reason I forgot that voices carry and people could hear you when you talked. "You wondered about me?" he asked.

"Just your eye color." Now it was my turn to be grumpy. How could I keep him at arm's length if I was waxing all poetic about his eyes?

His phone buzzed again and he glanced at the screen before letting out a sigh and placing it down.

"Girl trouble?" I couldn't help but ask.

"Yes, but not the kind you're thinking of. Sophie is the trouble."

"Sophie?" I looked out at the playground, where she was sitting at the top of the jungle gym, having what looked to be a serious conversation with Milo. "How could she be trouble? She seems so sweet."

"Sophie is my favorite poppet in the whole world." The affection in his tone was obvious. "But we're here in Aspen to protect her."

"From what? Is she the key to some ancient prophecy and there's an evil sorceress trying to find her?"

He rubbed his jaw tiredly. "You're not far from the mark. Not the prophecy part, but the evil sorceress. My grandmother."

"What does your grandma have to do with it? Is Sophie a gold digger?"

My teasing fell flat, given that he shifted away from me and didn't respond. His body language was closed off—arms against his chest, legs crossed at the ankle, not making eye contact with me. At first I worried that I might have said something to upset him, but I got the sense that things went much deeper than that.

My curious nature threatened to overtake me, wanting to pepper him with questions, but I stayed quiet, knowing that the best way to get people to speak was to remain silent.

Another fun fact I'd learned from my mother. It wasn't all that surprising that my brain went to her, considering we were talking about evil sorceresses / terrible people.

"The thing my grandmother cares most about is our reputation. And the older Ollie and I became, the more we publicly messed up, the more she has threatened to cut us off."

"Cut you off?" For some reason I was picturing an elderly lady with an axe aiming for Griffin's knees.

"Financially," he said with an odd look, as if I should have automatically known this. As a pretend rich person, I probably should have. "After my last . . . indiscretion she let us both know that we're on our last chance."

I actually knew what he was talking about. A few months ago he'd been dating a British reality TV star who had leaked private pictures of Griffin. There had been a lot of stories about it online, talking about how he'd shamed his family name.

"Wait. Sophie's five. It's not like she was just born. She's been around for a while," I said. "Unless you kidnapped her and that's why your grandma will be mad."

"I haven't kidnapped her. Ollie fell madly in love with a French model when he was at university. Sophie came along nine months later. He told me 'procreate in haste, repent at leisure.' Not that he doesn't adore Sophie, he does. He and Gisele were much too young to become parents. But they've done it and managed to keep it all secret. Nobody knows about her. Gisele was worried about her career, and Ollie was afraid Granny would find out and disinherit him."

"Wow." Five years was a long time to keep a secret, especially one of this magnitude.

"Ollie's been looking for a way to ease Granny into the situation, but six weeks ago Gisele decided she didn't want to be a mom any longer and dropped Sophie off at Ollie's door. They've always shared custody, but she won't respond to any texts or phone calls."

I looked over at the kids playing again. "That poor little girl."

"Gisele's timing couldn't have been worse. Granny's decided that since Ollie's old enough to gain access to his trust fund, he needed to do his duty." At my blank expression he added, "Join the boards of charities, be a more responsible figure in public. She's demanding all of his time. And since he supposedly doesn't have any other responsibilities . . ." He trailed off.

"But why come here? Couldn't you have just stayed in England?"

"The paparazzi is far more interested in me than Ollie. Eventually someone would have photographed Sophie if we'd stayed. The entire country would know. And regardless of what Ollie thinks, Granny will not take this well. I can already hear her now, railing about him 'besmirching' the family name by impregnating an 'entertainer' out of wedlock."

I digested this for a second and then asked, "But you're on thin ice with your grandma, too. If she finds out that you're involved with the cover-up, you'll be in trouble."

He nodded. "True. But the last thing my father ever said to me was to protect my little brother. So that's what I do."

"You're going to risk your inheritance for him?"

"Of course. I'd do anything for him."

I had never been more attracted to him, and I hadn't realized that was possible. "I get that. I feel the exact same way about my sister. And now I understand why you didn't want me to tell anyone that you were here."

"Yes. Things were actually going well. I was pulling it off. Until this morning. When Sophie's nanny quit."

He seemed so serious that I wanted to make him laugh. "Why? Did you use the raisins/dates line on her?"

Griffin didn't respond to my joke. "No, her boyfriend finally called and proposed after seven long years and she ran home to marry him before he changed his mind. Now I'm the one responsible for Sophie's care and I don't know how to entertain her. I'm guessing that it's not a good idea for her to sit in front of the telly all day."

"Can't you call an agency or something?"

"I don't know that I can trust someone new like that. I can't afford to have anyone living with us that hasn't been vetted already. Sophie is not very discreet."

I'd noticed. "What about your secretary?"

"Louis has informed me that while he doesn't mind watching over her while she's sleeping, he was not hired to 'care for small persons.' Which is true, and so it puts the responsibility of it all on me." He let out a deep breath that sounded frazzled. Like he was overwhelmed. "Apologies. I don't mean to unload all of my problems on you. We don't do that in my family. Have to keep a stiff upper lip and all that."

Reaching out, I put my hand on top of his forearm, squeezing it gently. His skin was so warm, and rough blond hairs on his arms tickled the underside of my palm. He looked at my hand in surprise, and then up at my face. I withdrew quickly, reassuring myself that it had just been one friend comforting another friend. Nothing more.

Because he needed some compassion. I kind of liked seeing him this way, though, out of sorts. It was a contrast to the perfect man I'd seen so far with his perfect hair and perfect teeth and perfect lips and perfect forearms and what was probably a perfect chest, which I couldn't verify as I hadn't actually seen it yet, but I wholeheartedly approved of what I could make out and . . . I stopped my train of thought from totally derailing and tried to get it back on track. Griffin needed help.

"The Crawfords travel a lot and I'm helping out with Milo." I didn't mention that I'd been compensated to do it.

Before I could continue on with what was about to be an insane offer, he said, "You seem to do a lot of favors for the Crawfords." I couldn't read his tone, but there was something there. Was it residual anxiety from his current family situation? Something different? I brushed it off, but now I felt the teensiest bit uneasy.

"Maybe because I'm a nice person," I said defensively. "Okay, I'm not actually a nice person, but I'm trying to be."

His face softened at that. "I think you're very nice."

Why did that thrill me and make me feel warm all over? It shouldn't have. "You don't even really know me."

"Not in the way I'd like, no. But you are nice and it's not up for discussion."

Well, okay then. I preened internally over his words. Not wanting to keep going down this road where he said sweet things to me that would eventually weaken my resolve, I asked, "How long are you planning on being in Aspen?"

"Ollie and I had originally hoped for Sophie and me to be here for a fortnight."

Confused, I asked, "Like the video game?"

"No," he said with a smile. "It means for about two weeks."

I frowned. That didn't feel long enough. I wanted him to stick around. "Then you should have just said two weeks. Anyway, the Crawfords and—" I cut myself off. I'd almost said "and I," which would mean that I'd been a part of it. Which I had been, but I didn't want Griffin to know that. "The Crawfords have a really good schedule set up for Milo with lots of activities. I could email that to you and maybe you guys could tag along and the kids could spend more time together. They seem to be getting along really well."

"That would be brilliant!" Griffin's relief was evident and he looked over at the kids, who were currently on a teeter-totter. "It would be a shame to split them up. They seem to be kindred spirits."

Then he turned his gaze back to me and I suddenly got the distinct impression that he was talking not about Milo and Sophie, but about us.

"Playdates are not actual dates," I told him, ignoring the way my pulse was dancing. "Don't get any ideas about them being dates in sheep's clothing."

He held up both hands, as if under arrest. "I hadn't thought anything of the sort."

This was all for the kids, I told myself. It had nothing to do with me wanting to see him and spend time with him. Nothing. "Okay. Just so long as we're clear on that."

I figured one of us should be.

"Truly, you're saving my life here. Thank you."

"What does one get for saving an earl?"

His eyes darkened—shifting from a viridian green to a dark forest green—and my breath caught in my throat when he said, "Anything you desire."

I gulped at his words and told my throbbing pulse to knock it off. Because my body apparently had all kinds of desires that it wanted to share with him. I coughed once, trying to clear my throat so that I could speak. We were not going to talk about what I wanted. I deflected by asking, "So, are you worried about losing all your money?"

His mouth twitched, like he wanted to smile. "You change the subject a lot."

Admittedly, I had been doing it in a fairly obvious way, but people usually didn't notice. Everyone liked talking about themselves and when you asked them a personal question, they assumed you found them just as fascinating as they found themselves. It surprised me that Griffin seemed a bit resistant to it, and that he'd noticed I was doing it. It said a lot about the kind of person he was. Not as self-centered as you'd expect a guy like him to be. "You didn't answer the question."

"I suppose I have to answer since I do owe you one . . . Am I worried about losing all my money? Probably more than I should."

I wanted to tell him money didn't matter, but how could I? In my current situation money was the only thing that mattered. "I know I should offer you some pithy quote. But all I can come up with is 'money doesn't buy happiness.'" It did, however, buy kidney-transplant surgeries, and at this point it was basically the same thing as happiness.

"What about 'money is the root of all evil'?" he offered.

"If that's true, then I guess you'd be better off without it."

"It's just difficult to have your whole life be one way and then be faced with the prospect of it all going away and everything being totally different."

"I know exactly what you're talking about and honestly? It's not so bad. You learn and adapt," I said.

"Like I mentioned, I'm not always quick at the adapting-to-change part. I just don't want everything to fall apart around me."

I felt that same urge from earlier to reach out and reassure him. Instead I said, "Again, I know exactly what you're talking about."

It was kind of eerie how he was saying things that perfectly expressed how I was feeling. I didn't want everything to blow up around me, either.

Which I needed to keep in mind when it came to Griffin. I tried not to think about how he'd shared something really personal about himself, something that I could have used to make money. He probably thought it was safe to tell me because if I were also wealthy, I wouldn't be tempted to call a tabloid and offer this whole story to them for a payout.

Obviously, there was no way I'd do it. I couldn't hurt him like that. For a moment it looked like he was going to ask me what I meant, but then it passed and he didn't say anything. Maybe I should have told him something private about me. Evened out the playing field between us.

Or I could give him a way to help me out. "If you owe me one, I know how you can repay me."

"Oh?" This interested him, his eyebrows raised in anticipation, that seductive smirk of his twisting his mouth to one side.

I told my hormones to behave. "Not that."

"If it is ever that, just let me know."

"Not going to happen. Anyway . . . can you teach me how to ski?"

That sexy expression slid off his face and he asked in shock, "You came to Aspen in January and you don't know how to ski?"

"No," I said defensively. "I mean, I understand skiing in theory."

"There isn't a ski theory. You either do it or you fall. There's not much philosophical wrestling happening out on the snow." He flashed that grin at me again, the one that made me weak-kneed and caused me to forget all of my good intentions.

"Milo's parents want him to learn but he's pretty resistant," I offered, turning my gaze away from him. Why was he so tempting? "I said I'd help out, but he won't tell me why he doesn't like it."

"The best thing to do with boys to get them talking is to be doing something else while you chat."

"Does that work on you?"

He let out a short laugh. "We're busy watching children and meanwhile I'm here confessing all my family secrets, aren't I?"

"Fair point."

"One of my nannies did that with me growing up. She would get me out playing football and then talk to me about my problems. It was really effective."

I drew in a sharp breath. Was it my imagination or had he emphasized the word *nannies*? Maybe my guilty conscience was getting the best of me.

Or was he saying that he knew I was a nanny? I turned back to look at him, but I didn't see any accusation in his eyes.

He added, "I'll look at the schedule when you send it over and we'll find a time to practice skiing."

Griffin said it in such a definitive way that it felt like I was being told instead of asked. "Is that a royal decree?"

"I'm not allowed to issue royal decrees. Just noble suggestions."

I laughed at that, but my uneasiness remained. I needed to put some distance between us. "I'll do that later on tonight. But for now, Milo and I should be heading back upstairs." I grabbed the tote bag and stood up.

He stood up, too. "So soon?"

I ignored his question and yelled Milo's name, waving at him. He and Sophie ran over together and Milo's little grin could have lit up the whole room. "Sophie taught me about rogue black holes! If one opens up near the earth we'll all be swallowed up!"

The very last thing I needed was for Milo to get caught up in another obsession. "How interesting! We need to get going. Your mom is going to be home soon."

"Aw," Milo whined, clearly not wanting to go.

"Sophie is going to come to our painting class tomorrow, and maybe some of our other activities for the next couple of weeks. What do you think about that?" I asked, hoping to appease him in this moment so that I could escape.

"That's awesome!" he said. He turned to give Sophie a high five. "See you tomorrow!"

"Bye, Milo!" she said, slipping her hand into Griffin's.

I didn't say anything to Griffin—I just walked off with Milo. Mostly because I was afraid of what I might say or do.

As we headed for the elevators, I couldn't help but think of the situation Griffin and Sophie were in, how sad everything was with his grandmother. And how even if I never would have admitted this to Alice, there was some stupid, very small, very tiny part of me that imagined a fantasy world where Griffin and I could be together.

There was no way he could find out about my past now. His grandma would probably show up and try to feed me to her pet dragon. I'd never be good enough for him and his family. Any sliver of hope that I might have entertained about Griffin chucking his fortune out the window to be with me was destroyed.

Realizing this should have been a relief, as it would keep us firmly in the friend zone, but instead it was strangely depressing.

CHAPTER ELEVEN

Milo talked about Sophie for the rest of the afternoon. He informed me that she was allergic to the color green, pine nuts, ice cream, and asteroids crashing into Earth.

"The color green, huh?" I asked. "That must make walking on grass difficult."

He nodded. "Yes. That's why she likes it here. The snow covers all the grass."

I was glad that things had gone so well for the two kids, but now I had to be worried about all the time I was about to spend with the Earl of Strathorne.

Sheila arrived home and she seemed alert and fresh and very happy to see Milo. He told her all about Sophie as the two went to have dinner. She invited me to join them, but I declined. I heated up some microwave macaroni and cheese and went back to my room. After I finished eating, I decided to take a long, hot bath. Where I read my entertainment magazine and did not think about Griffin Windsor. At all.

After I finished, I dried off and got into some sweats and a T-shirt so old it was in danger of falling apart. I loved how soft it felt. I twisted my hair up into a bun on top of my head and then checked the clock on the bedside table and saw that it was late enough in Florida that the twins would be asleep and I could call Alice.

She was going to be so happy with today's update.

It was then that I realized I didn't know where my phone was. I got up and checked the bed, pulling the covers straight. Nothing. Maybe I'd put it in the kitchen? I stuck my head around the corner to make sure it was empty and searched there. Not on the counters. Not in the tote bag I'd used for snacks. I tried to remember the last time I'd had it, but I couldn't.

I went back to my bedroom and searched my dirty clothes, checking the pockets. Not there, either.

There was no way I could go to the Crawfords and tell them that I'd lost the brand-new phone they'd just given me. I got on my hands and knees and had started searching under the bed when I heard Sheila calling my name. She knocked on my door and I jumped to my feet.

"Come in!" I pasted a smile on my face, hoping she wouldn't notice my panic.

Sheila opened the door and said, "Hey, Diana. There's someone here to see you."

I started to ask who, but quickly realized I didn't have to. Griffin. He was the only person I knew here. I looked down at what I was wearing and wondered if I had enough time to change.

"You look fine," Sheila said, as if she could read my mind. "You definitely don't want to keep your date waiting."

Did she think I was dating? I wasn't here to do that. "He's not a date. Just a friend."

"If that's your idea of just a friend, I can't imagine what your actual dates look like."

This. This was why I couldn't get close to him. He'd met Sheila and won her over with all his charm and handsomeness. Who knew what they'd said to one another? Had she told him I was the nanny? Had he referred to me in some way that would have caused her to correct him?

Too late now. Time to face the music, I supposed.

For some reason I thought she might follow me to the front hall-way. My mom would have. Instead Sheila walked toward Milo's room without another word. If anything had happened, her reaction said to me that nothing had changed between us.

But with Griffin? What would he say when he saw me?

My legs felt jittery, my heart jackhammered in my chest, and I real-ized that I was completely panicked as I walked toward where Griffin was waiting. The two worlds I had created for myself in Aspen had just collided in a big way. I looked toward the front door—he wasn't there. Maybe he'd left and I was safe.

"Diana?" The sound of his voice sent a shock wave through my system. Even though I was expecting him, it still caught me off guard.

Sheila was much more polite than me and had shown Griffin into the living room, where he was waiting for me. I straightened my shirt, as if that could fix the way I looked. But he didn't comment on my appear-ance, and he didn't look at me in a way that made me self-conscious. He just seemed happy to see me.

The feeling was kind of mutual.

"What are you doing here?" I demanded, annoyed by my joy at seeing him. I folded my arms as I entered the living room. I kept my voice lowered so that no one would overhear us.

"Why are we whispering?" he asked, leaning in so that I could get a whiff of how delicious he smelled.

"Milo is going to bed," I said as an explanation.

He reached into a pocket inside his coat and said, "I would have called first but . . . lose something?" He pulled out my cell phone.

My body slumped with relief and I let out a shaky laugh. "Yes! I haven't had a phone for a few years and I guess I'm out of the habit of making sure I have it with me." I must have left it at the playground. But given my state of mind there, it was understandable that I'd for-gotten it. I guessed that Griffin most likely had the ability to make me forget my own name if he wanted to. "So, by fairy-tale law, what do I owe you now?"

"I'll take a date, if you have a spare one."

Too adorable for his own good. "I have so many dates just lying around—" In trying to play his game I realized just how pathetic I'd made myself sound. I couldn't tell him all the reasons why we couldn't date, including my job. He still assumed that I was a socialite. "Dating's not really on my agenda at the moment. I'm using my free time to . . . relax."

"I've found dating to be very relaxing."

Not registering the seductive tone in his voice, I scrunched up my nose. "Really? Not me. It's all awkward and weird small talk and getting dressed up for no reason."

"Perhaps you haven't been doing it right. I happen to be an expert dater. I could show you."

"That's not really a selling feature," I told him.

"Not yet," he teased and the unspoken promise was making my skin feel tingly.

"Maybe I'll just turn some straw into gold and we'll call it good," I said. I held my phone up, as if we'd both already forgotten why he'd come. "It'll be good to have a phone again."

"I can't believe you went without one for years. I've always admired people who could do that," he said. "Completely disconnect from the world by not having a mobile."

I hadn't really had a choice in the matter because my cell provider had unilaterally decided to disconnect my service due to non-payment. Plus, my second-to-last boyfriend had stolen the phone and I hadn't had the money to get a new one and pay the activation fee.

"Well, thanks for returning it to me." Those words made me think of when I'd returned his scarf to him, and I could see from the expression in his eyes that he was thinking about it, too.

I couldn't quite breathe as my blood thickened, warming me all over. Thankfully, he still had his powers of speech.

"I would have returned it sooner, but Sophie was the one who found it on the bench at the playground. She put it in her backpack and she showed it to me just before she went to bed. I figured you would want it back. I think in all her excitement about making a new friend today she forgot about it."

"Understandable. Milo's pretty excited, too."

"Good. I'm glad they get on so well."

"Yeah, it would make hanging out pretty awkward if they didn't like each other. Is your secretary watching Sophie now?"

"Yes, since it's very easy to do. She's a champion sleeper. She reminds me of Ollie. He can fall asleep anywhere, anytime. I figure with all that energy she expends through the day, along with her constant vigilance over worrying about the end of the universe, she must exhaust herself."

"I guess it makes sense that she would focus on the earth being destroyed. Given the way her own world has been upended."

He raised both of his eyebrows in surprise, like this was something he hadn't considered. "It may well be."

"At least she doesn't think she's about to die of some tragic disease every few minutes. I've never even heard of half the illnesses Milo thinks he has."

"Must make life interesting."

Oh, my life was very interesting at the moment. Maybe a little too interesting. I held my phone up. "Now that I have this back I can text you the link to the Google doc with the schedule."

"Looking forward to it. If nothing else, at least returning your mobile gave me a *raisin* to see you again."

"Okay, you need to stop. The line doesn't work." Not true. Him bringing it up again made a dent in the cement wall I was trying to build around my heart.

Griffin shrugged one shoulder. "Disagree. Let me reiterate, a hundred percent success rate."

I should not have found this cute. Time to bring this to an end before I tackled him to the floor with Sheila in the next room. "Thanks for stopping by. Let me walk you out." I didn't give him a chance to respond and headed for the front door, holding it open for him so that he could see himself out.

He stepped in the hallway and said, "You know, Bunny, you don't need to keep leaving your things behind to get my attention. You already have it."

Then he started whistling as he walked down the hallway to the elevators. Not caring who else heard, I yelled after him, "That's not what I was doing! And we're just friends!" before slamming the door shut.

Well, pushing the door shut hard. The automatic hinges wouldn't let me slam it.

Much less satisfying.

I probably should have also told him not to call me Bunny but, well, I kind of liked that.

Turning around I shrieked when I almost ran into Sheila. "Sorry!"

"No, I'm sorry," she said. "I thought you were calling me."

Nope. Just making a public fool of myself by yelling things at the hot guy outside the hotel room door. "I was saying goodbye to Griffin."

"Your *friend*?" she asked, teasing me.

Was every older woman in my life determined to misunderstand me? "Yes. I met him at the charity event the other night and then ran into him again today at the playground."

"Oh? Good thing you went to that event instead of me."

Debatable at this point. "He's also Sophie's uncle."

"The infamous Sophie? How fun!" she said. "I've heard so much about her today."

It suddenly occurred to me that I had made these plans to hang out with Griffin and Sophie without checking in with Sheila to see if it was okay. I should have done that. I was just so used to making decisions for myself without anybody else's input that it honestly hadn't even occurred to me.

If she said no, I was going to have to call him and say we couldn't hang out. It might make me a little sad, but I owed the Crawfords my full attention. They deserved to have everything I could give them. Not hanging out with Griffin was the least I could do. "Are you okay if we have playdates with them? Sophie and Milo seemed to get along really well."

Sheila let out a strangled sound, almost like a sob. Oh, wait, she was crying. I wasn't sure what to do so I awkwardly patted her on the shoulder and asked, "Are you okay?"

"I'm sorry." It took her a bit to get the words out. "He was so sick for so long. When he left the hospital I was so worried about him catching something and not being strong enough to fight it off that I kept him home when I shouldn't have. I didn't let him have any playdates or go to school. Then he told me he didn't like being around other kids because he was an introvert and I thought I was doing him a favor by not forcing him to play with anyone else."

I gently reminded her, "He also told you he had the plague."

Sheila quickly caught on to what I was telling her—that Milo had lied to spare her feelings. "I'm the worst mom."

"You are not! You're the best mom ever. I would have given anything to have a mom who cares as much as you do."

Then, without warning, she grabbed me and pulled me into a hug. I'd never been a hugger and at first it felt foreign and strange, but as I settled into it—it was nice.

She let go first and I stepped back. "I'm sorry I'm such a mess," she said, wiping the mascara from her eyes. I walked over to the coffee table and grabbed her a tissue. She followed me into the living room and accepted it gratefully.

"You're entitled after all you've been through," I told her.

"Well, I hope you spend as much time as you can with that Griffin. Life is too short. I appreciate you running it past me, but it wasn't necessary. You're a grown woman, Diana. I trust your judgment."

She shouldn't have. I had terrible taste in men. "I didn't know if you and John would be okay with me having a . . . friend."

"Why wouldn't we be?" She asked this like I was being totally unreasonable in my hesitation.

"I'm working," was the only reason I could come up with.

"Eleven hours a day. What you do with those other thirteen hours are up to you. Have all the friends you want. Honestly, with as pretty, smart, and kind as you are, I'm surprised there haven't been a line of suitors knocking on our door. Oh, excuse me, not suitors. *Friends*." Her wink tempered her slightly sarcastic tone. "Good night. I'll see you in the morning."

Sheila turned off the light in the living room, plunging me into darkness. It suited me due to the kind of thoughts running around in my head.

I recalled her kind words with discomfort because I'd never been very good with compliments. My own mother had torn me down for so long that emotionally I was in a place where the things that Sheila said couldn't be true because . . . they just weren't. Like my brain couldn't conceive how she might be right. Her words had made me uncomfortable, but I had to remind myself that it was just my own insecurities rearing their ugly heads.

I realized that this must be what it was like to have a normal mom. Someone who encouraged you and cared about your well-being. Who rooted for your success, who thought you were good at things and that of course other people wanted to be around you.

Milo was the luckiest kid in the whole world.

Thinking of Milo made me then think about our playdate tomorrow, which inevitably led my thoughts back to Griffin.

The last thing I needed was to get that kind of blanket permission from Sheila where Griffin was concerned. It was one of the things holding me back, telling myself I needed to focus on Milo and being a good employee.

Obviously, I still needed to do that, but she'd just made room for something more. I could practically feel my subconscious mind plotting ways to make this thing work out with Griffin.

This was . . . not good.

CHAPTER TWELVE

I needed to talk to someone about this. There was too much chaos in my brain to figure it out myself. Time to call Alice. I realized that I didn't have my phone on me and looked around. I'd dropped it on the couch. I really had to be better about not leaving it behind.

When I picked it up, I saw that there was a text from Griffin that read Can't wait to see you tomorrow. It was sweet. Simple. But it did make me melt a little inside.

As I walked to my room, my next thought was to wonder whether he'd gone through my phone. The Crawfords hadn't password-protected it, and I hadn't seen the point of doing it myself. I was going to now, obviously, but Griffin could have perused my apps and files. Not that there would have been anything for him to see. No pictures, no social media.

He could have seen my texts to Alice and those would be embarrassing (both for me and for her) but I knew, in a way I couldn't have explained, that he hadn't invaded my phone. He just wouldn't do that. I was suspicious of everybody all the time, so this was a new feeling for me. To trust that somebody was exactly who they appeared to be and that they would behave in a moral way . . . outside of Alice, I'd never had that before.

I closed the door and sat on my bed, choosing Alice from my contacts list and pressing the button. I needed her opinion. Maybe other people were seeing things that I couldn't.

"Are you married yet?" she asked when she picked up the phone.

"No. But I need to talk to you about that."

She let out a loud, dramatic gasp but I stopped her. "It's not like that. I just need to get your opinion. So let me tell you what's been going on."

Even though I'd previously been holding things back from her, this time I decided to lay all my cards on the table. I knew she wouldn't be unbiased, but she was the only person who knew the entire truth about me, so she was the only one I could go to for help. Recognizing that the story would be long, I reached for my sketch pad and a pencil. Having my hands occupied helped keep my mind more focused.

When I finished telling her absolutely everything, including Sheila Crawford saying it was fine to date and hang out with Griffin and Sophie, this time Alice let out a happy sigh. "I just want you to know that I love everything about this guy already. Especially the stuff he says. He's so romantic. I want you to give me his phone number."

All the snow would have to melt off that mountain behind the hotel before I did that. "Why?"

"I want to leave him a voice mail that's just three straight minutes of me applauding him."

I had to laugh at that.

She added, "By the way, I knew you'd been editorializing when you talked to me. That there was more going on."

What could I say? She was right. I made long strokes on the sheet of paper in front of me. "Maybe that was because I knew you'd jump to the wrong conclusion."

"The one where you like him even though you're trying to deny it? Oh honey, I've been there since the first night. I don't need to jump because I've already hurtled out of an airplane ten thousand miles up and am currently plummeting to that conclusion."

"Pull that rip cord because nothing is going on."

"But you want it to."

"I . . ." What was I supposed to say? We couldn't be together. "That's not . . . I don't . . ."

"Oh, I see. We've entered the delusional part of the evening."

"I'm not deluded," I protested. "Just . . . unsure of what the right thing is to do here."

"Well, regardless of what you're telling yourself, this man is already deep in like with you."

She wasn't even here. How could she possibly know that? "It's only been like, three days."

"So? You're living the Cinderella story here. The prince fell in love with her after one night. As far as I can tell, Griffin is within the right time frame."

"As he keeps reminding me, he's not a prince, so your analogy doesn't work."

I could almost hear her shrugging over the phone. "Close enough. What does he have to do? Hire a skywriter? He's been very obvious with his intentions."

Shaking my head, I briefly closed my eyes and took a big breath. "That fairy-tale story has absolutely no bearing on my reality. I wouldn't want to date him unless I was being honest with him. And I am being so dishonest. The sheer magnitude of the lies! I mean, it's not just a string quartet of lies. It's not even a K-pop boy band of lies. No, this is the Vienna Boys Choir and accompanying orchestra of lies."

She was silent for a moment before she said, "Again, so?"

My hand stilled. How could she not be taking this more seriously? "Last time I checked, and as you keep reminding me, lying is bad. Things never work out once you finally get caught."

"Don't get caught, then. Tell him the truth now."

A panicked feeling wrapped itself around my heart, squeezing tightly. My pencil responded to my feelings, scratching on my sketch pad. "I don't want to do that. Then he won't have anything to do with me."

"You keep telling me you don't like him, so what would it matter if he stopped talking to you?"

The thought of not speaking to Griffin again crushed me, but I tried to ignore that feeling. "Well, I wouldn't want to keep Milo away from—"

"Don't you 'Milo' me. This was never about him. You offered to let Griffin come on those playdates so you could spend time with him. Because you like him."

Her words shocked me, even though some small part of my conscience suggested that she was right.

"Before you start deluding yourself again, and even though you are dismissive of my example, please allow me to point out that Cinderella lied. She lied and lied. She wore a beautiful gown that didn't belong to her, rode in a carriage made from a large orange-yellow gourd, pretended she had servants. The prince thought she was a princess or a noblewoman. She one hundred percent lied to that dude. She had a great backer in her fairy godmother, but the entire thing was one long con from the beginning to the end of the night. And do you know what the moral of Cinderella is?"

"Always wear great shoes because great shoes can change your whole life?"

At that Alice laughed. "No."

"Don't be mean to your stepdaughter because someday she might rule over you?"

"Okay, Miss Comedy, besides being kind to everyone and treating them the same whether they're an earl or a nanny, the moral of this story is that if Cinderella had been honest with her prince upfront, she would have saved them both a lot of heartache and misery. And to be specific to you, the prince didn't care that she'd lied. He loved her anyway. Even if you want to deny it, you and Cinderella are the same."

"Not true," I said, being stubborn because I didn't want to admit to the potential insight in her words. "Cinderella had small feet."

At that Alice laughed so loud I worried she might wake up her kids. "Look out, straws! Hide! Diana's grasping at you again!"

Now I joined in with her, and the laughing was strangely cathartic. I felt better. "He sees me in this expensive suite at this luxury hotel, going to a charity ball in a designer dress. He thinks we're the same, but we're not."

"It doesn't matter," she said gently. "If you were living in, well, your old apartment, he'd still like you. He doesn't care where you live. Tell him. It's better if it comes from you and he doesn't find out in some shocking way."

Like Sheila inadvertently telling him? "What if I confess and he thinks he has some moral responsibility to share it with the Crawfords?"

"You know that's stupid, right? That you're literally now making up reasons to stay away from him that have no bearing on reality?"

Okay, so I was being a little Pandora-esque, hanging on to my box tightly because I didn't want hope to escape.

"So maybe he won't tell anyone." I sighed, not sure what to do. "I also don't want to keep lying to him." This scruple that I had where Griffin was concerned was annoying and inconvenient, but definitely there.

"That's a good thing! It's what we like to call growth. You're becoming a better person, despite Mom's best intentions."

Her mentioning Mom put me on a totally different track, and had me thinking about a concern I had with Griffin. It made me confess something that I'd been secretly thinking but hadn't ever said. "He confuses me. I can't figure out what his angle is."

Now it was Alice's turn to sigh. "Not everyone has an angle. Mom did such a number on you."

"So far she's been right. You married a man who turned out to be garbage."

"True," she acknowledged, "but he didn't have an angle. He wasn't trying to use me or take anything from me."

"Just the best years of your life," I muttered.

"He also gave me Jenna and Jasper, and I'll always be grateful for that. The best things in life sometimes come from the absolute worst experiences. He and I were in love and it didn't work out. It happens. Maybe if I hadn't been so desperate to prove that I wasn't like Mom, I wouldn't have married him. There were warning signs about how selfish he could be, but I ignored them. That doesn't mean he was trying to con me, though."

It was really hard to see the world through such dark lenses all the time. I was trying to be better, but considering being vulnerable made all the fears so much more intense.

When I didn't say anything she continued on, "I worried about how the split might affect you. Chad and I were your only real-life experience with a married couple. But Griffin is not Chad. And you're not me. You wouldn't settle for anything less than you deserve."

I shifted on the bed, changing my position, moving my sketch pad. "That's probably part of the problem. I don't feel like I deserve anything good in my life. Do you think I'll ever stop feeling this way?"

"Only when you're able to forgive yourself. It's okay to want something good because you are a good person."

Alice's words made my throat feel thick, like there were unshed tears stuck there. "But I need to focus on what's important. To make sure that you're taken care of."

Her voice softened so low that it was almost hard to hear her. "Diana, I love you so much. But I don't want you to stop living your life trying to save mine."

"How can you say that to me? You know you and your kids are my whole world."

"You're allowed to enjoy the attention of a beautiful man and have fun. And if you're not ready to tell him the truth yet, which for the record I think is a mistake, no one would begrudge you living in a fantasy world for a fortnight."

I never should have told her that word. I had the feeling she was going to be using it a lot from now on.

She added, "You're not like Mom; this isn't the same thing. You're not trying to cheat or steal from him. Just have some fun. Believe me, if I could trade places with you, I would."

There were so many thoughts going through my head, all competing for attention, that it was hard to focus in on one thing. My pencil dropped out of my hand, landing softly on the floor.

Alice coughed, clearing her throat. "I know how hard it is to live your life with a ton of regrets. I think you'll regret it if you let this chance pass you by. Enough lectures from me! I'm going to go to bed. Have fun tomorrow, and I want to hear all about it! Love you!"

I said good night, told her I loved her, too, and hung up.

Glancing at my sketch pad, I realized what I'd drawn. It was a picture of Griffin, smirking at me from the page. I closed the cover. Left to its own devices, my subconscious had drawn him. I didn't know what that meant.

I decided that it had happened only because we'd been talking about him. No other reason. At least not one that I was willing to admit to. Mostly because if I was totally honest with myself, I'd disregard the rules I'd put into place to protect myself and my job. I couldn't risk everything for a cute boy.

But Alice's words and advice so closely mirrored some of the rationalizing thoughts I'd had, that I could just have fun with Griffin without it meaning something more, and it made me wonder whether I should consider that option more seriously.

I couldn't discount the real possibility of there being problems. Even if he didn't run and confess everything to the Crawfords, it didn't mean that he wouldn't accidentally say something when he saw them. Because he would see them. Especially if he was coming over with Sophie so that the kids could spend time together. I didn't know how feasible it would be to keep the Crawfords and Griffin apart, but I was guessing it would be difficult. That wasn't even taking into account them accidentally running into each other at a restaurant or on the slopes or some other rich-person place.

Maybe, if I told him everything, then there wouldn't be any slipups. He was obviously good at keeping secrets. He'd kept Sophie a secret from his grandmother for the last five years. That, if nothing else, indicated his trustworthiness.

Although that could be evidence of his dedication to his brother, and not to general secret keeping.

Could I risk it? Should I? I didn't want to do a bad job for Milo and the Crawfords. Well, a worse one than I was currently doing. Although I was trying my best. But would hanging out with Griffin make me unfocused? Distracted? Would it be completely selfish?

"Argh." I gritted my teeth together in frustration. My conversation with Alice hadn't made any of my choices clearer.

If anything, it was all muddier than before.

CHAPTER THIRTEEN

Milo and I used a rideshare service to get to the art museum. When we got inside signs pointed us in the right direction and we found a room with a bunch of kids and adults doing various projects. I had thought it would be more of a guided sort of class, but it looked like they'd just put out supplies and canvases. I initially felt uneasy at how many people were here, but given that most of them were kids, I figured I didn't have to worry about feeling like anyone was watching me.

"Hi, I'm Betty." A very pretty twentysomething blonde with a huge smile stopped in front of me and Milo. Confirming my evaluation she said, "There's cubbies over there for your coats and we have smocks hanging up. We have a picture up front of yellow daisies in a blue vase to copy if you'd like, but please grab whatever you need and feel free to make whatever you want. We're very informal here—we want to inspire as well as create. Let me know if you have any questions!"

Thanking her, I helped Milo get his coat off and we put them in our cubbies. The general chaos of the room seemed to overwhelm him a little bit, so I hurried up and grabbed our smocks and found a quiet table up near the front. I grabbed a couple of canvases and two easels, setting them up before going over to a nearby table to get our other supplies.

"What are you going to paint?" I asked Milo. Without thinking, I began to line up my brushes and paints in order. I grabbed a cardboard palette and decided I'd go ahead and paint the example. I didn't want my rogue thoughts to paint a picture of Griffin without my permission. That's all I needed him to see when he arrived.

Milo tapped a clean brush against his chin. "I don't know. I'll have to think about it."

"That's the great thing about painting. You don't have to make it look like something. There's no rules. Just do whatever feels right to you." I didn't know a lot about the things I was teaching Milo, but here at least I had some level of expertise. All self-taught, but it was better than how I pronounced "Où se trouvent les toilettes," which I believed to be French for "Where is the bathroom?" I couldn't be a hundred percent sure, though.

I began squeezing colors onto my palette while Milo pondered what his work of art should be. I saw the moment when inspiration struck his elfin face.

He turned the canvas toward me. "Look! I made mountains covered in snow!"

I smiled at him. "If you want to do that, there's some white over here. You could probably add in some grays and blacks, too."

"No. I think I'm going to paint the ocean and the sky together."

"Good plan," I told him, squeezing out some shades of blue. I tried to show him how he could lighten or darken the shades, but he wasn't listening.

Instead he announced, "I'm pretty good at this. It's surprising that I can paint so well even though I have dysentery."

"If you had dysentery, we wouldn't be sitting here having this conversation." I didn't add that he'd be stuck on a toilet—that was not something he needed to add to his repertoire.

I watched him paint for a bit, loving the look of concentration on his face as he covered an entire canvas in one shade of blue.

But I noticed something that seemed a little off. Milo frequently switched which hand he painted with. "Which hand do you prefer using? Like when you draw or eat?" I asked casually.

"I'm both-handed."

"Like . . . you're ambidextrous?"

Milo stopped what he was doing and looked at me in anticipation. "Is that a disease?"

"No, it means you can use both hands equally." He went back to his short brushstrokes. I was probably worrying over nothing, so I thought I would take Griffin's advice since Milo was occupied with something else, and ask him about the skiing thing.

"So, Milo, I was talking to Griffin about skiing. Sophie loves it. It might be fun to go with them."

"No thanks."

"What is it you don't like about skiing?"

He shrugged. "I don't like doing things I don't know how to do. Or going fast."

That dinged an alarm bell in my head. I'd already noticed that he struggled a bit with his writing and had tripped a few times over the rug, but I'd dismissed those moments. What if it was connected? "Going fast? Like when you ride a bike?"

"I don't like bikes. My dad tried to teach me, but I hated it."

"What about swings?"

"I don't like those, either," Milo said. "The slide's okay, but only if I can see the end of it. I don't like when I don't know what's going to happen next."

That made me think that roller coasters were something he wouldn't enjoy, either. His explanations reminded me so much of my nephew that I wondered if there was something else going on besides simply disliking skiing. I didn't want to rush to any conclusion without knowing more, but it was something I definitely wanted to bring up with Sheila the first chance I got.

"Miss me?" Griffin's voice broke into my thoughts, scattering them like marbles.

It was weird seeing him again. I'd been thinking about him so much, talking about him with both Sheila and Alice, that it felt strange to have him standing there looking implausibly handsome. As if he hadn't been consuming my thoughts and making it impossible to sleep.

But when I saw him, that muddied, confused feeling went away and I just wanted to be near him and talk to him.

Sophie had thrown her arms around Milo's neck, nearly crushing the poor kid. Milo said, "You need a smock to paint," and led her to the pegs near the cubbies to get one.

They had a very intent conversation on their way over, and in an effort to distract myself from how much I also wanted to throw my arms around Griffin's neck and hug him, I asked, "What do you think they're talking about?"

"The heat death of the universe and what disease Milo will have when it happens."

That made me laugh in a way that surprised me, and he grinned at my response, enjoying it. My knees had come up and hit the easel I was using, knocking one of my brushes to the floor.

He reached down and grabbed it before I could, handing it back to me. I made sure that our fingers did not touch because I'd do more than almost flatten my easel if they did.

When I'd put the brush back down he said, "I see you're still trying to set lures for me by dropping your accessories."

"Nobody's trying to trap you, Your Royal Stalkerness."

Milo and Sophie returned and were going through the different supplies that had been set up at the table nearby. Griffin grabbed a stool and sat next to me. Too close, but I wasn't going to complain. "I'll remind you that I was invited here today. By you, if memory serves."

Fine. He had a point. "I'm just glad that you finally showed up. You're late."

"I was practically on time. Fifteen minutes is not late," he said.

"It is." I was the kind of person who was compulsively on time. I didn't like the idea of wasting anybody's time. Just another reason things could never work between us. We were too different. He was private jets and caviar and I was bologna sandwiches and public transportation. We wouldn't have anything in common.

But then he leaned in close, and all those resolutions fled. He was so broad and strong and I really did want to wrap myself around him.

"We could have driven over together if you're concerned about my timeliness."

Oh. That actually hadn't occurred to me, although it probably should have, given that we were staying in the same place. I didn't know how that would work, though. It was bad enough being with him in a room filled with screaming children and bored parents. I couldn't imagine sitting close to him in a tiny, enclosed space. "Why? Did you have plans to show off your shiny sports car?"

"I do have some beauties back home, but we're relying on a car service here."

Ha. I knew he was a car guy. Totally called it. "Sorry, I've never cared much about cars."

"You will when we're going two hundred kilometers per hour on the Autobahn."

"Is that a lot?" I asked. "I don't know anything about fake measuring systems."

He straightened his shoulders. "The metric system is far more precise . . ." His voice trailed off when he realized I was teasing him. "Very funny. But you would be impressed."

"The only way your car would impress me is if it was a taco truck. Maybe an ice cream truck."

His eyes danced, as if he were highly amused.

"I love ice cream!" Sophie announced.

"I thought you were allergic," I said, my gaze moving over to Milo, who didn't look the least bit guilty about the list of allergies he'd made up for Sophie.

"If she is, she'd be dead by now with the way she eats it," Griffin said, as Sophie turned toward Milo to show him something. "So, Diana Parker, what would it take to impress you? Are you saying the royal connection doesn't work at all in my favor?"

"I've had a couple of brushes with a monarchy before. My mom used to date the Used Car King of New Jersey. Oh, and I won the spelling bee in seventh grade. Which technically made me the Queen Bee."

"I don't think that's how it works."

"You're not American, how would you know?"

He let out a dramatic, fake sigh. "I can't believe I don't possess anything that impresses you."

I was impressed with his kindness and thoughtfulness and how much he cared about his family. That he was funny and clever and looked like someone had lovingly carved him out of marble and breathed life into him didn't hurt things, either.

"I'm so sorry that you have to go through life with absolutely nothing in your favor," I told him.

Griffin smiled at me and then reached for a canvas. He held it up slightly and said, "Look. I painted a mountain covered in snow."

At that I laughed long and loud, not able to help myself. It was probably the hardest I had laughed in a long, long time. He was confused at first, but that boyish nature of his made it impossible for him not to join in.

When I finally caught my breath again he said, "I appreciate the support, but it wasn't that funny."

I lifted my paintbrush and started painting again. "Somebody beat you to that exact punch fifteen minutes ago. Milo said the same thing to me when he picked up a canvas."

"Just my luck. Upstaged by a five-year-old." He watched me and I felt surprisingly self-conscious. That wasn't something that normally happened when I painted. I was able to tune out the entire world and center everything around my paintbrush stroking against the canvas.

"You enjoy this. It makes you happy," he commented.

I considered his words, but *happy* didn't quite cover it. "This guy I used to date asked me once when I felt most like myself." It had been a hard question to answer at first because I'd spent so much of my life pretending to be someone I wasn't. "This. This is when I feel the most like me. Like . . . I've found my calling. What I'm supposed to be doing with my life."

Things felt too heavy, too serious, so I added, "Of course the only reason he'd asked me that question was because he wanted me to know that he felt most like himself when he was hooking up with multiple women, so . . ."

"He sounds delightful. What a fun mistake for you."

"I don't really make mistakes so much as date them. The last guy I went out with was basically a pile of red flags in a trench coat."

Griffin nodded, not saying anything for a moment. "How does it make you feel? The painting, not the git you dated."

"It's hard to describe. I will feel this urge that doesn't go away until I paint it. Sometimes I sketch but it's not the same as this. When I'm painting it's like I channel all of me into it and I shut the rest of the world out. It's relaxing, takes away my stress. I feel calmer and happier when I'm painting. There's even this rush when I'm finished, like an endorphin high."

"I know other ways to accomplish the same thing," he said, waggling his eyebrows at me.

"I bet you do." And again, I had that unfounded but certain knowledge that he'd be really, really good at helping me de-stress.

He grabbed a spare easel and placed his canvas on it. "Sounds like something I should try. I'm always up for relaxing, easing stress, and getting an endorphin hit. What should I do now? Where should I get paints and brushes?"

Had he not noticed the table where Milo and Sophie had grabbed their supplies? I was about to point out where everything was when Betty appeared, swooping in like a giant bird of prey who had been waiting for this very moment. "Hi! I'm Betty, the assistant teacher. Can I help you with anything?"

"Hullo, Betty. I'm Griffin and I don't know what to do to get started."

"Let me help you with that!"

He stood up and she slipped her arm through his, angling the side of her body against him. She didn't let go of him once they reached the table. My hand froze in midair as I watched them. She kept touching him and laughing at everything he said. It was irritating me.

I'd never known I was a jealous person. Whenever I'd been cheated on in the past (which was repeatedly), I'd just cut my losses. I certainly hadn't gotten upset about it or mad at the other woman before. What was the point?

So this was all new to me and I didn't much care for it. Not for the churned-up way it made me feel or what it said about my possible feelings for Griffin.

Betty patted him on his forearm and it infuriated me. In an I-wanted-to-jam-the-pointier-end-of-this-paintbrush-through-her-esophagus way. That didn't seem like a normal impulse. I had no right to be jealous. Griffin and I were just friends. He could spend as much time as he wanted with handsy blondes who didn't know how to keep their insipid giggles to themselves.

Here I was sharing my love of painting with him, opening up, giving him a piece of me, and he'd taken up with some art teacher. Assistant art teacher, at that.

All they were doing was talking, and I felt stabby. I didn't want to imagine what I'd do if someone else were kissing him. Maybe these surprising and totally unexpected feelings were something I should consider further. Betty finally pried herself free from him and I lowered my eyes back to my canvas so that he wouldn't see me watching them.

He sat down next to me and began to set up his workstation. Then he casually announced, "You're jealous."

CHAPTER FOURTEEN

"What?" I protested, nearly screeching the word. "I am not jealous!"

There was that smile that said he didn't believe me. He shouldn't, but that was beside the point. "I have some experience with jealous women."

My fingers tightened against my paintbrush. Now I just wanted to knock his ego down a few pegs. "There actually are women who don't want to date you and don't care who you talk to."

"Yes, but so far none of them are in this room."

Was he teasing me, or was he that sure of himself? "You really just go through life confident in yourself and your place in the world, don't you?"

"When it comes down to it, isn't that all we have? A belief in ourselves and where we belong?"

Maybe that was part of my issue. Until Alice showed up on my doorstep when I was sixteen, I'd never felt like I belonged anywhere. It was also strange that here, with the Crawfords and Griffin, in a life so completely different from my own, I'd started to feel like I did belong.

When I didn't respond he said, "I know we haven't defined the parameters of our friend relationship, but I am allowed to have other friends."

Of course he was. "Obviously. And I hope you have a wonderful, lifelong friendship with the very beautiful Betty. She seems really, really smart. And so successful as an *assistant* art teacher. I'm sure your grandmother would welcome her to the family."

It was a cheap shot, brought on by my newfound insecurity, and Griffin didn't let it slide. With an arched eyebrow that indicated disapproval he said, "You don't strike me as the type to say unkind things about other women. Are you saying you think she's not good enough for me?"

"I'm not saying it. I'm implying it passively, like a normal person." *Who is not at all jealous.* I didn't remark on his comment that I didn't normally say bad things about other women. Completely true. Other than my mother, but I knew that wasn't what he meant. I just did not know what to do with all these new feelings and they were pouring out of me like hot, steaming, ugly lava, making me say not-nice things.

"Sorry," I added on. I shouldn't have been mean.

"So who do you think I should be with, then?" He said it lightly, in a tone that suggested all was forgiven, but that's not at all how it felt. His question was heavy, weighing against my chest. I didn't have a good answer for him. Betty looked in our direction and it was obvious that she wanted a reason to come talk to him again. I felt like barking at her to stay away.

Instead I answered his question. "That's up to you. It's none of my business who you are or are not friends with."

I tried to keep my eyes on my own canvas, but I couldn't help but notice how he smiled secretly at my declaration. He wasn't buying it.

"Are you an artist?" he asked.

Grateful that we were no longer dwelling on the jealous pangs shooting through me. "Like, as a job? No."

"But you'd like to be."

"More than anything in the world," I said, the words tumbling out of me. I'd never even told Alice about how much I wanted to be a professional artist. She knew I loved art, but not that I wished it could be my career. She wasn't aware of the fact that I had all kinds of unrealistic dreams about having my own show in a gallery someday. It was so fantastical, so outside the realm of reality, that I didn't usually share it with anyone.

"What's stopping you?" he asked.

"My own crippling insecurity and impostor syndrome that my work's not good enough and never will be?" Something else I'd never said aloud. What was it about this man that made me want to tell him things?

Not everything, though. I didn't tell him how I couldn't buy supplies to paint. Or that having to work in order to eat and have a place to live made it so that I didn't have enough free time to devote to my art.

"You're incredibly talented," he told me. "I can see the joy it gives you, so I hope you do keep pursuing it. And if you're ever in need of a model, let me know. I specialize in nudes."

At that, I laughed so loud that everybody in the room turned to look at us. I immediately stopped, and there was a momentary awkward silence, like a record had just scratched while a raven cawed in the distance.

My cheeks went pink and I tried to cover up how embarrassed I felt by asking, "What about you? What would you be doing if you weren't busy earl-ing?"

He put his paintbrush down, seriously considering my question. "I think I would have liked to sell real estate."

It's not what I would have imagined for him—but the truth was, he would make a truly fantastic salesman. As my mom used to say, the kind of man who could sell ketchup Popsicles to a woman wearing white gloves. "Really? You could choose any job in the world—astronaut, famous neurosurgeon, NASCAR driver—and that's what you pick?"

"NASCAR—isn't that the one where they drive fast in circles?"

"Mr. I Drive 150 Kilometers an Hour doesn't like car racing?" He shrugged in acknowledgment and I realized how much I liked learning new things about him. Especially things that didn't line up with the image I had of Stuff Griffin Likes in His Regular Life. Now it was my turn to put my brush down. "Why real estate?"

Griffin smiled. "I think I'd be good at it. I've always loved old homes and discovered I also enjoy fixing them up. I have an estate in Nottingham that I've been renovating."

"Nottingham? As in, Sheriff of?" A Robin Hood connection inexplicably made Griffin even more attractive. The Disney movie of that story had been one of my favorites when I was a kid. Probably because he was the opposite of my mother. Robin Hood gave the things he stole to poor people and my mom just kept the money for herself.

"Yes, that Nottingham. The upkeep is expensive and I want to rent the manor out to help subsidize the cost. Especially since I spend most of my time at my flat in the city, but my grandmother is opposed to it."

"Renting out your house is sullying the family name?" I asked.

"Yes. Apparently it is beneath the Windsors to let out their country estates for weddings and other events." He took out his phone and flicked at the screen a couple of times before handing it to me.

His fingers brushed against mine, sending tingles in shock waves from my fingertips to my elbow. I swallowed against the sensation and took his phone, moving my body slightly away from his. I looked at the first photo and drew in a small breath. "This is your house?"

While it apparently wasn't an actual castle, it was freaking close enough. It was beautiful and stately, made out of gray and white stone with actual spires and turrets.

"That's Ashwood Manor." He said this with a note of pride, which he was more than entitled to. "If you want to scroll there's more pictures of the renovation."

Ashwood Manor. I repeated the words in my mind. It was the perfect name. I saw a bunch of different rooms, some of them decorated with older furniture and antiques, others with walls and ceilings missing as they underwent renovation. There was a long hallway with multiple portraits. "Maybe your grandma would let you host an art show. You could use this as a gallery. Like for a charity event?" That was more upscale and refined, wasn't it?

"With you as the resident artist?" His voice was teasing, but there was a note beneath it that said something more.

The next picture on his phone was of the backyard, and I could picture myself there on that terrace, near the rose gardens, painting to my heart's content. This idea did not terrify me, which was interesting as I'd always thought myself heartily opposed to any kind of commitment, given how badly it had worked out for everyone I was related to. "I'm not sure your grandma would approve of me."

"True, but you know that only makes you more appealing, don't you?" He was the most flirtatious man I'd ever met. No wonder that wannabe poacher Betty was still making eyes at him from across the room. "I'm not sure I'd want to end up with the kind of woman my grandmother wants for me. It would give her too much pleasure."

I understood that sentiment. My mother would be doing cartwheels in her prison cell if she knew that Griffin was interested in me. Maybe that was another reason I was keeping him at bay. I didn't particularly want to make her happy. "What kind of woman is that?"

"Wealthy, exceptionally good breeding, went to the best schools."

"Is your grandma going to check your future wife's teeth, too?"

"Negotiable," he said with a wink.

I had none of those things. That thought made me a little sad. "Have fun finding a wife like you're shopping for a luxury car."

"It's one of the reasons I'm still single even with my grandmother constantly pressuring me. It is rather hypocritical of her to have those kinds of restrictions, given that her own family is common. Very wealthy, though, which is why my grandfather married her. You think she'd be welcoming to others. Instead it's like now that she's arrived at this exclusive club she's bound and determined to keep out any new members."

I wondered if Griffin would eventually give in and marry the blue blood his grandma picked out and brushed off the fact that it annoyed me that he might.

"I'm so glad you're hiding from that woman," I told him. I handed him back his phone and picked my paintbrush up again, dipping it in the yellow paint to start work on the flower petals.

"I'm not hiding. I've temporarily moved to a location that she's unaware of. That sounds more manly."

I smiled at him, shaking my head. He did not need any help being more masculine. Everything I could see was working for him. Every muscle, every vein that showed on his forearms and hands, his strong jawline, his—

"What about me?" he asked, interrupting my soon-to-be-illicit thoughts. "Would your family approve of me?"

"You mean Alice, who has basically already printed up our wedding invitations?"

He laughed at that, and didn't run from the room screaming, which I found interesting. I'd met a man at work a few weeks ago who'd flirted with me, but he'd taken off like I'd set his clothes on fire when I'd asked for his last name.

"And your parents?" he asked.

"I have some."

He laughed again. "That wasn't what I meant."

"My mom would like you." That was the truth. She would adore him. She'd just rob him blind the first chance she got. I also didn't feel like mentioning that I had no idea who my father was.

"And?" he prompted, hearing that there was something I'd left out of my declaration.

I shrugged in response, worried that I wasn't hiding my true self from him very well.

You don't want to hide, a voice whispered. That was stupid. Of course I wanted to hide. There was no way for me to be honest with him.

He studied me for a moment before saying, "Maybe someday you'll tell me."

Maybe someday I would.

Whoa—that thought had come out of nowhere. If I told him about my mom, this . . . flirtationship would be officially over. No way would he trust me to be anywhere near his impressionable niece. And he might feel obligated to warn the Crawfords, too.

Wanting to take the spotlight off me I said, "Speaking of parents, I'm sorry about you losing yours."

"Thank you. But it was a long time ago."

"Do you want to tell me about it?"

He did. We sat side by side, working on our paintings while he told me about his parents. How his father would fix them breakfast on Sunday mornings and they would sit around the kitchen table and do the *Times* crossword puzzle. The picnics they'd take when the sun was actually shining. His mother's love of the color purple and how his father would bring her irises once a week. How they would always slow dance in the kitchen together. The way they adored each other and their children. He talked of a happy childhood surrounded with love and comfort and happiness. I couldn't even imagine.

They'd died in a car accident on the way to a friend's chalet in the Swiss Alps. His grandmother had brought Griffin and Ollie to live with her and everything in their life changed. She was obsessed with status and had constant, unrealistic expectations for Griffin and his brother. He told me how they'd both found ways to quietly rebel against her iron fist.

I got that. Not in the same exact way, but I'd also had a life full of expectations that I'd rebelled against. Although his were to do things like keep that castle in his family and mine were, well, to get a guy like him to sell that castle and give me all the money.

I finished up shading my painting, and sat back, satisfied with it. I looked over at Milo and Sophie. They had started new paintings, and while Sophie kept her paintbrush in her left hand the entire time, Milo continued to switch back and forth.

"You look concerned. What is it?" Griffin asked.

Outside of Alice, I'd never had anyone who could assess my moods and thoughts so accurately. Who'd cared enough to. I pushed away that annoying "in like" feeling and answered his question. "It might be nothing. But there's been some things that Milo's said and done that make me wonder if he might have mild dyspraxia. My nephew, Jasper, has it."

"You have a nephew?"

I realized that I hadn't brought up the twins before. "And a niece. They're twins. They're Alice's kids."

"Whenever you say your sister's name, I can tell how much you love her."

My eyes went a bit watery and I blinked several times. Again, I felt seen, even if I was trying not to be. "I do. I'd do anything for her."

"I understand that." He gestured over toward Sophie. "Just as I would do anything for my brother."

Griffin was proving that fact by putting his entire life on hold to keep his brother's secret child safe. I might have repeatedly denied to anybody who would listen that I liked Griffin, that I could like him, but that moment? When I saw that we shared the same loyalty to our loved ones? Something inside me burst to life.

"You were saying about your nephew?" Griffin said, making me realize how long I'd been sitting there thinking about how much I liked him.

"Dyspraxia manifests in different people in different ways. Jasper describes it as not knowing where his body is in space and having a hard time getting it to do everything he wants. Like he has a hard time in sports because his body doesn't always cooperate."

"You think Milo might have the same issue?"

I frowned. "Sometimes when somebody in your family has a specific diagnosis, you start seeing it even when it's not there. Like if I told you the number twenty-one was significant, suddenly you'd start noticing that particular number all the time."

"Just because you're predisposed to look for it, that doesn't mean your intuition is incorrect."

"My intuition has been incorrect for a very long time." I didn't trust myself very much, in nearly every area of my life.

This time he was the one comforting me. He reached out, taking my hand and squeezing it gently. The contact of his skin on mine, that electric charge that filled my entire body—would I ever get used to that? Would it go away?

Did I want it to?

He took his hand away and I very nearly grabbed it back.

To distract my traitorous hands I spoke. "If it's correct, I think that's why he's afraid of skiing. He doesn't like that fast motion where he feels out of control."

Griffin looked at me with that calm, strong gaze of his. "What would you do if it was your nephew?"

"Jasper can do things like that as long as we go through each step with him. We find ways to work around what he doesn't like. But only if it's something he wants to do. We'd never want to force him. I don't want to force Milo, either."

We both turned to watch the children and the way they were happily interacting with each other. I couldn't make it out properly, but it almost sounded like they were singing a song. I didn't recognize the tune, and the room was too loud to be certain.

Griffin said, "When I researched this hotel I found out that they have an excellent adaptive program for people with special needs. Perhaps Milo might prefer that."

I was touched by his suggestion, and the fact that he was enough of a dork to do research before going somewhere. That was something that I would absolutely do. Had done repeatedly. "You did research?"

"Technically, Louis did the work. But I read it."

The reminder of Griffin's employee, one who apparently did research for him, made my pulse spike. What if Louis chose to check out my background? "It's kind of weird that you have this old guy who lives in your suite and looks stuff up for you."

"'Tis," he agreed. "But that's how things are. My family has employed him for decades and he's very loyal."

"To you?"

"Of course."

Everyone had a price, even this Louis guy. He could be gathering research that he intended to send to Griffin's grandma to get in her good graces. Especially if she was the one who had all the money. But it was none of my business and I didn't want to trigger any alarm bells with Griffin that might lead him to ask Louis to look into my past, so I said nothing.

He shifted in his stool, straightening his back and shoulders, like he was preparing for impact. "I looked at the schedule and I noticed that you didn't have anything planned for this evening. I thought I could teach you to ski, once Sophie's in bed. I could come by your suite at eight fifteen or so, if that's agreeable to you."

"Just me? Alone?" That felt like we were entering into date-like territory.

"Well, I would be there, too," he said with a wink that made my knees feel like jelly.

Betty had locked her predatory gaze on him again, making my jealousy spike, and the next thing I knew, I was saying yes.

"Okay," I agreed, ignoring all of my internal systems that were flashing red and screaming at me *abort, abort!* I wanted to go, even if it might not have been the smart thing to do. "What do I need to ski? Can I rent everything? Like those puffy pants and stuff?"

He wore an odd expression. "You don't have any sporting equipment?"

"No. Uh, there was this mistake I went out with that stole all my sporting equipment and I haven't replaced it." I didn't tell him that my sporting equipment had consisted of a tennis racket missing most of its strings and a chewed-up Frisbee.

"I will take care of everything," he said. "As far as your previous mistakes go . . . you have heard that making the same mistake over and over is called a decision?"

I nodded. I should know that, because I'd been making a lot of bad decisions, too.

Then he added, "You could make a different decision. Just so you're aware."

I wanted that. I wanted to decide to be with someone like him. But that might make my entire currently complicated life fall apart and I couldn't risk that.

He was leaving in a fortnight. My hormones reminded me that I could have fun with him for two weeks. Keep it light and casual and not let anything get out of hand. "I know. But you're just teaching me how to ski. Nothing else." At least one of us should remember that.

"Wouldn't dream of it," he said with that disarming smile of his.

He didn't have to. I was daydreaming about it enough for the both of us.

CHAPTER FIFTEEN

After the art class finished, we all took the same SUV back to the hotel and it was every bit as awkward as I'd feared it would be. Milo and Sophie chatted the entire time, but now that I'd agreed to spend time, alone, with Griffin, I found myself feeling shy. So I just looked out the window at the snowy landscape instead.

I could feel his eyes on me, but he didn't say anything.

We all rode the elevator together and when they stepped out onto their floor Griffin stopped, put his hand against the door so that it couldn't shut, and turned toward me. There was an intensity there that made my breath hitch. I envisioned him coming back into the elevator, grabbing me close, crushing his mouth to mine . . .

But all he said was, "See you tonight."

The doors slid shut and Milo asked, "What's happening tonight?"

"Griffin's going to show me something." I clamped my lips together at how suggestive my meant-to-be-bland explanation sounded. If I'd said that to Alice, she would have made all sorts of inappropriate suggestions.

Milo and I headed back to our suite and worked on his lessons. I'd found out the name of the French school he was going to attend and had researched their standards for his age group (with my browser translating everything into English). All of that insomnia was finally good for something.

Most of the skills they wanted him to have he already possessed—he was a whiz at math and reading books meant for much older kids. Hopefully, he was getting something out of the subjects we covered. I felt like I was learning alongside him.

The door opened a few minutes before six o'clock. Sheila was home. "Diana? There's a package for you."

Weird. I wasn't expecting anything. I came into the front hallway and she was holding a large box wrapped up with a purple velvet ribbon.

My heart thudded hard. It had to be from Griffin. Who else?

I took it from her and carried it into the kitchen. Sheila and Milo both followed me. I considered taking it into my bedroom so that I could have some privacy, but given the expectant looks on their faces I felt like I had to open it here and now. They wanted to share this moment with me and I didn't have it in me to deny them that.

There was a card attached to the ribbon and I opened it. It read:

For tonight—G

I undid the ribbon and lifted off the top lid. I moved aside tissue paper and found . . . shiny purple material. I reached for it and lifted it up. Pants. Purple, puffy pants.

"Snow pants!" Sheila said. "You'll need those for skiing."

At that word Milo made a face and left the kitchen.

"I'm going skiing. Later tonight. If that's okay," I told her.

"Diana, you don't have to run anything by me. But I hope you and . . . Griffin, I'm assuming?" When I nodded she continued, "I hope that you two have a wonderful time. And maybe you'll come up with a way to get Milo interested."

Now my stomach was doing queasy little flips. I wanted to talk to her about what I'd noticed with Milo and now seemed like a perfect time, given that he wasn't in the room. It made me nervous, though. "Sheila, can I talk to you for a minute?"

She set her laptop bag down on the counter, sitting on one of the stools. "Sure. What's up?"

I couldn't help but hesitate. I didn't have any kind of medical expertise. Maybe I shouldn't say anything. It wasn't my place.

While there was part of me that wanted to hold back, I found that there was more of me that wanted to tell her about everything. About Griffin, how I was afraid to get close to him, how I didn't know how to actually do anything, and that everything she thought to be true about me was a lie.

This wasn't about me and my needs. This was to help Milo.

"I've been noticing some things about Milo. How he doesn't have a dominant hand, doesn't like doing things that are motion intensive, struggles a little with writing." Now my heart was beating so loud that my head was almost ringing with the sound. The words *this is none of your business* echoed through my mind, but I pressed on. "He reminds me of my nephew, who has dyspraxia."

At first I'd worried that I was going to have to explain what that meant and freak her out further, but the expression on her face helped my stomach to settle. She said, "Milo has an informal diagnosis of dyspraxia. His pediatrician told us about it when we mentioned some of the same things to her, and on her recommendation he had some occupational therapy when he was little to help with his fine motor skills. He has caught up developmentally, so we haven't worried too much about it. We do make accommodations where needed, though. That's why his shoes are Velcro instead of laces."

I nodded. "I know it's none of my business and—"

Sheila leaned over and took my hand in hers. "It absolutely is your business, Diana. You're basically family now."

It was the second time today I'd felt like crying, but I pushed the tears back down my burning throat. "I was bringing it up because I think that's why Milo doesn't want to ski. Griffin mentioned that the hotel's ski school has an excellent adaptive program."

"Griffin mentioned it, huh?" she said, wearing a pointed smile.

That threw me off for a second. It was bad enough getting it from Alice. I didn't need Sheila to keep encouraging this. "Yes. Anyway, if you're okay with it, then I'd like to see if Milo would be interested in something that's slower paced and geared more toward him and his needs."

"That sounds wonderful. I wish John and I had thought of it. I wish I had the time to try it out with him myself." The regret was evident in her voice. "I don't know why I didn't connect these dots earlier. I should have realized why he's been so reluctant. Sometimes it helps to have an extra set of eyes, I suppose. You'll have to tell me how things go."

See? I didn't need to be an expert skier who'd almost qualified for the Olympics. I could just take advantage of the resources around me to help Milo.

That kind of justification was how I made myself feel less guilty.

"I'm going to take a quick shower and then have dinner with Milo. Do you want to join us?" she asked.

"Thanks, but I'll just grab something quick. I want to call and check on my sister."

A look of concern furrowed Sheila's brow. "Is she okay?"

My first instinct was to lie. To smooth the situation over. But maybe because I'd lied about so many things so often, in this area I wanted to be truthful. "She's struggling. She needs a kidney transplant."

Now her brows shot up her forehead. "Diana! I'm so sorry. Is there anything I can do?"

"You're kind of already doing it," I told her. "Her ex-husband is trying to keep her off his insurance and I'm using my salary to help pay for her operation."

"Will it be enough?" she asked, seeming extremely worried. "Do you need more?"

That big round baseball was taking up residence in my throat again, making it hard to talk. "No, we'll be okay. I can't thank you enough for everything. This job really does mean the world to me."

She came over and hugged me, and her touch was so soothing and comforting that I leaned into it, letting some of my worry and concern pass over to her.

Releasing me she said, "I'm serious. If you need anything—to go home and see her or if you have an unexpected expense come up—please tell me."

"I will," I said, knowing I wouldn't. The Crawfords were already giving me so much, under false pretenses, that I couldn't take more from them.

She grabbed her laptop bag and started walking out of the room. She paused at the door. "We're here for you, Diana. Anything you need." She left to go shower.

And now I felt about a thousand times worse.

Feeling like I didn't deserve hot food, I grabbed a can of soup, a spoon, and my gift from Griffin, and headed to my room. I called Alice and as soon as she answered, I poured my heart out to her. Talking about how guilty I felt with the Crawfords and how I wished things could be different.

I expected her to lecture me about telling the truth, but she didn't. She just listened. It was so unlike my older sister that it threw me off-balance. "No sage words of wisdom?"

"You're a grown-up, Diana. You can make your own choices. You know the right thing to do."

That was somehow infinitely worse. "I'm disappointed in you but I'm going to express that disappointment by not saying anything" had never been a fun thing to deal with. Alice hadn't done it very often to me in the past, but it was effective.

So effective that I found myself offering up new intel just to appease her. "Griffin and I hung out today and we're going skiing in a couple of hours and he sent me snow pants as a present."

This seemed to work. Everything shifted and I could practically hear her trying to contain her giddy excitement. She confirmed it by saying, "I know you can't see me right now, but I'm gleefully rubbing my hands together like a villain from an old black-and-white movie. Because you're going on a date? With Griffin?"

"It's not a date," I told her.

"Two people meeting for a fun activity where one of them sent a gift to the other beforehand? Correct?"

She asked the question like she was a TV lawyer cross-examining a witness. "Yes, but—"

"And who is going to pay for you to ski?"

"You have to pay to ski?" For some reason I thought it was just available because the slopes were on a mountain. Like if it was in nature, it shouldn't cost money.

"Yes. And to rent skis and poles. So again I ask, who's paying?"

I could see where she was going with this and I didn't like it. "I guess he is."

"Do you think you'll laugh, enjoy each other's company, get to know one another better?"

I almost said, "That's what friends do," but even I was tired of hearing that we were "just friends." I didn't want him as only a friend, no matter how many times I told everyone else that I did.

"Alice, I know what you're—"

"Is he picking you up?"

I paused. "We live in the same place. We're walking down together. He's not driving me anywhere."

"Doesn't matter. You fall well within the parameters of things being an actual date. Ergo, a date. You are about to date the Earl of Strathorne. Even if you are being delusional about it."

I couldn't argue with her assessment. "I resent that remark. I'm not in a position to dispute it, but I resent it."

"*Really?*" There was far too much delight in her voice. "Give me a second. I'm going to go grab a slice of delicious gloat pie."

"Ha-ha. Fine. Gloat. But I don't know how to deal with any of this. Things are different with him. I don't like when he talks to other women. I've never been jealous before."

"You've never really cared about a guy before."

"I just met him," I protested.

"So? There's no set timetable for these things to happen. Tell me you don't care about him and his niece."

"I—" I opened my mouth but nothing came out.

"You can't," she retorted smugly.

"Why are you like this?"

"Like what? Right?"

Alice wasn't getting it. "Things can't work out between us."

"Says who?"

"Me. And him, if he ever finds out the truth about me."

There was a long and impatient sigh before she said, "I can't have every conversation with you end up with me telling you to *tell him* the truth. I'm going to bore myself."

Much as I didn't want to admit it, she probably was right. "You really think if I tell him that he'll be fine with it?"

"Only one way to find out," she said. "Also, if you're going to be such a chicken about everything, you could give me his number and we could pretend we were in middle school and I could text him to see if he liked you and he could reply yes or no."

"Okay, okay," I mumbled. I got it. I was being immature. But in my defense, I had a lot of emotional trauma and legitimate reasons for being messed up and not having had a normal relationship with a man ever.

"Although it is probably a good thing I don't have his number. Not only because of the applause voice mail I'd leave him, but because I'd want to call and introduce myself as Alice, Diana's sister, and one of his bridesmaids."

I shook my head, chuckling. She joked, but I could see her actually doing it. "You'd be the maid of honor, you know that."

There was a noise on her end, like the hinges on a door squeaking, and she said, "It's Jenna. She needs me, so I've got to go. Have the best time tonight!"

When we hung up I thought about her advice and what I should do. Instead of shoving everything down into a deep, dark hole inside me, I decided to examine why I really thought things wouldn't work out with Griffin.

There was the obvious—that we were from completely different worlds, and there wouldn't be any way for us to feel comfortable in one another's lives; that a shared sense of humor and attraction weren't really enough to build a relationship on; that he wouldn't be able to accept my lying.

Or that we had a deadline for when we were going to separate, so what was the point in getting involved with someone who was just going to leave?

Although . . . Alice had offered a solution for that problem. To have an emotion-free fling. Enjoy the time we had and then let him go.

He wasn't the only person I was going to have to walk away from. I was attached to Milo, but I knew that he was going to leave with his family to live in France. It didn't stop me from caring about him, or wanting him to have the best possible life. It wasn't like I held back a part of my affection because I didn't want to get hurt. I was going to enjoy caring for him for as long as I was allowed to and miss him when he left.

Why couldn't I feel the same way about Griffin?

Probably because a piece of me recognized that there were feelings here that I'd never felt before. There was something special about this man. Something that kept me wanting to be near him even as I was keeping him at arm's length. A quality, or emotion, that called to me, much as I wanted to ignore it.

I was normally so good at protecting myself. Which was due to the fact that I assumed every man I met was going to screw me over at some point and I hadn't been disappointed in this belief yet.

Only I didn't expect that from Griffin.

Which was weird. He was a gorgeous, worldly, charming man. He, probably more than any other guy I'd gone out with, had the capacity to wreck my life. To get me to fall for him before he then blissfully moved on to the next woman.

I looked over at the pants he'd sent me. There was probably some royal protocol or etiquette rule that said I shouldn't accept clothing from a man I'd met only recently. But it was thoughtful and considerate and I was struck with the urge to know why he'd done it.

Picking up my phone, I selected his contact info and pressed the "Call" button.

CHAPTER SIXTEEN

I could have just texted him, but I didn't do that. I wanted to hear his voice. Needed to hear it, actually. Like on a chemical level. This was bad. But I couldn't help myself.

Griffin answered immediately. "Bunny?"

That sent actual shivers dancing along my nervous system, giving me the endorphin reward that I'd hoped for. "Diana, actually."

"That's what I said. How are you, darling?"

Why was his voice so silky and seductive? I could picture him lounging on his bed, talking to me. Then I imagined myself lying next to him, him pulling me close and then whispering words against my skin. The mental image made me feel light-headed. I scooted until I was lying down, waiting for the feeling to pass.

It didn't pass.

"You sent me pants," I finally said when I realized he was still waiting for an answer.

"Pants?" he repeated. "I didn't send you underwear."

My cheeks flushed and it took me a second to realize that he was teasing me. "*Pants* means *underwear* in England?"

"Yes. Usually. What you call pants we call trousers. Although what I sent are referred to as ski pants. Don't ask me to explain why it's not ski trousers or something else. But I am responsible for sending them to you, along with a warm hat, ski gloves, and my scarf."

What? I hadn't even seen those. I rolled over and pulled the box to me, pushing the pants aside. There were the things he described—the gloves, the hat, and his Burberry scarf.

The scarf.

The one that had made me nearly kiss him. The memory of being that close to him gave me tingles in all the right spots. I put it up to my nose. It smelled faintly like him.

Was he trying to deliberately remind me of that night? Of the connection that we'd both felt? Or had he done it without thinking?

Feeling flustered I said, "You can't just send people pants," remembering only after the words were out that *pants* meant something entirely different to him.

From the lilt in his voice, I could tell it amused him. "I can, actually. I did."

That made me fall silent for a moment. He was right.

"You said you didn't have the proper kit for skiing, so I thought I'd send some things over."

"Most guys just send flowers." Not any that I'd ever gone out with, but I'd heard that such a thing could happen. I wouldn't mind getting flowers.

"Noted," he told me. "Did you want to be ungrateful for any other kind gestures I've made, or shall I just see you in a couple of hours?"

"I'm not trying to . . . I do appreciate . . . I mean, that's not . . ." I had a hard time completing my sentence, or arranging my thoughts into something organized. He'd done it again. Made me flabbergasted. As someone who had been able her entire life to talk her way out of almost any situation, this was a brand-new feeling. I didn't like it.

Or maybe I secretly did enjoy it, that he was clever enough to get the best of me. To not be fooled.

"Sophie is waiting for me to help her finish this puzzle we're working on, so I need to go." He hesitated for a beat before adding, "While I'm glad you called, you didn't have to. You could have just texted me."

Embarrassed that he'd picked up on my secret desire to speak to him so easily, I said, "I know!" and hung up the phone.

Again I was left feeling like everything was all confusing and jumbled up and I didn't know what to do.

~

I found myself freaking out waiting for him to show up. I'd been on lots of dates and had never once felt this way. This mixture of anticipation and slight nausea because I was both thrilled and anxious . . . I didn't know what to do with that.

Maybe it was like what Alice had said: that I was all churned up and excited because I'd never cared about anyone as much as I did about Griffin. And whatever tonight was—returning a favor, gratitude for helping him out, mutual fun between people who had clearly decided to be only friends, or a disguised date, I still wanted it to go well and I had so little experience in dates going well. I didn't know how to make tonight go smoothly and not be awkward.

Because despite all of my denials, I wanted him to like me the way I liked him.

On the surface, it seemed like that was already the case. But what if he was just a flirt? What if he smiled and sent articles of his clothing to every woman he came across? What if he had a skiing date with Betty tomorrow night and she was already in possession of her own snow pants?

I didn't like the idea that I might not be special to him when he'd somehow become really special and important to me.

So I told myself it wasn't a date. Just him teaching me to ski.

My subconscious did not buy this, and my insides continued to twist up in anticipation of his arrival.

Griffin didn't show up at 8:15, which I should have expected. It was actually 8:24—and I know that because I was standing next to the door, waiting for him. I wasn't going to risk him having another run-in with Sheila.

I opened the door immediately, instead of waiting a few seconds like a regular person would.

He didn't seem to mind, though. "There you are."

"Here I am!" I echoed, a little too brightly. "We should get going." I stepped out into the hallway, closing the door behind me.

"Right." He should have stepped back, to allow me some personal space in the hall, but instead he stayed close.

Too close.

His heat, his scent, caused a slow, delicious burn in my stomach. I heard his sharp intake of breath as he reacted to our nearness, and that sound made heat prickle along the back of my neck.

There was an entire electrical storm taking place between us, crackling and sparking, even though we weren't touching.

I swallowed hard and saw him do the same. I saw how his breaths came hard and fast and wondered if I was breathing the same way.

"Diana . . ." His voice was low, almost pleading.

Waiting, I realized he wasn't going to say anything else. I couldn't kiss him. Not while I was lying to him. So I acted, because I needed to put some distance between us or I'd never be able to keep things on a platonic level. "If I could just get past you . . ."

The hazy look fell from his face, his eyes widening. "Yes. Of course. Yes."

He stepped back and gestured with his arm toward the elevator. If this was an indication of how this night was going to go, I was about to be in a lot of trouble.

I stood in front of the elevator doors and saw us in the highly reflective surface. The first thing I noticed was my flushed skin. The second was how good we looked together. Like a real couple.

There was a ding from the doors opening that startled me, even though I was expecting it. "I didn't thank you earlier."

"For what?" he asked.

"For the pants. I mean, trousers. No! It's ski pants. These." I gestured toward the purple snow pants. "Thank you."

"You are welcome."

We rode in silence until we got to the lobby, which surprised me. Griffin always had some story to share, some joke to make me laugh. It wasn't an awkward silence, more of a tentative one. As if we both had things to say but were afraid to share.

While I thought of the things I wished I were brave enough to tell him, I fingered the soft ends of the scarf he'd given me, inwardly smiling that he'd been so thoughtful. I shifted my weight. That made the waterproof material of my pants rub together, creating a plasticky sound. I glanced down at them and again wondered how many other women he had given Burberry scarves and purple snow pants to.

That jealousy returned, sharp, vicious, green.

"There's a long hallway on the north side of the hotel that leads to the rental place," he said. I nodded, following along.

"Do you do that often?" I asked, not able to contain my curiosity any longer.

"Offer directions?"

"No. Buy gifts for . . . the numerous women you spend time with."

He looked over his shoulder at me. "I feel as though I'm being accused of something."

"I'm not accusing you of anything. Just stating the obvious. I have eyes and they have witnessed the many, many pictures of you and the entire female population of England on the internet."

His steps faltered for a second and I almost smacked into his back. "You looked at pictures of me?"

"Only to try and figure you out." I probably shouldn't have admitted it. I didn't want him trying to research me and discovering that my supposed wealthy background was all a lie. Not before I figured out a way to tell him first.

"You can't believe everything you read. If I so much as say hello to a woman, the tabloids assume we're dating. When you're stalked like a wild animal, you're not entitled to much privacy."

I noticed that people in the lobby were swinging their gazes our way. Not because they recognized Griffin, but because he was so magnetic and charming that people who hadn't even spoken to him couldn't help but look. I got the impulse.

These were all strangers who didn't care who we were. I couldn't imagine if there were reporters and cameras involved. "So if there was paparazzi here . . ."

He started walking again, and it was easy to keep pace with him. He said, "You'd be all over the internet by tomorrow morning as my latest fling."

Those words should not be exciting. "Is that what you are? A flinger?"

"I don't typically fling anyone. I'm not the serial dater they depict me to be. I've been too busy. It's actually been a long time since I've even wanted to ask someone on a date."

We'd arrived at the rental place. He opened the door and held it for me. I stopped at the threshold and peered up at him. Why was he acting like it was some rare thing for him to want to go out with someone? "But you ask me out all the time."

Griffin didn't say anything, he just looked at me with a secret little smile. I walked through the door, my heart pounding at the implication of his words.

The rental shop was busier than I would have predicted. It was dark outside. Didn't most people prefer skiing during the day? For some reason I had imagined a quiet and dark slope that we'd have to ourselves. It didn't look like that was going to happen.

The shop seemed a bit understaffed, so we got in line and waited. Which surprised me. Griffin had the kind of background where I could easily see him throwing his weight around and demanding attention.

Again, this patient and deferential behavior was not typical for the kind of men I'd chosen to spend time with in the past.

"Did you imagine that I was a womanizer?" he asked.

Yes. "No. I mean, not exactly." Even though that was precisely how those websites had painted him. Like a bee going from flower to flower, unable to stay with one person for longer than a day or two. "You don't really seem like the kind of guy to be in a long-term relationship."

"I have been."

"Really?"

"My first girlfriend and I dated for several years."

Jealous, jealous, jealous. I wanted to know everything including her name and Social Security number. For reasons. Until I remembered that she was probably British and they didn't have those. The numbers, I mean. She probably had a name. Something dumb like Petunia. "Oh. Why did you break up?"

Because if they hadn't broken up or were in one of those light bulb relationships where they were off and on again over and over, I was going right back upstairs.

The customer at the front finished and we moved up a spot. "She wanted to be an actress and Granny deemed that as an unsuitable occupation."

Ha. I wondered what she'd think of a former con artist / lying nanny.

Griffin continued, "That was back when I used to listen to my grandmother. I was eighteen when we broke up. I hated how everything happened."

"Do you regret that things ended?" Did he stay up at night writing bad poetry for this Petunia? She had to have an unattractive name. My jealousy couldn't cope otherwise.

"I regret that I didn't stand up to my grandmother, but not that Isla and I broke up. We wouldn't have made each other happy. We fought constantly because she thought drama meant passion, and it was exhausting."

But wasn't there some saying about first loves being the most powerful? What if he realized he couldn't live without this obviously stupid Isla person? "What happened to her?"

"She didn't become an actress. She married someone else and has two children."

And just like that, my newly awakened jealousy monster lumbered back to her cave to hibernate.

"What about you?" he asked, and I quickly realized that by focusing on my delight that this Isla was out of reach, I'd set myself up for him to ask probing questions.

So I deflected. "I'm not an actress, either."

"I meant, any long-term relationships in your past? Ones that I might possibly be jealous of?"

Again I wondered how he'd done that. I'd always thought I had a pretty good poker face, but his perceptiveness had me questioning my own skills. Because somehow I was showing every idiotic emotion in my head on my face. "I've never been in a relationship that lasted longer than a month."

Now it was his turn to look surprised. "I have a hard time imagining that."

Another customer paid for their skis and we were now second in line. "Well, that's not true. I dated Donnie Silver for three months, but that was only because he moved out of state and didn't tell me and so we technically never broke up."

Apparently not seeing the dark humor in my situation, he pressed on. "But why haven't you been in a longer relationship? A fear of commitment?"

"Not so much a fear as not ever finding anyone that I wanted to be with." That, and my previously terrible taste in men.

"A commitment virgin?" he asked with a charming half smile that broke down another one of those walls I had around my heart.

Then it was our turn to get equipment. The staffer and Griffin spoke in a sporting language I didn't understand and basically tuned out because I was busy admiring the way that Griffin filled out his ski outfit. It was all arranged quickly while I enjoyed my view.

Griffin pulled out his wallet to pay for everything, and I wondered whether I should make the pretense of protesting; given that he didn't look back at me, I decided not to make the effort. I expected to be left out of the process entirely since I had no idea what they were talking about, but Griffin turned to introduce me.

"This is Diana. She has a young friend who might be in need of your adaptive services."

The staffer shook my hand. "Hi! I'm Carl, and I'm one of the people who work in the adaptive program." He handed me a business card from the counter. "Whenever you guys want to arrange a private lesson, let me know and we'll get it all set up."

"Thanks, that would be great." I put his card into my pants pocket. Now all I had to do was see if Milo would be interested.

Carl then said, "If you want to have a seat over on that bench, I'll go grab your gear and we'll make sure we get everything to fit right."

Griffin and I seated ourselves on the bench and we sat so close that our thighs pressed up against one another. I didn't know if he even noticed, but I was aware of every single contact point between us, even if there were layers of thermal underwear and nylon/polyester clothing keeping us apart.

"Since we're offering up our appreciation," he said, "I never got to thank you."

It was then that I realized that I'd been staring at our legs. I forced myself to look at him. "For what? Deigning to be your friend? Allowing you to finance our entire evening, including my clothes? You're welcome."

He shot me that disarming grin of his. "No. For sharing your concerns about Milo. It means a great deal to me that you thought I was worth confiding in."

My throat tightened as my pulse hammered in my wrists. He was right. I had confided in him. I hadn't even shared my thoughts about Milo with Alice, who was the one in an actual position to help. I didn't know what that meant. "Oh?"

"There is something very trustworthy about you, and I'm honored that you see the same quality in me."

For a second I couldn't quite catch my breath. "I'm the last person you should trust."

I owed him that much honesty, at least.

But Griffin didn't take my warning seriously. Instead he wrapped his hand around mine and I couldn't even think of the effect it was having on me because I was so focused on the fact that he thought I was an honest and trustworthy person.

I wanted that. I wanted to be the woman he imagined me to be.

Gripping his hand tighter, realizing this might be the last time I ever got to touch him, I gathered up what little courage I had and said, "Griffin, I think there's something I want to tell you."

CHAPTER SEVENTEEN

His hold on my hand tightened. "I hope you know you can tell me anything. That your secrets will be safe with me. Just as I know that my secrets are safe with you."

Gah, he was making it worse. Did he really not see how he was making it worse?

Griffin had trusted me from the beginning. When he told me all about his messed-up family situation and how he was protecting his brother, I could have so easily called a tabloid and ratted him out. I never would have done that, though. I would never do anything to hurt him or Sophie, something he couldn't have known but instead intuited. It meant a lot to me that he thought I was worth trusting.

I could do this. I took a deep breath. This was so scary. Why was it so scary?

Because now you have something to lose, an internal voice whispered.

"There are things I want to tell you. But if I tell you, I don't think you'll like me very much after."

He sported a very serious expression until he asked, "Did you kill a man just to watch him die?"

"What? No."

"Harm any animals or small children?"

"No!"

He pulled my hand up to his mouth and pressed a soft kiss against it. Every bone in my body lost all of its mass, reducing me to a puddle of gooeyness.

"Then I can't think of anything you could say that might make me possibly dislike you, because you are kind, loyal, clever, funny, and beautiful. Everything I see in you is amazing."

My breath caught in my throat, feeling like it would be permanently lodged there. I tried really hard to ignore the fluttering feeling in my chest. He thought I was beautiful. There had been other things he mentioned, but that was all I could focus on. I'd never felt especially pretty, but his words made me feel like it was true.

I looked into those gorgeous green eyes of his and something was happening between us. Something I couldn't have put in words. Like the universe had connected our souls and I was an idiot to keep resisting him.

Carl interrupted us, returning with boots and skis and poles, and when Griffin let go of my hand I totally chickened out. Like an oversize, nervous, scared chicken afraid of her own shadow.

I tried paying attention to the conversation Carl and Griffin were having, but I was having a difficult time concentrating. Instead I looked at the sharpness of Griffin's jawline, the brownish-blond hairs in his scruff, how inviting his lips were. I was fascinated with the shape of them as they moved and formed words.

"How long have you two been dating?" Carl asked.

"Oh, no, we're not dating," I told him, if only to distract myself from making a mental inventory of Griffin's gorgeous features. "Griffin's just a friend. He's teaching me to ski."

Carl nodded and then asked, "Is this your first time in Aspen?" I didn't know who he was talking to, but Griffin answered.

"It is. I tend to holiday in warmer spots. Ibiza, Mustique, Aruba—"

I couldn't help myself. "And Jamaica?" At Griffin's questioning eyebrows I added on, "Like the old Beach Boys song? Never mind." I guessed transatlantic humor didn't always translate well.

"What about you?" Carl asked, and this time it was definitely directed to me. He knelt by my feet, making sure my boots fit into the skis properly. "Where else do you like to vacation?"

I'd never been on an actual vacation in my entire life. So instead I listed places that I'd lived. "Um, Southern California. Florida. The coast of Maine."

"I love Maine," Carl said. "Best lobster I've ever had."

"Yeah, you can't swing a dead cat there without hitting a lobster," I told him, and Carl chuckled as he stood up.

"If you want a personal tour guide while you're here, give me a call," Carl said with a wink. "You've got my number."

Now I realized why he'd asked how long Griffin and I had been together. I looked over at Griffin, and a brief and envious expression flashed across his face, one that now felt too familiar—he didn't like Carl flirting with me. It was his turn to be jealous. I found myself bracing for his reaction.

But instead of making a scene or yelling at me or Carl, Griffin remained kind and polite through the rest of the interaction.

Something else that had never happened to me—I'd had several men I'd dated who got angry if another man so much as made eye contact with me. Those were the ones I'd dumped the fastest.

Griffin didn't really have a right to say anything or be upset. We weren't dating. Not like that technicality had stopped other guys in the past. I decided it was pathetic that my expectation for men's behavior was so low.

I did like that he finally felt something of what I'd been feeling earlier that day. It helped to wipe away my fears that this was just a distraction or a flirtation. It was like I did matter to him.

Continuing to be the gentleman, Griffin shook Carl's hand and thanked him for all the help.

When Carl had left, Griffin stood up, helping gather my gear. "Shall we?"

"We shall," I agreed.

"This way to the slopes."

We walked out a side door and I was hit by a blast of frigid air. I spent so much time indoors I often forgot how truly freezing it was outside. I let out a yelp and said, "It's so cold out here I could fart snowflakes!"

Perfect. Just what you wanted to say to win over the inconceivably handsome man. Discussing gross bodily functions.

Fortunately for me, this somehow seemed to be the funniest thing I'd ever said and Griffin laughed. His laughter was so infectious that I couldn't help but join in.

When he finally stopped, he said, "Diana, have I told you how much I enjoy being in your company?"

"You might have mentioned it. Although personally I think you might be using me for my child-oriented schedule."

He swung around so that the material of our coats rubbed against each other. "I'd never use you."

Again, my anxiety over his intentions was soothed. But he needed to move away or else I was going to lean forward and fuse our mouths together. "You're, uh, standing really close to me. If you get any closer, you're going to have to buy me dinner."

Defying the laws of physics, he managed to somehow move closer without actually touching me. "You know I'd love to buy you dinner."

I audibly gulped. I hadn't intended to, it just happened. "You should, uh, probably back up."

He did, and I was both relieved and annoyed. He said, "My apologies. I was just overwhelmed by your loveliness and was powerless to resist."

"Are you flirting with me to get out of trouble?" I asked.

"Bunny, I'm flirting with you to get *in*to trouble."

Another gulp and warm, fuzzy tingles on my end.

He didn't seem to be affected in the same way. "You may want to put on your hat and gloves."

Right. I should bundle up. Although it felt unnecessary because suddenly it didn't seem so cold. Probably all my blood heating up inside me in anticipation of his touch.

I was in so much trouble.

He pointed up and I wondered how far we were going to go. "This way to the bunny slope."

I paused with my right glove only halfway on. "You're making that up."

"I'm not. They do call it the bunny slope. It's where I'm going to teach you to ski. It's just a bit up this way."

He was either following signs or had been here before, so I just trudged along behind him. "I thought we were going on one of those ski-bench things."

"The lift? That's only necessary for courses farther up the mountain."

I couldn't see the top of the mountain in the dark, but I had a hard time imagining traveling all the way up there just to hurl myself down while strapped to a couple of planks of wood.

He turned his head slightly and said, "There's also a restaurant at the summit that's supposed to have spectacular views. Maybe we could check it out some evening."

"I'm not great with heights," I confessed. "I don't freak out or anything. It just makes me uneasy."

That wasn't really a *no, I don't want to go to dinner* response—a fact he seemed to pick up on.

"The gondolas are enclosed and I would be there with you through it all."

He said this like his presence would solve every problem. I imagined that might actually be true. That it would be easier to get through things that scared me because he was with me.

I didn't know how to process that bit of insight.

When we got to the spot Griffin declared was the place, he handed me my skis. He put his own on, then crouched down to make sure that I'd done mine correctly. I looked at the top of his hair, wondering if it felt soft. I had lifted my hand, ready to take off my gloves and find out for myself, when he smiled up at me.

"You should be all good." He stood up, grabbed my poles, and handed them to me.

I didn't feel all good. It felt awkward having these sticks on my feet. I lifted my right foot slightly. "I feel like I'm about to go to clown college."

That threw my whole body off-balance and I started to lean sideways. Griffin grabbed my arm, righting me.

He showed me how to properly grip the poles and I lifted one up to look at the bottom. "What are these spikes for? Do I use them to stab you for making me fall?"

"That almost fall wasn't my fault. In case you're unfamiliar with it, I was helping you. To not fall." He pulled his woolen cap out of his pocket and pulled it down on his head. Sad. No inadvertent hair touching for me.

I turned to survey our surroundings. The slope was lit up by massive floodlights. We were the only ones here, though. That probably meant the other night skiers were looking for courses with more difficulty. So while it wasn't dark, at least we were alone. Half of my romantic fantasy had occurred.

Unfortunately, Griffin was all business. "You're not going to be happy about this, but one of the first things I need to teach you is how to fall."

"Why do I need to learn that? Are you anticipating that I'm going to be falling down a lot? I bruise easily. Like a ripe peach."

My heart fluttered when Griffin sent me a look that told me he wouldn't mind taking a bite out of me. "I'm teaching you how to do it right because I don't want you to get hurt."

Oh.

I was so intoxicated by his sweetness that I let him show me the right way to fall. No wonder Milo didn't want to do this. What kind of sport forced you to learn the right way to mess up before you even started? Like it was setting you up for failure.

Griffin seemed to be enjoying himself, so I kept my snarky commentary to myself. I had to squat down and fall on my side several times. The only good part was that he always helped me get back to my feet and I enjoyed how strong he was. I wasn't light, but he didn't seem to notice.

When I'd bruised my shoulder enough times to make him happy, he said, "Now that you've got that down, let's go over the basics of how this works. Fortunately for you, I'm an excellent skier and fairly good at instruction."

"Your humility is the most attractive thing about you," I told him. "When she was busy warning you about Cinderella, didn't your grandma also talk to you about being too egotistical?"

"I don't believe she'd think such a thing was possible." He pivoted gracefully on his skis, coming around to my right side. "I'm not really the arrogant sort. I'm more like one of those animals who show off to land a potential mate."

"So you're peacocking me?" I asked, ignoring the thrill his words gave me.

"Only if it's working."

It was working. "We're here to ski, remember? I hope you're as good at this as you say you are."

"There's a list of things that I excel at. Polo, driving, mudding and taping drywall. That's not all—I'm good at a great many things. One in particular."

That peach-biting look of his was back, and it gave my bones that gooey, meltable feeling again as I imagined just what else he was good at. His gaze was hot and sexy and I was frankly surprised at the amount of willpower I apparently possessed.

Especially given the thought of him doing construction work, all sweaty and muscled, wearing a white T-shirt that he'd have to take off because oh no, it was too hot, and he'd slowly pull it up and . . .

"Ready?" he asked.

Since he was unaware of what was happening in my head, he was all business. He threw around a lot of explanatory words like *wedge* and *shifting weight* and *bending knees*, and I honestly felt cheated. He didn't touch me, not once.

Every rom-com I'd ever watched had told me that this was where he was supposed to put his arms around me in order to help me. Like when the heroine had to learn how to shoot an arrow and her love interest put his arms around her to get her positioning correct? Sliding down a mountain seemed a lot more dangerous and in need of physical intervention than shooting a pointy stick at a target.

Maybe if I accidentally threw my stabby pole, he'd come over and show me the right way to do it.

"Try going a few meters," he said. "I'll stay right next to you."

I pointed the tips of my skis toward each other and pushed slightly with my poles. The slant here wasn't very intense, hence why it was used for kids and beginners, but I was definitely moving. Slowly, like he'd instructed, so that I wouldn't travel fast before I was ready for it.

"You're doing it!" he said. Like I wasn't there or something.

"I noticed!"

"Okay, come to a stop."

I turned my skis even more inward and came to a stop.

Griffin halted alongside me. "That was an excellent first attempt. I'm rather surprised you didn't fall."

"I happen to have incredible flexibility and balance." I said it because if he was going to brag about how awesome he was, maybe I should brag a little, too.

He had that peach-biting look back on his face and I realized what I might have implied. Especially when he asked with great interest, "Really? Does that apply to other areas of your life?"

I knew what he was hinting at but pretended I didn't. "Yes, you should see me walk a tightrope or play hopscotch."

Grinning, he said, "We should discuss your skills further tomorrow night at dinner."

I didn't remember agreeing to that. "Aren't you supposed to ask me?"

"Ask you about what?"

"Dinner?"

"Thank you for the invitation. As I mentioned earlier, I'd love to have dinner with you."

I pressed my lips together so that I wouldn't smile the way I wanted to. He probably thought he was so clever and charming.

Okay, he was, but that was absolutely beside the point.

Sensing that I was receptive to his sneaky invitation, he said, "There is a restaurant in town that serves a Domaine Leroy cabernet sauvignon that I think you would love. You know, if you combine *wine* and *dinner*, the new word is *winner*."

"I'm not sure I should drink around you," I told him.

"Why is that?" The twinkle in his eyes was unmistakable. He knew why. He was panty-melting hot sober. I would have no ability to resist if I lowered my defenses even slightly.

Not willing to admit what he'd apparently already figured out I said, "Don't you guys call it *supper* instead of *dinner* in England?"

"We do in my family but *wupper* isn't a funny pun. Come on, we'll just eat. It will all be very innocent."

"Said no innocent person ever."

He did manage to arrange his features into a wholesome-like expression. "Shall I list more things to recommend me?"

"I get it. You're fantastic. You don't need to keep flattering yourself."

Now he looked slightly offended. "I've only done that three times tonight since you seem incapable of appreciating what an incredible catch I am."

I couldn't help but laugh. "I know what kind of guy you are." A far sweeter and better one than he probably realized. The sort of man who would go to a foreign country to protect his brother and niece. Who would take the time to teach a woman he'd just met to ski. Who sent that same girl thoughtful gifts.

The kind of man who had me rethinking all sorts of things.

"Yet despite all that, you like me, Diana Parker."

"What's the word when you're not right?" I asked, ignoring the way my cheeks were warming up despite the cold.

"*Left*?" he offered.

"No, I believe the word is *you*."

That smile on his face let me know that I wasn't fooling anyone on this slope. "Tell you what. Go five meters without falling and we will go to dinner."

"Is that far?"

He rolled his eyes at my latest dig at the metric system. "I'll tell you when you've reached the mark."

"What if I can't make it?"

"You can." He exhaled slowly, his breath turning into a tiny mist of vapor that hung there between us before it dissipated. "I think you could do anything you set your mind to. But if you fall, well, then I'll have my answer, won't I?"

I had a decision to make. I was a fast learner—something that had been necessary in my previous line of work. So I pretty much had the hang of this staying-upright thing. I was fairly certain I could safely ski for however long five meters was.

Should I do it?

Or should I fall and keep this friends-only pretense going?

CHAPTER EIGHTEEN

The decision was actually pretty easy to make. I skied the five meters, going until Griffin called out to me to stop. It took him a couple of seconds to join me, and his grin was so wide that it made me smile shyly back at him.

"Supper tomorrow night, then. Same time?" he asked.

"You Europeans and your late dinners," I said with a shake of my head. "But yes. I can do that."

His eyes flicked over my face, and I wondered what he was looking for. What he hoped to see. "It's getting cold. I think you've got a handle on this. May I walk you back to your room?"

"Sure."

We removed our skis and he asked me, "Do you feel adequately prepared now?"

"I do. At the very least I have a better idea of what I'll be asking Milo to do."

The snow crunched under my boots as we returned to the ski shop. The warmth that enveloped us when we walked inside was so very welcome. Carl took our equipment and I gave him a bland smile when he reminded me that I should call him.

As we headed back toward the lobby Griffin asked, "So are you going to call Carl?" His question was meant to be disinterested, but I could tell it mattered to him.

"I'm not." No question. There was only one guy I was interested in, even if we shouldn't date.

He nodded, and he seemed pleased.

I felt like I needed to explain things further. "I told you, I don't really have time to date."

"And yet . . ." He didn't finish his sentence, but his implication came through loud and clear. Yes, I was being wildly inconsistent with my story. But that was because I was trying to rationalize why hanging out with him was a good idea.

He cleared his throat, then asked, "Speaking of you not dating, was tonight awkward?"

"Not until you asked me that question."

"Did you feel stressed?"

Where was he going with this? "No." At least, not for reasons I could admit out loud.

"Did you get dressed up for nothing?"

Obviously I got dressed appropriately for our activity. I was about to tell him no when I realized what he was doing. I'd complained to him earlier that dates were awkward and stressful and that I got dressed up for no reason. This clever boy had figured out a way to give me a date where none of those things were true.

It didn't strike me how high school–esque our evening was until we started walking down the hallway toward the room. He was literally walking me to my door. I thought he was just going to ride the elevator to his own floor and wish me a good night. I didn't need him to walk with me, but it was very sweet that he was. Another novel experience for me.

We stopped in front of the door and I took out my keycard. I fiddled with it, not sure what to say to him. He stood there quietly, like he was waiting for me to take the lead. To say or do something. Again he had that intense gaze, the soul-burning one. I was starting to heat up everywhere, and it wasn't just due to all the layers I had on.

"I should probably . . ." Now I was the one not ending my sentences. I waved my card next to the pad on the door and wrapped my fingers around the handle. "Thanks for tonight."

Then I turned and slammed face-first into the door. The card apparently hadn't registered and my muddled brain didn't register the fact until it was too late.

"Are you all right?" he asked, reaching out and putting both of his strong hands on the sides of my face. He peered at me with such concern, and my skin was prickling with electricity where he touched me.

"Fine." Totally and completely humiliated, but fine.

"I do hate when doors just leap out at you like that."

Still embarrassed, but grateful that his joke made things not seem so bad. He had a talent for putting me at ease.

Then he did something that made all of that go away. He let go of my face, apparently satisfied that I didn't have a concussion, and took my right hand. He pulled it up to his mouth and said, "Thank you for this evening."

He kissed the back of my hand, his lips feeling warm and soft and sending zings of sparkly energy through my veins, threatening to short-circuit my nervous system.

I opened my mouth to thank him but all I could do was stare.

It was over quickly, too quickly, and I leaned against the door for support.

And very nearly tumbled into the hallway when Sheila opened the door behind me.

"Oh! Diana! Griffin!" She sounded shocked and mortified as I straightened up, wondering how many other embarrassing things I could do this evening. "I'm so sorry. I heard a noise and I thought somebody was knocking—"

Griffin handled this like he handled everything else. "Just us. How have you been?"

Sheila smiled at him. "We're doing well. Things wouldn't be nearly as great without having Diana here."

I was alarmed, ready to intervene, but Griffin just said, "I certainly understand and share in that sentiment."

This time I was the one putting my hands against my face, like I could contain the blush happening there through physical force. He had to stop saying sweet things to me. It was more than I could take. I didn't know what to do with so much niceness.

Sheila said, "I meant to ask you when we first met, and I know this may seem like a strange question, but by any chance are you related to a Wilhelmina Windsor?"

I saw the moment when the light left his eyes, leaving behind a fake-looking smile. "Yes, she's my grandmother. Why do you ask?"

Total and utter panic bolted through me. Did she know the Windsors? Did they have some personal connection I wasn't aware of? Was everything about to blow up in my face?

"She offered to invest in my company a few years back, but we declined."

I relaxed slightly. A missed business opportunity wasn't that serious.

"My grandmother only backs sound investments, so your company must be quite successful. What is it you do?"

Sheila explained about her organic meal delivery service with Griffin nodding politely. But it was too easy for me to see where this conversation would go and how things could potentially go bad for me. My heart began to beat at a slow but hard pace. I wondered if they could hear it and would figure out how much I was starting to freak out. I knew they were just making small talk, but this could turn awful quickly.

Sure enough, as soon as she finished she decided to boost my anxiety level up to a hundred by asking, "And what is it you do, Griffin?"

"Philanthropy, mostly. And whatever it is that my grandmother requires."

I could see what was coming next, like the girl in that chess movie who could envision all the plays in her head before anyone made them.

He was going to ask me what I did, to include me in the conversation, and there would be no way for me to get through this without either Sheila or Griffin realizing that I'd been lying to both of them.

I fake yawned, stretching my arms above my head. "Sorry, it's getting late. We should probably call it a night."

At that Sheila brought a hand up to her mouth. "I didn't mean to interrupt you. I'll let you two . . . uh . . . as you were."

"As we were" was me running into a door while Griffin had to question his own life choices by being interested in someone who was assaulted by inanimate objects.

Sheila stepped back into the hallway, and I caught the door before it swung shut completely. I'd rather not have a repeat of the last time I'd tried to go through it.

"She's a nice woman," Griffin remarked, and I wondered if she was still within earshot.

"The best," I agreed. "I really am tired, though."

"Yes, you should go. Get some sleep."

Instead of taking the out he offered me, my mouth decided to spew some truth at him. That directly contradicted what I was trying to say. "I don't actually sleep very much. Sleep and I broke up about two years ago."

Now he looked worried. "You don't sleep? Why?"

"If I knew the answer to that and how to fix it I'd be . . ." I trailed off. I'd been about to say that "I'd be rich." Which would have been a bad thing to say, considering that he assumed I was already wealthy. I didn't need to worry about Griffin or Sheila to mess things up for me. I was fully capable of saying something revealing all on my own.

"I'll be hoping that things improve and you get the rest you need."

"Thanks." It wasn't going to happen, but it was kind of him to say that he wished things would get better for me.

I'd been into superheroes and comic books as a kid, and I'd always wondered what my kryptonite would be.

Turned out it was men who behaved decently.

Not willing to tempt fate any further, I said, "I should go. I guess I'll see you tomorrow."

He put his arm out, resting his hand against the door that I held in place. He didn't push on it but instead briefly stopped me from going inside. Then he did that thing where he stood oh so close without actually touching me and my lung function entirely ceased.

His mouth was close to my cheek, his breath almost caressing my skin. "May I ask you one question?"

Please don't ask me what I do, please don't ask me what I do repeated in my head on a loop.

"Yes."

"Am I alone in this?" he asked. "In what I feel—this connection between us?"

I knew the answer I should give him.

I also knew the answer that I wanted to give him.

Ducking my head, I went under his arm. I walked around to the other side of the door, placing it between us. I couldn't say what I wanted to say with him being so near.

"You're not alone," I whispered to him, then closed it.

I rested my forehead against the cool surface of the door. No more delaying. I had to tell him the truth. Maybe not about my famous felon mother, because that was too awful to talk about with anybody who wasn't related to her, but that I was a nanny and not the rich person he assumed me to be.

Because at some point, Griffin was going to blow it for me. Inadvertently, but it would happen.

I needed to tell him about my situation, about how this was all for Alice, and hope he would understand. I'd beg him not to rat me out. He was a good man—that much was obvious. He would get it, right?

While I couldn't accurately predict what his reaction was going to be, I knew I'd have to be brave and face whatever consequences would come. If he stopped hanging out with us, I'd find Milo another friend. And I would move on. Most of the walls surrounding my heart were still intact. I could get over this.

Maybe.

No, not maybe. If I had to, I would. I was strong enough to do that. This could be a story I'd tell at parties or something. Someday when my heart stopped hurting.

I closed my eyes against the pain of not having Griffin in my life anymore.

If that was the price I had to pay, then I was willing to pay it.

~

The next morning, Griffin and Sophie showed up to the movement class fifteen minutes after it started. From reading the description, I had thought it would be a tumbling, rock climbing, walking-on-balance-beams sort of thing, but apparently today it was all about dancing.

A current pop song I recognized played loudly over the speakers, but it was sung by little kids. Children of all ages were spread out in the middle of the room, having a blast.

"Do you want to dance?" I asked Milo.

He shook his head and moved closer to me. I rested my hand on top of his head. "Then you don't have to."

I didn't know what part of it made him uncomfortable, but the reason didn't matter.

Sophie had no such reluctance. As soon as she and Griffin arrived, she dragged her uncle out to the middle of the dance floor. They both danced enthusiastically, Griffin in an exaggerated way that made both me and Sophie giggle. He definitely didn't care who was watching or what anyone else thought of him. He grabbed both of Sophie's hands, helping her to shake and groove. She threw her head back to laugh, obviously having the best time.

He was so adorably cute with his niece that it made my uterus hurt.

Sophie saw us and pointed at me. "Ask Diana to dance!"

Following her instructions, he bounded over and offered me his hand. "Dance with us?"

I looked down at Milo, who had pressed himself against my side. He needed me here with him. I wasn't going to let him be left out. "Not this time."

Griffin took it in stride, shooting me a quick grin before returning to Sophie.

"Dancing can be hard," I said to Milo. "There's stuff that scares us, and you can stay away from it if that's what you choose. But sometimes there's things we can try out, even just once, and see if we might like it."

He turned his expressive eyes up at me, curious.

"Last night I did something that was really hard for me. Griffin taught me to ski." There was every chance that Milo would tell his mom I didn't know how to ski, but I was gambling on the fact that it was a subject he didn't like discussing with her. "It was hard, and I fell down a few times, but it was fun. I think you might like it."

I expected him to immediately shut me down, and when he didn't, I pressed on. "I met someone last night who is an expert at helping kids who don't like skiing. He can make it really safe and will be there with you every step. I'll make sure you don't get hurt, either. Just think about it. Sophie loves to ski and I think it would be fun if we all went together."

He was silent for a beat, considering this. "My dad loves to ski, too."

"I know. It would be fun if you could do that with your parents."

Milo twisted his mouth to one side, but he didn't say no. So I suggested, "Maybe we can just go look at the slope when we get back to the hotel. And I can introduce you to Carl, the skiing expert. If you want."

"Maybe," Milo said, and I wanted to pump both of my fists into the air. First step! We'd made a first step!

"Cool." I was trying to be nonchalant, but I was so excited by this tiny bit of progress that I was full-on chalant.

Milo never did join in during the dance class, and we spent the entire time on the sidelines. When the instructor led the kids through the steps of "I'm a Little Teapot," I could feel his body swaying next to me. He wanted to join in, but this wasn't the moment to push him.

One thing at a time.

The class ended, and Sophie and Griffin came to join us. Some of the tips of Griffin's hair had fallen forward, brushing against his forehead, and I wanted to reach out and move them.

He did it himself and I tried not to sigh in disappointment that I was denied the opportunity.

"Where are you off to now?" he asked.

"I was thinking that maybe I could show Milo the bunny slope back at the hotel." I ignored the knowing grin Griffin shot at me when I said *bunny*. "Just to let him see what it's like."

"We can go with you!" Sophie volunteered.

"Yes, let us drive you," Griffin added.

I turned to Milo. "What do you think?"

Wearing a determined little face that made me melt, he nodded. "Let's go see it."

I could not have been prouder of him.

~

Later that evening, I gave my sister a call and filled her in on everything that had been going on.

"Wait, wait, wait," Alice said. "You ran into the door? Do you have a huge bruise on your face?"

"No." I'd checked. Multiple times.

"Then what happened?"

"Griffin made sure I was okay. Then we said good night and he, um, kissed my hand."

"He kissed your hand?" she shrieked.

"Yes." Why had I thought it was a good idea to call Alice right before I went out on my first official date with Griffin? She was somehow managing to make me more nervous. At least I looked okay, if nothing else. I'd told Sheila about my date and the name of the restaurant, and she'd insisted on lending me a black cocktail dress. The matching shoes were too big again, but I was going to suck it up. I wasn't going to wear this dress with my hiking boots.

"Where was your hand when he kissed it?" Alice asked suggestively.

"At the end of my wrist!" I told her in exasperation.

"You're so going to kiss this boy soon."

"I'm not," I said, trying to remove the image of doing just that from my mind. "I can't. Not until I tell him the truth."

"Tell him, tell him, tell him," she chanted like she was at a ball game.

"I will. Tonight."

"Because you like him," she crowed. "Have I mentioned how much I love being right?"

Then she literally cackled.

And I couldn't deny what she'd said. "Okay, you can rein in your evil-scientist laugh. I thought you'd give me a bigger reaction to telling him the truth about me. That I'm not rich. And why I'm doing all this."

There was a moment of hesitation and I wished I could see her face. Alice had always been so easy to read. "You're not going to tell him about Mom?"

Telling him that I was poor and had faked my way into this job wasn't enough? "I'm not ready to have that conversation with him." I hadn't had that conversation with anyone in years.

"I suppose that'll have to do for now," she said. "Also, I think I should definitely have his number. Someone needs to call him."

"Why?"

"There are things I need to know. Like, what are his intentions? Are they honorable?"

I shook my head. "Nobody asks that anymore. And we're just having dinner. We're not going to a ball in the Victorian era."

"Fine." She drew out the vowels in the word like an annoyed teenage girl. "Have the best time. I want all the details."

I promised I'd give them to her, and after saying our love-yous, I hung up. I glanced at my phone. It was eight fifteen, but I wasn't expecting him quite yet. I walked out to the front living room, planning on waiting for him there. I couldn't risk another run-in with Sheila.

But as I went to sit down, there was a knock at the door.

He was on time? That was surprising. Him behaving unexpectedly made my anxiety kick up a notch. I grabbed my coat, putting it on. Then I walked to the door and caught a glimpse of Sheila coming out of her bedroom to give me a thumbs-up.

For some reason that gave me the courage I needed in that moment. Because this was it. I was going to tell him.

Letting out a deep breath, I opened the front door.

CHAPTER NINETEEN

Griffin was wearing a black Tom Ford suit with a crisp white dress shirt and a red silk tie. This wasn't the same getup from the charity event. Which meant he'd come to Aspen for a couple of weeks and had brought at least two different suits.

And even though I'd already seen him in a suit, it was like I'd forgotten how handsome he was. Clean-shaven, his hair styled. I liked everything I saw.

He put a hand out, like he was going to reach for me, and at the last second changed his mind. He put it against his chest instead, as if feeling his own heartbeat. "Diana . . . you take my breath away. You are stunning."

Suddenly self-conscious, I waved my hand toward my outfit. "It's just the dress."

"It most certainly is not the dress," he disagreed.

It was probably one of the nicest things anyone had ever said to me. I realized that I should let him know that I liked how he looked. It would have been rude not to say anything, right?

"You, um, you look really nice." Weak, not how I truly felt, because he took my breath away, too, but I didn't know what was going to happen after I told him I was a nanny, so I was playing it close to the vest.

"Thank you." Why hadn't I ever learned to take a compliment as well as he apparently did? Then he waved his hand down toward his legs. "You like this old thing? I've had it forever."

I understood he was joking, but I felt an urge to explain why it was working for me. "You have really nice suits. That you wear well. You know, I heard a quote once that said for women, a man wearing a suit is like what a woman wearing lingerie is for men."

He hadn't even been here for a full two minutes and I was already saying stupid things.

"So if I wear a suit in the future that means you'll wear—"

I cut him off by pushing against his forearm. "Griffin!" Sheila might be six feet behind me for all I knew. He captured my hand with his, holding it in place.

This time, he didn't let go.

I swallowed against the sensation, which was telegraphing a message to my nervous system to start shooting off sparks of electricity.

"Are you ready?" he asked, and this time he stepped away from the door so that I could leave, but he was still holding my hand.

"Yes."

I wanted to tell him the same thing he'd told me, that I liked how he looked regardless of what he was wearing, but I was pretty sure that was going to lead to some remarks from him about being naked and I wasn't equipped to deal with it. We walked down the hallway to the elevator, hand in hand. There was a warmth and a strength to him that I just could not get enough of.

He was the one who broke the silence when the elevator arrived and we stepped into it. "Today with Milo seemed promising."

"I think so, too." I nodded. Carl had met us at the bunny slope after I texted him and he was wonderful with Milo. He made Milo laugh and showed him some of the equipment they used, like a harness that would make sure Milo didn't fall or go too fast. They also had a special slope that they would use without any other skiers on it, except for people with special needs.

All on his own, Milo told Carl he'd like to try it out. I had felt giddy. Carl had said he didn't have time right then, but that we could make an appointment for tomorrow. I was partially afraid that Milo might change his mind, but he didn't mention it again the rest of the afternoon.

Griffin offered to bring Sophie along to our appointment, and I had accepted. The four of us had an official ski date.

But I had this dinner date to get through, first. We walked through the lobby out to the front door, where a very expensive red car waited for us.

I came to a stop. "What is that?"

He tugged on my hand, pulling me over to the car. "That is a Lamborghini Huracán Performante. An excellent piece of Italian art and machinery all in one."

"Did you go out and buy this today?" He'd been pretty clear that all of his cars were back in England.

Griffin opened the car door for me, and assisted me in getting into the car. Which was necessary, given how close the seats were to the ground. It was hard to maneuver myself to climb in properly, especially with shoes that were too big.

He closed the door and then ran around to the other side, where he handed some money to the waiting valet and got into the car. He revved the engine a few times and then shot me a mischievous grin that did funny things to my lady bits.

The smile, not the car.

"I rented it," he said, pulling out to the road and turning left.

"Not willing to settle for the two-door economy automobile?"

"Louis found a luxury-car rental place. I wanted something sporty, although given the possibility of snowfall and icy roads, I probably should have picked an SUV. Anyway, I wanted to show you what you're missing. Being as dismissive as you are of supercars."

"Supercars? Do they have little capes that they wear on the road?"

He chuckled. "Not quite."

I looked around. It all looked costly and high tech. "Aren't you trying to keep a low profile? Wouldn't this car tend to draw attention to you?"

Griffin pointed out the window. "That mountain over there is called Billionaire Mountain, home to some of the most expensive homes in your entire country. If you hadn't noticed, my car blends right in with everything else around us."

He was right. Cars had never been my thing, so I hadn't paid close attention, but looking at the other automobiles on the road and those parked along the sidewalk downtown, they obviously all cost more than I normally made in a year.

"It's the reason we chose Aspen," he said. "It's full of wealthy people and I knew Sophie and I wouldn't stand out."

With his personal secretary and car service and designer clothes, it seemed like a logical conclusion to make. And given that we weren't being followed by any paparazzi, he'd been right about blending in. He added, "Don't think I haven't noticed that you still haven't given me your opinion about the Lamborghini."

What was I supposed to say? I settled on, "It's a very nice car."

"That's it? Nice?"

"Um, the seats are soft?" I opened the center console and reached inside. "Look! Little bottles of water! That's cool."

"The engine. Don't you hear how powerful it is? How it purrs?"

That made me think of him doing things that would make me purr and I might have tuned him out for a bit while he waxed on about the incredible features of this all-wheel-drive luxury sports car, something something horsepower and something something else carbon fiber, so that I could daydream about kissing him.

His excitement over his Italian supercar was adorable, and my vivid imagination had given me a thoroughly delightful kissing scenario—it involved him pulling this car over to tell me he could no longer fight his feelings for me—but there were other issues I needed to focus on. Like what I was planning to do. When did I tell him the truth? At the end of the meal? Maybe he'd feel cheated, like I'd used him for a nice dinner and then revealed my treachery. In the beginning? But that might ruin the whole night. Although maybe that was what I deserved. To not get this night with him before everything fell apart.

We arrived at the restaurant and there was a valet shivering out front. Griffin handed him the keys, then ran around to help me get out of the car. Which was a good thing, because the sidewalk was slippery. He put his hand on the small of my back. The pressure was slight, but I felt very elegant and mature as we went inside.

A hostess waited for us but I quickly realized the restaurant was empty. "Are we late? Did they already close?"

"Mr. Windsor? Right this way, please," the hostess said, answering the question for me.

She showed us to a table in the center of the room. There were white tablecloths and tiny candles on each table. The overhead lighting was soft and the whole place felt romantic and cozy. Griffin pulled a chair out. I assumed it was for him and went for the other one. "No, Diana, this is your seat." He sounded very amused.

"Okay. Um, thanks." I didn't get it. I sat in the chair and scooted in, with him kind of assisting? I had to assume this was some British-etiquette thing I was unaware of. It was a good thing I planned to tell him about the real me so that I wouldn't have to keep pretending like I knew more than I did.

Confessing didn't actually feel like a good thing, but I told my nervous stomach it was in an attempt to calm it down.

The hostess gave us menus and Griffin and I thanked her.

When she left I leaned in to ask, "Why are we the only ones here?"

"Because I rented out the restaurant for two hours."

"What does that even mean?" I asked.

He held his menu up to his face so that I could see only his forehead. "It means we're going to be the only customers for the rest of the night."

"But . . . why?" Wouldn't that have cost a small fortune? I grabbed my glass of water, needing a drink because my throat suddenly felt so dry and tight. Was he embarrassed to be seen with me?

At my question he put the menu down on the table, his eyes soft. "I've noticed that you seem uncomfortable in crowds and I thought this would put you more at ease."

He was right. I did feel a bit unbalanced around lots of people. In large part because I had this constant, irrational fear that someone might possibly recognize me, but also lately because people seemed to stare at Griffin when we were together. Not with recognition, but like they were drawn to him, too. Which I understood. But I was worried that some of that attention might blow back on me.

And even though he didn't know any of the reasons, he'd gone out of his way to make me comfortable. The gesture was unbelievably sweet. "Why the car?"

At my question he shrugged, embarrassed. "Too much? I apologize if this all seems over the top. My father loved supercars, and I've collected a few in his honor. I suppose it makes me feel close to him."

I wondered what that would be like. To have a parent you wanted to be close to, even if they were just a memory.

"And . . . ," he continued, glancing down, "I rented the car because I wanted to share something that was important to me with you."

My heart leaped at his words. I was incredibly touched. "You didn't have to."

"I won't do it again," he said. "Just with it being our first official date and all, I may have been a bit extreme. Which earned me a phone call from my grandmother. She oversees my trust and rang to ask what these expenses were for, and I had to give her an explanation she wasn't happy about."

I understood what he was saying. He didn't just have this money lying around—he'd had to undergo an interrogation in an attempt to woo me.

Despite what he might think, I was totally out of my depth with this level of wealth. It felt like I was in a movie or something. "You don't have to go to bat for me with your grandma. And you definitely don't need to spend money on me."

"It's not as if I bought you the water rights to Liechtenstein," he joked but all my brain could think of was that he probably was rich enough to buy the water rights of a small country. "And of course I would stand up for you when it comes to Granny. Despite what she thinks, I am old enough to make my own decisions."

Alice had talked to me once about love languages, citing it as one of the reasons her own marriage hadn't worked out, and I remembered that one of them was gift giving. Maybe that was a way that Griffin showed affection and I should graciously accept his kind gestures.

But I wanted him to understand that he didn't have to spend money to win me over. "Thank you for being thoughtful and sharing something important to you with me. But your money isn't what impresses me. You, today with Sophie—that impressed me. How caring you are. How you were willing to make a fool of yourself to make a little girl happy."

"Good to know that you see me as more than just good posture and charm. Although I will note that you weren't impressed enough to accept my invitation to dance." He was being good-humored, but there was a slightly wounded tone underneath it, which surprised me.

"I wasn't rejecting you. Milo didn't want to dance and I didn't want to leave him alone."

"Oh. I hadn't realized."

"No, but I did."

He gave me a soft smile. "Milo's lucky to have a friend like you."
This was it. I had to tell him.

"About that—" But I was cut off by the appearance of our waitress, who introduced herself as Jolene and asked if we had any questions for her with regard to the menu.

"No, thank you. Could we have a few minutes?" Griffin asked.

Jolene nodded and said she'd be back.

I had folded my hands in my lap, looking down at the floor. My palms were completely sweaty, my heart racing, like I was standing on a rope bridge over a seven-hundred-foot-deep chasm.

"Diana?"

This was it. Now or never. "Ask me again," I said.

He paused. "Ask you what?"

"Ask me to dance."

He didn't speak for a moment and I raised my gaze to his face. There was such tenderness there, such affection, that it made my nerve endings short out.

"Dance with me." His voice was low and utterly intoxicating.

"Yes."

He stood up first, offering me his hand.

I wiped my hands on my dress before accepting. I got up and Griffin pulled me in close. I wrapped my arms around his neck, enjoying his broad shoulders. He put his hands at my waist, pressing me against him, and I let out a sigh of relief when I finally had the full breadth of him against me. It was delicious.

I'd assumed he'd turn on some music from his phone, but he held me tightly as we swayed. "There's no music," I said against his jawline.

His lips were right next to my ear, and his hot breath and words were like a caress. "We don't need any."

I'd thought this would be better—if we were dancing, then I couldn't see his face. I wouldn't have to deal with his disappointment when I told him everything. But this had not been a good plan. I wanted to melt against him, have him support all of my weight as I drifted in a hazy cloud of want.

"Do you . . ." It took me a second to find my voice because he'd moved one of his hands to my shoulder blades and was running his fingers up and down my spine. "Do you think maybe it's better not to know things? Ignorance is bliss and all that?"

"I don't think that's necessarily true. If ignorance is bliss, then why aren't more people happy?"

It was my one last out and he hadn't taken it. I tried building up my confidence, but I was so distracted by everything—his clean and expensive scent, his muscles pressed against me, the way he kept breathing softly on my ear. How my entire body had turned into one giant heartthrob, blood pounding hard through my veins.

"Remember how I said yesterday there was something I wanted to tell you?"

"Yes."

"I'm ready to tell you now."

I half expected him to make a joke as his body stilled, stopping our rhythmic swaying. He didn't. He pulled his head back so that I could see his serious expression. "All right."

"Only . . ." I trailed off. "I'm not really sure how to say it."

"In my experience, it's best to put words together in order to form a complete sentence," he said with a wink, and he led me back to my chair and then seated himself across from me.

My voice box suddenly felt too big for my throat, like I couldn't swallow. This was ridiculous. I was strong enough to do this.

"Despite what you probably thought—what I let you think—I'm not rich like you. I'm poor."

I tensed, waiting for his reaction, but his expression didn't change at all. "Oh, I'm sorry, is this where I'm supposed to feign shock? Should I gasp?"

"What?" I demanded. "You knew? How?"

He twisted his lips to the side, as if trying to come up with a diplomatic answer. "When you're surrounded by ostentatious luxury your entire life, you notice when someone doesn't . . ." His voice trailed off, as if unwilling to finish his sentence. Then he added, "Your clothes."

I glanced at my dress. "But this is Carolina Herrera."

"I'm not speaking about tonight. The first night we met, when I helped you with your coat . . ."

The coat. Of course.

That made me think of how careless I'd been around him. His assessment was entirely accurate. I thought of the superstore jeans I'd been wearing earlier. Had this been an actual con, I would have taken care of all those details. I would have considered how important it would be to dress a specific way to fit in. Hadn't I repeatedly noticed his designer clothes? I mean, mostly how well they fit him, but I'd been trained to look for those kinds of things. It just hadn't occurred to me that he had been, too. For very different reasons, but the end result was the same.

I'd totally misread him. I had assumed he'd thought I was like him. Living in an expensive suite, wearing fancy clothes. But he'd known. The. Whole. Time.

While I'd been freaking myself out, worried that he was going to uncover my secret, he'd known all along.

I was . . . bad at this. At conning people. I realized that I was out of practice. Completely rusty. I'd been so worried for so long that I'd end up like my mom, promising Alice I'd be honest so that I wouldn't end up like her and . . . it had worked, apparently.

Somehow I'd imagined that I was going to waltz into this situation having everything in hand, totally confident in my apparently nonexistent abilities. Instead I'd misjudged so much, including my total lack of skills.

It was very disconcerting to see yourself one way and realize you hadn't been that person in a long time.

My mind raced with how bad all of this was, because this meant the Crawfords might also have figured everything out.

I quelled the panic rising up inside me. That wasn't possible. As I sat here and ran through everything that had happened, the way that Griffin had talked to me, the things he'd said, I could finally detect that pattern. That he had figured out this truth about me a long time ago.

But the same couldn't be said for the Crawfords. They hadn't given me any indication that they knew I'd been lying to them from the beginning. The rest of my life was safe. It had to be, because I had to take care of Alice.

But Griffin . . . I had to respect that he'd been quick enough to figure things out. There was still the fact that I felt like he didn't understand just how poor I was. That this was a bigger deal than he seemed to realize. "The last apartment that I lived in had actual vermin in it, and I had two roommates and two jobs and was barely getting by. I didn't graduate from high school. I don't know what the British equivalent is for that because my only familiarity with your educational system is Harry Potter and I'm guessing you didn't go to Hogwarts."

He reached across the table and I accepted that connection eagerly. I wanted to touch him and have his strength to rely on, as nervous as I felt.

"Why do you think I'd care?" he asked.

Why did I think the billionaire who drove luxury cars and rented out restaurants would care about my background?

Griffin continued, "You just said my money doesn't matter to you, so why did you think your lack of it would matter to me?"

This was not going at all like I'd anticipated. What would he do with the next thing I had to tell him?

I glanced down at our joined hands and said, "It's more than just that. I lied. I'm not friends with the Crawfords like I told you. I'm their nanny."

CHAPTER TWENTY

Griffin still didn't look surprised. "Yes, I surmised that, too. Plus, Milo might have confirmed my suspicion when he mentioned that you were indeed his nanny yesterday to Sophie."

Now my mouth was hanging open in shock. He'd known that, too? I'd been hysterical over nothing? "Why didn't you say anything?"

Shrugging, he said, "Because I'd hoped you would know that you could tell me yourself."

How could he be so calm? "I've been freaking out this whole time, afraid that you'd say something to Sheila about me being a nanny and blow this all up."

He furrowed his eyebrows. "Don't the Crawfords already know that you're their nanny?"

"Yes, but they think I'm . . . more."

"More how?"

I explained their ridiculous list of requirements and how I'd lied and faked some social media profiles and references in order to get hired.

"I hate lying to them," I said. "Especially since they're such fantastic people. Not at all what I expected."

There. The truth. Now he'd get upset. Now he'd realize what a mistake he'd made. That I was a bad influence and shouldn't be allowed to be around the kids.

Instead his hand tightened around mine. "I know the kind of person you are. You must have had a good reason for doing what you did."

No one had ever believed in me like this. Not even my own sister. She wanted the best for me, but she was just as worried as I was that I would backslide. We were both operating from a place of fear. Because despite what had just happened, I had been good at all of this. I knew Alice felt like she had to monitor me, watch over me, remind me to be good.

Even though she loved me, the message was that I wasn't to be trusted.

And here was Griffin, saying that he didn't think any of that was true.

I put my free hand over my stomach, dragging in a shaky breath. "Alice is sick. She needs a kidney transplant or she's going to die. Her ex-husband is keeping her off his insurance despite a court order and I need forty thousand dollars to pay for the surgery. The Crawfords are paying me that much to watch Milo for the next few months."

"You must allow me to pay for your sister's surgery," he said and tears filled up my eyes, but I couldn't afford to let them out. If I started crying, I might never stop.

"I can't. I won't take charity."

"It's not charity," he insisted. "We could set up a payment plan, if you are determined to pay me back. Which wouldn't be necessary."

"No."

Griffin finally gave me the reaction I'd been waiting for. Shock. "Why not? You just told me you're unhappy with lying to the Crawfords. Me covering the surgery means you could tell them everything."

That was true. And I didn't know if I could properly explain to him why I couldn't take his money. Even though I'd just discovered how very bad at it I'd become, my worst fear in the entire world was becoming my mother, who used romance to trick men into spending all their money on her. I knew I wasn't conning Griffin, but if I took his money?

Then I would be.

I needed to prove, to myself at the very least, that I wasn't using him. He wasn't my mark, and I wasn't going to turn him into one, even accidentally. I would not be my mom.

"I'm not happy about lying," I told him, "but it's different. I'm working for them. I teach and watch Milo eleven hours a day, sometimes longer if they're traveling, and the fee they're paying me is what they paid their previous nanny. Who did not have any of the skills they wanted me to have."

"Do you worry that you're justifying it? Rationalizing? I don't believe you have to. Sheila seems like a very kind person. I think she would understand."

That might be true, but I wasn't willing to risk it. "Or she'd fire me and I'd be left with nothing."

He leaned forward. "I'd make sure you weren't left with nothing."

"That's not your responsibility." I took a deep, cleansing breath. Even if he wanted to, I was pretty sure his grandma would put a stop payment on any check or wire transfer he tried to give to me.

"You don't have anything set aside for a rainy day?" he asked.

"Just an umbrella. No, wait, I left that behind when I came out here."

"But—"

I raised one hand and cut him off. There wasn't a solution he was going to be able to come up with that I would agree to, and if I let him go on too long he'd probably talk me into taking money from him. I couldn't do that. "You've respected my boundaries. Please respect this one, too."

Griffin looked like he wanted to argue with me, but he didn't. His expression turned wistful. "Are you certain I can't slay this dragon for you?"

"Sorry, but I heard you have to have a special license for that."

He smiled, but there was a touch of sadness to it. "Is this why you've held back? With us?"

There wasn't an easy answer to that one. "It's one of the reasons."

"There are others? Do you want to tell me about them?" he offered.

"Not tonight." I'd done enough for one day. "I'm sorry for not being honest with you about this stuff. Also, I apologize that whenever I've talked about my past, there's been so many plot holes."

That smile turned into a real one and he reached over to hand me my menu. "If you ever change your mind," he said, "I'll always be here to listen. Whatever you need."

I thanked him, and we both turned our attention to the menus. We studied them, quietly. It wasn't uncomfortable, but I did find myself wondering what he really thought and if he was okay with everything that I'd shared with him.

Jolene wisely chose this moment to return, asking if we were ready to order. Griffin said to me, "They have a tasting menu here. It means we could try a bit of everything."

"That sounds really good. Let's get that." I almost didn't agree with his suggestion, because I wanted to keep Jolene at the table for a bit longer. If Griffin pressed me harder I'd have to tell him about my mom and it was too much. Anyone who'd ever found out about Margaret Fox had stopped being my friend immediately.

And while I'd been willing to let go of Griffin for choices that I'd made, I wasn't willing to lose him for something that wasn't my fault.

Jolene asked what we wanted to drink and despite his endorsement last night of a particular wine they offered, he said he was driving and asked for water. I asked for the same. I still needed my wits about me.

She left to put in our order and I said, "When I was looking through the menu, that tasting thing was exactly what I would have chosen."

"I believe you and I are on the same wavelength," he told me.

"Even though our lives are totally different?"

"We didn't have to grow up the same way to be kindred spirits," he said. "We don't have to have everything in common. We can enjoy each other's humor and outlook on life. I like seeing the world through your eyes."

"My cynical eyes? I like the way you see things better. Full of possibilities. Optimistic."

"I don't know how true that is, but I like that you see me that way. And I like being hopeful," he agreed. "Speaking of being hopeful, does your sister have a donor yet?"

"Yes. Me. I was worried we wouldn't be a match because we have different fathers, but we are."

"That's very noble of you to give your sister one of your internal organs."

"Well, I have another kidney, so it's okay. And she needs it more than I do."

At that he smiled. "What do your parents think about this?"

He said it casually, but there was definitely a probing element to his question. Now that I'd let down one of my walls he wanted more information. I couldn't blame him for that. I wanted to know all about him, too.

"My mother wouldn't care and I don't know who my father is. My last name is made up. My mom thought Diana Parker sounded good. It's something that's always bothered me, actually. Not knowing where I come from. It was humiliating when I had to do those genealogy projects at school."

Our server returned with the water, placing the glasses on the table while Griffin looked adorably confused. "I've never done that sort of project. There are people who keep track of those things and my family line is all recorded."

Right. Once again, the stark contrast between our lives reared up. Reminding me that I was stupid to think there could be something more here, despite his sweet reassurances. "For those of us not related to a royal household, the teachers wanted us to tell stories and have pictures of grandparents and great-grandparents, aunts and uncles, and I had to make it all up. The family I wished I had. I wanted a last name of my own that I could be proud of."

"Living up to a last name is not always all it's cracked up to be," he said. "I understand how you feel, but the pressure of having to carry on a line, the constant expectations and demands, the invasion of privacy, the judgment . . . it can be quite a lot."

I'd been so caught up in admiring all the trappings of his life that it hadn't ever occurred to me that there were parts of it that might be difficult. I knew his grandma was obviously challenging, but there was more to him than that. I'd overlooked the other trials in his life.

"I'm sorry—"

But he interrupted me, apparently not wanting to dig more into that particular pain—an impulse I understood all too well. "Tell me more about Alice."

Jolene brought out a wooden board with meats, crackers, and cheeses on it as an appetizer, along with two small plates. It looked like a more sophisticated version of a Lunchable. She told us to enjoy and we thanked her. Griffin released my hand so that we could eat, and I pushed down the keen sense of disappointment that we were no longer touching.

"About Alice . . . well, she's funny and so motherly and wants the best for me. She rescued me."

I realized my mistake but before I could take it back he said, "Rescued you? How so?"

How much should I tell him? "I was in a bad living situation and when I was sixteen, she came and got me and took me home to live with her. She's the first person who ever chose me."

We were both getting some food and putting it on our plates and even though I'd just been holding hands with him, when our fingers brushed against each other it still sent a jolt of sensation through me.

I looked into his eyes and saw that he was feeling the same thing. He cleared his throat. "What do you mean she *chose* you?"

"My whole life, when I actually went to school, I was the kid picked last for teams in PE. The one who sat alone at lunchtime because nobody wanted to be friends with me. I was always the outsider. Alice chose me. She wanted me and made me a part of her family. I would do anything for her."

As if she'd sensed that we were talking about her, my phone buzzed and I turned it over to look at the screen. It was a text from Alice:

Did you tell him yet? Is he your boyfriend? Have you smooched him?

"What's that look for?" he asked.

"Does your family drive you crazy?"

"That's what families do. At least all the ones I've been a part of."

I held my phone up. "Are they trying to get you to date a British nobleman?"

"No, but have I mentioned just how much I like your brilliant sister? In days of yore I would have knighted her for her service to the crown."

"You're not a prince," I reminded him.

"In days of yore I think I would have been."

"And I would have been a scullery maid."

"No." He paused, thoughtful. "A housekeeper, at least."

That made me laugh and he added, "I do understand what you're experiencing. The dowager countess often drives me mad."

I asked him what that title meant, being unfamiliar with the term. He explained that his grandfather had been the Earl of Strathorne and his wife the countess, but that when he died and Griffin's father took the title, his grandma became known as the dowager countess since Griffin's mom had become the current one.

"Here's what I don't get," I said. "It's duke and duchess, viscount and viscountess, but earl and countess? How does that make sense?"

"It doesn't. Along with much of the English language."

True. It also meant that I'd been technically right when I'd called Griffin a count the first time I'd spoken about him with Alice.

I asked him what it was like growing up as an earl, and he was telling me about his best friends at boarding school (which meant that I'd also been right about the Hogwarts comparison) and a prank they'd played on their headmaster during something he called Upper Sixth that involved a group of pigs and red paint when he was interrupted by the growling of my stomach.

It was then that I realized that we'd been so busy chatting that neither one of us had eaten anything yet. I'd never had this experience, either—being so excited to talk to someone and find out about them that I'd forgotten to eat, wanting to share parts of myself as well.

I routinely forgot to do many things during the course of a day, but eating had never been one of them.

"We should dig in," Griffin said.

He reached for the blue cheese.

"Ugh, blue cheese?" I said. "You were so perfect until this very moment. You could have been everything. Why would you go and ruin all that?"

He laughed, but then he took a bite. "Blue cheese is delicious."

"It's like a crime against humanity. Mold wasn't meant to be eaten. That's why it looks the way it does. So we'll stay away."

"There must be some blue food you eat. Blueberries."

It was a relief to be able to not have to hide my life, to be able to talk with him in a way that was much more honest. "Blueberries are expensive and, like most fresh fruit, go bad fast."

"Blue M&M's," he offered.

"That's unnatural food dye, which is fine," I told him. "Blue cheese is totally natural."

"That's what makes it good. Try some."

I refused, and he spent the next five minutes trying to talk me into it, and he was so persuasive I very nearly gave in. I was saved by the next course, which was salad, and then there was fish and finally the main course, a filet mignon.

"This is one of the best things I've ever put in my mouth." I moaned after my first bite. "It's seriously like crack made out of steak."

He looked at me appreciatively. "You must be fun to cook for."

"Anytime you want to cook for me, I'm there." I'd been eating pretty well with the Crawfords, but I didn't really ever have hot food. Unless I'd heated something up in the microwave. I didn't want to intrude on their family dinnertime.

"If only I'd known earlier that the way to your heart was through your stomach."

I knew he was teasing, but he wasn't wrong. Which Jolene proved ten minutes later by bringing out the best piece of layered chocolate cake that I'd ever had in my entire life.

After my first bite I told him, "This is so good I'm about to pass out."

Griffin then managed to raise his ranking in the running for favorite person in my life by asking Jolene if we could get the rest of the cake to go. Seriously, Alice and the twins were in trouble here.

Jolene brought the cake in a box and handed it to Griffin, who quickly passed it over to me. I was so happy and stuffed. "Thank you for this," I told him. "This might have easily been the best meal I've ever eaten."

"I definitely plan on feeding you again." He stood, that twinkle in his eyes doing funny things to my too-full stomach. "It's getting late. We should go."

Nodding, I got up and grabbed my coat. I put it on quickly before he could offer to help. As we walked toward the exit, he said, "That's a beautiful Steinway."

He nodded his head toward the piano that was set up in an alcove away from the dining room.

"Do you play?"

Griffin shrugged. "A bit."

He walked over and sat down at the piano, running his fingers on top of the keys. He shot me his mischievous grin and I expected him to bang out "Chopsticks." Instead, he started playing a complicated and hauntingly beautiful piece of music.

I stood there with my mouth slightly open. I didn't know much about music other than what pop songs I listened to online, but there was something emotional in what he played. It tugged at my heart, and then I felt it in my very soul.

When the last note had trailed off, he looked at me expectantly.

"Who wrote that?" I asked him, wanting to download it immediately.

"I did."

"Seriously?" My esteem for him went up several more notches.

"I'm a bit insulted by your amount of surprise," he said with a grin as he stood back up to join me.

"I just had no idea. You're so good. So good."

"Thank you."

He started to walk away but I put my hand on his chest to stop him. "I don't think you understand. You're amazing."

An expression flitted across his face so quickly I couldn't tell what it was. "That's what I think about you."

Nothing I'd ever done was as amazing as that song he'd just played. Not a single one of my paintings could ever compare. "Well, you'd be wrong."

"I'm allowed to draw my own conclusions."

It was refreshing to think there was a man who would think good things about me and there was nothing I could do to convince him otherwise.

Well, I could bring up my felon mother, but other than that, he seemed to be on board.

We went back to the front door and the valet had the Italian super-car waiting for us. Griffin helped me into the car again and I settled back, putting on my seat belt.

Time to go back to the hotel. Back home. He would, I assumed, walk me to my door.

Where I would finally get my fairy-tale kiss.

CHAPTER TWENTY-ONE

"How long did you take piano lessons for?" I asked.

Griffin's gaze was turned toward the road as he maneuvered out of the parking lot. "My entire childhood. Ollie hated it, and he fought it, but I loved learning. My instructor thought I might be good enough to travel, perform, and compete. But Granny said no. I had responsibilities. Duties."

He wasn't serious like this very often, so I knew this restriction had hurt him. "Can't you do all that now?"

"No. I'm too old and haven't kept up with the kind of training that would require. My grandmother doesn't mind me going on holiday, but she would very much mind me devoting most of my time to music."

"So? She's not actually the boss of you."

"She might disagree with you. My life is not always my own."

My life had been very much my own for so long that I couldn't quite comprehend what his regular day-to-day back in England must be like. "Well, I think you should stand up to her and do the things you want to do. Rock that boat."

"Do you know what happens when you rock boats? You fall out."

While I tried to figure out his precise meaning, he changed the subject on me. "What was it like when you moved in with your sister? Back when you were a teenager?"

He'd apparently figured out that all he had to do was bring up Alice and I would willingly talk about her. Pretty clever of him.

I did oblige him, though. I told him how bad things had been at home—the electricity had been off for a month and the water had turned off the day before because I didn't make enough money at my fast-food job to cover the bills. I didn't tell him that my mom had been living with her latest conquest and had forgotten that I needed to be taken care of. Then Alice came in on her white horse and took me away.

"She wanted me to go back to school, or at least get my GED, but I fought her on it. I wanted to get a full-time job and take care of myself. With money that I had earned." Not money that I had stolen.

"Where was your mother?"

"Gone. She did that a lot. But I'd relied on her to take care of me and she'd let me down. I never wanted to be in that position ever again."

He made a sound as if he suddenly understood something about me that he hadn't before. "It's very important to take care of yourself, isn't it?"

"Isn't that important to everyone?"

"You'd be surprised," he said.

We pulled up to the hotel, handed off the keys, and Griffin assisted me through the lobby. Once we were inside, I took off my uncomfortable shoes.

He smiled at my bare feet but didn't comment on it as we went to the elevator. The doors opened and we stepped in.

"Anyway," I went on, "Alice was right. I should have at least graduated. And even though I couldn't have gone to regular college, there were art schools that I could have applied to, and if I'd been accepted there would have been scholarships to pay for everything. It's my biggest regret."

The doors opened on my floor and we walked out together. He said, "You could take your own advice. Go to school now."

"Yeah, maybe I'll get right on that after Alice is safe." I was being sarcastic. I couldn't imagine going back to school with a bunch of nineteen-year-olds. "I did audit some art classes before Alice got sick, and it wasn't as informative as I'd hoped it would be."

"That's because you're already so naturally talented."

"Says the man who composes his own classical music."

We stopped in front of the door. "That's why you should believe me. From one artist to another."

Suddenly everything felt entirely awkward. How did you say, "Hey, remember how I said we'd never date and never kiss? Yeah, never doesn't last nearly as long as it used to! So pucker up, baby!"

Because tonight, everything was different. It had changed in a way where I couldn't have changed it back, even if I'd wanted to. I was never going to be just his friend.

There was too much between us now.

"So in the spirit of radical honesty . . . ," I said, looking down, "this was the best first date I've ever had."

He raised both eyebrows in amusement. "You're calling it a date now?"

"That's what it was." My heart beat slow and hard, as I was now the one maneuvering my way closer to him. "And at the end of the date, you say goodbye."

Something bright flared to life in his eyes. "I know of a perfect way to do that."

He put his hands on my shoulders and then leaned in. I closed my eyes in anticipation, my pulse jumping and jolting with joy at his touch.

But he didn't kiss me. At least, not on my lips.

Instead he pressed a kiss against my right cheek. It was a fleeting sensation and not at all what I had wanted, but the skin underneath his mouth tingled and warmed up in response.

He kissed my left cheek, where I had the same response.

And then he was done. He left me breathing heavily and wanting so much more.

"That's how the French say hello and goodbye," he said.

Was he . . . *teasing* me? "That's not the kind of kissing the French are famous for," I said.

There was a moment of interest in his eyes as his gaze was drawn to my lips, but he stepped back instead. "I'm not going to kiss you."

I wanted to whine "Why not?" like a little kid. I considered throwing myself at him, planting my mouth on his, but that suddenly felt very pathetic. What if he didn't want to kiss me? I wasn't going to make him do it.

But if this was some kind of pride thing, that should be easy enough to circumvent. "That's okay. I heard earls aren't very good kissers, anyways."

He wasn't falling for it. I could see it on his face. He smiled at me. "Normally I would ask to defend my honor, but not tonight."

"Sounds like I wouldn't be missing out on much."

He moved close to me, exciting every cell in my body. "Diana, if I kissed you, you'd be begging me to never stop."

I one hundred percent believed him, but wasn't about to agree. He might assume I disputed his statement and then kiss the ever-loving life out of me to prove his point, and I wasn't going to say anything that might get in the way of that happening.

Despite me invoking radical honesty earlier, I wasn't going to do that now. Just in case.

He didn't take the bait, though. "I'm not going to kiss you because you are the one who set the boundaries. You said we were just friends. I would never cross that line. Bunny, you are going to have to be the one to kiss me."

My fevered brain and desperate body eagerly accepted this solution. Kiss him! Of course! I could do that right now!

But he kept talking. "It has to be your decision. And when you do, it'll be to show me that things have changed and you want to be with me. That we're more than friends."

It was like being doused with a bucket of ice water. Was I ready for that? I had accepted that we could have a casual fling that lasted for about two weeks and then he would go back to England.

But even as I thought it, I knew it wasn't enough. If I kissed him, let myself develop deeper feelings for him, how could I ever let him go?

As if he sensed my indecision, he took several steps away from me. "Thank you for a perfect evening, Diana. You are right, best first date ever. And, as I'd promised earlier, an innocent evening."

Well, crap. I'd just been blown up by my own bomb. I watched him walk down to the elevator, waiting until he was gone from sight before I let myself into the suite.

My boundaries. Ha. I'd done this to myself.

If I hadn't been feeling so frustrated, I might have been amused.

~

Things were business as usual with Griffin the next morning at story time. Other than the fact that he kept giving me funny looks and I didn't know what he was expecting—did he think I was going to leap on him like a lion pouncing on a gazelle? In a room filled with young mothers and very small children?

I had some dignity. Not much, but some.

We made plans to get together later to ski with Milo and I checked my phone to see a text from Sheila. She routinely texted me throughout the day—to ask how Milo was doing and how things were going.

But this text was unusual.

The second you step foot in the suite, I want you to call me immediately.

I texted her back:

Is everything okay?

I saw the three dots as she typed her reply.

Everything's fine. Just call.

That seemed weird. I did as she asked, though, and as soon as I got through the door I called her.

She answered immediately. "Hi, Diana! I needed to ask you to check and see if we have any flour."

I helped Milo get his coat off and hung it up. Flour? That was kind of a weird question. Maybe she wanted to make cookies later. "I'll check."

"Good. Keep me on the phone while you do."

"Okay." I headed through the entryway to the hall on the right and went into the kitchen.

The kitchen that was full of purple irises. Every countertop was covered with irises in vases, and there was a lot of countertop space.

"Oh my . . ."

"Sorry, I didn't mean the baking kind of flour. I meant the flower type of flower! Ack! Sorry for the trick, but look at how many flowers you got! They arrived right after you guys left this morning."

No wonder Griffin had been shooting me funny looks all morning. He probably wondered why I wasn't mentioning it.

Sheila was so excited you'd think they had been sent to her. But I was stunned as I connected what this meant.

These were the flowers that Griffin's dad used to bring to his mom every week, to show her how much he loved her.

I'd told him he didn't need to try to impress me, but this wasn't about the money. This was about what those flowers meant to him.

What I meant to him.

"All this is for me?" I asked, overwhelmed by his gesture.

"They're not for me."

There was a little white card attached to the vase nearest to me and with trembling fingers I opened it. It read:

Thinking of you—G

P.S. Please note that I didn't send ownership of the water rights of any small nations.

No water rights, but he had easily emptied out the iris stock of every flower shop from here to Denver.

How was I supposed to react to this? He was being completely adorable and sweet and did the flowers mean more than just hey, thanks for all the fun?

Did they mean Griffin had deeper feelings for me?

That he might even love me?

That thought hit me square in the chest and then sent off ripples of emotion through my body.

"Are they from Sophie's uncle?" Sheila asked. "Her very, very cute uncle?"

"Yes, they're from Griffin."

"Does this make him your official boyfriend?"

"We're just friends," I said, but it was reflexive. Out of habit.

But clearly untrue.

"Yes, I can see that. All of my friends send me dozens of bouquets. I hate to tell you this, Diana, but you are being seriously wooed. I have to get back to work. Enjoy your flowers!"

She hung up and I stood in the kitchen, unsure of what to do next.

It was probably a good thing he hadn't sent these to me yesterday. I might have thrown all caution to the wind last night and laid a big old kiss on him. Screw worrying about the future and getting my heart broken. His money still didn't impress me, but this gesture, the one that meant something special to him?

That wasn't something that would be easy to ignore.

~

It was also a good thing that he hadn't been anywhere near me when I got the flowers. If he'd asked me to date him, for real, I would have done it. Now that a few hours had passed, and Milo and I had worked on the lesson plan for today, I'd had time to settle down and let my mind consider all the possibilities.

I could have a brief fling with a British nobleman who was going back to his own country soon.

Or I could be just friends with that same man, focusing my attention on letting Sophie and Milo spend time together.

Then there was the third option—I could go ahead and kiss him and hope for something more. Something that might last beyond this one vacation.

But how could I know if that was possible? Even Alice had been urging me down the fling road. To just enjoy whatever time I had with him and then let him go.

Keeping him at a distance would make that easier to do. Like how I adored Milo but remembered that he was going to leave. I had that thing in the back of my mind that reminded me from time to time that the Crawfords had an expiration date and this would all end.

I couldn't imagine doing the same thing with Griffin. I had the distinct feeling that when it came to caring about him, it was going to be all or nothing.

That when he left me, it would absolutely shatter my heart.

I wasn't sure I could take that.

So now I had to be resolved. To do the best thing for everyone involved. We could be friends, but I would keep my distance. Last night had to be a one-off. It didn't matter how attractive he was or how much I wanted him. I had to be smart here. Think about Alice.

Remembering Alice didn't help matters because every text from her was some variation of *did you kiss him yet?*

Her words were still in my head while I got Milo all bundled up to take him to our ski appointment. I knew I was going to have some time before Griffin and Sophie showed up and I planned on using it to remind myself that I was going to be strong and not fall for a guy who wasn't going to stick around.

Unfortunately, Griffin had decided to mix things up again and he and Sophie were waiting for us at the adaptive slope. Griffin was speaking to Carl and hadn't noticed us yet.

I thought I had adequately prepared myself to see Griffin again, but I hadn't. Even though he was all covered in puffy clothes and had on a pair of what looked to be Cartier sunglasses, he was still hot enough to melt all this snow around us.

That would certainly make our lesson end early.

Carl saw us first. "Hi, Diana! Hey, Milo! Good to see you again, little man." He held out a fist to Milo, who bumped it back after a moment's hesitation.

"Hi. I have cholera. From eating blue M&M's," Milo informed him solemnly.

The ski instructor looked up at me with concern and I waved my hand. "He doesn't. He's fine."

At some point Griffin had come over to stand right next to me. "I told you those blue M&M's were unsafe."

"You were pro blue food," I reminded him.

"I was kind of hoping you'd forget that for the sake of the joke," he said and I couldn't help but smile back at him and question all of the resolutions I'd just made.

Sophie came over and tugged on my hand. "Diana! Did you know that the moon will wobble in its orbit and it could make sea levels rise and flood coastal cities?"

"I did not," I told her.

She ran to Carl and Milo, joining in.

"Just great," I said to Griffin. "One more thing for me to worry about. Shouldn't the moon not wobble?" Like I didn't already have enough going on.

"She's exaggerating," he said. "There's plenty of other things that will destroy the planet long before the moon does."

"Thank you," I blurted out, worried that if I didn't say it to him now, I might be too chicken to say it later. "Not for reassuring me about the moon, but for the flowers. They are beautiful."

"I'm glad you like them."

I could feel his gaze on me, like he wanted to say something else, but I didn't encourage him and he stayed quiet.

Leaving it up to me to say something.

What I wanted to do was ask him why he had chosen the irises, what they symbolized for him, but that was a door I needed to keep shut. "It was a really kind gesture, but you know that we can't . . . that we . . . what I'm trying to say is . . ." How was I back here again? Giving him sentence fragments that I couldn't finish? "You're leaving in a week."

That should be enough of an explanation.

"I'm not."

"What? Why not?"

"Because of how much we're enjoying the crisp mountain air?" he offered, but he could see that I didn't believe him. "I spoke with Ollie last night and we agreed that I should stay here. Things with Granny are tense, apparently."

This Ollie was a bit of a coward. I couldn't condemn him, though. I was very often a huge scaredy-cat myself.

"That sounds tough." I looked over at Sophie, and the sun chose that moment to hit her golden blonde hair perfectly so that she looked like a little angel.

"It's easier for me than Sophie, obviously. She misses home. She misses her parents."

"Has there been any contact with her mom?"

"None." The word was terse, and I understood how much Sophie's mom abandoning her upset him.

"Sophie is such a great girl. I can't imagine how anyone could walk away from her."

"Neither can I," he agreed. "Personally, I don't make a habit of walking away from fantastic people that I care about."

Those words were directed at me, and they wounded me. Unintentionally, because what he was saying was a positive thing, but even if he didn't want to leave me, he was going to eventually. Maybe not as soon as I'd thought, but at some point his grandmother would make him come home.

I'd be nothing more than a fond memory.

And that wasn't good enough for me. Not anymore.

CHAPTER TWENTY-TWO

We walked over to join Milo, Carl, and Sophie. We listened while Carl explained the equipment he was using, how it all worked, and patiently answered every question that Milo had. When Milo indicated he was good with getting all geared up, Carl then explained in excruciating detail everything they would do, how to move, how to stop, how to shift his weight to turn. He also promised Milo that he wouldn't let him fall and that they wouldn't go too fast.

Carl asked, "Are you ready?"

Milo nodded, and then Carl gave him a tiny push and Milo . . . was doing it! He was skiing! At a snail's pace, but it was happening! I pulled out my phone and started filming him. This would make his parents so happy.

Pressing a few buttons, I texted the video to Sheila. She answered thirty seconds later:

I am full on crying in this business center. Thank you, Diana.
Thank you.

Her words made my heart swell up. It was amazing to know that I'd helped to make her that happy. It certainly soothed my guilty conscience.

"Look, Diana! I'm doing it!" he called over his shoulder to me.

Milo was such a rock star. I was incredibly proud of him and how brave he was being. "You're doing so awesome! Great job, Milo! What do you think of it?"

"This is cool! Let's go faster!" he told Carl.

"We can do that. Tell me when you want to stop," Carl said. They picked up speed slowly, but it was happening and Milo looked thrilled.

I was so glad he'd tried this. That he'd given it a chance.

That made me think of Griffin and I glanced at him briefly. I wanted so badly to give this thing between us a chance, but there were only so many times a heart could break before it stopped working altogether. He already meant more to me than any other man I'd gone out with. I couldn't love him and then lose him.

Sophie had strapped on her own skis and joined them. She giggled with Milo as they skied at a very slow but steady pace. Carl stayed close, giving him more step-by-step instructions.

"You did that," Griffin said. "You put that look on his face."

His words made me feel like my soul was smiling. "Not just me. You and Sophie are a big part of that. Carl, too."

Carl led the kids over to where we were waiting for them. I couldn't help myself—even if it embarrassed him, I had to hug Milo. He hugged me back tightly.

"What do you think about skiing?" I asked him when I let him go.

"It's cool! And later we get to read *Principles and Practice of Infectious Diseases*, right?" he asked.

"Two pages, like we agreed on," I told him.

Sophie said, "Come on, Milo! Let's ski some more!"

The trio skied off and Sophie said something to Milo that made him grin. They had become the best of friends so quickly. I didn't want to potentially mess that up for him by dating Griffin and having every-thing fall apart.

"I may not know much about parenting," Griffin said, "but aren't you not supposed to bribe them?"

"It wasn't a bribe. Not really. More of an incentive for something he already said he would do. An additional bonus to make it win-win for both of us. We both got something we wanted out of it." Not to mention that I'd at least accomplished one of the things the Crawfords had asked me to do. Which felt like such a relief.

"Speaking of getting what we both want, what time are you done with work?" Griffin asked.

Oh no. "Six. Why?"

"Would you like to come over? I could make you dinner. My skills are limited, but you sound like you're not all that picky when it comes to food."

That was true. And I did want to go over to his suite. With every fiber of my entire being.

But I couldn't. "Not tonight."

His eyes shuttered. "Oh, I see."

I didn't mean it as a total rejection. Just a course correction. "No, it's not like that. Things between us . . . even if you're staying for a bit longer, this will end."

"That's not necessarily true."

"We live on entirely different continents. You said it yourself. You have responsibilities and duties." Not to mention that his grandmother would probably have a coronary if she found out about me. "I have people here who need me. And if things went badly—"

"Why do you assume they'd go badly?" he interrupted me to ask.

"They have in every relationship I've ever been in."

"It only takes once," he said in a soft voice that made my heart feel woozy. I reminded myself to stay strong.

"If things went badly, I don't want to be the one responsible for breaking poor Milo's heart." I gestured toward them, where the kids were having such a great time together.

"Nor I Sophie's," he said. "What if we promised that no matter what happens with us, we wouldn't let it affect their friendship?"

That was so tempting. "Maybe we should stay just friends." There was absolutely no conviction behind my words, because that wasn't what I really wanted.

Which he seemed to get. He studied me for a bit and then said, "It isn't what I hoped for, but if that's what you choose, you know that you can trust me to respect your wishes."

"Thank you. Definitely friends." Nope, still not buying it. I held out my hand to him.

He reached for it and part of me thought he might kiss it again, like he had the other night. Instead he shook it like a friend would, and there wasn't any time to enjoy how amazing it was to have his skin pressed against mine, to fawn over the strength of his grip, or how large his hand was, before it was over.

His phone beeped and he glanced at it. "We have a scheduled call with Ollie in a few minutes. Sophie and I should go."

"Oh. Okay." I was disappointed, hoping they'd stay awhile longer.

"Sophie!" he called, waving her over. She sat down to remove her skis and Griffin turned toward me. "Diana, I hope you don't mind me saying this, but I need to say it. And then I won't bring it up again."

My heart slammed violently against my rib cage as my breathing went shallow. This was it. He was going to say something to totally change my mind.

I actually welcomed him doing just that. Because despite all my recent resolutions, I would have loved an out.

"I understand that you're protecting yourself. I may not understand all the reasons why, but I know that you have this rough exterior to safeguard your tender heart. A heart that's been damaged. And I promise that I would be careful with it, should you choose to trust me with it."

Oh. My entire body flooded with those oxytocin hormones that made you feel all affectionate and lovey-dovey to the person you were looking at and stop being noble or smart.

Sophie came over, handing her skis and poles to her uncle. "Is it time to talk to Papa?"

"It is," he said. "We should go. We'll see Milo and Diana soon."

They left, with Sophie chattering to Griffin as they walked away. He glanced over his shoulder at me and that wave of want hit me again.

Soon. He was planning on seeing me soon.

I was not strong enough to resist this for long.

~

Over the next couple of days there ended up not being much to resist. Griffin pulled back a little. He was still friendly and kind, he still laughed and teased me, but there was no more flirting. No mention of dates or kisses or anything else.

It also sucked because the more time I spent with him, the more I liked him, despite my best efforts not to fall for him. His intelligence and wit, the way he didn't care what anybody else thought of him, his kindness, how everybody from old ladies to babies fell in love with him as soon as they met him. I loved his curiosity and how he wanted to learn everything, like when we went on a museum tour with the kids and he spent the entire time chatting up our tour guide with questions about all the exhibits.

He'd never be mine.

All of it made me so sad.

Which made no sense because I was the one who had said this was how things had to be. I had no right to be hurt by him doing exactly what I'd asked him to do.

Sometimes he would slip, and I enjoyed those times more than I should have. Like the afternoon we got together at Griffin's place to play board games. I had explained to Sheila that the games would teach strategic thinking and problem-solving, along with social skills like taking turns and losing gracefully. She thought that sounded great.

Milo and I arrived at Griffin's suite and knocked on his door. I expected him to answer, but a middle-aged man with a large nose and a receding hairline opened it and said, "May I help you?"

This had to be Louis. The secretary/valet/butler guy. "Hi. We're here to see Griffin and Sophie."

"Do you have an appointment?" he asked, looking down his nose at me.

"It's all right, Louis. These are our guests." Griffin came up behind him and pulled the door all the way open. "Come in, please!"

Louis sniffed at us, then exited the room.

"He must be fun at parties," I said in a low voice and Griffin grinned at me.

"He usually stays in his room when he's not lecturing me on proper behavior or helping to arrange my schedule. I suspect he might also report on me to my grandmother."

"Wow." From what I could see, Griffin didn't have much of a schedule beyond Sophie, and the only unsavory activity he was getting up to was hanging out with me. "He has got to be bored. Do you think he's told your grandma about Sophie?"

"I know he hasn't because if he had, she'd be here already."

Fair point. "What do you think he does in his room all day?"

"Plot to overthrow the British monarchy? I don't know. I find it better not to ask," he said.

"Maybe he has a video game console in there," I suggested.

"I have a hard time imagining Louis playing *Grand Theft Auto*."

This back-and-forth almost made me feel like we were us again. I'd missed this.

"Where's Sophie?" Milo asked, interrupting our banter.

"In the WC," Griffin said. At our blank expressions he added, "The loo."

"What?" I asked.

"The toilet."

"Oh. You could have just said she was in the bathroom. Why do you Brits have such weird words for things?"

"No American should ever say that. Your lot has positively butchered the language."

That made me laugh.

"This way," he said, leading us into the sitting room. There were several different age-appropriate board games piled up on the coffee table. "What catches your fancy, Milo?"

Milo looked through the boxes and grabbed one. "We should play Twister!"

"What do you call that in England?" I asked Griffin.

"Stretchy Toddlywinks," he said.

"Really?"

"No, we just call it Twister." I nudged him with my arm and caught a fleeting glimpse of an expression I'd seen several times already.

It was sadness.

A feeling I understood all too well.

When I caught him looking at me that way, it was like a light had dimmed. Not that he was punishing me or trying to manipulate me, but I still felt guilty anyway. We were both sad and both missing each other, even though we were physically together.

Which was, as Alice had put it, "a special kind of stupid."

Sophie ran into the room like a ray of sunshine and greeted us. "Twister? I love that game! I'm the spinner!"

She helped Milo to open it and got the plastic sheet on the ground for people to stand on. "Off with your shoes!" she said.

We did as she directed. Milo kicked his off and one of them went flying and hit Griffin in the head.

Milo looked mortified. "Sorry! Sorry! I didn't mean to!"

"It's fine, Milo," Griffin said.

"You should be more careful in the future," I told Milo. Trying not to laugh, I touched the side of Griffin's head where the shoe had made contact. "Are you okay?"

"I'll live," he said.

I couldn't help myself. I let my fingers linger on his skin and then reached up to feel his hair. Just as I'd suspected. Soft as silk. I trailed a path down the side of his face, feeling the roughness of his stubble, loving the contrast.

He sucked in a harsh breath and I tore my hand away. I shouldn't do that. It wasn't fair to either one of us.

"All ready!" Sophie declared. She was holding the spinner. "Okay, everyone, left foot blue!"

I chose a spot and realized quickly what a dumb decision it had been agreeing to this game. Griffin was right next to me, Milo on the far edge behind him. Griffin and I faced each other. It might have been smarter to go back to front, but it was like I lacked that filter in my brain that should have stopped me from doing dumb things.

"Right hand red!" Sophie called out.

Milo fell immediately, leaving me and Griffin alone.

"Are you okay?" I asked Milo.

"I'm fine." He went over to join Sophie as co-spinner. She let him have a turn and he said, "Right foot yellow."

Both Griffin and I had to slide our feet over to make that connection, and our bodies were dangerously close together.

Sophie continued to trade turns with Milo to call out moves and it didn't take long for my legs and arms to be intertwined through Griffin's. I tried to keep my breathing and heart rate normal, but nothing was working. I probably should have learned how to meditate at some point.

I could feel his chest moving in and out and noted with both delight and alarm that he was breathing heavy, too.

Okay, that could have been from trying to hold these insane yoga positions, but I was choosing to believe that I was the cause.

"Left hand yellow," Sophie said.

I went to reach for a spot and made contact with Griffin, which seemed to startle him and he lost his balance, pulling me down with him so that I landed on top of him.

And I was too shocked to respond. I could only look down into his eyes, see the desire and affection there, my body pressed against his as we breathed in and out together.

"Diana wins!" Sophie declared.

"I rather think I'm the winner," Griffin said quietly, so that only I could hear.

Why had I thought staying away from him was a good idea? "I should get up," I whispered.

"You don't have to." He put one hand on the small of my back, and with the other pushed back my hair that had fallen on the right side of my face. He traced the outline of my ear and I felt that tingling, prickly sensation all the way to my toes.

That was the problem. I didn't have to get up, and I didn't want to.

People talked about playing with fire but with Griffin, it was more like . . . playing with lightning. There would be this electrical explosion that gave me goose bumps, made my ears ring, my heart thud painfully. It could strike anywhere, anytime, and it would hit me hard and render me immobile, like now. I felt like I had no control over it.

I should probably get out of the storm.

So I reluctantly pulled myself free of him, turning to one side and then climbing to sit on the couch. "What should we play next?" I asked, ignoring the way my heart raged and thundered in my chest. Even though we were no longer touching, it was like I could still feel him.

After that we played some non-contact board games and I kept my distance.

Unfortunately, those moments between us, where that connection we had roared back to life, were too few and far between.

And it was all my fault.

Until I did something supremely stupid that threatened everything I'd so carefully planned.

CHAPTER TWENTY-THREE

Milo and I had gone to our art class that morning, where Griffin had made the entire room laugh by painting his own face. I realized that it had been exactly two weeks since he and I had first met, but I didn't bring it up. I just enjoyed the time we were spending together, even if I was secretly longing for more.

I found myself thinking about Griffin the entire day. I mean, I usually thought about him pretty regularly, but this was different. I couldn't get him out of my mind. Sheila seemed to notice my restlessness when she returned from work and asked me if I wanted to go downstairs and pick up food she'd ordered at one of the restaurants. I was pretty sure the hotel had people to deliver it, but I was grateful for the chance to stretch my legs.

Milo begged to come with me, and I had a hard time refusing him. It didn't take long for us to get everything and go back upstairs. When Milo and I returned to the suite, we found a strange man standing in the hallway. I didn't know whether to scream or grab Milo and run back out, but Milo solved the problem for me.

"Dad!" he called, running over to throw himself into his father's waiting arms.

I felt stupid that I hadn't recognized John Crawford—he looked so much like Milo that I should have known.

"You must be Diana," he said, holding out his hand to greet me while still holding Milo.

"And you must be John. I was beginning to think you were fictional," I told him as we shook hands.

He laughed. "I was thinking the same thing about you. Enchanté de faire votre connaissance. Comment allez-vous?"

I froze in place and I could feel sweat breaking out on my hairline. This. I had been so worried about this very thing. That at some point the Crawfords would test or challenge me in some way. Put me on the spot and make me prove my value. Or want Milo to give a demonstration showing what he'd learned. While he'd definitely been engaged with our lessons over the last couple of weeks, he was a little kid who would have rather been doing anything else besides schoolwork.

But it wasn't Milo in the hot seat—it was me.

And I didn't know what John had said or what he'd asked me. I'd been focusing primarily on vocabulary with Milo. If John had shown me a picture of a dog, I could have easily told him that it was *le chien*.

But this? Was it a yes-or-no question? I realized that I'd been silent for too long and needed to answer.

Ignoring the sweat trickling down my back, I answered, "Très bien." I figured *very good* would cover a multitude of questions.

I had to hope that my accent, questionable as it was, held up.

"Good to hear!" John gave me a smile that reminded me so much of Milo. "That's the full extent of what I know how to say in French: *nice to meet you* and *how are you*."

I should have known that. I'd have to start studying simple, common phrases with Milo, too.

John was still talking. "Wait, that's not true. I can also ask where the bathroom is. Which is more useful than you might imagine. I've been using one of those apps that promises to make you fluent in three months, but it is really difficult to learn a new language as an adult."

"I know exactly what you mean," I said, relief spreading through my limbs that I'd narrowly missed being exposed.

"Speaking of new things, what's this I hear about you skiing?" he asked Milo.

"Skiing is fun. We should go," Milo said. "But first do you want to see my new LEGOs?"

"I sure do!" John placed his son on the floor. "It was good to finally meet you, Diana."

"Same," I told him. They went to Milo's room with Milo chattering away, telling him about our art class and how he had recently contracted measles.

My heartbeat hadn't completely settled into a normal rhythm yet, so I went into the kitchen to grab a bottle of water from the fridge and to search for some chocolate. Sheila stood next to the island and she looked extremely annoyed.

"Hi!" I said. "I met John." I set the bags with dinner onto the counter.

"That's good." Not just annoyed, but distracted and unhappy, which surprised me. It wasn't exactly the face of someone whose beloved husband had finally returned home.

"Are you okay?" I asked.

"Just feeling a little stressed out and I think it's taking a bit of a physical toll. We have to go see Milo's grandparents in Wyoming."

I opened the fridge and got my water and then sat down at the island across from her. "That sounds fun. I've never been to Wyoming."

She frowned slightly. "Oh. I didn't mean that you would have to go with us. We weren't expecting you to come."

I was staying here? They were going to pay me to hang out in a fancy hotel suite and eat? I was okay with that. "Are you sure? I can obviously go with you. My schedule is pretty clear."

But she didn't respond to my joke. "They've been in Argentina for the last few months and decided to go back to their ranch in Wyoming and when they call . . . we come."

I twisted off the bottle cap with a satisfying snap. "I'm guessing these are John's parents?"

"How could you tell?"

Other than the amount of annoyance and disdain in her voice? "Just a guess."

"John finally has time off and we have to spend it with his parents. They snap their fingers and we have to come running. Every time. No matter what else we've got going on in our lives." She said this more to herself, so I wasn't sure if it was appropriate for me to respond.

But if she didn't like her in-laws, I guessed that meant I had a new enemy now. Obviously there wasn't much I could actually do, but if she needed me I would one hundred percent have her back.

She turned toward me, and she switched from a frown to a smile. "Us being gone will give you more time to spend with Griffin."

"That didn't, um, didn't really work out. We decided to stay friends."

Sheila blinked at me slowly, like I was stupid. "The charming, thoughtful man who sent you a kitchenful of flowers and looks like he walked out of the pages of a fashion magazine—you want to be just friends?"

"We're . . . we come from very different backgrounds. I don't know how that would all work outside of this little vacation bubble."

She seemed to be considering my words. "Things like that work out all the time. John comes from old money. We met in college at his country club, where I was working as a server to help put myself through school. My mom was a librarian and my dad was a janitor. They saved their whole lives so that my sister and I could go to college. You couldn't pick two people with more opposite upbringings. But John and I fell in love and have been together ever since."

"I didn't know that." I had assumed that Sheila had always been rich.

"I'm just trying to tell you that I know what it's like to date someone whose background is wildly different from your own. I'm also proof that it can work out. And that you, too, may someday be subjected to having to spend four days with people who think you aren't good enough for their precious son, no matter how successful you become."

"Griffin only has his grandma. His parents passed away when he was young."

"That's so sad." She paused. "And please don't think I'm terrible, but not having in-laws would be a check in the pro column for me."

All of this was so unlike the positive woman I usually saw. John's parents had to be awful. I was on her side even more now.

She pushed a paper over to me. "This is our itinerary. I just found out that we're leaving in about an hour. I hope you enjoy your break. Call us if you need anything."

"You can call me if you need to vent," I said.

"I just might take you up on your offer."

Looking over the paper, I realized that I couldn't remember the last time that I'd had time off, with nothing to do. I couldn't even look forward to it because I was pretty sure that I was going to be thinking about Griffin the entire time with nothing else to distract me.

"You are officially off duty. We have to go pack." Sheila passed a pair of tiny pink gloves over to me. "Sophie left these here during her last playdate with Milo. Maybe you could return them to her."

Yes, yes, yes, a reason to go over to Griffin's! And tell him about all that free time I was about to have!

Why were all of my initial impulses bad? I couldn't do that. I had to stop looking for reasons to open doors that I'd slammed shut.

Staring at the gloves I said a bit desperately, "Don't you want me to stay here and help Milo pack?"

"Nope. We've got this."

As she left the kitchen, some detached part of my brain wondered if she and Alice had been chatting behind my back in a dual attempt to plot against me. I shook my head. The very idea of that was ridiculous.

Also ridiculous: my current lack of impulse control.

I grabbed the gloves and headed down two floors to Griffin's suite. I found myself knocking on his door before I had really registered what I was doing. What was I going to say?

Griffin answered, but he looked flustered and upset. He was on his phone, and he waved me inside.

He was pacing back and forth and I could hear someone talking to him. I took Sophie's gloves and laid them on a table in the entryway. He ran his fingers through his hair, gripping it tightly.

"Yes. Yes. I understand. I'll be there. Goodbye." He hung up his phone and let out a growl of frustration.

"What's wrong?" I asked, a little alarmed.

"I've been summoned," he said, walking into the living room and collapsing on the couch. He let his head loll back and he closed his eyes.

I followed him in and sat on the couch next to him. "Summoned by who?"

At my question he opened his eyes again. "My grandmother. She knows I'm in the States and wants me to come to this fundraiser in New York for a children's charity she's involved with. I would want to help the group regardless, but I dislike how she demands things and I have no say."

"She knows you're here?" For some reason I had thought his grandma was unaware of his location.

"Not in Aspen specifically. But as I mentioned, yes, she knows I'm in America."

"What does she think you're doing?"

He sighed deeply. "To quote a movie, sowing my royal oats, perhaps? As long as I don't end up in a tabloid, she doesn't care."

I knew exactly what it was like to have your one parental figure not care what happened to you. I reached for his hand, and he held on to me like I was a life preserver.

"When do you go?" I asked.

"Later tonight. The private jet is being made ready. I have to be at an event in the morning, then a gala that evening, and I can fly home the following day. Granny has asked to have a private breakfast with me, so I should be home that evening."

That was basically three of the four days that the Crawfords would be in Wyoming. Now I felt totally deflated. I'd come over hoping . . . well, I didn't know exactly what I had thought would happen, but I could have hung out with him and Sophie all day for the next four days if I'd wanted to.

But he was leaving.

This felt like some kind of karmic punishment by the universe: lie to everybody and no getting to hang out with the hot boy who should be photographed for a calendar without a shirt and holding a puppy.

"Louis is coming with me," he said. "But Sophie can't. My grandmother will expect to see him there and will be rather upset if she discovers anything about Sophie." He looked bleakly at his phone. "Which means I'm going to have to hire a service to take care of her and that puts us all at risk."

"I can do it." The words left me without hesitation. Maybe this was a way of balancing out the cosmic scales. Instead of goofing off for four days, I'd spend the time helping someone else. "I can watch her."

"How? Won't the Crawfords mind?"

"They're going to visit Milo's grandparents, so they'll be gone for the next four days. I can take care of her."

"Oh, Diana." He leaned in and hugged me tight. This whooshing feeling rushed through me and then I was leaning into him, my face against his neck. I sighed and relaxed, wrapping my arms around his broad chest. Why did he have to smell so amazing? It made a girl forget all her good intentions.

And why hadn't we been hugging this entire time? I had been seriously missing out. He was an excellent hugger. I snuggled further into his warmth, tightening my hold on him.

I could have stayed like this happily for the rest of my life.

It was as if him holding me flipped some switch inside me. Why was I denying myself something I wanted? Because I was afraid of getting hurt? What if I didn't get hurt? What if things could work out for us? Maybe I shouldn't be imagining that this was all going to end before I'd even given it a chance.

I should give us a chance.

But only if he wanted the same thing.

His cheek was against the top of my head and I realized that if I lifted my face I'd be in a position to be closer to his mouth. The prospect of it made my own lips tingle and twitch, like they were preparing to make contact. To do what he'd asked—show him that I wanted something more.

But he said, "You have no idea how much this helps. Thank you," and he let go of me.

I nearly said, "That's what friends are for," but I didn't. It hadn't been friendship that had brought me down here with Sophie's gloves. I had missed him, missed the way we were together, even though we'd been with each other every day since I'd told him it couldn't be anything more.

Time to stop sending mixed signals.

It took me a second to register that the hug had ended, because I was enjoying it so much that I didn't release him right away like a normal person.

No, I had to make it weird. I slowly pulled my arms back, wondering if he would tease me about it, but he didn't. Instead he leaned forward, resting his arms on his knees. "Would you like to stay here?

You could sleep in my room. Or in Louis's, if you'd prefer. There's only three bedrooms."

"Your room," I said immediately. I didn't want to go into Louis's room at all. I feared what I might find in there.

There was an awkward moment. There shouldn't have been—it wasn't like we would be sleeping in the bed together, but it still signified something. To both of us.

Griffin cleared his throat and spoke first. "Any expenses, charge them to the room. I'll call the front desk and let them know to allow you to do that. You should also let me pay you for watching her. How much do you charge for three days? What about a thousand dollars a day? That adds up to . . ." He held up his fingers like he was doing some calculations. "Forty thousand dollars total, correct? Let me get my checkbook. I'll write you a check right now." He made like he was about to get up.

"Nice try. I see that math isn't your strong suit," I said, putting my hand on his forearm. Why did he have such sexy forearms? I'd never noticed that on any other guy before. All strong and corded and . . . I shook my head. I had been explaining something to him before he'd distracted me with his masculine wiles. "You're also not going to pay me. I'm doing this because we're . . . because I want to and you need me."

"I do. I do need you."

That wasn't about Sophie. Even my in-denial brain could see that.

Maybe things should change. I certainly wanted them to. "Griffin, I—"

Sophie chose that moment to come running into the room. "Diana! Is Milo here?"

"No, he's going on a short trip with his parents."

"So is my uncle! And Louis." She dropped her volume. "I don't mind if Louis goes."

I tried to hide my smile from her.

"And while we're gone"—Griffin jumped in—"Diana has agreed to stay here and look after you."

Sophie's eyes went wide and she began to jump up and down. "I hope we're still here when you return because if there's a nuclear attack, ninety percent of all life within a four-kilometer blast radius will die. But if we are around, then Diana and I are going to be the best of mates and have so much fun! Can I do your makeup?"

"Maybe tomorrow," I told her. "But for now I need to go back upstairs and pack my things."

"This is so exciting!" Sophie shrieked, running from the room. "I'm going to get all of my things ready!"

I wondered what things she had to prepare for me to come over, but figured I'd find out soon. I stood. "I should go upstairs. When I get back you can show me where everything is and fill me in on all the need-to-know Sophie details." I started walking to the front door and I felt him following behind me. "What time are you leaving?"

"We need to be out the door by nine o'clock. Sophie will be in bed by then. If you want to come down around eight thirty I can show you everything."

"Okay."

I opened the front door and walked out into the hallway.

"Thank you," he said. "You're saving me. Again."

"You know, Cinderella's not supposed to save her prince."

His eyes lit up with interest. He'd most definitely noticed that I'd used a possessive word, like I was saying he was mine. I held my breath, wondering how he'd respond. But all he said was, "The prince is very grateful."

"I'd do anything—" I stopped myself. He had to go and this could wait until he got back. He had other things to concentrate on at the moment. "When you get back, can we talk?"

He raised his eyebrows at me. "About?"

"I'll tell you when you get back."

234

"A surprise then?"

"Yes," I told him.

"One I'll like?"

"Are you unfamiliar with how surprises work?" There. That was the grin I'd missed and had been waiting for. "Don't worry about me and Sophie. We'll be fine. Enjoy your trip if you can, and I'll see you when you get back."

"I'll be counting the minutes, Diana."

He closed the door then and I found myself sad that he hadn't called me Bunny.

Maybe it was time to change that.

CHAPTER TWENTY-FOUR

The Crawfords were running around getting ready and I had my own bag to pack. I didn't need a whole lot of stuff, the basic day clothes and things to sleep in, some toiletries. I could always run back upstairs if I needed to. I explained to Sheila what was going on and while she tried to remain cool and nonchalant, she was obviously excited about this new development. I promised her that if anything changed, she only needed to call me and I'd be there. Possibly with Sophie in tow, if necessary.

"I can't imagine how that would happen. Have the best time," she said. "Especially when Griffin gets back." She raised her eyebrows in an exaggerated way, and I couldn't help but laugh.

I found Milo sitting on his bed with a suitcase. He had his iPad out and was playing a game.

"All packed?" I asked, leaning in the doorway.

"Uh-huh."

"Are you excited to see your grandparents?"

His eyes still on his screen, he shrugged one shoulder. "I guess. They're not nice to Mom. They make her sad."

Now I knew it was bad, if even the five-year-old had picked up on it. "I think it'll be okay."

"Maybe there will be some new disease in Wyoming," he said, sliding his finger across the screen.

I walked across the room and sat next to him. "Do you think that maybe the reason you like diseases so much is that you got a lot of attention when you were sick?"

Another single-shoulder shrug. "I don't know."

"Lying's not great," I told him. Saying this stuff probably made me the world's biggest hypocrite, but I didn't want Milo to suffer the same way that I had. I wanted better for him. "It can hurt other people when they trust you and you lie to them. You can also hurt yourself. When you keep telling yourself things that aren't true, it can make you miss out on some pretty great stuff."

He paused his game to look up at me. "Have you done that?"

"I have." Still was. "Have you ever heard the story about a little boy who cried wolf?"

"Why did he make a wolf cry?"

"That's not what that means. It was about how he kept telling people in his village that there was a wolf and everybody would come running to stop the wolf from hurting the sheep. The little boy thought it was funny, until one day there really was a wolf and nobody listened and the wolf ate all the sheep."

Milo blinked at me a couple of times. "I would have fought the wolf."

He was missing the point. "That story's about how the little boy lied over and over again, and then when he told the truth, nobody believed him."

"Okay." He returned to his game.

I sighed, seeing that he wasn't getting it. I figured at least one of us should learn that lesson before metaphorical wolves started eating sheep. When something bad happened.

With the Crawfords, with Griffin.

Technically I wasn't actually lying to Griffin anymore. I'd told him the truth of my background and what I was doing here. But I was definitely still keeping things from him. He didn't know about my mother.

What would he do if I told him? Maybe it was a good thing he was going for a bit. So I could think about my options.

Instead I thought about how much I was going to miss him while he was gone. How much I'd miss him when this whole nanny thing ended and I went to Florida and he went back to that almost-castle he lived in. When we didn't get to see each other all the time.

"Are you going to miss Sophie?" I asked Milo.

"I'll see her again when I get back."

"No, I meant when your vacation is over and you go to France and she goes back home to England."

"We can still be friends. We can talk online and play Roblox together."

True. It was sad that he had figured out a way to keep his own friendship going and yet I was so afraid of the possibility of being apart that I hadn't even considered taking a risk to be with Griffin. Considered ways that he and I could see each other after our time here ended.

Milo's outlook had me thinking about possible outcomes with Griffin. I had been so worried about making things worse, getting my heart broken. But Griffin had already removed what I said was our biggest obstacle—he'd promised that nothing would change with Milo and Sophie no matter what happened with us.

Acting on our attraction might not make things worse. It might even make things better. How had I not come to this conclusion before?

If Milo could figure out a way to stay in touch with Sophie, surely Griffin and I could do an even better job. Griffin was rich. We could visit each other. Video chat and text and find a way to make things work.

Some anxious part of my brain worried that I was getting ahead of myself, but I reminded it that Griffin had already said this wasn't a fling. That he was looking for something more serious.

Given that I'd already decided to keep him at arm's length, I could just as easily decide that I'd changed my mind and the version of me who'd made that earlier choice was clearly an idiot who didn't appreciate what she was missing out on.

Sheila called for Milo, and I grabbed his suitcase and joined them in the front hall. Sheila and Milo gave me a hug goodbye, while John waved to me.

Then they were gone.

I still had about an hour and a half until Griffin was expecting me. I could have gone over earlier, played with Sophie, maybe had my talk with him. But there would be distractions and I wanted the chance to tell him that I wanted things to change when there wouldn't be any interruptions. No snooty secretaries or bouncy little girls.

Actually, I didn't know exactly what I wanted to say to him yet. So I should wait. I would have a few days to work it out. Then I'd have a movie-worthy confession that would blow him away and we'd get our happily ever after.

It was a good thing I'd been denying myself things so much the last couple of weeks, because my willpower was nice and toned and strong. I could be patient. I waited until eight thirty, and then with my duffel bag in one hand, I knocked on his door with the other.

"Sophie's in bed," Griffin told me. "Come in." He was on his phone again. "Give me a moment."

I thought he was talking to me, but it was directed at whoever was on the other line and he addressed me. "There's not much to know about Sophie. She's easy to take care of. She goes to bed at eight. If she stays up she will fall asleep wherever she is. She showers on her own and she'll eat just about anything you put in front of her. Easy enough?"

"Yes," I said, nodding.

"Any questions?"

Nothing that pertained to Sophie so I said no.

He went back to his call. "Ollie, I'm here. Yes, I understand that. But there is no good way to tell her. The longer you keep this from her, the angrier she'll be." He paused. "Yes, it's possible you might be able to wait her out. But her own mother lived to be ninety-four. The women in her family survive on pure spite."

Griffin walked out of the room and I sat on the couch, unsure of what I should do with myself and wondering why he was arguing with his brother.

While I was shamelessly eavesdropping on Griffin's call, Louis walked into the living room. He made me uneasy, and I wasn't sure why. I didn't like being alone with him. I wished that Griffin would return.

"Miss Parker."

"Mr. . . ." I couldn't remember his last name. Griffin always called him Louis. "Mr. Louis."

"It seems to me that you have some affection for Lord Strathorne."

It took me a second to realize he meant Griffin. "Yeah." And?

"While you seem like a very nice . . . person, you must know: nothing can come of you and Lord Strathorne. He has an important lineage to live up to and there are many expectations on him for the kind of women he can court."

There was a sick feeling in my stomach, like a large stone sinking from my chest down to my stomach. "What are you saying? Do you think I'm not good enough for him?"

"I wouldn't put it in quite those terms, but you have to be aware that you are entirely unsuitable. There is no romantic future for the two of you. He is a peer of the realm."

What the actual . . . I stood up. "I don't know what that means, but it is absolutely none of your business if Griffin and I spend time together."

While nothing had technically changed between me and Griffin yet and we were basically still in the friend zone, Louis's disapproval was shoving me over the line I'd already planned on crossing.

I also wasn't going to lie and tell Louis what he wanted to hear. That wasn't me. I mean, obviously, I was okay with the lying, but I wasn't the kind of person to say what some snobby lackey wanted to hear. I didn't like confrontation, but I didn't like people telling me what to do more. Unfortunately for Louis, I wasn't the meek sort and wasn't about to walk away because this old guy decided it was necessary.

"I am only trying to save you future heartbreak, Miss Parker. I think you know Dowager Lady Strathorne would not approve."

Was that a threat? I folded my arms. "I don't need anyone's approval. Not hers, and not yours. Whatever happens is between me and Griffin and is nobody else's business." It was a very bad thing to challenge me. I tended to do the opposite of whatever I was being told to do.

"You may think that now, but you don't understand Lord Strathorne's life. I'm sure you're perfectly fine, but you are the last thing he needs. Another scandal will ruin him. We won't let that happen again."

The implication that I would deliberately hurt Griffin was infuriating. Especially because I'd been so good at staying friends with him and not dating him like I wanted to. As if I were here just to chase after Griffin. Which, to be fair, I kind of was, but it was almost like this Louis had some kind of sixth sense and was able to read my intent.

Which also annoyed me.

"Griffin is old enough to make his own decisions."

He stared at me unkindly and whispered something under his breath that sounded suspiciously like "ill mannered," but then he said, "My suggestion was only meant as a kindness."

Louis left the room.

A kindness? *A kindness?*

Griffin came into the hallway, pulling a suitcase. I almost called his name, wanting to tell him about what had just happened. I knew he would console me and tell me he didn't care what anyone else thought, but he was still on the phone. "No, I don't think Sophie's admittance to university would be the time to tell Granny about her. And how do you propose hiding Sophie for the next thirteen years? You're barely managing for a few weeks, relying totally on me with Gisele out of the picture."

I had all this indignant outrage that I couldn't release because he was busy talking to his brother.

Griffin went back to his room again and I sat down, hard. Stupid Louis. Trying to control Griffin.

I started thinking about what Louis had said, running it through my mind. Maybe I was being defensive when Louis really was just trying to protect Griffin. Perhaps I should take a more charitable approach to his words. This really could be just about Griffin's reputation. About him not being able to take any more public hits because of how it would affect his family.

And if I was going to be honest, Louis wasn't wrong as far as I was concerned. If it came out that I was an unqualified nanny and the daughter of an infamous con artist . . . it would leave Griffin's reputation in tatters.

That did make me second-guess myself.

I wondered how Griffin would feel about it. If he knew.

There was no chance to ask him, though. He continued arguing with his brother and came in and out of the living room. He brought in a carry-on and one of those suit bags, putting them in a pile on his suitcase. He was packing a lot of stuff for a few days.

"Fine. We will discuss this later, Ollie. Not making a decision is still making a decision," he said and I felt the guilt of that to my bones. That was something I'd done far too many times in my life.

Griffin turned off his phone and announced, "I need a drink."

There was a bar set up next to the fireplace. I had to keep busy so that I didn't start blurting things out at him. "I'll get it. What's your poison?"

"Women afraid of commitment, apparently."

He did not just say that. I turned to look at him, raising both of my eyebrows, and he held up a hand, like he was apologizing. "Sorry. Anything's fine." He sat on the couch, staring at the fire.

I grabbed a bottle of bourbon and filled a tumbler a quarter of the way full. I walked over and handed it to him.

"Thank you."

"You're welcome." I sat across from him, not trusting myself to get too close. "Your conversation sounded pretty intense."

"My younger brother does not live in the real world. He never has. He seems to glory in his ability to be totally irresponsible." He held the rim up to his lips and knocked back his drink. It was actually kind of impressive.

"I take it he didn't tell your grandma."

"No." He cradled the tumbler in his hands. "He let her come to the States without even a hint of what's happening. He has to tell her. Ollie moves through his life not aware of the messes he makes and leaves it to other people to clean it up."

"Maybe you should stop doing that. Force him to deal with the consequences of his actions."

"The only problem with that is now it affects Sophie. I can't allow her to be harmed. To be splashed across the front page of every British tabloid."

"At some point that might be out of your hands," I told him. "It might happen even if you don't want it to. You don't get to control everything."

"I don't want to control everything. I just want to keep Sophie safe."

I bit my lower lip. I wished there were something I could do to help. "I'm sorry. That has to be hard."

He set his drink down on the coffee table. "Diana, I know you said that you wanted to talk when—"

"Lord Strathorne?" Louis had joined us. My heart rate sped up as I wondered if he was about to warn Griffin to stay away from me, too.

"Yes, Louis?"

"I've just been notified that our car has arrived a bit early downstairs, my lord."

It was kind of weird to see someone being so deferential to Griffin. While I understood that he had this title and importance, he was a regular guy to me. One who was too handsome for his own good and made my ovaries celebrate, but still Griffin.

"Thank you." Griffin stood up and took something out of his back wallet and handed it to me. "A keycard for you. My room is the second door on the left. Please call if you need anything. Anything at all."

"I will," I said.

Louis helped Griffin with his multitude of bags and I walked with them to the front door. Louis opened it and went into the hallway, and Griffin paused.

"I'm serious, Diana. Call for any reason."

Was he trying to tell me something else? "I will. But don't worry about us. I promise not to call any tabloids!" Wow, was that the absolute worst thing to say. "Obviously, I won't do that. I'm sorry. I don't know what made me say that. I was just trying to be cute."

He smiled at me, despite his obvious weariness and concern. "You don't have to try. You just are."

How did he always know the sweetest thing to say? I put my hand over my chest, like I could keep my heart from leaping clear.

"Keep both of my favorite girls safe," he said, reaching out to cup the side of my face. "I'm looking forward to our talk."

So was I.

He left and it felt like he was taking a piece of me with him.

CHAPTER TWENTY-FIVE

I stayed up for a while, running over the entire situation in my head and trying to figure out what to do, and then decided to get ready for bed. Sophie's room was the farthest one, and I poked my head in just to check on her. She was snoring and it made me smile and then I started wondering if her uncle snored, too, and whether I'd ever get the chance to find out.

Closing her door, I doubled back and found Griffin's room. He had his own bathroom, just like I did. I had half hoped to find out what kind of cologne he used, you know, just for research purposes. Or so that I could maybe put some on my pillow at night or something. But that was a bust. He'd taken it with him.

A wave of fatigue hit me as soon as I finished brushing my teeth. I turned off the light and headed into the bedroom. I plugged in my cell phone charger and then put the phone on the nightstand. The sheets were all tucked in tightly, and I had to yank them loose to get in.

The second my head hit the pillow, thanks to my old pal insomnia, I felt wide awake. Here I was, just lying in Griffin's bed. It was weird and intimate all at the same time. It didn't smell like him or anything because the housekeeping staff changed the bedding every day, but being here, where he spent his time alone, I found it comforting.

I glanced at the clock. It was late in Florida. I wondered if my sister was awake. I texted her:

You up?

Alice called me immediately. "Is this a booty call?"

"You're hilarious. Guess where I am right now."

"Drinking caviar and eating champagne or purchasing islands or whatever it is that rich people do?"

I pulled the covers up to my chin. "Not even close. I'm in Griffin's bed."

There was a long pause. Then she whooped so loudly I was shocked she didn't wake up the twins. She excitedly asked, "Is he there with you? Put him on the phone. I'm definitely finding out what his intentions are now!"

That made me laugh. "He's not. Even if he was, there's no way I'd let you talk to him." I told her about the current situation that had led me to stay here with her interjecting noises of disbelief and glee the whole time.

"That brother of his sounds like a piece of work."

I felt oddly compelled to defend Sophie's dad. "We don't have all the details. It's not really fair to judge him because we don't know him."

"But that's when I do my best judging!" she protested.

I smiled and shook my head. "Anyway, that's why Griffin is on his way to New York. And is most definitely not here with me. I'm sorry if that ruins your day."

"My day was already ruined, so I'm so happy that you called to tell me about this." Her voice broke on the last word.

I sat straight up. "What's wrong?"

"It's just been difficult lately. The clinic has started asking for payment in full."

My heart started to thump in my ears. "I thought the dialysis clinic understood? That they were going to wait to get paid until you are rightfully put back on Chad's insurance?" I had been counting on that. There was no way I could come up with the money for dialysis, too. Unless I convinced the Crawfords to take me with them to France for another few months.

But it was going to be hard enough to keep this pretense up for three months. I couldn't imagine doing it for six. Or nine.

Maybe I really should charge Griffin forty thousand dollars for watching Sophie. As soon as I thought it, I immediately disregarded it. There was no way. I couldn't take his money.

"I'm going to get things worked out," Alice said. "You don't have to worry about it. Don't go to the nearest hospital and tell them you're a neurosurgeon or something to try and make the money."

Biting the inside of my cheek, I nodded. Even though she couldn't see me. "I want to help."

"The best way for you to help is to tell me everything that's been going on."

So I did exactly that. Told her everything, including how I'd been going back and forth on whether to try having a romantic relationship with him.

"I don't know how to tell you this, Diana, but Professor Plum called and he'd like you to get a clue. You're already in a romantic relationship with him. You might not be kissing him, but there are so many feelings there."

Opening my mouth, I meant to protest. I'd worked hard to keep us at a friend level.

But she was right. "I don't know why I'm being so indecisive when it comes to him. I'm not normally like that." In the rest of my life I planned out what I wanted to do and then I did it. This second-guessing thing was so unlike me.

"I refer you to my earlier statement that things are this way because you really, really like him and it's freaking you out. I am so glad that this is happening. You're like my own personal telenovela. I already bought my ticket for this ship, but you've got me wanting to upgrade to first class."

"What does that even mean?" I asked.

"It means I am *here* for all of this!"

I turned on my side, drawing my knees up to my chest. "But how does this work? It's like that whole fish-loving-a-bird thing. What do he and I have in common? I don't toss polo ponies or kayak up mountainsides or whatever it is that his people do."

"What do you have in common? Uh, you both like to eat; you're both artists; you're both good with children; you make each other laugh; you love your families; you're both extremely loyal; you adore spending time together; I'm guessing he likes to watch movies like ninety-eight percent of people in this country, and I know you love them. Do you want me to go on?"

"No." I got it.

"Why are you trying to talk yourself out of something so great?"

A question I had asked myself many times. "Because it would hurt too much to fall for him and have him leave."

She made a huffing sound. "You can't live your life in fear. You'll miss out on a lot of really great things if you do that. That's a lesson I've had to learn the hard way."

"I know." I played with the edge of the blanket. "But if you don't hope for anything, then no one can hurt you."

"Oh, sweetie, I understand that, but if you don't take a risk, then there's no joy, either."

Again, her words made me uncomfortable. "I was trying to protect myself."

"Yes, Captain Obvious, we all know you were trying to protect yourself."

"Maybe I have a good reason for doing that. He doesn't know about Mom yet." At least, I had to assume he didn't. He knew other stuff about me that he'd kept quiet until I'd shared it with him. What if he already knew everything?

"I'll go back to my old standby of 'just tell him.' Better for him to find out now than having some reporter shove a microphone in his face and ask him about it. You're not responsible for what Mom did. You need to exorcise her from your life."

"Exercise?" I repeated, confused. "Like you want me to jog her around the prison yard?"

"No, exorcise. Like, banish her from your thoughts. When she creeps in, send that thought away. It will take practice and it's hard, but you can do it."

Even though the room was dark, I put my spare hand over my eyes. "I've been thinking about her almost constantly lately. More than I have in years."

"Probably because you're in a situation where you're lying and of course that's going to make you think of her. But, Diana? It's time to stop letting Mom take up so much of your headspace. She doesn't deserve it. You need to move on and get your own happily ever after."

"How does someone like me get the fairy tale?" I asked. It felt like I had lifetimes of bad karma to work through.

"Fairy tales aren't quite all they're cracked up to be. Getting married is like a fairy tale in reverse—you start out at a ball in a gorgeous gown and then spend all your time cleaning up after little people. So you better be sure that the person standing at your side is your partner and teammate and someone you adore, because it's difficult. Promise me that you'll do that."

"I promise." I lowered my hand, wishing Alice were here with me so that I could give her a hug.

"Don't settle for anything less."

It seemed so important to her. "I won't."

She then said it was late and that she needed to go. I told her good night and hung up. I was glad I had Alice to tell things to.

If I wanted things to change with Griffin, I had to tell him everything. Give him the option to decide whether he wanted to be with me once he had the entire story.

It was time to stop putting it off.

~

Sophie was like a firework that had been turned into a person. I adored her. Not as much as Milo, but it was close. It was also nice to spend time with her without the added pressure of keeping a secret or trying to educate her. We could just do stuff she enjoyed doing. I think she got a little frustrated with me when it came to skiing, but other than that we had a good time.

Griffin called every day to talk to Sophie. He would say hello to me, but he never asked to chat with just me. And coward that I was, I didn't ask for that, either. It seemed like he was taking the whole "wait to talk until you get back" thing pretty seriously.

Then my anxiety-ridden brain started coming up with alternative explanations: What if he was pulling away from me? Had Louis gotten to him? Convinced him to end things now before they went any further?

Maybe now it was Griffin's turn to start second-guessing everything.

I couldn't even blame him. He didn't really know what he was in for when it came to me.

Those two days flew by and I found myself missing him in a way I didn't know was possible. I wondered if this was how people with addictions felt when they went through withdrawals. I ached for him. It was like a part of me was missing.

It didn't help to be staying in his hotel suite, surrounded by his things and someone he loved. I didn't stop thinking about him.

Especially when it got closer to the time he was supposed to return. To distract myself I packed up all my things, putting the duffel bag by the door, and then I ordered room service for Sophie and me.

Sophie and I finished our dinner and had moved into the front room to do some coloring when we both heard the front door open.

We looked at each other and she reacted first. "Uncle Griffin!"

She went running toward the door and I heard his grunt when she launched herself at him.

"Hullo, poppet!" he said and his voice . . . it was almost my undoing. It hadn't been that long. How could I have missed him this much?

I came around the corner and saw him. And my heart stopped. He was rumpled, tired, but how had I forgotten how completely gorgeous he was?

Without thinking I walked toward him. He was watching me with interest, as if he knew what I was about to do even though I had no idea.

I pressed my lips against his, strong and firm. It was quick and completely unplanned. I couldn't help myself. All the blood in my body rushed to my lips. It was a heady feeling to finally be kissing him.

Before he could react, I stepped back, putting distance between us. What had I just done? I put one of my hands over my mouth. I had forgotten that there were two other people staring at us. Including one who very much wanted me out of the way.

"Hello to you, too," Griffin said, grinning at me with self-satisfied confidence.

"Diana just kissed Uncle Griffin!" Sophie said in a stage whisper.

I did. I really did. My entire being felt light, like I was having an out-of-body experience. I was still tingling, everywhere. This was all so bad. I hadn't meant to do that.

Louis harrumphed and walked out of the entryway. Sophie stood there with her eyes wide, watching us carefully.

"At the risk of sounding stereotypically British, what's all this then?" Griffin asked, and I could tell he was trying to make me laugh. To break the tension.

The tension felt entirely unbreakable. Reaching for my duffel bag I said, "Sophie missed you. I should let the two of you catch up. I'm going to go."

I grabbed the handle and somehow managed to get the door open. Which was surprising, given how shaky all my limbs felt.

I just kissed him, I just kissed him ran on a loop through my brain. I wanted to talk to him, tell him everything and let him make the choice before I took it away from him. Bad. This was all bad.

When I got into the hallway Griffin was right behind me. "Diana, wait. Stay so that we can talk."

"I can't." My heart beat so hard in my chest I was worried it was going to fracture my ribs.

Somehow I made it to the elevator and pushed the right button to go back up to my suite. I got inside and dumped my bag in the hallway. I went and sat on the couch.

It was just a kiss. A friendly greeting. No big deal, right?

Unfortunately it felt like the biggest deal ever. There were conditions that he'd attached to that kiss. And I couldn't ignore that.

My phone buzzed. There was a text from Griffin. Just one word.

Coward.

He was right. I was a big lily-livered scaredy cat. He kept saying that I could trust him, that he wanted me to do that, and I rejected it. Why? Because I was so scared that he'd reject me first? Choose his family and his money over me?

I just sat there on the couch, ruminating over everything, when my phone beeped again. With surprise I noted the time. It had been two hours since I'd left Griffin's suite.

But the message wasn't from him. It was from Sheila. She'd messaged me:

You do such great work!

There were two video clips. One was of Milo singing the theme song for *Paw Patrol* in French. Which shouldn't surprise me, given how often we watched that show in French, but it was still sweet. The next was of him and John at dinner with Sheila prompting him, "What did you just say to your dad?"

"I said 'passe-moi le lait, s'il te plaît.' It means *please pass the milk*."

Milo spoke in French. I hadn't taught him that. Where did he learn it?

I was so dumbfounded by what I was seeing that when there was a knock at the door, my distracted brain didn't register who it obviously had to be. I opened the door and there he stood.

Griffin.

"Diana, I think we need to talk."

CHAPTER TWENTY-SIX

Nodding, I let him into the suite. We walked into the formal front room together. He sat down on the sofa and I debated where I should sit. Next to him? I wasn't sure my senses could take that kind of overload, so I perched on the wingback chair across from him. My finger accidentally slipped in my nervousness, touching my phone screen and replaying the video that I'd just watched.

I made a noise of annoyance and embarrassment as I went to shut it off.

"What was that?" Griffin asked.

Feeling grateful to be talking about this and not something else, I said, "A video Sheila sent me. Of Milo speaking French by asking for the milk to be passed. I don't know how he learned it. I didn't teach it to him."

"Sophie did."

"What?" I asked, feeling very confused, and more than a little off-balance with him sitting there right in front of me, just out of reach. This all kind of felt like a fever dream.

He gave me an odd look, which I probably deserved. "Sophie's fluent. Her mother is French. Gisele?"

Although he'd told me that information before, for some reason it hadn't registered. "Sophie's been teaching him French?"

"Not all the time, but yes. You said he needed to learn it."

Griffin had done that for me. Encouraged his niece to speak to Milo in French for me. To help me.

It was even more romantic than the room full of irises.

I got up, went over to the couch, and tackled him in a bear hug, throwing my arms around his neck. There was no hesitation this time, and his arms immediately went around my waist.

"Thank you. That means so much to me. Thank you."

"You're very welcome."

I held on tightly, not wanting to let go. He seemed to share my impulse. He murmured, "I missed you," against my right temple.

That made me pull back. "Then why didn't you call or text me?"

"You said you wanted to talk when I got back and I was trying to be patient. Which I knew I wouldn't be if I chatted with you."

I lightly slapped his right shoulder. "That's not what I meant! You didn't have to stop talking to me altogether."

He grabbed his arm, making a cartoonish look of pain. "You wound me, madam."

I almost offered to kiss it better, but I refrained. "How was the charity gala? Did you eat a lot of gross cheeses and talk about how rich you are?"

Griffin didn't fall for my delay tactic. "Why did you run away earlier?"

Okay, radical honesty. "Because I don't like confrontation. I freak out and run away when things get tough. If you lined up all of my exes, you'd have a flow chart of my bad taste in men and cowardliness. I end things so I don't have to deal."

"Are you going to do that with us? End things?"

He had his hand on his knee, and I reached for it, lacing my fingers through his. "I don't want to. But I'm scared."

"It's a bit scary for me, too," he confessed. "But I'm willing to try if you are."

"I want to."

"I'll never hurt you," he said, and my throat suddenly felt thick.

"You can't promise me that."

"I can." I so wanted to believe that. Wanted to believe in him. Trust him. He shifted his position, closing the gap between us. "So we're resolved—we're together?"

There was nothing I wanted more than to lean toward him, but I had to put all my cards on the table. Time to be brave. "Wait. There's something else I have to tell you. I want you to see me. All of me."

He raised his eyebrows with interest. "I am in favor of the plan where I get to see all of you."

Leave it to Griffin to make a joke. It wasn't enough to distract from my fear, though. I concentrated on pushing my shaky breaths in and out of my lungs, trying to ignore the way my heart thudded hard in my chest. This was it. I was going to tell him and would have to deal with whatever the repercussions were. "Not like that. I have something else I've kept to myself that I want to share with you. My mother . . . is the Honey Bandit."

"I beg your pardon?"

He had no idea what I was talking about. Maybe that was a good thing? "My mother is a con artist. A notorious one who cheated a bunch of men out of a lot of money. She has dozens of aliases, but the name she prefers is Margaret Fox. That's not even her real name. She named herself after one of the most infamous female con artists of all time. A little inside joke that no one else understood. The police suspect that she committed more crimes under her real name, probably as a juvenile, so there's no records or fingerprints or anything. But Margaret Fox is the name on my birth certificate. Not that that part matters." I let out a breath. I was really losing the story here. "Basically, she's a really terrible person."

It was hard to describe the expression on his face. I had expected horror. Or shock. Instead, he just looked concerned. "How did that affect you? Having a mother like that?"

"How did that affect me?" I let out a half laugh. "My entire life revolved around this woman and her cons. I was her unwitting accomplice. It was just regular life until I got older and realized it was wrong. She kept me out of school as much as possible so that I could help her run her schemes. It was probably also so that I wouldn't be exposed to other kids and figure out what she was doing."

His eyebrows furrowed. "Didn't you say you won the spelling bee? In seventh grade?"

"It was one of the few times my mom left me in school for almost a year. Her mark had a daughter my age and she wanted us to be friends and so sent me to the same school. Bad move on her part, because her fear about me realizing what she was doing was wrong came true."

Then it hit me that I'd told him the spelling-bee thing in passing. How had he remembered something so inconsequential about me? It made me feel important. Like what I said mattered to him.

Another entirely new and heady feeling.

But he should still know what he was getting into. "My mother always said that having a kid along made her seem more trustworthy. So I'm a liar. Which you've probably already figured out. And a thief. I helped her hurt people."

There. Now he would cut me off forever and be done with me. Not good enough for him, definitely not good enough for his blue-blood family.

"It's why I love reading so much," I continued. "It was a way to escape the reality of my life. Not to mention that it's one of the few hobbies a kid can have when there's no electricity in the house."

His hand tightened around mine. "Where is she now?"

"Locked up, and will be for decades to come. She committed crimes for years, leading men into what they call a honey trap. She would get them to fall in love with her and then she would empty out their bank accounts. There were warrants out for her arrest all over the country. Then she found a mark that she thought would be her golden goose: an extremely wealthy CFO. She got nailed for fraud, embezzlement, insider trading, plus a mountain of other illegal things she was doing."

He sat there quietly, and I didn't know if he was waiting for me to say more, or if he wanted to say something but didn't know how to phrase it.

"You're dying to take out your phone and look her up, aren't you?"

The edges of his eyes crinkled as he smiled. "Little bit. But right now I'm more concerned about you. Do you see her? Speak to her?"

"No."

"Do you miss her?"

The question shocked me so much that it left me feeling a bit winded, like something large had just slammed against my chest. "I miss that I didn't have a real mom who cared about me. I guess I love her in a Stockholm syndrome–y kind of way, but I wish that I'd had a regular childhood."

He lifted my hand and pressed a kiss to the back of it, as if he were using his warm lips to pass along some of his strength.

It seemed to be working. "I think about her all the time. Everything she did colors my life. I wish it didn't. I wish I was stronger and could just forget about it."

Griffin was studying my hand, not looking at me. "Our past shapes us into who we are. And I'm sorry for what you went through. You deserved a proper mother. But I'm glad for the experiences that led you here to me and made you into the person you are." He raised his gaze to mine. "Because I . . . I really care about that person."

I closed my eyes against his words. How was he the most romantic, sweetest man to have ever existed? I made myself open my eyes again because I wanted to see his face when I told him what scared me. "Do you know how many friends I lost as a teenager when they found out about my mom? Even before she got arrested, we were constantly moving, never had a real home, and if I did make a friend I'd lose them a few weeks later."

"Like me."

"Like you." He was going to leave me, too. He had to.

"Diana, unlike your young friends, I have resources. We can see each other again, even when our time here is up. If you'd like that."

"I would like that." There, I'd said it. My body slumped from the relief flooding through me. I'd done it. I'd told him everything that he needed to know. "That's all of it."

"All of it?" he repeated. "No other secrets? You aren't secretly married with twins?"

"That's Alice, not me."

He winked at me to let me know he was joking, but then his expression sobered. "I feel very honored that you would trust me enough to share your true self with me."

"I know you're someone that I can trust. I know that it's taken me some time to get here, but my worst fear is turning into her. When Alice rescued me, we made each other a promise. Radical honesty from then on. So we wouldn't end up like Mom." I was afraid it was somehow genetic and would be passed down. Like nice silverware.

"You're not your mother."

"How can you know that?"

"Because I know you." He paused before asking, "When I offered to pay for your sister's surgery, what would your mother have done if she were in your shoes?"

"She would have taken all the money you offered. Then she would have figured out how to get more."

He nodded. "Which you didn't do. I recall you being rather adamant in turning me down. If you really are a gold digger, you are very bad at it."

"Is it sad that that's one of the nicest things anyone has ever said to me?"

"It's very sad," he agreed. "You should be surrounded by people singing your praises. A religion should be started in your honor. Diana-ism. It will essentially consist of me worshipping you."

"I'm pretty sure there are temples dedicated to the goddess Diana in Italy."

"Excellent. A place already set up for worship services."

He reached up to brush some hair away from my face, tucking it behind my ear. Then he leaned in and brushed his lips across my right cheek.

If he was about to "French goodbye" me, we were going to have words.

Only he said just what I wanted to hear: "Bunny, may I kiss you?" He murmured his request, his breath hot against my skin. A jolt of electric pleasure followed his soft kisses.

The sensations he was causing made my breath stutter in my lungs. It was like I couldn't quite catch it and wasn't sure I wanted to. I closed my eyes and gulped. It was like my entire life had been leading up to this very moment. I had been waiting for so long to kiss him that it had felt like an actual eternity.

"Please."

That was the only word he needed. He pulled back and put his hands on the sides of my face, holding me there. He gazed into my eyes and that intense look of his, the one that was pure want, made my stomach feel like it had turned into a helium balloon and was about to float away. The man was bewitching my hormones.

Electricity pulsed on my skin where he touched me, and then he was moving his mouth closer. There was a charge in the air, like just before a storm. It was both terrifying and exhilarating. Closer and closer . . . until finally his lips fused with mine.

It was like being struck with lightning. Blinding, brilliant, burning. Filling up all my senses so that nothing else in the world existed beyond him.

There was sheer power and heat everywhere, traveling along my nervous system, threatening to make my heart explode. We were going to burn down this entire room around us.

He stopped kissing me for a second, long enough to ask in a low and strangled voice, "Do you feel that?"

"Uh-huh," I said. This wasn't the time for speaking, so I yanked him back to me. Now that I had him, I wasn't going to let him go.

He groaned at my actions, and the sound rumbled in his chest like thunder. His kisses were hot, insistent, unrelenting. But he went back and forth, between soft, gentle, tender kisses and demanding, incendiary ones. Like he couldn't settle on which type he preferred. Or like he was testing them all out.

I was very grateful to be the recipient of his experiment.

A detached part of my brain was asking me why I had been denying myself this for so long. Obviously, I was a very, very stupid woman.

I moved closer to him, wanting to be connected by not just our lips, but our hands, and arms, our chests pressed together. I put my arms around his neck, letting my hands drift up to play with the ends of his hair.

His mouth slanted against mine, demanding my attention. I abandoned his hair and instead curled my fingers against the back of his neck. As if I could pull him closer. Because I needed him to get closer.

It wasn't possible, but I still wanted it.

I wanted him.

He kissed me with a devastating thoroughness. Every part of me was affected. Synapses and nerve endings I hadn't even known I possessed were shooting off sparks that sent waves of sensation through me, over and over.

His kiss was a study in opposites—primitive yet refined, fiery yet shivery, sweet but spicy.

Just as I was reveling in experiencing each of these feelings that he invoked, inexplicably, he withdrew from me again. He was panting, and so was I. "I need you to know that this is real. I'm real."

I rested my hands on his broad shoulders. "I can feel how real you are."

"That's not what I—"

But I cut him off by kissing him, moving my mouth against his so that I had him shaking against me. Everything I did affected him, the way he murmured words I couldn't hear against my lips, how he growled at the back of his throat, the way the air pumped in and out of his chest, the thundering of his heart against my palm.

And I couldn't get enough of the fact that I was the one causing his reactions.

His kisses were exquisitely hot and intense, making my blood thicken inside me, and my heart race so fast that I was actually worried it might never go back to a normal rhythm ever again. I was overheated, dizzy, and floating. His hands in my hair, his lips on mine—those were the only things keeping me tethered to this world.

At some point I realized that I was having the hardest time catching my breath. Although, currently, oxygen seemed totally overrated. Who needed to breathe when there were kisses like these in the world?

As if he sensed the lack of air to my poor overstimulated brain, he moved his lips to my cheek, feathering delectable kisses along my cheekbone. I kept my eyes closed, reveling in his devastating tenderness and the spirals of sensation that radiated out from my skin, down through my quivering stomach, into my limbs.

"So lovely," he murmured. "So soft, so exquisite. I don't think I'll ever be able to get enough of you."

I managed to choke out, "Back at you," because there was no way I could have uttered more than three syllables.

Griffin had been seriously underselling his skills. He'd said he was good at other things, but this wasn't just good. This was an earth-shattering, sell-your-soul, give-up-your-firstborn-child variety of fantastic. He had marked me, marked my skin. I was worried that I'd never feel like myself again without his touch.

He was cradling my face, while my lips ached for him. I opened my eyes slowly, feeling like I'd been drugged, my vision hazy. It took me a second to focus on him.

There was something in his eyes I hadn't seen before. It was more than just affection. More than just tenderness.

"Diana," he said again, like a breathless prayer for the new religion he planned on starting.

"Bunny," I corrected him.

He grinned at me, a smile so knowing and confident that it fed the already consuming fire in my veins. He pressed his lips to mine again, but this time he wasn't trying to discover anything. He had apparently figured out exactly how to kiss me, how to make my bones melt.

There was still heat, and there was still passion, but something shifted. He kissed me like I was precious to him, like he never wanted to let me go.

It was entirely different kissing someone you cared about. Someone you were falling for. It was . . . more intense and deeper, like I felt it in my soul.

My heart stumbled all over itself, tripping and falling down a path that led directly to him.

I wanted to show him how I was feeling, and what he meant to me.

Mostly, I wanted more. More of everything. Especially more of his skin. I started exploring him, my arms moving down his impeccably sculpted chest, to a stomach that I would have liked to wash laundry on, and then under the hem of his shirt, brushing my fingers against the warmth I found there.

He sucked in a sharp breath, his stomach tightening, and then he took my hands in his. He pulled away from our kiss and lifted up my hands, kissing the backs of them, one after the other.

Then he said the worst thing ever.

"Bunny, I think we should take things slow."

CHAPTER TWENTY-SEVEN

That was it. Obviously Griffin was trying to kill me. Slow? "You're not secretly a monk or a priest or anything, right?" It was the only explanation that made any sense to me. We were alone, recently committed, and in a very empty hotel suite.

Oh, and he was the sexiest man I'd ever known.

He smiled. "No. Far more sinner than saint, I'm afraid."

"Okay." I wasn't getting the problem. "Do I get a say in this?" I had so much built-up frustration that he was making so much worse.

"Of course you do. But so do I and I think if one person wants things to move slowly, the other person should respect that boundary."

He had not just used my own words against me. "But why?"

"Because I want this to last, Diana Parker. We have plenty of time."

That was the problem. "No, we don't."

He kissed my hands again. "We do. I want us to really get to know one another. You've had so much chaos and unpredictability in your life; I want to show you that I'm not one of those things. I'll be here. You'll see that this means more to me than some vacation romance. That I want you. I want us."

What could I say to that? I wanted to disagree, but I appreciated the gesture. That he wanted to prove his intentions with his actions, and not just his words.

He released my hands and stood up. "I should go, because if you keep kissing me the way you just were, I won't be able to resist you for much longer."

I reached for his hand. "You don't have to go."

"I do." He pulled me up from the couch and then walked with me to the front door, holding my hand.

When he opened the door, he turned to kiss me briefly, and that flash of atom-rearranging electrons emerged, fizzing through me hotly.

A sensation he seemed to share in, since he made a sound of frustration and regret when he pulled back.

I was glad that I wasn't alone in this.

"Good night, Diana."

As I was contemplating just how many cold showers I was about to take, he paused. "By the way, what did I tell you about that raisin/date line? One hundred percent success rate."

He flashed me a wicked, mischievous grin as he walked toward the elevator.

I couldn't even be indignant. Because he was right.

~

Another two weeks passed, and it really was like living in a fairy tale. We did take things slowly, mostly out of necessity. We were never actually alone, as there was always somebody nearby basically chaperoning us. Louis in particular seemed to take great joy in reminding Griffin just how late it was and how Miss Parker should be returning to her own room.

We spent time with the kids and hung out together every evening. It was almost like he was trying to make up for the time we'd lost when we weren't dating and kissing.

It also felt a bit like playing house when it was just us with Sophie and Milo. I felt like we balanced each other out so well—I was strict while he was the fun one. I'd get stressed, and he was always there with a joke to lighten the mood. We were a good pair.

Alice was, predictably enough, beside herself. When I'd texted her about the kiss and then complained about him wanting to take things slow, she'd responded:

Ugh. What a total jerk. Want me to fly out there and kick his butt?

I'd ignored her sarcasm.

The main thing she and I talked about was the fact that I'd never spent this much time with someone else and still looked forward to seeing them again. Even Alice had started to annoy me a couple of days into living with her. I was grateful for my breaks from Milo.

But Griffin? I felt like I could be with him morning, noon, and night and never, ever get tired of him.

At the one-month mark of me starting to work for the Crawfords, I woke up late. My alarm hadn't gone off. I smelled something delicious cooking, and ran to the kitchen. The whole family was gathered there.

"I'm so sorry," I said. I'd never accidentally slept in before. "I overslept."

"You're fine," John reassured me. "Come in and have breakfast with us."

I noticed that there was an unmistakable air of excitement.

"What's going on?" I asked.

"We're celebrating!" Milo shouted. "Mom's pregnant!"

Since Milo was the one sharing the news, I didn't know if it was true. But given the exhilarated expression on Sheila's face I realized it was. I knew she'd struggled with infertility and I was so excited for her. She beamed at me. "The doctor called early this morning and confirmed it!"

"Congratulations, you guys!" I said, hugging her.

John smiled at me, then asked if I wanted any pancakes. I told him absolutely.

"We decided to go on a family outing today," Sheila told me. "There's a winter festival downtown."

"That sounds fun. Have a good time!"

Sheila frowned slightly. "Diana, you're part of the family. We want you to come with us."

That made my heart feel a bit too big for my rib cage. "Oh. Sure!"

"Pancakes," John announced, putting two down on a plate and passing it to me. I sat next to Milo at the island.

I poured a river of syrup over the hot food in front of me. "That will definitely make your move even more interesting. Adding a new baby to the mix."

Sheila put her hand on her stomach. "That's why I've been traveling so much. I'm shifting into more of an advisory or consulting position at my company. Still retaining my ownership, but I want to enjoy this phase of my life and spend time with my kids."

We ate and talked about baby names, with Milo suggesting Bonzo Rex or Chlamydia as options. I nearly choked on my breakfast, given that I was the one who had been reading pages from that infectious-diseases book to reward him for a hard day's work. The Crawfords didn't freak out, though. We finished eating and all headed to our rooms to get dressed. I texted Griffin to let him know that my plans today had changed, and that I would see him later.

He didn't answer.

When we arrived at the festival, Milo wanted to look at the ice sculptures first. We headed that direction and I was confused when I saw Griffin and Sophie standing in front of the sculptures, waiting for us.

"Surprise!" Sophie called out, her exuberance overflowing.

I was totally confused. "What are you guys doing here?"

"We invited them," Sheila said. "I ran into Griffin this morning and we exchanged numbers. We had to include them, too!"

I didn't know how I felt about Sheila and Griffin being in contact. I knew he wouldn't reveal my secrets to them, but I liked keeping them in two separate boxes.

Griffin kissed me hello, a brief kiss, given all the sets of eyes watching us. It still managed to make my toes curl.

"Now let's go see the animals in the petting zoo!" Milo said, running in the opposite direction of the sculptures. John trotted after him and the rest of us followed. It took us a few minutes to find the heated barn where the animals were kept, and Milo was already petting sheep and goats. Sheila and John joined him.

"Look!" Sophie said, pointing to a hutch with rabbits. "Bunnies! Aren't they so cute?"

"I happen to adore bunnies," Griffin said, before dropping a kiss on the tip of my nose.

Sophie came over to grab his hand so that he could pick up one of the rabbits for her.

As I stood there alone, I realized that my earlier inclination had been wrong. I liked seeing the separate parts of my life coming together. It made me wish that Alice and the twins were here, too.

"You have a beautiful family," a woman behind me commented.

"Oh, we're not a family."

She pointed at Griffin. "You're not with that guy?"

"Yes, we're together, but we're not married."

The woman smiled. "I just assumed that was your little girl. She kind of looks like both of you."

Why did part of me want that to be true? "Nope. I'm a nanny for that boy over there." I pointed at Milo.

"I'm Carrie, by the way. Carrie Bogdanovich."

"I'm Diana Parker. Nice to meet you."

She gave me a thoughtful look. "You're staying at the Royal Paramount, right? I've seen you there at the playground. I'm here with my daughter, Paisley." She called out, "Paisley!" and a little blonde girl turned and waved.

"I am." It was honestly no surprise that I hadn't noticed Carrie at the playground, because Griffin made it hard to notice anybody else.

"You snagged the only hot single dad here," she told me ruefully, her gaze going back to Griffin. It was making that jealousy beast of mine start to grumble.

Which made me defensive. "He's not a dad. That's his niece." He also wasn't single, but there was no reason to emphasize that again.

"Well, you are lucky."

"Thanks."

"Nice to meet you. I'll see you around!" She walked away to join her daughter, and I realized she was right. I did feel incredibly lucky.

Griffin came back over and, seeing that we were alone, dragged me behind a stack of hay bales, kissing me long and hard, leaving me shaking.

"Do you know how wonderful it is to kiss a woman I care about in public and not have anyone care? No photos, no tabloid headlines?" he asked, holding me close so that I could feel his quick heartbeat.

"We're not in public at the moment," I told him. "But we should get back to it. I'm still on the clock."

Hand in hand, we returned to where I'd been standing. Sheila approached us, smiling, and said, "We were going to take the kids to the ice-skating rink and see if Milo wants to give it a try. Maybe get some hot chocolate after."

"That sounds fun," I said.

"I was thinking that maybe you and Griffin could go off together. We'll keep an eye on Sophie."

"I'm your nanny," I protested. Even if I wanted to jump at her offer. "You're not supposed to watch other kids so that I can hang out with my . . . person." Was he my boyfriend? We'd never discussed terms, but it seemed like he was.

"Have fun," Sheila told me, exchanging a secretive glance with Griffin. "We'll meet up later."

It took me until that moment to realize that this was something else Sheila and Griffin had set up. But the chance to be alone with him? With no kids or secretaries lurking in the background?

Yes, please. "Okay. But call if you need me."

She waved and both Griffin and I thanked her as we left. "What do you want to do now?" he asked.

"I'm kind of in the mood for hot chocolate."

He checked his phone and then said, "Let's go."

There were hot chocolate booths set up everywhere and we found one close to the petting zoo. We got in line and Griffin had his arms around me, in an attempt to ward off the cold.

But I didn't ever feel cold when he was near me.

There was a sign that said CASH ONLY. Griffin followed my eyeline and said, "I'll cover it."

"Okay. Hey, do you remember when you asked about my mom's cons? Do you want to see one?"

His eyes lit up. "Yes."

"Do you have a fifty-dollar and a five-dollar bill?"

He reached into his back pocket and there was a thick pile of cash in his wallet. "Why are you carrying around that much money?" I asked. "Is it just in case you have to pay for Sophie's ransom?"

He gave me a half frown. "It's not that much. Here." He gave me the bill. "Is that it? The con? Having people hand over fifty-five dollars?"

"No. Watch." I took the five-dollar bill and folded it twice.

It was our turn and the teenage boy behind the counter looked extremely bored. I held up the fifty dollars, making sure the kid got a good look at it. "Can you break a fifty?"

"Sure."

"Good. This is my last fifty so . . . what do we want?" I pretended to read the menu. "I think we'll just take two hot chocolates."

"That's four dollars." While looking at the menu I had put the fifty-dollar bill into my back pocket and handed him the five. He didn't realize that I'd changed out the bills and handed me back forty-six dollars.

I thanked him and then said, "I am so stupid. Sorry, but I gave you a five instead of a fifty." I gave him all the cash back.

Griffin and I walked away. "That seems like a tremendous amount of effort for a small amount of money."

"It's called change raising. And you can do it with larger denominations. Not every con is huge."

"I also didn't get my fifty dollars back," he teased.

"Price of doing business," I told him and he stopped to kiss me again. While he was distracted, I put the fifty in his pocket, imagining his look of surprise that I'd slipped it back to him without him knowing.

We walked through the festival, checking out all the different craft items offered in the booths. He offered several times to buy me something but I refused. I felt like I already had everything I needed.

He took out his phone and glanced at it again. "Come with me. I have a surprise."

Taking me by the hand, he made his way through the festival, not hesitating, knowing exactly where to go. I held my hot chocolate aloft, making sure it didn't spill.

Griffin stopped short and told me to close my eyes. "Just follow me."

We walked for a bit and I kept my eyes shut, even though I wanted to peek. He stopped and told me to stay put. Then he walked behind me, and I felt him wrap his arms around me and he put his lips against my ear. He knew how that drove me absolutely insane.

"Do you remember the first night we met? When I told you a carriage coming to take you away would be a sign?"

"I remember that there was no carriage."

"Open your eyes, Bunny."

I did, and saw a white horse hooked up to a matching white carriage. I wanted to legitimately swoon. Lie down on this street limply, unable to move. This was amazing.

"A carriage, but not a pumpkin," I teased.

"They wouldn't paint it orange and I offered them a great deal of money." He sounded annoyed and it made me laugh.

"So you asking me what I wanted to do was all for show?"

His mood instantly shifted and he grinned. "Yes."

"This is perfect, thank you."

"Now I can finally say, 'My lady, your carriage awaits.'"

He helped me climb in. The bench was red velvet and there was a faux fur blanket to put on our laps. The driver made a clicking noise and the horse began to move, his hooves clopping against the street, the sleigh bells on the reins jingling with each step.

It was beautiful—the snow sparkling on the sides of the street, the kids who saw the carriage and pointed at us, waving. I waved back, feeling like I was a princess in a parade.

Griffin reached for my hot chocolate, and put it on the floor next to his. Then he slid his arm around my waist, pulling me close. "Do you know how much the time we've spent together has meant to me?" he asked.

"I do, because it's meant a lot to me, too."

"Being here with you, Milo, and Sophie . . ." He trailed off, looking at the people walking on the sidewalks. He took a deep breath, like he was gathering his courage. It was a sound I recognized all too well. "It's very tiring living up to constant expectations—from my grandmother, the rest of my family, from the public. I don't get many chances to be me. Being here with you has allowed me to be myself, without pressure."

"I'm glad, because I really like no-pressure you."

He smiled and went on. "And getting to be me has led me to question the things that I want. I knew I'd have a family someday, but it always felt like a very distant thing. Something that happened to other people, but not something I could imagine for myself. These last few weeks have made me realize that this is something I want. A family of my own. Do you think you want that, too?"

He looked at me, all seriousness, and my heart jumped up into my throat. Was this like, a theoretical situation or a precursor to a proposal? I waited, expecting to panic, but to my great shock, I didn't.

"A few years ago I would have said no, because I thought if I had a child I'd become like my mom. And I didn't know how to give a kid the life they deserve. I'd never want them to worry about food or shelter, or whether their mom would still be there when they got home from school. You're right, though. Being around Milo and Sophie, I see that there's another way, and I can see a brighter future, too."

Griffin kissed my cheek. I wondered where he was going with this. He reached up to turn my face toward his, and the expression in his eyes was nothing short of pure magic.

Then he said, "I'm in love with you."

CHAPTER TWENTY-EIGHT

There was this loud white noise, like a clap of thunder. My heart throbbed painfully, my breath coming out in short bursts. "What?"

"I understand that it hasn't been very long, but I love you," he repeated.

"How do you know?" I whispered. "I've never been in love before."

"Nor I. But I just know. You are the best thing in my life and I never want to be without you. I want to go to sleep with you every night and wake up to you every morning. I want to have a family with you someday. I want to buy you an art gallery so you can exhibit your paintings. I think about you all the time and whenever we're apart I feel as if a piece of me is missing. I don't feel completed until you're with me."

I just reacted. I kissed him, and while the feel of his mouth on mine was like a star going supernova, again I felt that bond to him, like our souls were connecting. His arms tightened around me and when someone yelled, "Get a room!" in the distance, I reminded myself that we weren't alone.

We were both breathing heavily when we pulled apart, the white puffs of our frozen breath hanging in the air between us.

"Then . . . I think I might love you, too."

"You're not certain?" he asked, a teasing glint in his eyes, but I saw hope and joy there as well.

"I don't know. But I feel the same way that you do."

"Was that hard to say?"

It was a fair question, given how terrified I'd been of every step in this relationship. "Surprisingly, no. You make me feel safe and like everything's going to be okay."

"Everything will be okay." He hugged me to him, holding me close while our breathing started moving in sync with one another. "I don't think I've mentioned it yet, but Louis caught an early flight to New York this morning."

"Why? Isn't he your personal employee?"

"My grandmother employs him. His job is to assist me. I assumed she's summoned him, but he didn't say why and I didn't ask. The point, though, is that if you would like to come to dinner tonight, he won't be there."

I widened my eyes. "So . . . there won't be any chaperones once Sophie's in bed?"

"Not a one," he replied, his eyes burning with that intensity of his that I loved.

Because I loved him.

"I'll bring dessert," I told him.

"Will you?" he asked with interest and it made me laugh.

"Actual dessert. It should be fun."

"Oh, there's no question of that," he said and I'd never been so excited for a dinner date ever.

~

I went down to the lobby, where they had a little Italian bakery. I had them give me an assortment of cookies and they told me the ingredients and taught me all the names—anginetti, baci di dama, pignoli, pizzelle.

All different colors and shapes and textures and I couldn't wait to try them all.

I felt nervous and excited. Alice hadn't helped with any of my over-wrought emotions—after the carriage ride I'd told Griffin that I needed to use the bathroom, but I'd actually snuck away to call her.

She was in dialysis when I called. "So, what's new?" she asked.

"Griffin said he loves me and I told him I loved him, too."

Alice shrieked so loudly that I had to hold the phone away from my ear. "You are giving me heart palpitations with this!" she exclaimed.

"You probably shouldn't be raising your heart rate while you're doing dialysis."

"Then don't call and say you're falling in love with the Earl of Strathorne. People can't maintain normal heart rates when they find out that their little sister is about to become royalty."

"Not technically," I reminded her.

"Shh. In my fantasy you're getting married in a castle and wearing a tiara."

This was the image I had in my head as I went up to Griffin's suite. Me in a wedding dress and a tiara. I wondered what he would think of that.

Something told me that he probably wouldn't mind.

I still had the key he'd given me when he'd gone on that trip to New York a couple of weeks ago, so I let myself in. "I'm here!"

Sophie hug attacked me. "What's in that pink box?"

"Cookies. For dessert."

Griffin walked up behind her, leaning in to kiss me hello. It was probably a longer kiss than it should have been for a greeting with a small child in the room, but I wasn't complaining.

Sophie reached for the box and ran off toward the kitchen.

"Those are for after dinner!" Griffin called out, sounding surprisingly tired.

"I know!" she responded in a singsong voice that indicated to me she had no plans to wait for dinner.

He rubbed the back of his neck as we followed Sophie into the kitchen. She'd put the box on the counter and was going through the cookies, inspecting each one.

"What's wrong?" I asked him, keeping my voice low just in case.

"Ollie called me early this morning and left a voice mail. I just listened to it a few minutes ago. Apparently Gisele came to him last night and said she made a mistake and that she's desperate to see Sophie again, so they got on a flight this morning. They're coming here to get her."

I wrapped my arms around his waist. He seemed so sad. "That's a good thing, right?"

He hugged me back. "It is. I'm just . . . I'm really going to miss her." His voice caught and I understood his emotions completely. I was going to miss her, too. Sophie had become an important part of my life.

As had Griffin.

"Ollie and Gisele should be arriving soon. I don't know if their flight is on time or how long it will take them to get here from the airport."

"So we're still being chaperoned," I said in a light tone. "No alone time for us."

"I'm afraid not."

"What's the plan then? Are they taking her back right away?"

"I think so."

Sophie had turned her back to us and I realized that I heard chewing noises. Sure enough, she had been secretly eating cookies this whole time.

"What did I tell you?" Griffin said. "Cookies are for after dinner. We ordered takeaway from that Chinese restaurant down the street. It should be here soon."

"I'm sorry, Uncle Griffin." She gave us big puppy-dog eyes, peering up at us through her lashes.

"It's fine, poppet. Go wash your hands."

She ran to the bathroom and Griffin leaned against the counter. I ran my fingertips along his scalp, wanting to soothe him. I knew how hard this had to be.

"What does this mean for you now?" I asked. "Are you going back to England?" I hated the idea that he would go, my heart clenching at the prospect, but we were in love. We would work things out. It would be okay, even if he left.

"I'm not certain. I'll have to discuss things with Ollie and Gisele to see where we go from here."

"Isn't he worried about your grandma finding out?"

"Because she's still in New York, he thought it was safe to come."

That made me pause. "Do you think that it's a coincidence that they're coming here from England just as Louis went to New York?"

Griffin shook his head. "I don't think that the two events are connected."

"I guess I'm just naturally paranoid," I said.

Sophie walked into the kitchen, her face a pale white and what looked like a rash around her mouth. "Uncle Griffin? I feel funny. My throat. I can't breathe."

"Lay down, Sophie," I said to her, rushing to her side and helping her to get on the ground. "Concentrate on breathing in and out. Breathe with me." I kept my voice level so that she would stay calm. "Griffin, I think Sophie's in anaphylactic shock. Does she have an EpiPen?"

He stood there, his mouth agape, eyes wide. He didn't respond.

"Griffin!"

"Uh, not that I'm aware of. Is she going to be all right?"

"I need you to call the concierge to see if they have any epinephrine. Then I need you to call 911 and tell them we need an ambulance."

He was still frozen in place, unmoving. I yelled his name this time and added, "Hurry!"

That seemed to work. He got his phone out and started making phone calls. I focused all of my attention on Sophie, getting her to keep breathing with me.

"Am . . . I . . . going . . . to . . . die?" she asked, wheezing the question to me.

I tamped down the sense of panic I was feeling. She needed me. "No. You are going to be just fine. I promise you."

There was a flurry of activity as hotel staff arrived, including the on-site medic. He had a shot for her, and within seconds of getting it her breathing improved.

"The ambulance should be here soon," the medic told me. "Do you know what she's allergic to?"

I glanced over at Griffin, who still seemed to be in shock, crouching by Sophie's feet. He had told me he wasn't great in a crisis, and he hadn't been kidding. "Does Sophie have an allergy, Griffin?"

"Ollie never mentioned one."

Alice was right. We were totally within our rights to judge Ollie. Poor little Sophie had a major allergy and he failed to say anything to his brother? Who was taking care of her?

That sparked a memory for me. Milo had told me. I just hadn't believed him. "Pine nuts," I told the medic. "I bought some cookies downstairs. The pignoli cookies are made with pine nuts and she's allergic."

The EMTs arrived then with a gurney for Sophie. Griffin and I stepped back to allow them to work. Now that professionals were here, I could let go. A wave of nausea slammed into me as my adrenaline subsided, and I found that I was shaking.

"How do you know what she was allergic to?" he asked, arms wrapped around me, holding me tightly. It made the shaking subside.

"Milo told me she had allergies. But the other ones were ridiculous, so I just dismissed it. I should have listened to him. I brought that cookie here. It's like this is my fault."

"Your fault? You saved her. You were bloody brilliant. How did you know what to do?"

I shrugged, but the weight of my guilt over not believing Milo was pushing down too hard to raise my shoulders very high. "I worked as a lifeguard a few years ago. We had first aid training, and a kid went into anaphylactic shock once. I've dealt with it before."

He kissed my forehead. "I'm so glad you were here."

"Only one of you can come on the ambulance with us," an EMT said. "We're taking her to the hospital and the doctors will probably want to keep her overnight for observation, given her age."

Obviously Griffin was going to be the one to go. I said, "Let me grab some changes of clothes for both of you and I'll meet you there."

He nodded and then followed everyone out to the elevator. I rushed to Griffin's closet and found a little Louis Vuitton suitcase and grabbed some pants and a shirt from his drawer. Then I went into Sophie's room and did the same thing, making sure to grab stuff that I knew was her favorite. She would want something bright and sparkly to put on in the morning.

I left the suite and got my phone out to get a rideshare, but instead I decided to go upstairs. I wanted the Crawfords to know what had happened. That Sophie had been hurt, and that she would be leaving soon because her father and mother were coming for her.

When I got to the suite, the first thing I noticed was a bunch of suitcases in the hallway. Not just a couple, like they were going on a short trip, but a ton. Weird.

I found Sheila cleaning up the leftovers from dinner and Milo was watching French *Paw Patrol* in the living room.

"I have to talk to you," I told her in a soft voice.

She looked stricken. "You know."

"I know what?"

Sheila picked up a dishrag and twisted it in her hands several times. "I've been trying to figure out how to tell you for a couple of days."

I was totally dumbfounded. I had no idea what she was talking about. "I was going to tell you about Sophie. First, that she's leaving, and second that she just went into anaphylactic shock from an allergy to pine nuts. I'm going to go to the hospital, but I wanted to tell you guys first."

She gasped. "Is Sophie going to be okay?"

"The medics said she's going to be fine, but the doctors at the hospital will probably hold her overnight for observation."

Milo came into the kitchen and said, "Who's in the hospital?"

My first instinct was to lie. To spare his feelings. He might be really worried.

Sheila went over and crouched down next to him. "Sophie had an allergic reaction tonight. She had to go to the hospital so that the doctors could help her. But she's going to be just fine." She hugged him tightly, but Milo just looked confused.

"I know you tried to warn me about the pine nuts," I told him. I didn't want him to think he was to blame.

"But you didn't believe me," he said sadly.

Sheila released him and stood up. "Do you want to talk about it? Do you have any questions?"

Milo just shook his head.

A phone started ringing from another room. "That's probably John," Sheila said. "I'll be right back."

Milo wandered over to the island and climbed up on a stool. He sat with his elbows on the countertop, resting his chin against his hands. He looked so defeated. "You didn't believe me about Sophie's allergy because I tell lies all the time. I'm like that little boy who beat up wolves."

"Cried wolf . . . Never mind. I hope you know this isn't your fault. If anything it's more my fault. I should have listened to you. I wish I had."

"Sometimes I say things that aren't true," he acknowledged. "I should tell the truth more."

His declaration hit me like a thunderclap, suddenly making everything completely clear. While I'd always known that it was wrong to lie to the Crawfords, hearing him say it made everything plain and simple.

I had to come clean with Sheila. She might fire me and kick me out, but it would be what I deserved. I couldn't keep lying to them. Not when this little five-year-old boy was vowing to be honest. The very least I could do was keep up with him. "I'm going to tell the truth more, too. Let's make a pact." I offered him my hand and he took it. We shook.

"Deal," he said.

"Since we're telling the truth, Sophie's mom and dad are coming from Europe to be with her. I don't know what's going to happen, but she's probably going to go back with them."

He took in this new information. "I'll miss her."

"Me too," I told him. Milo was another person I needed to be totally honest with. "But that's kind of the deal, right? Pretty soon you're going to leave, and I'm going back to my sister's house. It will be okay, though! You'll have so much going on! There will be new friends at school, your parents, a new baby brother or sister. Your life is going to be so busy you won't even have time to miss me."

"That's not the truth, Diana."

My heart swelled up with love for this kid. I kissed him on the top of his head as I hugged him tight. It was going to be so, so hard to leave him.

Sheila came back into the kitchen. "Sorry, that was John. I needed to fill him in on what's going on. Are you doing okay, sweetheart?" she asked Milo.

He gave her a little smile. "I am fine."

No disease, no pretend illness. Milo was going to be just fine.

"Why don't you go have some screen time?" Sheila asked. "I'll be there in a few minutes and you can show me what you're building in Minecraft."

"Okay!" He jumped off the stool and shot out of the room.

"Diana, can you take a seat?" she asked.

"Sure."

That nervous look on her face had me feeling anxious. My first thought was that she'd found out about me, but I shoved that away. I was done letting my fears and dishonesty control my life. "There's something I want to tell you," I said.

"Me first, if that's okay. I've known this for a couple of days and I haven't really been sure how to bring it up with you." She took a deep breath. "Our plans have changed. The tenants in our house in France have vacated early. John's company has agreed to let him start his new position immediately, and I've tied up all the loose ends I have here in the States. We're ready to move on to the next part of our lives."

I was glad she had me sitting down. "Oh. I don't have a passport." But as soon as I said it I realized why she was telling me.

Because I wasn't going with them.

They no longer required my services.

I wasn't going to get the money I needed for Alice. For a moment it felt like the world was spinning around me and the only thing keeping me grounded was the incredible ache in my chest.

I'd failed my sister.

CHAPTER TWENTY-NINE

Sheila appeared worried about me, but she was trying to put a positive spin on things. "This is going to be so great. We'll be able to enroll Milo in school right away so that he can catch up with his peers. We'll hire tutors if he needs them. Everything is set up and ready to go."

"All that was left was telling me."

She nodded, still looking miserable. "My timing obviously couldn't be worse. But we're leaving tomorrow evening."

Wow. She really hadn't given me much notice here.

"The suite is reserved for the rest of the week, so you can stay here until then if you need to. I know I should have told you earlier," she said. "I wanted to. But you've become so important to us that I didn't know how to break it to you."

"That's fine. I understand." I was the absolute last person in the world who should be judging anybody for keeping secrets. But I had worked one month for them, so I would have to return at least five thousand dollars of the twenty she'd already given me. If not more. "How much of the money do you want me to give back to you?"

Now she looked confused. "None. You're getting the salary we agreed on. Forty thousand dollars. I've already transferred the rest of the funds to your bank account."

That pierced my gut like a hot lance. Again I was grateful that I was already sitting down. "I didn't keep up my end of the bargain. I don't deserve the full amount."

"Well, considering I'm the one who decides what your salary is going to be, that's what I'm paying you. We'll think of it as a nice severance package."

"No, Sheila, you can't do that." I paused, trying to ignore the way my limbs trembled, because I knew this had to be done. Alice and I would figure something else out. "You shouldn't pay me at all. I'm not who you think I am."

"What do you mean?"

"I don't know French at all. I can only ski because Griffin taught me, and I barely passed algebra. I lied about my qualifications and experience to get this job. I've been lying to you this whole time and I am so, so sorry."

There. It was out. I'd done it.

She didn't say anything and my entire body felt heavy, making it hard to move. I did manage to stand, pushing against the counter for support. "So I'll go pack up all my stuff and leave. I'll return all of the money to you. Is it okay if I say goodbye to Milo first?"

"Diana, none of that matters."

I blinked slowly, unsure I'd heard her right. "What?"

"Do you know what matters most to me in the world?" she asked.

"Honesty?"

"My family. Everything else comes second. Milo is my world. I would do anything to protect him. Make him happy. You won't understand what that feels like until you have a child."

This was the lecture I deserved. I swallowed down the burning sensation in my throat and nodded.

"And the last few weeks . . ." She paused until I lifted my head to look at her. "This is literally the happiest I have ever seen him. And you did that. You've given Milo everything he needed. You loved him. You taught him to be a friend. You got him to try skiing, helped him get a familiarity with French. Last night the teacher from his new school did an evaluation of his academic skills for placement in her class, and she told us that he was very smart and right where he should be. You did that. You did everything we asked you to do and more. He has blossomed with you as his nanny."

She was giving me too much credit. "I'm not responsible for any—"

But she cut me off. "You are. Where you come from, who you were . . . doesn't matter."

It was at that point I realized that she probably had done a thorough background check on me. Yet she'd still hired me. "Why?" I asked. "Why did you give me the job?"

"I rely a lot on my instincts. And when I first talked to you, I knew that you were the right person. I had a good feeling about you. You needed us, and we needed you. It feels like it was meant to be."

"And knowing everything that you know, you're still going to give me the money? You can't do that."

"Why not?" she asked. "I can easily afford to pay you what we agreed on."

I cleared my throat, willing myself not to tear up. "Because . . . I don't deserve to be rewarded. I should be punished. I have to . . . pay for my crimes."

"Oh, Diana, sweetheart." Sheila came over and pulled me into a fierce hug. "I get the feeling you've been doing that for a long time already."

I nodded, willing myself to not cry, to ignore the lump in my throat, the way my chest ached. I was glad I couldn't see her face, or I probably would have lost it. I'd never had anyone, outside of Alice and Griffin, treat me with this kind of compassion. And understanding.

"You're a good person, Diana. You deserve to be happy." She kept hugging me, just as she'd hugged Milo earlier.

I clung to her. I wished I'd grown up with this, had this kind of support in my childhood.

"And if you won't do it for yourself, do it for your sister."

Ouch. She had found my weak spot. For Alice, I could say yes.

Sheila stepped back and brushed some of my hair away from my face. She took an envelope from the counter and handed it to me.

"This is a gift card for an airline ticket. I know it'll be last minute, so there's extra on there just in case. And maybe once you get a passport, there should be enough left over for you to come visit us in France. Okay?"

I nodded, still not trusting myself to speak.

"You are family now," she told me. "No matter where we are in the world, if you need something, John and I will be here for you. Always."

"Same," I said, that one syllable all I could let out.

"Mom!" Milo called from the other room. "Come see my base!"

Sheila smiled at me. "Duty calls."

I stayed in the kitchen for a little while, still hanging on to the suitcase that I was supposed to bring to Griffin and Sophie. I felt really overwhelmed and I didn't want to go to the hospital while I was feeling so churned up.

Heading to my room, I closed the door and called Alice. I had to unload. And she was always the best listener.

As soon as she picked up I told her all about what had happened with Sophie and with the Crawfords. She listened without saying much, which kind of surprised me. Because even when she was letting me vent, she usually still made little sounds of encouragement or shock.

This time? Total silence.

When I finished I said, "Are you okay? You're unusually quiet."

"I'm taking it you haven't been online."

"Not really. I've been kind of busy."

"Hold on," she said. "I'm sending you a link. Check your messages."

There was a buzz and I saw her text. I clicked on it and it led to a website.

A website that had a picture of me and Griffin on it. Kissing in the carriage. And a headline that read:

ENGLAND'S MOST ELIGIBLE BACHELOR DATES THE HELP!

Oh no.

My heart sank to my feet as I began to read the article. "American nanny Diana Parker confirmed that she was in a relationship with Griffin Windsor, the Earl of Strathorne. She also exclusively revealed that the earl's younger brother, Oliver Windsor, has a secret love child."

What? What, what, what? "I never told anyone any of this!" I exclaimed.

I scrolled up to see the name of the journalist.

Carrie Bogdanovich. The woman I'd spoken to at the winter festival. My heart beat loud and hard, and I felt nauseated. I'd thought she was just some stranger. But she'd known.

She'd even taken the time to tell me her full name. So that I would know it had been her. To make me aware of just how easy I'd been to take advantage of.

How had I not figured it out? The person who'd always been suspicious of everyone around me, the one trained to look for things other people missed?

That woman was a reporter and I felt idiotic for not having realized it. I'd put my guard down so much that this had happened.

"This is my fault," Alice said.

"Your fault? I'm the one who talked to her. She was that mom from the festival today."

"You know how sometimes you call when I'm in dialysis? One of the women there was listening in on our conversations and her daughter,

Carrie, went to school to become a journalist but hadn't been able to break into the market. Denise told her about your situation and . . . I guess she found you to get the story and make a name for herself. I'm so sorry. You told me not to tell anyone. And I didn't tell her, but she overheard everything and . . . please tell Griffin I'm sorry."

I sat down hard on my bed. This woman must have gone straight from the festival to write the article and sell it to the highest bidder.

Griffin had done everything he could to protect his brother and his niece. And now the entire world knew about Sophie. It was the one thing he hadn't wanted.

And I was responsible for it happening. "What am I going to do now?"

"That place is about to be swarmed with paparazzi," Alice said. "If it isn't already."

"Griffin is ruined. His grandmother will see this and she's going to disown him. I don't even know what to do. There's no way to fix this." How could he possibly forgive me for this?

"Hold on," she said and I heard typing sounds. "You said Sheila gave you a gift card for travel? There's a red-eye out of Aspen tonight that connects in Denver and then comes straight to Miami. Come home. It's the best place to hide out. And bring Griffin with you."

"Wait, wait," I said. "Everything is happening too fast." I couldn't just hop on a plane and go back to Florida. I had to know what was going on with Griffin and Sophie. I had to see if Griffin would still speak to me, let alone fly across the country with me to Alice's house. I had to say goodbye to Sheila and Milo. It all felt like too much.

"There's a few seats left on the flight. I'm going to get you a ticket. Give me the number off the gift card."

Feeling a bit numb, I read the number to her.

"There. Your ticket has been bought. Your flight leaves in three hours. You can do this, Diana. If our mother was good for one thing, it was for teaching us to be adaptable. Pick yourself up. Go pack your belongings. Say your goodbyes. And bring that handsome man of yours home with you."

My sister was right. I could do this. And I did need to get out of Aspen. Not only for Griffin's sake, but for the Crawfords'. They did not need to be implicated in any of this and have their names dragged through the mud. They were professionals with reputations to protect. After all they had done for me, there was no way I was going to let this blow back on them.

If Griffin would just listen to me, understand what had happened, we could be okay. We loved each other, right?

I thanked Alice, told her I would see her soon, before hanging up the phone. Here I'd thought I was going to let her help me get in a better mood before I went to see Griffin, but now everything was a thousand times worse.

Taking her advice, I packed up quickly. I uninstalled the apps I'd put on my phone and left it on the nightstand. I found Sheila and asked if I could talk to her and told her a brief version of what had happened, and that I was going to leave tonight. She hugged me again and reiterated that they would help in any way they could. I promised to write and then went to chat with Milo. He was distracted by his game, and he kept showing me all the stuff he was working on in Minecraft.

"So, I have to leave tonight," I told him. "I'm sure your mom told you but you guys are heading out tomorrow to go to France."

"I know. It will be fun to go to school."

"It will be," I agreed. "But I'm really going to miss you."

"I'll miss you, too."

I felt like my heart was breaking, but he was happy and chipper and kept telling me more Minecraft facts. I hugged him goodbye and I wondered if he realized that he wouldn't see me again. He was probably used to people leaving, with his parents traveling so much, but they always came back.

I sat on that couch and thought about how all of the Crawfords meant so much to me.

Somehow I did manage to leave, even though I wanted to stay in that room with him and listen to him talk about his game. I reminded myself that Griffin was waiting for me and that I had to tell him about this article before he found out another way.

I considered calling him to tell him about it before I'd left the hotel. Because there was no way his grandmother was unaware of this. I was sure Louis had personally hand-delivered it to her. But I wanted to tell Griffin in person so that we could hopefully figure out a way to deal with it. Together.

The ride to the hospital was quick, and the nurse at the front desk gave me Sophie's room number. It was easy enough to find.

But when I walked into Sophie's room, it wasn't just Sophie and Griffin.

Her parents were there.

Gisele had elfin features, with hair the same pretty blonde color as Sophie's. She sat at Sophie's bedside, holding her hand. Sophie was good and passed out. I wondered if the doctors had given her a sedative.

Ollie was like a less handsome version of Griffin. A bit shorter, his hair and eyes darker than his brother's. Maybe I was being ungenerous because I was still mad at him for not telling Griffin about Sophie's allergy.

"This is Diana Parker," Griffin said, coming over to hug me hello. "She's the one who saved Sophie."

Gisele got up and kissed me on my cheeks. "Thank you so much. I made such a big mistake. I don't know what I would have done if something had happened to her." Her French accent was soft and I couldn't help but notice how Ollie watched everything she did. I realized that he was still in love with her.

"You're welcome," I said.

Ollie added, "Yes, thank you, Diana. We'll never be able to repay you." His voice was so much like Griffin's that it was weird. I nodded at him.

"I need to talk to you," I murmured to Griffin.

"What is it?" he asked.

"Um, can we step outside?" This was not a conversation I wanted to have in front of his family.

My heart beat hard and fast as he followed behind me. It was difficult to swallow or to catch my breath as I realized just how bad this was all about to be, and that I was the one who'd caused this. Inadvertently, but I was still responsible. I felt sweat on my hairline, and trickling down my back.

I had to hope that he'd forgive me.

"Can I see your phone?" I was never going to forget the name of the website that would be responsible for hurting Griffin and his family. I located the article quickly and handed it back to him.

He began to read the story and I saw his face pale. "How did this—"

"Today, at the petting zoo. This woman was talking to me and it all seemed so harmless and I told her we were dating and that you were Sophie's uncle and, Griffin, I am so, so sorry." My throat felt too thick to talk. "I did this. I didn't mean to, but I did."

I thought he might get angry with me. Yell. Tell me how upset he was. Instead he took one look at me and hugged me tightly against him. "Everything will be all right, Diana. I know you didn't do this on purpose. We'll figure out a way to deal with it. Together."

My relief was instant, warming my insides. "Thank you. I was so afraid that . . ."

"Afraid of what?" he asked, kissing the top of my head. "Nothing will ever come between us. I told you I was serious about you. That I'm in this for the long haul, and I meant it. Nothing's changed. But I have to let Ollie know what's occurred."

He hugged me one last time and then went back into Sophie's room. He handed the phone to Ollie, who didn't look quite as surprised by the article.

"Granny already knows about Sophie," Ollie told his brother before giving the phone back.

The shock on Griffin's face was clear. "When did you tell her?"

"I sent her an email this morning just before I texted you."

Griffin said incredulously, "You emailed her?"

"I'm not going back to England any time soon. I'm going to let her cool off first. Better to deal with her wrath at a distance." Ollie shrugged. "Gisele and I are taking Sophie to France as soon as the doctors release her."

"So you're running away," Griffin said.

"She'll get over it eventually," Ollie said. "Granny can't stay mad forever."

"Have you met the woman?"

"Sophie is her only great-grandchild. That will have to matter to her. You know how important bloodlines are to her. That there be an heir for her massive fortune."

"You are gambling on Granny to take this well and I think we both know that won't be the case. That's why I brought Sophie to Aspen in the first place!"

Ollie folded his arms. "It's not your problem, Griffin. I'm Sophie's father and I'll decide what's right for her. And my relationship with our grandmother is also my problem. You can't be the big brother who rescues me forever. You have to let me do things my own way."

Finally, Ollie had stepped up. It was about time. I felt how Griffin tensed beside me, and although Ollie wasn't going about things the best way, he was right. He and Gisele were the ones who had to make decisions about Sophie. Which Griffin must have realized, because he relaxed and didn't argue with his brother.

"Call me when you land in Paris and let me know where you're staying so that I can come visit my niece." Griffin reached into his pocket and pulled out a keycard. "I'm in the Mountain Suite. Whenever you want to head over there, you can pack up Sophie's things so that you can take them with you."

Then Ollie and Griffin shook hands. It was a bit formal, but I figured that was probably normal in his family. Then Griffin went over to the hospital bed and kissed Sophie's forehead. He whispered, "Goodbye, poppet."

He took me by the hand and led me from the room. I called out, "Nice to meet you!" over my shoulder, but we went down to the lobby and then outside the hospital. It was freezing, but I got the feeling he didn't want to be around people at the moment.

He got out his phone, and I guessed it was to get a car.

"I'm sorry," I told him. "I wish there was a word more powerful than *sorry*. Because I did this. I can't believe how that woman tricked me." The same woman who had followed us and taken pictures of us without us knowing. It felt so creepy. No wonder Griffin hated all this paparazzi stuff so much.

"This isn't your fault," he assured me, sounding exhausted. "I don't blame you." Then he kissed me to show me that he meant what he'd said.

"But it's your last strike. Your grandma is going to kill you."

"I will blow up that bridge when I get to it," he said. "A problem for another day."

We were interrupted by a taxi pulling up to the front of the hospital. The driver rolled down his window and asked us, "Did you need a ride?"

"No, thank you," Griffin told him. "We're waiting for a car."

I wondered where Griffin planned on going next. And whether I was part of his plans. "What are you going to do now?"

"Go back to the hotel to get my things. And then . . . I don't know."

There was a silence, one I rushed to fill due to my guilt over the article. I told him everything that had happened since he'd gone to the hospital, and how I was going to be leaving in a few hours.

Then I added, "I want you to come with me. Alice's house will be the perfect place to hide out. We have different last names and hopefully the press won't find us." Neither Alice nor I maintained any social media accounts. We knew better.

"You think Alice wants to meet me?" he teased.

"I think she'd give up both of her kidneys for the chance," I said and he laughed. I was glad he could still laugh despite all of this.

"You want me to meet your family," he said with a smug smile.

"I do."

"Because I love you so much, I promise to never take you home to meet the rest of my family," he said, kissing me briefly. "What flight are you on?"

I gave him the information that I'd written down on a piece of paper. He booked himself a ticket on his phone. "Then I suppose we're both going to the airport. Ollie has the right idea. Clear the country before Hurricane Granny makes landfall."

A black SUV, which I assumed was our ride, pulled up.

Griffin swore and I was confused. Was something wrong with the car?

The back door of the SUV opened and an older woman climbed out. "Hello, Griffin."

"Grandmother."

CHAPTER THIRTY

Now I knew why he'd cursed. His grandma was actually here. She looked like a villain who had walked out of a Disney movie: silver hair pinned tightly back, a black Chanel dress paired with strands of pearls that were real, an actual mink fur coat.

"How did you know we were here?" Griffin asked. It was a valid question. There was no way for her to have known we'd gone to the hospital. Not unless Ollie had told her.

I caught a glimpse of Louis smirking at me from the back seat. I wouldn't have put it past him to put a tracker or a bug on Griffin's phone.

"The means are not important. What matters is that I stop you before you make a grave mistake."

Griffin took my hand and squeezed it. To let me know that he wasn't going anywhere. "I'm not making a mistake. I'm in love with Diana."

"How can you be in love with a woman you don't even know? Has she told you of her sordid past? Her mother is in prison and she doesn't know who her father is." She spat the words out. "I warned you about this kind of gold digger, Griffin. She's little more than a viper looking to slither her way into our noble family tree."

Even though I was well aware of my own unsavory backstory, it was still painful to have her throwing the harsh realities of my life at me. As if each word were designed to pierce my skin and leave marks.

"You mean like you did?" I asked her and she whirled on me, her eyes flashing. No wonder Griffin was scared of her reaction.

"No one gave you permission to speak."

"You will not talk to Diana like that," Griffin said and I squeezed his hand.

"I will speak to this person any way that I wish," she snapped back. "She is nothing to me and does not deserve my respect. At least your brother had the decency to find a woman who is descended from an Italian visconte before impregnating her and then failing to inform me. After I've dealt with you I will deal with him next. Along with his illegitimate child."

She really was about to disown everybody. All of Griffin's concerns had been totally justified.

"Sophie doesn't deserve your anger," he said. "She had nothing to do with Ollie's actions and she shouldn't be disinherited."

"Do not concern yourself with my plans for your brother." She sighed dramatically and then said, "I tire of these games and of your rebellion. You have brought shame to our name, once again. I told you this was your last chance, and I was quite serious. I will not let you make us a laughingstock by courting the help. So, grandson, it is time to choose. I will let you make the decision for both yourself and Oliver. Do you choose the girl, or do you choose your fortune and family?"

Griffin stood there, not speaking.

I looked at him, waiting for him to talk. To say he chose me. That of course he would choose me because he loved me.

But he didn't.

He ducked his head.

I realized the truth. Despite all his promises, despite all my daydreams and wishes, he wasn't going to choose me.

My chest felt tight, constricting my breathing. My stomach clenched so hard I was afraid I might throw up. It felt like I'd swallowed a thousand tiny knives and they were all stabbing at my insides at once. My heart actually ached, while dark pain bloomed inside me, spreading like a stain.

"Griffin?" I whispered.

He rubbed the back of his neck. "Diana . . . I have to . . . I can't just . . ."

But he didn't finish. Just stood there, not making eye contact.

"There, girl, you see? He could never pick you over his inheritance."

Anger flared up inside me. I was done with not being chosen. He couldn't really love me if his grandma's fortune was more important to him. She had ordered him to do as she said, and just as I'd predicted, he'd obeyed.

I had to get out of there. Had to leave all this behind. My chest was heaving and I was breathing so hard I worried I might hyperventilate.

That taxi from earlier was still idling and I walked over toward it, willing myself not to slip on the icy parking lot. I sent up a silent prayer to let me have some dignity and not let me falling be the last image that Griffin and his grandma had of me.

As I worried about slipping, I thought of the first night we'd met, how Griffin had said he'd be there to catch me.

And I'd thought I was the liar.

The taxi driver rolled down his window and I managed to ask, "Can you take me to the airport?"

"Sure can," he said.

I opened the door and threw my duffel bag on the back seat. I told myself not to, but I looked back at Griffin, still standing there with the dowager countess.

I'd been such a fool. Regret, despair, and anger threatened to swallow me up.

Looking away, I got into the back of the cab. It took the driver forever to put the car into gear and pull away from the front of the hospital.

Part of me hoped Griffin would come running after me, that he would bang on the window of the taxi and tell me to wait. That of course I mattered to him more than the money.

It didn't happen.

I hadn't let myself cry in years. Not since I was a little girl. I hadn't cried over any of the messed-up stuff my mom had done, not when she was sentenced to prison, not when Alice got her diagnosis, not when her husband left her. Never. I was always the strong one. I made plans and carried them out and took care of whoever needed me.

There had never been a relationship heartbreak, either. Not even with the one guy I'd imagined myself in love with, the one who had so many red flags he should have led his own red-flag brigade with a personal color guard who waved his monogrammed red flags. That guy had walked out on me and had stolen the three thousand dollars I'd worked so hard to save. Money that was supposed to help my sister.

I'd been pissed, but I hadn't cried.

But now, I cried. And just as I feared, it was like a dam breaking. I just kept sobbing and sobbing, nose running, chest heaving. My chest and throat started to hurt from crying so much, but I couldn't stop.

Griffin had let me walk away and I didn't think I was going to get over losing him. It was just as soul-shatteringly awful as I'd feared it would be. It felt like the entire world had turned to gray misery. That I was never going to stop crying.

That my heart would never stop breaking, over and over again.

The taxi driver asked me if I was okay, but I couldn't answer. I could barely breathe.

I could only cry.

He seemed relieved to drop me off at the airport and I sat outside the building, still crying. Several people stared at me as they walked by and one woman handed me a tissue and said, "I've been there, sweetie. It gets better."

I didn't see how. It was impossible.

When I had finally cried myself dry, I went into the airport to check in. I knew I had to be a mess, my eyes bright red, my breathing ragged, my cheeks tearstained. No one said a word.

I no longer had a phone, so I couldn't call Alice. She would have known the right things to say, the stuff to make everything better. Although I didn't think even Alice could fix this. So I got to sit with my despair, with my shattered heart.

I managed to make it to my gate and slumped into one of those plastic chairs. Even though I knew it was over, I still looked for him. In every crowd that passed down the hallway next to me, I searched the groups for his face.

But he wasn't there. He didn't come for me.

It was surprisingly pathetic for someone who should have known better.

I waffled between pain and fury. That Griffin wasn't the person I'd thought he was. That he would choose money over me. That I had meant so little to him, despite all his promises and assurances.

They announced that they were boarding the flight, and up until the moment that they closed the plane door, a part of my heart still hoped he would show up and beg for forgiveness.

When the plane began to taxi away from the gate, I could finally let that fantasy go. I didn't have much of a choice. I was leaving, and he wasn't next to me. But there were no more tears to cry, although the man seated next to me seemed extremely uncomfortable with the way I kept trying to catch my breath but couldn't. He kept shooting me worried looks, but I couldn't deal with anyone else's issues at the moment. I was barely hanging on.

Fortunately, the flight to Denver was a short one, and the layover even shorter. They were already boarding the flight when I got to the gate.

Which left me with hours until I got to Miami.

Most of the people around me were sleeping. I had a hard time going to sleep in a comfortable bed. In an uncomfortable airplane seat? There was no way.

Not to mention that I couldn't turn my brain off. At first my whole body felt like one giant exposed nerve, throbbing with pain until I started to go completely numb. There was too much pain to deal with.

I'd always been overly emotional. My mom had made fun of me for it.

No. I took Alice's advice and I shoved that thought out of my head. I wasn't going to let my mom's garbage get into my brain. I was emotional, but that wasn't a bad thing.

At least, it hadn't been until I got my heart shattered beyond repair.

As the flight went on, a back-and-forth began to happen in my brain. While I accepted the reality of my situation, there was still a tiny voice inside me that said maybe I'd misunderstood. That something more had been going on and I hadn't given Griffin a chance. That once again, I'd run away from a situation instead of dealing with it. Confronting it.

The louder voice told the quieter one to shut up. Griffin had been given a choice and had made it very clearly.

It was at least understandable. That was a lot of money to just walk away from.

But wasn't I worth it?

My mind wandered to the allergy incident with Sophie, and I thought of the way that Griffin had frozen in the moment when she'd needed him. What if I hadn't been there? What if he'd waited too long to get her help?

And . . . what if that was what had happened with his grandmother? Was that why he hadn't responded? He'd told me he was no good with snap decisions. What if this was all a misunderstanding? If he'd failed to react when I needed him?

No, I hadn't misunderstood. I was on this plane alone, wasn't I?

I had started the day off with the man of my dreams telling me he loved me, and I had ended it alone, life ruined.

That made me shake my head. I wasn't going to think about my mom anymore, but I could hold on to the few good things she'd managed to teach me. Like adaptability. Putting one foot in front of the other. Faking it until I made it. I told myself that my life wasn't ruined. I was going to save Alice and then figure out what I wanted to do after that. I'd devote more time to painting, because I loved it. And it wouldn't ever destroy me the way that Griffin had. I'd spend more time with Jasper and Jenna. Maybe I'd get my GED.

Everything was going to change.

And I'd keep telling myself that until I believed it.

~

I arrived in Miami early in the morning. I called Alice from a pay phone to let her know that my flight had landed safely and that I was on the way to her house. She sounded sleepy and I felt guilty for having woken her up. But she assured me she was so excited to see me. Something to look forward to.

I went outside the airport and the humidity slammed into me, reminding me why it had been an easy decision to move up north. And it was only February. It was going to be so miserable in the summer. My shirt was clinging to my back as I got in line to hire a taxi to take me to Alice's house. She lived about an hour away and we thankfully avoided most of the morning rush-hour traffic, but my driver didn't have air-conditioning and not to be overdramatic, but I felt a little like I was going to die.

When the driver pulled up to Alice's house, a sense of relief overcame me. I was back with my sister and her kids. Things had to get better. I paid the driver, and when I climbed out of the cab, Alice was waiting at her front door for me.

I ran up the sidewalk and hugged her, holding on for dear life.

"Come inside," she said.

The cool air of the air-conditioning hit me with a frigid blast, reminding me of where I'd just been.

I noticed that Alice had made up a bed for me on the couch. She asked, "Did you want to try and sleep? I'll tell the twins to be quiet when they get up, before they go to school."

The twins could be quiet, all right. Like a T. rex stomping through a minefield. "No. I'd rather talk, if you're up to it."

"What's wrong?" she asked. "Your eyes look puffy. And I thought Griffin was coming with you."

I'd spent so much time in my own head thinking through this situation that I had forgotten I hadn't actually told her yet. "Griffin and I broke up."

"What?" she demanded, pulling me over to the sofa and making me sit. "Tell me everything."

So I did. I gave her all the details.

When I finished she asked, "Is that it?"

What more did she need? "Yes."

"So . . . he never broke up with you?"

"He did. When he didn't choose me."

"No, he didn't. He didn't say the words. He didn't choose anything. You didn't give him a chance to do it."

I tamped down the dismay and annoyance I was currently feeling. "You wanted me to wait for him to say 'I pick the money, nice knowing you'?"

"I'm not saying that. I just . . . I don't know. I think sometimes situations aren't quite what they appear. And that we should give the people we love the benefit of the doubt. And not run away to Florida when things don't match the fantasy in your head."

"You told me to come here!" I protested. I wasn't running away. I wasn't.

"You should have let him make an actual choice. That's all I'm saying."

"Him not saying anything was the choice. Whenever he'd talk about Ollie he kept saying that his brother not making a decision was still making a decision. So Griffin made his decision to break up with me by not saying anything."

"Okay," she said with a loud sigh. I could tell she wanted to say more, but she was holding back.

It aggravated me that she wasn't on my side.

A loud thump signaled that her kids had woken up. The twins came into the front room, and their faces lit up when they saw me. I got tackled by them both as they ran over to hug me. "Aunt Diana!"

"Hey, you two."

"Let your aunt breathe," Alice said. "Go get ready for school and we'll get breakfast started."

I got up to help her make breakfast and pack lunches. I sat with them and ate, but the food didn't have a taste. It was like all the joy in the world, along with all the tastes, had been sucked out of my life. I tried to smile and enjoy being with everyone. But it was so strange to be here now—it was like waking up from the most intense, realistic dream ever and then returning back to your old life.

Being with the kids did make me miss Milo a little less.

It did not, however, make the ache over Griffin feel any less sharp.

Every time I breathed, it was like being stabbed by those tiny knives again. I wondered if there would come a point when it stopped hurting so much.

"Can we show Aunt Diana the surprise yet?" Jenna asked, bobbing up and down in her seat.

"Put your plates in the sink and then we'll show her," Alice said.

The kids got up and did as she asked, and then they grabbed my hands. "Come with us!"

They led me through the door into the garage. They'd moved aside boxes and made a little mini-studio for me. There was the easel I'd left behind, and several canvases for me to use, along with some new paint.

"The twins and I cleared this spot out for you last night. I know there's just that window on the side wall so the lighting's not ideal, but I figured it might work."

"It's perfect. Thank you." I hugged my family. This. This was what I had to concentrate on now. My loved ones and my art.

Alice told the kids it was time to go to school. She would drop them off and then head off to dialysis. I almost offered to go with her but that reporter's mother was in that group and I didn't need anyone to know that I was here in Miami. I figured it was better to stay at Alice's place and hide out.

The problem with staying here was that it gave me nothing but time. Time to think about everything, time to dwell on my pain and how much I missed Griffin.

I took a shower and then wasn't sure what to do with myself after. I glanced at Alice's laptop. I didn't want to go online and see the fallout from the article or inadvertently find out what Griffin was doing. I didn't need a computer to fill in those blanks for me. I was sure he had flown back with his precious grandma to England to visit their massive bank vault and swim around in it like Scrooge McDuck or whatever it was that rich people did.

I picked up the remote but I didn't have the mental capacity to watch TV or stream something.

Or to even read.

And things had never been so bad that I couldn't read.

I was like some walking open wound, and I wondered how long it would take for these pains, which were somehow both dull and sharp at the same time, to go away.

The only thing I could do was paint.

Heading back to the garage, I sat down on the rickety stool and started to fill the canvases. Blacks, grays, purples. Things that reflected my mood.

But even painting wasn't the refuge that it normally was for me. Instead I was ruminating on Alice's words. What if she was right? Maybe I should have stayed and let him say out loud what his choice was. I had been overly emotional from the Sophie incident and the Crawfords leaving early. Then add in the tabloid issue, which had made me worry about both Griffin and the Crawfords, and I hadn't been in the right frame of mind to react logically. I had panicked.

Panicked and run.

I hadn't given him the opportunity to be accountable, and then made a rational decision based on what he said. I shouldn't have run away before he could even speak.

Alice was right again. I did take off when things got hard.

I resolved that I was going to stop doing that. Going forward, I would face things that were difficult for me.

Maybe I should call him. That felt too scary for the moment. I was too raw, too emotional. Alice always said things looked brighter in the morning. Maybe I needed a good night's sleep and then I could manage trying to talk to him. Because in the back of my mind, that voice of my mother's was there. Telling me that Alice and I were imagining things. That Griffin didn't really care about me. That I was so pathetic for believing that I'd somehow misunderstood our interaction.

Nope. Not going to let that happen. I cast the voice out. A good night's rest. Then I would stop running away from him.

But for now? I needed to get lost in some painting.

Hours passed, and the garage became more and more stifling. But that also fit my mood. I wanted to sweat and be miserable so that my outside matched my inside.

I was startled by the sound of the garage door opening. Why was Alice coming in this way? She usually went through the front door.

The automatic door opened slowly and I saw a pair of shoes. Definitely not Alice's.

I recognized those shoes. My heart started to thud low and hard in my chest.

Then jeans and an expensive-looking T-shirt.

Griffin.

He was here.

CHAPTER THIRTY-ONE

My pulse pounded so loud that for a moment I couldn't hear. Was I imagining this? So stuck in my own head and missing Griffin that I had started hallucinating him?

He stepped into the garage with a rectangular package in his hands. He looked hesitant, nervous. "Hello, Diana."

I stood up, knocking my stool over. "What . . . how did you . . . how did you find me?"

"I had some help." He stepped into the garage, but he left a large gap between us. "I tried calling your mobile but you didn't answer."

"Yes . . . I left it with the Crawfords. It was their phone. They just let me borrow it while I was working for them."

Nodding, he added, "Sheila answered it. She was able to look at your call logs and found Alice's phone number. I rang Alice and she gave me her address. And the garage door code, in case you didn't answer the front door. Which you didn't."

Was I going to be mad at Alice later? I wasn't sure yet. I couldn't really feel anything besides shock that he had shown up.

Griffin took a step forward. "I hope it's all right that I came here. I also hope that you'll give me the opportunity to explain."

I pursed my lips, unable to respond. Because I didn't know yet whether it was okay that he was here.

My instinct was to flee. To not let whatever this was happen. Because even though I wanted to be better, that evil voice of my mother's was still in my head, making me fearful. Telling me I shouldn't trust him with my heart. I reminded myself of my resolution. To face hard things. I took a deep breath that wasn't at all cleansing and turned toward him. At the very least I was going to get answers.

"Why didn't you choose me?" I couldn't keep my voice from breaking.

There was a look of such love, such concern, on his face, but he stayed put. "It's no excuse, because the moment my grandmother stepped out of that car I knew what was going to happen. And I didn't care what she did to me. I was happy to give everything up to be with you. But then she threatened Ollie and Sophie and I . . . I had to be there to try and defuse the situation. I realized as soon as you'd gone that it was the wrong choice, because I should have run after you. I did manage to focus all of her anger on me, though. She hasn't cut off Ollie."

That made sense. That he'd focus on protecting Ollie and Sophie, much as he had since I'd met him.

He looked down, clearing his throat. "My grandmother is the only parental figure I still have. She's trained me my whole life to please her and in that moment, I still felt compelled to do that. Awful as she may be, I didn't want to lose her. She's still my family."

As someone without any parents to speak of, I understood that impulse. I couldn't blame him for that.

"Not that it did me any good. She's cut me out of her life. Permanently." There was both relief and pain in his declaration and I folded my arms to keep myself from comforting him. "Both financially and physically."

"So she did disinherit you."

He nodded. "Yes."

"And you're what . . . fine with it?"

"I am."

I let out a sound of disbelief. He'd lost his last remaining parent and an incredible amount of money because of me. "You're so going to resent me for that. Maybe you think you won't now, but someday you will."

"That's not possible. You rescued me. Freed me. I didn't realize how tight those bonds were around me until they were broken. I've never been able to be myself, to live life as I choose. Now I can. And that is because of you."

He was saying all the right words, and I wanted so badly to believe him. "But you've lost everything. Because of me."

"The only thing in the world that matters to me is in this room." He took another step forward. "I've gained everything. For the first time in my entire life, I am my own man. I get to make my own decisions. The first decision I made was to come here and beg for your forgiveness. Because everything I've done . . . it will all be for nothing if you're not a part of it. If I could redo last night, I would have spoken up immediately. Of course I choose you. I will always choose you."

He moved even closer, and I felt those walls that I had been trying so hard to reconstruct since last night tumbling into pieces all around my heart.

Not because he had broken them down, but because I was choosing to let them fall.

"Please forgive me, Diana. I am so sorry."

"You hurt me," I told him. "You promised you wouldn't do that."

"I didn't intend to."

"Intentional or not, it still happened."

"I love you. I love you and don't want to live without you. Please tell me what I can do to make this up to you," he pleaded. "I'll do anything you ask. I'll grovel."

"Like, get-down-on-your-knees kind of thing?"

At that, Griffin did start to sink to his knees, but he was close enough now that I could touch him. I reached for his shoulder and said, "I was asking what you meant. I'm not asking you to get on your knees."

His gaze focused on my hand and I let it drop. I could tell how much he wanted to be touching me. It was an impulse I understood, because I felt exactly the same way. I had misjudged him and his intentions. I should have waited. I should have let him speak. I shouldn't have left.

I regretted my choice. But instead of telling him that, I fell back on my old standby. Deflection. "So . . . where's your grandmother now?"

"I presume flying back to London. Livid with me, no doubt. I don't expect she'll be speaking to me anytime soon."

I realized what I was doing. I was avoiding his question about whether I could forgive him by asking about his grandma. Something that didn't matter right now. It was just another way to run—changing the subject.

Time to woman up and face all of this. I had to know that he was sure of what he was doing. "Griffin, I know it will be hard to lose her. But the money . . . it's so much money."

"It doesn't matter to me. Only you do."

He'd done that for me. He'd sacrificed all his money and the only parent figure he had because he loved me.

Griffin had chosen me.

I closed my eyes, trying to give myself strength to do this. To not miss out on the greatest thing that had ever happened to me because I was too proud or unforgiving. "I can forgive you. Only if you can forgive me, too." Time to stop being a coward. "I should have let you explain. I shouldn't have run off. And even though there's this part of me still saying that I should run, I won't. I can't. Because I love you so much that I can't imagine a life without you in it."

Pure joy sparked in his eyes and he reached for me. He pulled me into a hug and there was such a sense of rightness and completeness by being in his arms again. I wrapped my arms around his waist and held on tight.

And I realized how gross I must feel, how sticky and hot. "I'm all sweaty."

He kissed my left temple. "I'm only sorry I'm not the reason for it."

That made me laugh, and it felt amazing to laugh again. He joined me, and I loved the way his chest moved against me as he chuckled.

"I'm sorry for any pain that I've caused you. I can't promise not to hurt you," he said. "I imagine we'll both do things that hurt and upset one another. But I do promise that I will talk everything through with you. Because we make a bloody brilliant team. We can overcome anything."

"I apologize again for leaving. For not giving you a chance to talk and to hear your side of things. So I promise not to run away. To deal with things that freak me out and to work everything out together."

He pulled back to look down at me. "If you do run, please leave your shoes behind so I'll know which direction to go and find you. And speaking of, I've brought you a gift."

Then he handed me the package he'd been holding. It was wrapped up in newspaper. I tore the paper off and then opened the lid of the box.

It was a man's shoe.

I raised both of my eyebrows in confusion.

"It should have been diamonds," he said. "You deserve diamonds."

"What is this?"

"I had your shoe, now you have one of mine," he said, a bit sheepish. "This seemed more romantic in my mind."

Now I got it. And it was pretty romantic. This was better than diamonds. "So, by fairy-tale law, you belong to me."

"Yes, my Bunny. Always."

My heart fluttered at his declaration. "And weren't you the one who told me that there's supposed to be some kind of marriage proposal attached to a shoe being returned to its rightful owner?"

"This is hardly the place for it." He glanced around and I laughed again. He'd probably never been in a garage full of stuff before. "Soon. And in a slightly better environment."

He took the shoe from me and put it on the floor so that he could hold me properly. Then he said, "I know you wanted a last name that belonged to you. I have a very old one that you're welcome to if you'd like it."

My heart fluttered with happy anticipation. No fear, no concern. I wanted to spend my life with him, too.

It seemed like he was going to kiss me, but I beat him to it. He drew me in, causing those flashes of light and heat that melted my bones and heated up my blood. He kissed me until he actually was the reason I was sweaty.

To my dismay, he stopped the kiss to tell me, "I love you."

Okay, that was a pretty good reason to pause things for a moment. "I love you, too." Him mentioning his last name made me wonder something. "With your grandma cutting you off, does that mean you're not an earl anymore?"

"She can't touch the title. I'm still the earl. Ashwood Manor is also mine. Those belong to me, along with the rents from the estate to help with upkeep. And now that I no longer have to cater to her, I can also rent it out and have all sorts of tacky events there."

I was going to be a countess. Alice was going to explode with happiness.

So was I.

"We are going to be quite poor," he said.

"It's okay. I'm good at it. I can show you the ropes."

"And I'll probably have to get a proper job. I mean, there's the inheritance from my mother's estate, but it's only a few million pounds a year."

I blinked slowly, not sure I'd heard him correctly. "Did you say a few million pounds? A year?"

"Yes."

That made me laugh again. "For someone who went to *Oxford*, you are dumb."

He looked indignant. "I'm poor, not dumb."

"You're not poor, either. That's a lot of money. People live really well on far less."

Griffin kissed my lips softly, once, twice, three times. "Do you think we'll be able to manage?"

I kissed him back. "I think we're going to be just fine."

EPILOGUE

Two years later...

It was an unusually sunny day and I'd set up my easel out on the patio in the backyard. *Garden,* I mentally corrected. They called it a garden in England. I liked being out here—it was all greenery and hedgerows and songbirds. It was serene and I'd discovered how much I loved painting landscapes.

Ashwood Manor was the perfect place to do that. Right now I was focused on the pond and the ducks swimming smoothly on the surface.

"Lady Strathorne."

Griffin walked out onto the patio and came over to kiss me. As always, he made my stomach flutter and my pulse race. Everyone kept telling me this honeymoon phase would end, but I saw no signs of it slowing down.

"My, Lord Strathorne, what did I do to deserve that?"

"You are you, my darling Bunny." He'd had one of the staff set up an extra chair for him whenever I sat outside. He studied my painting. "This is extraordinary."

I felt the blush rising in my cheeks. I still wasn't very good with compliments, but I was trying. "Thank you."

Putting down my brush and palette, I turned in my seat to face him. He had that canary-eating grin on his face. Which meant he had news that he couldn't wait to share. "Did you have that secretary of Ollie's run a background check on Alice's new boyfriend?"

"Yes. And I am pleased to tell you that Franklin is clean as a whistle. No red flags of any kind, as you were worried about. By all accounts, he seems to be a decent man."

"Good." In addition to the new man in her life, the kidney transplant had gone perfectly, and both Alice and I had recovered successfully within a few months. She had found a new job with excellent benefits, including health and dental, and had gone back to work. Chad had finally been forced to start paying child support and alimony by having his wages garnished, and was compelled by the court to put Alice back on his insurance. She'd been reimbursed for all of her medical expenses.

Griffin had also paid off her mortgage despite her protests, and I was glad he did it. That had to help ease her mind—that she would always have a home for her and her kids.

My phone buzzed and I reached for it. "Oh, it's from Sheila. She's landed with John, Milo, and baby Michelle."

"I'm excited to see them at the wedding," he said.

"Me too." I could hardly wait. While I'd kept in constant contact with them via email and video chat, it was going to be so fantastic to see them in person again.

Ollie and Gisele were getting married tomorrow and Sophie had insisted that her very best friend, Milo, and his family be invited. Probably due to some leftover guilt, Ollie and Gisele had a very hard time ever telling Sophie no.

Griffin's brother had also turned out to be less of a douchebag than I'd initially imagined him to be. Their grandmother had refused to come to our wedding a year and a half ago, but she was expected to attend Ollie and Gisele's tomorrow. Not only because of Gisele's "noble" ancestry, but because as Griffin had pointed out to her the night she'd chased me off, Sophie was her only heir. Wilhelmina Windsor had no intention of leaving her fortune to charity, so Ollie had kept his trust fund.

I leaned back in my chair and put a hand over my growing bump. It was hard to believe that this was my life, but I had become just a bit accustomed to it.

"You have news, too," Griffin said. He could read me just as easily as I could read him.

"Possibly," I teased.

He sat straight up in his chair. "Did the doctor ring?"

"He did."

"And he knew the baby's sex?"

"Yes," I said, drawing this out. I was twenty weeks along, past my morning sickness (all-day sickness, thank you very much), and was back to enjoying things like painting and tormenting my adorable husband.

He let out a playful growl and said, "Well? Did he confirm that you're having my heir?"

I waited another beat and then realized that it wasn't fair to keep teasing him. "I'm having your heiress," I told him.

Grinning, he leaned over to plant a kiss on my protruding stomach. "A little girl. Another Windsor woman to wrap me around her little finger. We should name her Wilhelmina."

"Over my dead body. I'd name her after my mom before I'd name her after your grandma."

He laughed, knowing just how unlikely that possibility was. "But then Granny might forgive and forget if we name a child after her."

I knew he was teasing, but I couldn't joke about this. "Doubtful." She was a petty, old, selfish woman and I was happy she was out of our lives.

He reached into his suit pocket and took out a business card. "There's something else I have for you, my darling wife."

"What is it?"

"I went into London today." He said this like I didn't know. He had started his own flipping business and it brought him immense joy to fix up old houses. His business had become very successful very quickly, and I had to imagine that part of it was the novelty of being able to say that the Earl of Strathorne had reno-ed your new home.

"Yes. And?"

"I ran into an old chum from Oxford. He apparently owns an art gallery downtown. I showed him some of your pieces on my phone, and he'd like you to do a show."

"Are you serious?" I shrieked.

"Always," he said and I got up to hug him. He stood so that I wouldn't knock both of us over in his chair. Which was a real possibility. I was always miscalculating my center of gravity.

"You are the best husband," I told him. "You've given me everything."

"You've given me everything, Bunny. I could hardly consider myself worthy of you if I didn't provide you with a happily ever after."

He kissed me and I knew, in a way I couldn't have explained, that what he'd said was completely true.

We really were going to live happily ever after.

AUTHOR'S NOTE

Thank you for reading my story! I hope you liked getting to know Griffin and Diana and enjoyed them falling in love as much as I did. If you'd like to find out when I've written something new, make sure you sign up for my newsletter at www.sariahwilson.com, where I most definitely will not spam you. (I'm happy when I send out a newsletter once a month!)

And if you feel so inclined, I'd love for you to leave a review on Amazon, on Goodreads, with your hairdresser's cousin's roommate's blog, via a skywriter, in graffiti on the side of a bookstore, on the back of your electric bill, or any other place you want. I would be so grateful. Thanks!

ACKNOWLEDGMENTS

For everyone who is reading this—thank you. I can't tell you how much your support means to me—it is often quite literally the thing that keeps me going when the writing is hard. Hoping that you will enjoy and laugh and swoon and that, for a short amount of time, I maybe made your burdens a little easier to bear.

A huge thank-you to Alison Dasho—this book is dedicated to you because I'm in awe of you as a person, as a mom, as an editor, and I'm very grateful that we're going on these fictional adventures together. I couldn't ask for a better editor. I'm beyond thankful that I get to work with you and the entire phenomenal Montlake team. And my eternal gratitude to Charlotte Herscher, who always has the best insights and suggestions and makes my manuscripts absolutely shine. Here's to both of us trying to figure out current grammatical guidelines for many more books to come!

Thank you to the copyeditors and proofreaders who find all my mistakes and continuity errors and gently guide me in the right direction. A special shout-out to Philip Pascuzzo, who always makes such beautiful covers for me.

For my agent, Sarah Younger—you've endured a pandemic and a hurricane while this book was being written, but somehow you always still manage to be a hundred percent professional and wonderful and give me the absolute best advice. I'm so thankful for your support and for always guiding me on the best paths.

Thank you to Dana, Julia, and Jordan of Dana Kaye Publicity for everything you guys do, the way that you keep me on track, and all of your fantastic advice.

Sending love to Christy, Amy, Nancy, Tiff, Kim, and Laura—you guys helped me during one of the worst times of my life and I'll never, ever forget your support and kindness. Thank you so much for everything.

For my kids—there aren't enough words to let you know how much you mean to me, and how much I adore all of you.

And Kevin, I know what you had to give up, and I'm grateful you chose me. I'll always choose you.

ABOUT THE AUTHOR

Photo © 2020 Jordan Batt

Sariah Wilson is the *USA Today* bestselling author of *The Paid Bridesmaid*, *The Seat Filler*, *Roommaid*, *Just a Boyfriend*, the Royals of Monterra series, and the #Lovestruck novels. She has never jumped out of an airplane, has never climbed Mount Everest, and is not a former CIA operative. She has, however, been madly, passionately in love with her soul mate and is a fervent believer in happily ever afters—which is why she writes romance. She grew up in Southern California, graduated from Brigham Young University (go Cougars!) with a semi-useless degree in history, and is the oldest of nine (yes, nine). She currently lives with the aforementioned soul mate and their children in Utah, along with three cats named Pixel, Callie, and Belle, who do not get along (the cats, not the kids—although the kids sometimes have their issues, too). For more information, visit her website at www.sariahwilson.com.